Everything

is

Horrible

Now

Edward Lorn

ISBN: 9781729437407

# Also by Edward Lorn

*Bay's End*
*Dastardly Bastard*
*Hope for the Wicked*
*Life after Dane*
*Cruelty*
*Fog Warning*
*Pennies for the Damned*
*Fairy Lights*
*The Bedding of Boys*
*Everything is Horrible Now*
*No Home for Boys*

## Collections

*What the Dark Brings*
*Others & Oddities*
*Word*
*There Were Other Versions of Us*

## DEDICATION

This one's for H Michael Casper, to whom I owe a great deal of gratitude. Thanks, brother.


This book would not have been possible without the help of Gregor Xane, Sarah Frost, and Thomas Strömquist. Thank you so much for your tireless attention to detail.

*"Nel mezzo del cammin di nostra vita*
*mi ritrovai per una selva oscura*
*ché la diritta via era smarrita.*
*Ahi quanto a dir qual era è cosa dura*
*esta selva selvaggia e aspra e forte*
*che nel pensier rinova la paura!*
*Tant'è amara che poco è più morte;*
*ma per trattar del ben ch'i' vi trovai,*
*dirò de l'altre cose ch'i' v'ho scorte."*
~Canto I, *Inferno*, Dante

*"The truth of a man is first what he hides."*
~*Antimémoires*, André Malraux

# 1. Father George Lets Everyone Down

There was something wrong with time. Something vague yet growing stronger. Futures came before pasts. Present passed in the past. Confusing. The very fabric of reality upset by...something. No. Some*one*. Someone she had not the slightest control over. Leave it up to Mankind to break everything they touched.

She watched it all unravel like a child watching a dismembered and de-winged fly struggling for flight. Utterly fascinating how all her hard work could be ruined so quickly, as if everything had been disorganized chaos from the beginning. As if nothing had ever made sense.

Nothing left to do but watch. After all, how bad could things get?

\*\*\*

The morning Father George let everyone down, Wesley Haversham was washing socks at the creek. Doug Opinsky, who was eleven like Wesley but a year ahead of Wesley in school, his parents had just this year purchased a machine that did all the washing for you. The Opinskys were what poor people like Wesley Haversham called *Rich Folk*, for washing machines were new to everyone yet affordable to few.

The boy ran a hand through his kinky, rust-colored hair, hair that his father said would've gotten him gassed under Hitler's rule. His father, Sean Haversham, was as Irish as a shillelagh, but Wesley's mother (God rest her soul) had been a Jew from a line of Jews running all the way back to Bethlehem and the death of Jesus. This was unverifiable information, of course, but it made for good bedtime stories.

Javelins of sunlight poked through the trees, alighting on Wesley's ear and shoulders. The cool autumnal morning spoke of yards painted orange with fallen leaves, wood smoke, and candy in potato sacks.

Wesley ground a particularly filthy sock across the rutted spine of the washboard. A rustling in the trees caught his attention, but he ignored it, figuring a squirrel as the culprit. A moment later, a girldog exited the woods to Wesley's left, her droopy stomach heavy with pink teats. Her white-and-brown coat shimmered like fresh paint where the sun touched her. Wesley knew the dog by name—Gethsemane. Not many people in Bay's End didn't know Father George's Australian shepherd, although most folks just called her—

"Gess? That you, girl?" Wesley rose from the creekside and wiped his hands on his jeans. "Whatcha doin out here? Get on home, now. Shoo!"

Gethsemane remained as tranquil and reflective as her namesake, the garden in which Jesus spent his last hours as a free man. Wesley approached the girldog tentatively. He'd been iffy on the subject of dogs absent masters ever since he'd been chased home in the third grade by a rabid German shepherd. That same German shepherd had bitten a kid, but that was after Wesley had escaped to the safety of his own house. The victim, Ralphie Sikes, had to have a million injections in his stomach to cure the rabies. Least that was how Ralphie told the story. Afterwards, some lab cut the beast's head off (the dog's head, not Ralphie's) and sent it straight to Hell. Again, these were Ralphie's words, not Wesley's, because it was Wesley's opinion that dogs had no souls which one could send to Hell. Dogs died and became dirt. The end.

Gethsemane stepped forward with short, nervous steps, as if she found Wesley as off-putting as he did her. Or perhaps Gethsemane was trying to ease the boy's fears by saying, in her own wordless doggy way, that she was no threat. See me as I ease forward, boy? I mean no harm. Let me drop my head, just so, to hide the mouth you believe wishes to tear you asunder.

It was then, with Gethsemane's head down and the back of her neck in view, that Wesley Haversham saw the bloody handprint on the back of her neck.

\*\*\*

Twenty minutes before Wesley Haversham noticed the bloody handprint on Gethsemane's neck, Father George stood behind his wife while she washed breakfast dishes. Molly was pretty in her cornflower blue dress with the white fringe, one of her favorite dresses. He snapped closed the freshly loaded double-barrel shotgun. Molly, smiling in her own sweet way, turned around to see what that metallic click had been, and her husband blew the smile right off her face. She crumpled to the floor, her sudsy hands and forearms pooling foamy soap.

*When had everything gone so wrong?* Father George asked himself as he left the kitchen, digging in his pocket for fresh shells, and headed upstairs, two at a time, to the second floor. He turned into the hallway and entered Georgina's room. The three-month-old baby girl slept in her crib soundlessly, and for only the briefest moment, Father George wondered if she were dreaming in the simple way only babies dream.

It wasn't so long ago that life had been good. Hadn't it been good? Hadn't it? But somewhere down the line a dam had broken and horrible things had come flooding in. The nightmares were bad. The worst, in fact. He recalled one nightmare (had it been last night's dream?) in which Georgina had crawled up his supine body, from crotch to chest, her pudgy little mouth filled with teeth like ivory nails. He'd awakened screaming. Molly had held him until they had both fallen asleep.

Why had he never trusted Molly? She was dead now, and he supposed such things didn't matter, but the question ate at him just the same. Molly had loved and cared for him, as she had their infant daughter in the short time Georgina had been alive, yet he'd never found it in himself to trust his wife in return. Even showing affection to Molly had seemed to be by rote, his husbandly duties forthcoming due more to expectation than his desire for affections. So was it any wonder everything had gone so wrong?

Still there had been a time when he'd loved her. If not emotionally, then physically. Here before him lay the proof of their coupling, a bundle of pink wrapped in pink—a study in pink, if you will. So benign and, to him, the very definition of femininity. They were so weak, females; each one of them born into and raised under the umbrella of male protection. The lucky ones were raised in such a manner, anyway. Sure there were the sluts and whores of the world—hadn't he preached on them dozens of times from his pulpit?—but Georgina would never have the chance to become one. His baby girl would be no Jezebel. No harlot. She would remain pure and innocent. Unlike him.

Father George reloaded the shotgun, raised the barrel, and took aim.

The blast shook the entire town.

Afterward, Father George reached into the crib, more to make real what he had done than to try to comfort the dead infant, or himself. She was nothing but blood now, seemingly skinless and boneless in her entirety. Father George snatched his hand away in revulsion.

Something nudged his hip. He dropped his hand to pet the girldog he knew would be at his side. He only touched Gethsemane briefly, but it was enough to apply a red handprint to the back of her neck. The gory palm and digits resembled a crimson turkey drawn by a child using their hand as a stencil. A blood turkey. *Gobble, gobble...*

Gethsemane licked blood from his wet hand. Appalled, Father George roared at the dog, "No!"

Gethsemane fled, tail between her legs, the red hand on her neck a bold accusation. He heard her thump down the stairs, then the squeak and clunk of the doggy door in the kitchen. Absently, Father George hoped Gess hadn't walked through Molly on her way outside.

"Good girl," he said to an empty room. "You don't need to see what happens next."

Father George reloaded his shotgun, headed downstairs and out onto the front porch.

\*\*\*

In hindsight, Wesley would think that maybe he should have gone for help straight away. Had he done so, things might have ended differently than they did.

His first thought after seeing the blood on the dog's neck was that she might be hurt. This, of course, was obviously not the case. By now the blood had caked to the point that anyone could tell, even a simple eleven-year-old farm boy like Wesley Haversham, that the blood had been pressed into the fur, leaving a clear handprint. Could someone have injured the dog and then tried to grab her to keep her from running away? Maybe. Another possibility was that she'd injured herself and someone had grabbed her to get her to hold still while they checked out her wounds. But, somehow, Wesley knew neither scenario was what had occurred. Something inside him felt the wrongness of the situation, as a mother might feel that her child is in danger, or a twin might sense that their sibling is in pain.

Everything about Gethsemane felt wrong. And that's why, when she trotted off into the trees, Wesley Haversham followed, close on her heels.

The girldog moved at a slow-but-steady clip through Marietta Wood, which had been named after Francis Bay's young wife. Folks said that Marietta had been a witch in her day, and that the town's burning of her and her husband—the founder of the town in which Wesley and a thousand other souls lived—had not only been warranted but desired by the populace. The way he'd heard it was, a bunch of kids had gotten sick and one of them wouldn't stop calling out Marietta's name. When another sick child began crying out the same name, locals hunted down Marietta. In his attempts to protect his young bride, Francis Bay fought tooth and nail, murdering with an ax two of the men who'd been sent after his wife. It would be later, but not too long, mind you, before Wesley would hear the rest, and truth of the story.

Gethsemane exited Marietta Wood and headed north on Highway 607. Not once on his way to the Georges' home did Wesley see a vehicle on the highway or think that what he was doing might be a bad idea. Those thoughts would come later; when his house was dark and only his thoughts and the creaking of floorboards could be heard. This didn't mean he wasn't scared or worried during his walk. He was both of those things, in equal measure, but Wesley Haversham, for all his faults and inexperience, was worried that there might be something wrong at the Georges'. Mostly, as children are wont to do when other children are involved, Wesley's concern for the safety of the Georges' new baby was at the forefront of his mind. He could almost see what had happened.

*Mrs. George, having heard Baby Georgina crying, has fallen down the stairs in her haste to see about her bawling child!* (Wesley saw this clearly, even if he had no idea what the inside of the Georges' house looked like and never would.) *She tumbles head over feet and lands in a pile at the bottom of the stairs. Her spine juts from the skin of her neck like the fork of a check mark. There's blood and guts everywhere.* (Although Wesley had no idea why this should be, given that Mrs. George has only snapped her neck, but okay, we'll go with blood and guts everywhere.) *Mrs. George tries to call for help but she can't because there's, you know, the hole in her neck caused by the jutting neck bone so all you can hear is wheezing. Gethsemane trots over to see about her mistress and that's when Mrs. George grabs Gess by the neck with her bloody hand and pleads silently* (or would it be wheezingly?) *with Gess to go, go find help! That's a good girl.*

Hey, you never know, right?

Wesley didn't consider where Father George was in this seemingly worst-case scenario, so when the Georges' house came into view around a bend in the road, Wesley was surprised to see Father George sitting in a wicker rocking chair on the front porch.

The Georges' house was set back off Highway 607 by about fifty feet, giving the family, in Wesley's opinion, a decent-sized front yard squared off by a white picket fence of the kind that were all the rage nowadays. To the left of the house, nothing but trees. To the right, the Georges' driveway. A brick footpath ran from the concrete driveway to the porch steps. The porch itself had bannisters painted the same bright white as the fence out front. It was this bannister that kept the boy from seeing the shotgun laid across Father George's lap until Wesley was in the driveway and right up on the picket fence.

"Good morning, Father George," Wesley said. The presence of the shotgun didn't bother Wesley in the least. His father owned a double-barrel just like this one, an old Remington father and son alike used to shoot geese and quail during hunting season. Seeing the shotgun laying across the preacher's lap no more upset Wesley than it would have had it been a bundle of laundry.

*Shoot,* Wesley grumbled internally, *I left the wash at the creek. Pop's gonna be hot over that.*

Father George mumbled something, bringing Wesley's attention back to the porch. Whatever the preacher had said, Wesley hadn't understood.

"What was that, sir?"

*Mumble, mumble...*

"Hang on. Lemme come where I can hear."

Wesley reached over the gate, undid the gravity latch, and walked across the bricks to the porch steps. Whereas the presence of the shotgun hadn't spooked the boy, Father George's bloody hand scared him plenty. Wesley froze solid on the spot; one foot on bricks, the other on the first step. He couldn't take his eyes off that reddish-brown hand where it lay across the barrels of the gun, limp at the wrist, fingers dangling, as if the hand and its owner had not a single care in all of God's creation.

Wesley scanned the rest of Father George. The preacher's white button-down was speckled with blood, like freckles on a redhead; Wesley was well acquainted with freckles, being the redhead that he was, and thought the simile worked well. Father George's blue jeans were equally dotted with specks of drying blood. His penny loafers, from what Wesley could tell, were free of any blemishes. Wesley's eyes lifted to Father George's face. The preacher stared off into the distance, his lips dry and moving almost imperceptibly. Blood splatter covered one cheek and temple and not the other as if something had shielded him on the left side of his face.

Then there was Father George's eyes. Wesley didn't like what he saw in them because what he saw was nothing. If the eyes were the windows to the soul like he'd heard so many grown folks say, Father George's soul had taken a leave of absence.

"You, um—you okay, Father George?" Then, inanely, Wesley added, "Didja cut yourself, sir?"

Father George spoke again, much clearer this time. Wesley heard the words that came from the man's mouth, but they made about as much sense to him as the mumbling had.

"What's that you said, sir?" Wesley asked, shaken but polite with good home-training. Because no matter how scary Father George and his crimson hand and blood-splattered clothes were at that moment, there was no call for forgetting one's manners. Not when one was so well programmed.

Sometimes, when adults knew you were scared, they'd cut you some slack. Wesley swallowed with more than a little difficultly, steeled himself and said, "You're scaring me, sir."

Father George's gaze drifted toward Wesley. Their eyes met, and the preacher spoke four words that would not leave Wesley Haversham until the day he died.

He said, "Everything is horrible now."

Father George kicked off a shoe, jammed the stock of the shotgun into the porch's floorboards, toed the trigger through his sock, and slowly applied pressure to the trigger. The thunderclap deafened Wesley as the wall of the house and the roof of the porch were painted the color of blackberry preserves. The rocking chair swayed three more times and came to rest with Father George's body slumped over the right arm. The shotgun clattered to the porch, where it sat, undisturbed for several hours.

Wesley ran home, screaming the whole way.

# 2. The Shot Heard All Round Town

Sheriff Harold "Hap" Carringer—*two Rs on that last name there,* he'd say to the uninitiated—stood over the bloody crib of Georgina George, thinking, *Who in the good goddamn names a child Georgina George?* He took off his wide-brim hat, frowned, and sighed. He put his hat over his heart and looked like he was praying, but a praying man Hap wasn't.

"Damn Greek tragedy, Hap," said Deputy Ronnie Sharp as he walked into the room. The deputy was five feet and halfway to six with a broad chest and thick biceps. Skinny chicken legs hid underneath Ronnie's uniform pants, legs Hap had seen too much of this past summer when Ronnie volunteered to lifeguard the annual city picnic at Lake Haversham.

"Huh?" Hap said, maybe a little too sternly.

"It's a tragedy, s'all I said." Ronnie stepped beside Hap, looked inside the gore-splattered crib, and covered his mouth with a fist. "Why ya think he'd go and do something like that? Father George, I mean."

"Phone's off the hook downstairs," Hap said.

"Yeah?" Ronnie said as if he didn't see the connection between what he'd said and how Hap had followed up.

"Prolly got a call from his mistress. She likely said she was going to tell Molly 'bout him steppin out."

"Father George was cheating on Molly?" Ronnie was comically shocked at this revelation.

Hap suppressed a grin and said, "No, Ronnie, I said *prolly* he was. What else makes a man, a man of God at that, go off the reservation 'cept scandal?"

Ronnie shrugged. "Maybe he was in debt? That could be it, too, right? I reckon that's another good reason, anyhow." Ronnie glanced into the crib one more time, his face sickened but his eyes shining with morbid curiosity. He'd not thrown up. Not when they found Father George on the porch, nor when they came upon Molly missing half her head in the kitchen. Even now, when faced with the shattered body of an infant, Ronnie Sharp remained as cool as a cucumber in a snowdrift—green as all creation, but nonetheless cool.

You could get sickened in this line of work. Nothing wrong with that. But you couldn't get sick. A professional always kept his lunch down. Hap respected Ronnie for that. He was a good kid, likely to go places, and Hap was glad he'd decided on hiring him.

"Who found them?" asked Ronnie.

Hap couldn't believe he hadn't mentioned it before now. "The Haversham boy. He run home from here, got his pa, and they both rode in to see me at the station. They ain't got no phone out where they live. Ma Bell ain't run a line out that far yet."

Ronnie nodded. "He tell you why he was out here?"

Hap laughed.

Ronnie gave the sheriff a curious look.

Hap said, "You think the Haversham boy had something to do with all this carnage? Is that it, Deputy Dog?"

Ronnie grimaced.

"Nossir. Just seems weird he'd be out this way, s'all."

"What's odder 'n that is what the boy said Father George said 'fore he blew his brains all over the porch."

"What'd he say?"

\*\*\*

"Everything is horrible now?" Beulah Blackwood said into the phone. She curled the cord around her finger, extracted her finger, wrapped it up again. "Why ya think he'd say something like that, Reeb?"

"I don't know, Beulah. Ronnie come home tonight jus' talkin up a ruckus. Said Father George shot the baby, Beulah. The baby!" Reba Sharp expressed her shock in a hissing whisper. "Imagine the kind of person could do such a thing as shoot a baby with one them huntin guns. Why, they'd be heartless, or filled with the devil, Beulah, and I don't recall ever thinkin Father George was either of them things."

"Just goes to show, you never do know nothin about another person. Not as well as you know your own heart and head, anyway. You hear about that Elvis. He done joined the army, or some such, is what I heard tell."

Reba tittered. "He gonna shake them hips at the enemy and shock 'em all to death? Next war we get ourselves into gon' be over in two shakes of ol' Elvis's pelvis."

Beulah laughed along with her young friend. Reba was forty years Beulah's junior but one of the old lady's best friends. Well, maybe not a friend in the classical sense of the word. They never went out together or shared a meal, but they did gossip. Lord how they gossiped.

Her grandson, whom Beulah had accepted guardianship of, stepped from the darkness of the hallway. The boy's prepubescent face warmed her heart every time she laid eyes on it.

"Hang on, Reeb." Beulah clapped a hand over the mouthpiece. "What is it, Petey?"

"When's dinner, Mama?" the eleven-year-old asked.

Beulah looked to the cuckoo clock on the mantel and saw it was half past seven in the evening. She grabbed her shirt as if clutching pearls.

"Oh my, Reba, I got to go. I forgot all about dinner! At this point, I guess we'll have sandwiches, which I hate, because a growin boy like Petey needs a good hot meal every night if he's gon' grow up big and strong."

"You do that, Beulah, and I'll see ya... Well, I was gon' say I'd see you at church, but I don't guess there's gon' be services this Sunday, now will there?"

"Unless one of the deacons decides to preach, I think you're right."

"The flock's gon' need new leadership—"

"Reeb, I really must go. Petey is just wasting away over here. Tootles!"

Beulah made sandwiches out of the leftover roast she'd cooked the night before, then slathered mayonnaise on bread, and finally used the lettuce in the crisper that she'd all but forgotten about; she'd needed to throw away the first ten leaves or so because they were slimy and brown, but the flesh under the rot was a pretty white and green.

They ate at the table, like they always did, and she pressed the boy for how school had gone today. Petey kept shrugging. She hated when he did that but would not chide him for not giving her a verbal answer. The boy had been through a lot since his parents—her daughter and son-in-law—had died three months prior. Beulah was surprised that Petey had wanted to go back to school so quickly after the funerals. Seemed wrong to restart life while still in the shadow of a tragedy, although there were times when she felt that her daughter's death had hit her harder than it would ever hit Petey.

Patrick Rothsberg had courted Beulah's daughter Joyce for almost two years before he popped the question. Joyce said *yes* right off, refraining from playing hard to get, which Beulah had found easy, but it wasn't Beulah's life that would be ruined by marrying the first man that came along, so she let it go.

Patrick did well for Joyce and their eventual child, a son named Pete, who Beulah would forever call Petey. Patrick did so well for the family that he eventually moved them out of the End and into a big fancy house in Columbus, where Joyce and he lived until their deaths.

On a summer's afternoon not unlike other summer days, Beulah answered the phone and accepted the news that both her daughter and her son-in-law had been brutally murdered in their home. Petey, the police said, had likely witnessed the double murder. Why the boy had been left alive was anyone's guess. This was before serial killers would become as American as apple pie and baseball.

Beulah did her Christian duty and took the boy in. In the past three months, the boy child had become her last connection to Joyce. Beulah never imagined that she would forget what her daughter looked like and was shocked when Joyce's face began to fade as soon as a month after her daughter's death. But, poor memory or not, Beulah had Petey to look at. All that was required was to catch him in the right light, under the globe in the ceiling of the kitchen worked just fine, while he was chewing. It was times like this, with his jaw working and his eyes downcast, that he resembled his mother. The resemblance was uncanny, really.

Beulah wiped a tear from the corner of her eye before it could roll down her cheek and continued watching the boy eat his sandwich.

He swallowed and said, "They call me Fatty."

"What?" Beulah said, shocked.

"They call me Fatty. Like it's my name. I told them not to, but they still say it."

"Who is this *Them* and *They*?"

"Everyone," the boy said, and took another bite of his sandwich.

"You can't mean *everyone*, Petey. Surely your teacher doesn't call you Fatty."

Petey gave her a look as if to say that was exactly how it was and then snatched another section off his leftover sandwich.

"I'll just have to call the school, then. Right? I mean, I won't be havin *Theys* and *Thems* calling my baby *Fatty*. Why, you aren't fat at all. Just a little big boned, is all. Don't be silly," she said, as if it were Petey himself who'd said something.

Pete finished his sandwich and asked to be excused from the table.

"I have a Conan comic to read."

"That's fine. Enjoy your funny book, Petey."

"Thanks... Mama."

He disappeared into the shadow of the hallway whence he came and Beulah was left wondering why he'd hesitated when calling her *Mama*. He hadn't before. Not that she could remember, anyway. Perhaps he'd been thinking about his mother and father as she herself had been doing. Perhaps not.

She sighed and got up to collect the evening's dishes. She washed up in silence, her thoughts pregnant with Joyce and Patrick and yes, even Petey. The boy child in her care. Her young man.

Petey Rothsberger.

No.

Petey Blackwood. She'd had the boy's name changed, of course. No need in him growing up under the name of the dead. Better for him to accept her own maiden name and grow up a Blackwood. Growing up a Blackwood had been good enough for her. Good enough that she'd reverted to the strong Cherokee name after the death of her husband, God rest his soul.

\*\*\*

Hap spent himself inside Janice Larson and collapsed atop the skinny woman's nonexistent breasts. She might not have any titties to speak of but the woman had a bear trap hidden between those chopsticks she called legs.

"You did it in me *again*?" Janice slapped Hap's sweaty back.

"I can't help it, Jan," he huffed in her ear. "That pussycat of yours was just beggin for some milk."

She smacked his back flesh once more. "You gonna get me pregnant, you fool! Then what am I gonna tell Eric? I ain't been with him like I been with you in a coon's age."

Hap never had understood that stupid saying. Exactly how long was a *coon's age*? Like those odd potatoes who said silly stuff like how there was more than one way to skin a cat. Odd potatoes, the lot of them.

"Let 'im lay between your thighs when he gets off patrol tonight. If you catch pregnant, you can blame tonight. If it's the only time you done fucked him recently, he's bound to remember it."

She pushed him off her. He rolled onto his back and listened as she struck a match. The room brightened briefly with flickering flame. She lit a Pall Mall and shook out the match. The ashtray clinked. The cigarette's cherry bobbed in the fresh darkness. She exhaled. The cherry drifted toward Hap. He pinched it between index and middle fingers and inhaled thick, soul-soothing smoke.

"You'd really share me with him?" she asked.

"Who?" Hap laughed. "Your husband?"

"Yes, you jerk. Eric. My husband. You wouldn't be upset if I made love to him and then made love to you again?"

Hap laughed harder. "Hell, woman, I thought that's what we've been doin this whole time! Didn't know till just now that you weren't fuckin him no more."

She slapped his bare chest so hard it stung. "Don't be crude around me."

"You like me crude and you know it." He passed her the Pall Mall.

"Hush."

"Shit. No wonder Eric's been in such a bad mood recently. If I came home to a cold shoulder, I'd be irritable, too."

He felt her roll onto her side in the dark. She blew smoke into his face.

"You really thought I was sleeping with the both of you at the same time? What must you think of me? Jesus, Hap, what am I to you? Some kind of whore?"

"You ain't no whore. Whores charge for what they do."

"So you think I'm a—*what*? A slut?"

"If the shoe fits."

She ground the cigarette out in the flesh of his hairy chest. The pain was instant and pure instinct caused Hap to snatch away from the source. He crashed onto the floor, striking a nightstand on his way down. Glass clattered and shattered.

"Fuckin hell, woman!" Hap hollered from the carpet.

The bed squeaked. A second later light blinded him. A door closed, and the room went dark, but not completely black. Hap pushed himself to his feet, using the bed for support. The outline of Janice's bathroom door glowed in the darkness like a doorway to another dimension. The door knob clicked and Hap knew she'd locked herself in.

Hap moved at a furious clip. He slammed the ball of one fist against the door while the fingers of his other hand massaged the burned flesh and hair where the cigarette had been put out on him.

The wound was raw and wet and hurt like an asshole full of concertina wire.

"Leave me alone!" Janice screamed through the wood, her voice equal parts angry and scared. She obviously knew what she'd done, how surely she'd crossed that line in the sand by harming him. He could hear the panic in her voice. Something about that sound excited him.

"You just gonna burn me and think I won't do shit to you? I ain't your mouse of a husband, Janice. You bring your ass out here and I'll show you how a real man deals with a bitch when she acts out of line!"

"*GO AWAY!*"

"Go away?" Hap laughed. "Bitch, I ain't goin anywhere."

He brought up a muscular leg and kicked the door in, like it was nothing more substantial than a door on a cardboard fort.

Hap dragged Janice, screaming, from where she cowered on the toilet. Her skin stuck to the toilet lid and brought it up. When her flesh peeled away, the lid slammed down with a crack like a gunshot. He tugged Janice to the bed and shoved her down, face first, into the sex-damp mattress. She kicked out. Her foot glanced off his thigh. He punched her in the kidney and all the fight drained from her like puss from an infected wound. She writhed underneath him as he raped her.

When he was done, he dressed while she lay quiet and still on the bed, and then he drove home. It wasn't until Hap was in the shower that he noticed the muddy-brown mess smeared on his penis.

He fingered the burn on his chest as he vigorously soaped his balls.

"Guess that'll teach her."

***

As the day drew to a close, Wesley Haversham knelt by his bed and prayed. He prayed that God would forgive Father George for what he'd done. As Wesley said, "Amen," he heard his father speak from the bedroom doorway.

"That's mighty big of you, asking for what you just asked for. Mighty proud of you, boy."

"Thank you, Pa." Wesley crawled into bed. Sean Haversham tucked his boy in.

"You too grown for a story?" Sean asked.

Wesley thought hard but not long. "I don't guess so."

It had been well over a year since his father had told him a bedtime story and Pa, if Wesley was honest, was rustier than an old well crank. Pa was halfway through with the story by the time Wesley realized that he'd heard this particular tale before, and from Pa no less. No matter. He loved the soothing sound of his father's voice, as deep and familiar as the tale he told. When Pa was done, he kissed Wesley on the forehead and made for the bedroom door. He shut off the light.

"Pa?"

"Yeah?"

"Why you think he done it?" Wesley tried to keep any emotion from his voice, for he didn't wish to sound weak.

Pa thought for a moment, striking a thick-chested shadow in the light coming from the hallway. Then his old man said, "We might never know the why of it, Wes. You might have to live with the mystery and misery of it all. I know that sounds rough, but not everything in this world can be explained. Like leprechauns, for instance."

Wesley couldn't see his father smile due to the backsplash of light from the hallway but he could sense a smile in Pa's words all the same.

"Leprechauns ain't real," Wesley said, just in case Pa's words had been a test.

"No, son, they ain't. But sadness is. And I suppose I believe that Father George was a very sad man. Sometimes sad people take permanent steps to cure a temporary mood. You followin?"

"Yessir."

"But, Wes, you gotta accept the fact that you might never know why Father George did the terrible things he done. And, more importantly, you need to understand that there's nothing you could have done to stop him."

"Yessir. I know."

"Do you now?"

"Yessir. Had you seen him—had you seen Father George and heard what he said, you'd've thought he wasn't gon' change his mind, neither. You know what he looked like, Pa? What he made me think? Afterward?"

"What's that?" Pa asked, although Wesley thought Pa had sounded like he'd give anything in the whole world not to hear, as if what he might hear next would change everything.

Wesley said, "Father George, he was dead long before I got there this morning. Weren't nothin in him, Pa. His eyes was empty. Just nothin there."

Silence lingered between father and son like a tangible wall.

Finally, Pa said, "I'm sorry you had to see that, Wes. I'm just so sorry. I like to think I can protect you from this world, but then you go an' see something like that and I gotta wonder if…"

"If what?"

"Nothin. Go on to sleep."

"It'll be all right, Pa. I ain't seen nothin like it before and I don't 'spect I'll see anything like it again."

Pa's laughter was sudden, bright and full of pride. "You've grown up so much. Your mother'd be proud of you, boy."

"Ya think so?"

"I know so. Goodnight, boy."

"Night, Pa."

The door eased closed and the hall light died a quiet death. Darkness swallowed Wesley Haversham. Something breathed in the corner. Something crept inside the walls. Something lurked upon the roof. But Somethings no longer scared Wesley. Because nothing was scarier than the nothing he'd seen in Father George. Before today, Wesley hadn't known just how scary Nothing could be.

Something howled in the night.

And Wesley Haversham rolled over and fell peacefully to sleep.

\*\*\*

Across town, in a similarly darkened room not unlike the one in which slept the Haversham boy, Kirby Johnson listened intently to the Coat Men moving about in his closet. The problematic ticking of clothes hangers were the only sounds in existence. They were everywhere. Louder than the entirety of the whole wide world.

Kirby tried his best to ignore the ticking of the Coat Men, but every time he closed his eyes he saw Father George's smiling face. Kirby didn't know what was more detrimental to his sleep: the Coat Men and their ticking; or Father George and his godawful smiling.

His mother had been part of the phone tag played earlier that day and throughout the night between the wives and mothers and all the other big-mouth gossips of Bay's End. Gossips with mouths like bass, and bladders that couldn't hold an ounce of water. Mother hadn't gotten off the phone until well after midnight according to Kirby's alarm clock. He checked it now in the glow of the streetlights coming through his bedroom window.

2:23

So many hours before sunrise. So many ticks from the Coat Men yet to come. Ticks as numerous as the stars in the sky.

"I can't do it," Kirby whined as he rolled over and tugged the cord on his bedside lamp.

Three svelte figures stood at the footboard of Kirby's bed. Three ghouls with featureless faces of smooth crimson skin. Three blood-red coats, as if the trio were doctors in Hell. On the breast of each, a number followed by a white cruciform. From right to left: 3, 14, 9.

"No, no, *nonono...*" Kirby mumbled and trembled in time with the Coat Men's ticking.

Number Three's face split, horizontally, just below where a normal human face might have a nose, and inside the fresh wound of a mouth there gleamed teeth like nine inch nails, the very length of the nails used by Roman soldiers to secure Christ to his cross, Kirby was sure.

Number Fourteen broke formation, gliding from in between his fellow Coat Men and drifting backward into Kirby's pitch black closet. Number Fourteen vanished into the void where Kirby's clothes should have been hanging.

Number Nine floated around the bed and came gliding up to Kirby's right side. Its hands came into view; too many fingers with too many knuckles. The fingers unfolded like worms uncoiling. The hand with too many knuckles reached to the waxy nothingness of its crimson face. With a swipe of a palm, Number Nine became Father George, just not all the way. It had Father George's face, yes, but the sides of the head were wrapped in dark red skin, as if Father George were trying to escape Hell, face first, but couldn't manage to remove any more than his face.

"Hey, Kirby," the face of Father George said. "Ready for today? Today's gonna be swell, kiddo. Just swell. Ain't you excited, Kirb? Ain't'cha? *AIN'T'CHA?!*" Father George snarled and roared and exploded into a million crimson fragments, like blood in zero gravity. Kirby instinctively raised an arm to protect his eyes. He stayed like that, forearm over his eyes, listening to his pulse throbbing in his temples.

Kirby peeked through his fingers.

Number Three hovered above him, sandwiching Kirby between itself and Kirby's mattress, smiling with its gash of a mouth filled with ivory nails.

Kirby, shaking violently, watched in horror as the Coat Man above him reached out, grabbed the pull chain on his bedside lamp, and dropped the teenager into utter darkness. Not the darkness of a darkened room, though. The dark of beyond. The soulless dark of the Void.

Kirby screamed.

Neighborhood dogs barked and howled. Lights came on in the windows of neighboring houses. A frightened cat bounded from a garbage can and dashed into the shadowy protection of a nearby hedge.

Kirby's mother rushed into her son's room, trailing blessed light in her wake: her bedroom light, the one in the hall, the bulb in the ceiling of Kirby's room, all aglow and shoving back the darkness, the Void.

Her hair in curlers, her face a splotchy mess, Donna Johnson dove into the bed beside her son. She hugged him and petted his hair and told him everything was going to be all right. Whatever had scared him, it was gone now. Mommy's here.

"It's g-g-getting worse. The t-t-ticking's getting worse," Kirby stammered, his words pushing into his mother's sweat-dampened neck, her flesh cold and slick with tears.

She caressed his long black hair. "Oh, what did they do to you? They were supposed to help you, not... not make you worse. Not make you like *this*."

And what was *this*, exactly? He'd told his mother of the Coat Men, but her response had always been that the men in the numbered coats were nothing more than bad wiring in his head, just like his unnatural desires. The staff at Humble Hill had promised a cure and had failed to deliver. His time at Humble Hill was over but Kirby was anything but better.

Donna Johnson loved her son and would do anything to see him live a normal healthy life. She'd tried her best to protect him and point him in the right direction, but Kirby seemed bound, set, and determined to make her life a living hell.

Hell. Father George likely resided there now, if there truly was such a place. Kirby certainly hoped so, because anything was better than here.

# 3. Hap's Tale in Retrospect

Sheriff Hap had always been what people called an *Old Soul*. Even in his youth, his questions and concerns were of an adult nature. When packing his lunch on his first day of kindergarten, his mother had been asked questions like, "Shouldn't there be fruit?" and "Might I have another slice of bologna on my sandwich, please and thank you."

At eight, he'd heard his mother and father arguing over financial worries that should have been of no concern to a child of his age. The next day, he asked the manager of Peaton's Grocery for a job. Henry Parks, a pudgy, balding man who would die in a car accident the scene of which Hap would one day work, looked down on the boy in a jovial manner.

"Why do you need a job, lad? What's happened to you parents? Can't they take care of you?"

Hap said, "Why should they take care of me when I can take care of myself?"

Henry Parks chuckled in the way adults chuckle when faced with the trivialities of silly children. He mussed Hap's hair and shuffled away. Hap watched the fat manager disappear into the back of the store, fully expecting Parks to return with a uniform and a scheduled start date.

Hap stood there, in the back of the store, by the entrance to the rear storeroom, suffering the curious stares of employees and customers alike. There he waited, his arms studded with gooseflesh—the air coming from the meat department chilling every inch of him. Eventually, a teenage girl dressed in the green vest of a Peaton's Grocery employee came out of the storeroom. Maybe Hap had seen her earlier, without the vest, on her way into the back to clock in? Hap didn't know for sure but she sure looked familiar.

"You lost, honey?" Her voice was sweeter than the syrup of canned peaches.

"I'm waiting on Mr. Parks to give me my uniform," Hap said with conviction.

"Honey, Mr. Parks has gone home this time of day. How... Just how long you been standing here?"

Hap turned and walked away. His foolishness scalded his cheeks. He felt everyone's eyes upon him, a thing to be mocked. Years later, when Henry Parks had a heart attack at the wheel and drove head-on into a station wagon full of the Clark family—all four boys, two girls, and both parents—newly appointed Deputy Harold "Hap" Carringer spat on the manager's mangled corpse before going to see about piecing together what was left of all those Clarks.

Hap lost his virginity when he was twelve. The girl had been a neighbor several years older than he. She liked to watch the boy as he cut the grass or performed other outside chores, like trimming the hedgerow and watering the lawn. She seemed to especially enjoy watching him wash his father's Hudson, shirtless. Eventually, Hap caught on to the girl's attentions. On that day, he sat down his hedge clippers and walked across the street. She eyed him with the cool calculation of an experienced predator sizing up its prey.

"Why you always watchin me?" twelve-year-old Hap asked the girl.

She smiled and held out a ruddy hand. "Name's Ethel."

He eyed her hand but didn't shake it. "Everyone with a pulse calls me Hap. Now why you been watchin me?"

Ethel lit a cigarette and blew smoke into the boy's face. Hap squinted through the bluish fog. Ethel glanced over Hap's shoulder and asked, "Your parents home?"

"No," said Hap. "Mom's shopping and my father's at work."

"Mm," she purred and held out her smoke. She raised her eyebrows as if to ask him if he wanted a pull. He took the cigarette, inhaled deeply, picked tobacco off his bottom lip, and blew smoke into her face, to return the favor.

"You've smoked before?" she asked after a moment of seemingly waiting for him to devolve into a coughing fit.

"My parents do. House is always fulla smoke." He took another puff before passing the cigarette back. Inch-long gray ash fell from the tip and exploded silently on the porch boards.

Ethel glanced around. She stubbed out the half-smoked cigarette and reached for Hap's hand. He slipped his palm into hers and she led him inside, where she allowed him to slip inside her.

By the time Hap hit high school, he'd become something of a presence, one who people blindly respected, no matter their age or station in life. The cocksure teenager was every bit a natural leader. People simply tended to follow Hap, be the journey difficult, or the destination troublesome. He landed the coveted role of team captain for his school's baseball team, the Enders.

Hap never wanted for attention, especially that of the female variety. And what attention he wasn't afforded, he took.

Senior prom, Hap arrived to the dance with a girl he'd been screwing nearly nightly by the name of Brenda Grant. Truth be told, Hap was tired of Brenda. The cat between her legs smelled like an old tire. The smell was even present the dozen or so times Hap had forced her into a shower while his parents weren't home. He'd be glad to move on from the stinking cunt. The only reason he'd stayed with her this long was because Brenda, for all her poor hygiene, was the first girl to put his penis in her mouth without complaining about how he *peed outta that thing*, or how the uncircumcised head was unbearably musty. One girl had commented that his dick smelled like an unwashed armpit. Thanks to Hap, the girl hadn't been able to smell musty cock or anything else for an entire month, not until the swelling went down in her broken nose. Brenda, however, always went the extra mile. The lovely soul would even swallow his junk. She'd lap at his dick like a kid at a drippy ice cream cone.

"It tastes like pickles," she'd say, and Hap, in his state of post-coital contentment, would cringe.

"I don't wanna hear that shit."

Years later, after Brenda had married and produced a litter of boys, Hap ran into her and her gang of ankle-biters in a hotel in Columbus. Hap was there for a fellow deputy's stag party and never bothered asking Brenda why she was there. They spoke only briefly, in the hotel's foyer, but long enough for Brenda to introduce him to her four boys—whose names he instantly forgot—and her husband to pop up brandishing a room key.

Brenda introduced the two men. The hubby was amiable enough, but Hap could sense how threatened the other man felt. A feeling of inadequacy radiated from the hubby's sweaty palm and up Hap's arm as they shook hands. Hap didn't like the feeling. It depressed him and he was not the depressive type.

"Nice to meetcha, Hap," said Hubby, and then Hubby turned to his wife to say, "Pickles, get the bags, would you? It was a pleasure, Hap."

Smiling knowingly, Hap watched the crew depart for their room.

*Pickles,* Hap thought. *Some things never change, I reckon.*

What Brenda Grant hadn't seemed to recall that day at the hotel was how Hap had disappeared halfway through senior prom. He'd left her by the punchbowl and approached the prettiest girl at the dance. Mary Robichaux was a vision in a pink dress tight enough to contain-yet-compliment an amazing pair of full breasts. Hap asked Mary to dance, and she frowned, something Hap had yet to experience when dealing with the fairer sex.

"Aren't you here with someone, Harold?" Mary Robichaux asked.

"So you've been watching me," Hap said. It wasn't a question.

"You're hard to miss." This did not sound complimentary to Hap. It was his turn to frown.

Confused, Hap said, "You sayin you don't wanna dance with me?"

"Yes, that is what I'm saying. I'm here with Charlie Marchesini, and I'm not someone to leave my date high and dry. Unlike *some* people I am unfortunate enough to know."

"What's that supposed to mean?" Hap shuffled his feet as if the world were quaking and affecting his balance.

"You aren't dumb, Harold. You're a lot of things, but dumb isn't one of them. You can figure out my meaning, easy."

Mary grabbed the sides of her dress and hiked the trim from the floor to keep from stepping on it. She drifted away on an air of self-importance. Hap watched her go, his pulse pounding in his head. Mary met up with her date as he was coming out of the boys' room at the rear of the auditorium. Charlie Marchesini looked like a sissy in his purple tux. At least Hap thought so.

Hap sniffed once at the sight of Charlie with Mary and headed outside to smoke and think. He sat in his father's Hudson Hornet, smoking with the windows up, peering through the gray-blue haze, never taking his eyes off the exit to the auditorium. People came and went, but Hap was only interested in one person.

Thirty minutes later, Mary Robichaux and Charlie Marchesini exited the prom, arm in arm. Charlie had the serious expression of a man with one thing on his mind. The front of his pants tented with the foreshadowing of pleasures to come. Mary laughed and played with her hair as she traveled with her beau through the school's parking lot. The couple entered an old rattle-trap and drove away. Hap started the Hudson and followed into the night.

Charlie drove recklessly past the rolled up sidewalks of Bay's End, swerving here and there, like a drunken idiot. But Hap was pretty sure Charlie hadn't been drinking. Ol' Chucky Boy was drunk on anticipation alone. Hap couldn't blame the guy. Chucky Boy was about to get his dick wet, likely for the first time, and Hap hated to interfere, but a man's gotta do what a man's gotta do.

Charlie pulled behind Peaton's Grocery. Hap parked on the side of the building. He waited a count of one hundred before getting out. He rounded the rear corner of the building and found Charlie's rattle-trap parked in the loading bay. The rear of the car danced with activity. Chucky Boy was really giving it to Mary. Hap would have to thank Charlie for preheating the oven for him.

Hap tugged open the back door of the rattle-trap, ducked inside, and yanked Charlie out, the guy's hips pumping even as he fell to the concrete, ass first.

Hap kicked Chuck's teeth in. Chuck's head snapped backward and his skull bounced off the concrete, knocking him cold.

*Well, that was easy.*

Behind him, Mary was screaming. Hap unzipped his pants and dove in on top of her.

Once he had her adequately pinned down, he whispered in her ear.

"You should've danced with me, Mare."

At some point she stopped fighting and took what he was giving. Whether or not she enjoyed herself was none of his concern. At least her cunt didn't smell like smoldering rubber. He shot his wad and climbed off her. He shoved himself up and gazed down; he could see her fine, even in the dark. She lay in the car, perfectly still, perfectly silent, her arms at her sides and her legs spread wide. It was, if Hap was honest, quite the inviting pose.

A thought that had gone previously unconsidered in Hap's short life on this revolving rock, third from the sun, bubbled to the surface of the usually calm water of Lake Carringer.

*She's gonna tell someone. You might even get in trouble.*

Well, he'd deny it. He was a popular guy. People liked him. They'd believe him over her.

Hap turned and looked down on the unmoving form of Charlie Marchesini.

*Fuck.*

Everyone in town would likely believe Hap over Mary, but Hap didn't like the odds of two against one.

*I might even go to jail.*

*Shit.*

*Okay. Calm down. You can fix this.*

Whether that last voice was his or not was anyone's guess.

He knelt beside Charlie. The teenager would be missed, that much was certain. The Marchesini clan procreated like drunken rabbits. Charlie was the oldest of four boys, not to mention the five sisters Hap knew about. Some of the girls were older than Charlie, some of them younger, but all of them doted on Charlie, the first apple to fall off the tree with a stem attached. If Hap asked around town he was sure everyone he could interview would say that Charlie was the favorite child out of the ten-head Marchesini herd. Charlie's yearbook photo caption had read: *I'm going to put bad people away.* Charlie had wanted to be a lawyer, if Hap recalled correctly. The kid was going places.

*Screw it.*

Hap reached down and pinched Chuck's nose closed. Chuck's jaw dropped open. Hap clapped a hand over the guy's mouth. In a minute or so, Chucky Boy started to buck. Not violently, but enough to be annoying. Hap stuck a knee in Charlie's chest to keep him down. Another minute or so later and Ol' Chucky Boy stopped moving entirely. Hap stayed in place for a bit longer, whistling Dixie. Finally he checked for Chuck's pulse but couldn't find it.

Chucky Boy was most assuredly dead. Hap didn't know how he felt about that. The murder didn't feel important in any way, not even in a first-time sense. If questioned on the topic of killing Charlie Marchesini, which he would never be, he'd have to say that the action of ending another person's life didn't affect him in the least. He was a little tired, sure, but shit, look at the night he'd had.

Hap stood and stretched and heard for the first time the slapping of feet on pavement. He twisted and looked into the car, where Mary should have been laid out.

Mary wasn't laid out.

Hap strode out of the loading bay and found her about thirty yards away and moving farther away every second. He sighed and sprinted after her.

He'd cut the distance between them in half by the time she vanished around the corner of the building. He couldn't tell if she was screaming or wheezing, what with the *eee-eee-eee* sound she was making.

Hap skated around the side of Peaton's Grocery. Mary had his car door open and was attempting to crawl inside. He slammed hip-and-shoulder into the open door, catching one of her feet in the jam. She shrieked like a tea kettle. Hap yanked the door wide, slid by, and ripped the squealing pig from his passenger seat. She hit the brick wall of Peaton's Grocery hard and her breath caught in her chest. She clutched at her breasts, seeking the air the impact with the wall had knocked out of her lungs.

Hap punched her in the face as hard as he could. No wimpy swing, this, but a full bore auger of impatience and entitled rage. He put every bit of her rejection behind that punch. He hit her with such force that he was shocked he didn't plant her fucking head in the wall. Yet, somehow, she managed to stay upright.

*Resilient little cunt, ain't'cha?*

He slammed a fist into her soft middle. Mary folded in half. A sound like a cold engine trying to crank came from her. He grabbed her by the hair and the back of her dress and battle-rammed the top of her skull into the Hudson's front, right fender. She collapsed, boneless as a marionette.

He dragged her back to the loading bay by her hair and stuffed her in the backseat, on her back. Then he shoved Ol' Chucky Boy in on top of her. Hap pulled his pack of smokes from his shirt sleeve and tugged the book of matches from the cellophane. He lit Chuck's pant leg on fire with the first match and used the next match to ignite Mary's satin dress.

He had a cigarette while he watched the couple cook like pigs in a smoker. Had it not been for the upholstery catching, the blaze might have gone out prematurely. Luckily for Hap that wasn't the case.

He drove home, coming to terms with the possibility of being caught and killed by the state for the crimes he'd committed tonight. These thoughts kept him awake until the sun came through his bedroom window the next morning. And then he went to work for eight hours.

On his way home that day, he dropped into Peaton's Grocery for a pound of hamburger and a little peace of mind. Everyone he passed in the aisles, which were admittedly sparsely populated for a Saturday, was talking about the tragedy that had befallen Charlie Marchesini and Mary Robichaux. One lady he passed compared the couple's deaths to those of Romeo and Juliet. Hap found that odd. Shakespeare's star-crossed lovers had killed themselves. Surely no one thought Chuck and Mary had set themselves on fire. He paid for his hamburger and headed home.

Monday morning's paper, *The End Times*, provided the details Hap had failed to procure from the gossips at Peaton's.

Nothing about the story made any sense to him. According to the front-page article, Chuck and Mary had perished in a car fire, yes, but those were the only details the paper got right. The blaze that took the lives of the young couple was blamed on faulty wiring in the engine. After reading that part, Hap had to drop the paper and stare at the wall for a time. When he finally looked back to the one-page write up, he read that the gas line in Charlie's car had likely leaked, making a small fire into a deadlier situation than it might have been otherwise. Then the car had exploded, killing both teens instantly.

*What?*

There was no mention of the car having been parked behind the grocery store, or that the couple had died in the backseat. The whole thing smelled, beautifully, like a cover up.

*But why?*

There was only one logical explanation for the missing information.

Someone was trying to save Charlie's and Mary's parents the embarrassment of having to explain why their kids had been in the backseat of a car shortly after leaving their senior prom. Anyone with a healthy sex life could put two and two together. By not mentioning how the couple was found, the article protected everyone involved.

Including Hap himself.

To think that someone would cover up a murder to save face was a realization that rocked Hap. The things someone could get away with if they had even a little dirt on their victims. The revelation changed Hap, and he never saw the world the same way again. It was the closest thing to a religious experience he would ever have.

\*\*\*

The day after Father George killed himself was a cold one. Had Hap not known any better, he'd have thought it was January and not late October.

Ronnie was already at the station when Hap arrived that morning. An urn filled with fresh coffee strong enough to strip the enamel from healthy teeth awaited the sheriff in the break room. A copy of that day's paper lay out on the counter next to the coffee pot. Hap poured himself a cup and sat down to spend a few minutes with *The End Times*.

Father George was front page news, which wasn't a huge shock. Bay's End claimed just over a thousand residents on its yearly census, so anything more substantial than a mouse farting in a field could steal the day's headlines. Unlike the fiery deaths of Charlie Marchesini and Mary Robichaux seventeen years ago, the story of the Georges' deaths was nearly note-for-note accurate, right down to the fact that no one had any clue why Father George would want to do the terrible things he'd done. Hap remained of the mind that the preacher had fallen into a sexual scandal of some kind that he hadn't seen a way out of, but it was more likely that no one, not even he, would ever find out the truth behind the double-murder suicide.

Infidelity, Hap thought, was the most-likely cause, because a sinner always projects their own sins on others. If no one else in the world knew that, Hap sure as hell did.

And then there was the only piece of evidence he had on the case: the phone off the hook in the main hallway downstairs. Either Father George hadn't wanted to be disturbed during his little killing spree, or the man of God had received a phone call that had acted as a catalyst to the bloody deaths of Molly and Georgina, and then Father George himself.

What Hap didn't want to think about until he had no other choice was how his town would react to losing a beloved religious figure such as Father George. Fact of the matter was that god-botherers tended to treat unkindly anything that tested their faith in the Almighty.

After all, what kind of god would allow the kind of death poor Georgina George had suffered? A three-month-old reduced to little more than raw hamburger by a shotgun blast was one of the few things Hap Carringer thought indefensible.

*Ya don't harm defenseless children. Ya just don't.*

Hap sipped his coffee and read the rest of the four-page paper. *The End Times* was normally a one-sheet affair, more of a muted bugle than a marching band in the world of news, but it made the residents of the End feel like they were part of something bigger; something big enough to warrant a newspaper.

Hap read past Father George's front page news. Japan was, just now after over a decade, starting to bounce back from the nuclear attacks they'd suffered in Nagasaki and Hiroshima.

Somehow *The End Times* had landed a phone interview with a white man who had been on the outskirts of Hiroshima at the time of the bombings, a priest named Malcolm Rodgers. Rodgers recounted how metal close to the blast had melted and fused like candle wax. But the most striking comment Hap read that morning had to do with what Rodgers called *Nuclear Shadows*. A picture that would've been front-page news had it been in any other issue of *The End Times* other than the Father-George issue showed the dark silhouette of a child on a cinderblock wall. The photo cited Rodgers as the photographer. Rodgers explained in the interview how the blast had been so bright as to vaporize anyone in the initial blast radius, but not before leaving behind their ghosts on the walls.

The longer Hap stared at the child's outline on the wall the more he could hear the child calling for help, as if their very soul had been trapped in the stone, where it would reside until kingdom come. The child's wailing echoed crystal-clear through Hap's mind. He squeezed his eyes closed and shook his head, hoping the shaking would dispel the haunting lamentations of a dead child whom he'd never met.

"Hap?" Ronnie said from the door to the break room.

Hap opened his eyes and cleared his throat.

"Yeah?"

"Beulah Blackwood's on the phone for you."

"Did she say what she wanted?"

"She only asked for you. Should I tell her you're busy?"

Hap exhaled at length, inadvertently blowing steam from his coffee in the process. The cloud blew out over the paper, fogging the print, and Hap felt thrust into a film noir. All he needed was a trench coat and a narrative voiceover to complete the vision.

"No. I'm comin."

He took the call at the reception desk.

"Carringer speaking." Hap yawned into the back of his hand and waited for Blackwood to start talking. He knew how the woman could ramble. Rambling seemed a potent disease in Bay's End. Female residents were especially susceptible to the sickness.

"Good morning, Harold."

"Mornin, Beulah. What can I do you for?"

"I'm calling in regard to Petey. He's not home this morning. Can't find him none of anywhere."

Pete Blackwood, who never missed a meal, went missing at least twice a week. It was for this reason and this reason alone that Hap sighed into the phone. Probably too forcefully for his own good.

"Why don't you ever take me seriously, Harold?"

The way she said his name like that boiled his blood.

"Because he's fine, *Beulah*." He spat out her name as if it were as foul to him as rancid cabbage. "He'll be home before the end of the day and you know it."

"I know no such thing and neither do you. There's no way anyone could know if he's safe. Other than him, maybe." Beulah sobbed. Hap thought the old biddy deserved some kind of acting award. Something shiny and heavy, so he could bash her over the head with it.

"If he's not home by the time the streetlights come on, call us back and I'll send a car out to look for him. Bye now, Beulah."

49

"Anything could happen to him between now and then!" she said it all so fast it were as if the sentence was monosyllabic.

"Bye, Beulah."

Hap hung up.

Ronnie said, "Pete?"

"Yessir," Hap said with a sad grin. "Gotta say, Ronnie, if I were that woman's ward, I'd run away every other day, too. That, or shoot myself. Poor fuckin kid."

Ronnie smiled in such a way that Hap knew he'd gone too far with his last statement.

Hap said, "Wanna hold things down for me while I take a drive?"

"Sure. Where ya headin?"

"Out to see about Pete."

"Thought you said he was fine?" Ronnie said with a knowing smile stretched across his face.

"Fuck you, kid."

Ronnie laughed as if Hap were playing with him. Hap wasn't about to tell the guy he meant every bit of the curse.

Hap didn't have far to look, or drive, for that matter. Pete Blackwood was where he almost always was: at Carringer and Sons, watching the hustle and bustle of the logging company. The company shared a name with Hap and little else at this point. His grandfather had started the company back in the thirties. Nowadays, his father ran the place. And by *ran the place* one could assume he did nothing but signed paperwork while the on-site manager, Thomas Strömquist, a Swede with a taste for soft women and hard liquor, made sure the place didn't burn down, or go bankrupt.

When Hap pulled up, Pete had his chubby face pressed right up against the chain link of the perimeter fence. The boy looked over his shoulder only when he heard Hap's door slam shut. Pete got an eyeful of the sheriff and visibly deflated.

"Your grandmother phoned."

Pete nodded, his cheeks jiggling like slugs in a paint mixer.

"You wan' go home?"

Pete shook his head.

Hap sighed. "Listen, kid. She calls me every time you do this. Why don't you just come out and tell her you need some air? It ain't healthy, no way, for a kid your age to be cooped up in a house all day. Want I should talk to her? Tell her so?"

"They call me fat?" Pete said, as if it were the obvious response to everything Hap had just said.

"Well, you ain't slight, that's for sure."

Damn kid looked like he was about to cry. Hap sighed again and inwardly told himself to stop all his fucking sighing.

"Who calls you fat?"

"Everybody."

"I haven't never called you fat, have I?"

"Nossir."

"Then not everybody calls you fat. Who especially calls you a porker? Gimme a name. Or names. Whichever it is."

Pete dropped his head, studied his feet as if they'd help him name the suspects. "Doug Opinsky. Ralphie Sikes. Marion Marchesini. Tommy Tucker. Bruce Dykes. Donald T—"

"These boys from your school?"

"Yessir."

"They always mean to you?"

"Mean?"

"Yeah, *mean*. Are they *mean* to you? Jesus, kid, are you all puddin in the head, too? You tell me they call you fat, and then you act like you don't know what *mean* means?"

"They ain't mean about it, nossir. They're laughing and such when they say it."

"Hate to spoil your milk, kiddo, but that's them being mean."

Hap couldn't understand what this kid was on about. If he didn't know these asshole kids were picking on him, what was the big deal? Either he knew they were being mean, and he didn't like it, or... Well, Hap didn't know what other options there were. If it didn't bother the kid in some way, he'd never have mentioned it. Or at least Hap assumed.

"They don't call anyone else fat. Not even other fat kids."

"So just you? They only call you fat?"

"Yessir. They don't even call Mr. Garland fat and he's planetary."

Hap guffawed. Big, soul-belching laughs that about doubled him over. "Oh, shit, kid. Pardon my French, but holy shit, that was funny. David Garland *is* swole as all hell, ain't he?"

Hap continued to laugh. Pete smiled a bit. Just a little. Hap could see the boy thought it was funny too. He simply didn't want to get in trouble for laughing.

"It's okay, kid. Laugh. It's funny. Boy, if Ronnie and Eric were here to hear that one. You said ol' David Garland was planetary. *Planetary!*" Hap howled with laughter.

Pete no longer smiled.

"You ain't gonna tell them, are you?"

Hap wiped tears from his eyes.

"Tell who, kid?"

"Those two names you said. Ronnie and Derrick?"

"Oh. It's Eric, but naw. I ain't gon' tell anyone what you said. Been funnier than hell had they been here. I know for a fact that Eric Larson don't much like David Garland. They've had bad blood since around, oh, since about the end of the second world war."

"Thank you," Pete said.

"What you thanking me for?"

"Laughing at what I said. I don't get much laughing at what I say. Mostly people just laugh at *me*."

"Well, you're a funny kid, kiddo. Least I think so."

"Do I really have to go home?"

Hap glanced around. Two men in overalls and conductor hats standing inside the fence waved at Hap and Hap reciprocated.

"I don't suppose so. I'll give your grandmother a ring and let her know you're okay. That all right with you?"

"That'd be fine, I guess."

Hap smiled. "You guess?"

"Yessir."

"You're kinda wishy-washy, ain't'cha." It wasn't a question.

"Wishy-washy?"

"On the fence."

Pete glanced over his shoulder to the chain link.

Hap said, "No, I mean... Shit. Um, on the fence can mean you're—damn it, what's the word. It's like when you're on the commode and you think you might be done but you don't want to risk getting up and messing yourself, but you don't wanna sit on the toilet all day, either. You're... *indecisive!* Christ, finally. What an elusive goddamn word. Pardon my French, of course."

"Adult words don't bother me any."

"Good," Hap said with a nod. "Stay that way. Some people are too gosh-darn sensitive for their own good. Folks like your grandmother."

Pete's eyes got big and his head nodded frantically, as if to say, *You sure are right about that!*

"She gives you a load of grief, don't she." Again, not a question.

"I don't guess she's all that bad. She's worse than my parents were, that's for sure. They were swell. Until they died. Now they're just dead."

"I had an uncle who died in a fishing accident. He's the only one I was ever close to who died. I've cleaned up dead people off the road before and it don't bother me none, but Hank, that's my uncle, his death rightly hurt. Stung." Hap tapped his chest over his heart. "Hurt right here. He used to take me fishing and hunting when I was a sprout, not much older than you. 'Bout twelve or thirteen, I was. Shot my first ten-point before the first hair sprouted on my balls."

Pete blushed but laughed. He was getting through to the kid. That was good. Maybe the little fucker would stop running off all the goddamn time if he knew not everyone hated him.

Pete said, "That's a funny word."

"What is? *Balls*?"

Pete chortled. "Yes!"

"Well, you got balls. I got balls. All us men's got balls. Just a load of balls swinging in the wind. Only thing holdin them back is your jockey shorts. But, sometimes, they'll escape and get all twisted up and you'll think your life is about to end if you don't find a restroom to sort yourself out in. So you do a little dance, like a tree frog with a stun gun up his asshole!"

Pete was all but rolling around in the gravel laughing. Tears coursed down the kid's chubby cheeks as he huffed and snorted and snot ran down his face. Hap thought the kid was all right. He might not be all right to everyone, but he was pretty all right to Hap.

When Pete was done laughing, Hap said, "You better now?"

Pete wiped at his face. "Yessir."

"How 'bout I don't call your grandmother. How 'bout you just head on home in, let's say, an hour? How'd that be?"

"That would be fine, sir."

"Good. You have a nice day, Pete."

"You too, sir."

Hap slid behind the wheel of his car and watched as Pete headed back to his place against the fence. What could be so interesting about watching men work? Was Pete Blackwood fantasizing about being a lumberjack? Was his life's ambition to chop wood to his heart's content? Hap didn't think any of that was right. The answer to Pete's fascination with Carringer and Son's Logging was likely far simpler than even Hap's estimations. It likely had to do with order and chaos. Things being torn apart and repurposed. Not necessarily becoming better. Just different. Trees were pretty things, tall and green and lovely smelling. But a nice piece of woodworking could be just as pretty. Pete might appreciate that, how things could change. How things might not always be the same. How you could be torn down to your most basic level and still serve a purpose.

Whether it was Pete, or Hap himself, who saw things this way, well, that was anyone's guess.

Hap glanced at his watch. 8:15.

# 4. On These Worn Knees They Pray

Pete Blackwood would never tell anyone the real reason why he liked watching the men working inside Carringer and Sons Logging because not even he knew his motivation.

He hadn't known what to say to the sheriff—whatever the man's name had been—so he'd tossed the cop the same lie he'd given his grandmother Beulah.

*They call me fat.*

Well, yeah, sure they did, but Pete was well ahead of his time and gender politics in the sense that when he said *They* he was referring to one person. *They* was actually a *Him* and Pete liked *Him* very much. *Him* being the toughest boy in the tri-county area, Rodeo Feldman.

First off, Rodeo had an amazing name. What guy wouldn't want to be named Rodeo? Pete knew he'd change his name to Rodeo in a heartbeat, given the chance, and Pete didn't even care about bulls and matadors and clowns and barrels, and whatever else they had at rodeos. He simply liked the sound of the name. *Rodeo*. It rolled off the tongue. Not like *Pete*. *Pete* sounded like something one did in a toilet. *Pete* sounded weak. *Rodeo* was anything but weak.

Second, Rodeo was older, and Pete had a fascination with all things twelve years old, as if reaching that age was the end-all-be-all of human achievements. Who gave a rat's behind about thirteen? You were a teenager—so what? Fourteen was for the birds. And fifteen? Well, ladies and gentlemen, fifteen was such a far off concept that Pete's imagination could only conjure images of him being imbued with wizard-like abilities the likes of which mankind had never seen. Such talents would include: learning to drive, high school, and possibly his first *piece of ass*, whatever that was. All the older boys talked about getting a *piece of ass*, and it sounded like fun, but it was yet another thing his innocent mind could not visualize. Certainly the term wasn't literal. No one was running around snatching the asses off people. Surely the term was one of those things people just said, something that sounded awful but was really quite pleasant. Anyway, maybe fifteen would be better than twelve, eventually, but as of right now, twelve was closer, and therefore of greater importance.

Thirdly, Pete didn't much care that Rodeo mocked him. Any attention from what he considered his schoolyard hero would have been welcome. And then there was the fact that, on occasion, Rodeo had stuck up for Pete, as if it were fine and dandy that he picked on Pete, but should anyone else do so, well, they would suffer his wrath.

One time, Doug Opinsky had called Pete a beached whale at the public pool and Rodeo had given Doug a wedgie in retaliation. You should've seen Opinsky dance and jive with his underwear up his butt. Pete had laughed and laughed, and then Rodeo had said, "What's so funny, Fatty?" and Pete had stopped laughing. Pete had wiped happy tears from his eyes and went on smiling, but he'd held in his chuckles after that, all while Doug Opinsky dug a good yard of Fruit-o-the-Looms out of his butthole.

Rodeo was great when his attention wasn't solely on Pete in the schoolyard. Rodeo was even better when he was picking on someone else entirely.

While Pete could not, at this time in his life, lock down what made him come out here to watch the men work, or from where stemmed his hero-worship of Rodeo Feldman, he knew well and good why he'd left the house this morning; he didn't want to go to church.

He hated that silly place, where a goofy man shouted from a pulpit, and a superstitious throng hung on every word. The Bible that these people read from was full of magic and other nonsense on par with the idea that a fat man in a red coat delivered candy and toys to all the good Christian children of the world in a single night. Pete never jived with the idea of Santa Claus, and had skirted religion for many of the same reasons.

His father and mother—may they rest in peace—had been adamant about their atheism. They'd taught Pete at an early age that God, like Santa and the Easter Bunny, was more idea than actuality. All three had been created to control a set group of individuals. Santa and the only bunny on the planet to ever have lain eggs, were there to make children behave. Plant good seeds and you will sow good things. Religion was that very same thing for adults. Don't be horrible, even though you tend to the horrible, and some deity will grant you eternal life.

This all made a lot of sense to Pete, a sensible kid raised by sensible people; sensible people who'd passed away too young. Sensible people who'd tried their best to remove him from the zealotry of his grandmother, only to die and force him to live with her. What kind of sense did that make?

Pete knew he couldn't blame his folks for leaving him with his grandmother. That had been the court's decision. Because there had been no will written up for a couple young enough to believe they might live long enough to enjoy seeing their child graduate high school, no one had been named to inherit the boy after their death. The judge gave him to his grandmother without a single qualm mentioned. Why not Grandma? She seemed as good as anybody, and lookey here, she's a stalwart Christian! All the better.

He could abide her near-constant praying and browbeating him into attending church, but he couldn't gel with worshipping alongside her. Besides, it didn't really matter, did it? He checked his watch. Quarter after eight. She'd be at church right now, he was sure of it, with or without him. So the concern that drove her to call the sheriff spoke more to her desire that he attend church moreso than it said anything about her concern for his whereabouts and safety.

He dropped his arm and tried to ignore the watch on his wrist. That had been a stupid idea, checking it when he'd been in such a decent mood. The day had started off rather poorly, with Mama hooting and hollering for him to get up and get ready for "the Lord's day!" Once he'd heard the shower start, he'd dressed quickly in jeans and a t-shirt, pulled on his sneakers, and sneaked out the back door. Carringer and Sons had been a fifteen minute walk, and Pete was well and truly tired when he finally arrived, but watching the men had put him in a great mood. Talking to the sheriff had somewhat mellowed his chill, but now that the sheriff was out of Pete's hair, his good mood had returned.

Then he'd looked at his watch.

His father's watch.

His *dead* father's watch.

Why it had seemed a good idea for the detective investigating the murder of Pete's parents to give Pete his father's watch, Pete would never know. It seemed the antithesis of a good idea. At least to Pete it did. The watch, for all the good memories it carried with it, ticked and tocked peacefully on his right wrist, reminding him with every single movement that its existence on his person had come by way of his father's brutal murder. And, of course, when he thought about that, he thought about the man in the mask; the man who'd diced up his parents as if they were nothing more than celery and carrots to be added to a pot roast.

*Stop thinking about it.*

His inner voice sounded a lot like his father's voice. That certainly didn't help matters. But, in the end, he managed to rip his mind away from his dead parents.

He had over four hours to kill before his grandmother came home, and his legs were already tired of holding up his chubby torso, so he turned and headed in the direction of home. But, halfway down Juniper, the road that led to Carringer and Sons, Pete made a right turn into sparsely packed forest, known colloquially as Marietta Wood. What led him in this new direction, in the exact opposite direction of home, he hadn't a clue. But to say he felt drawn would not be an exaggeration. He had no idea what awaited him through these trees, but he'd find out, sooner rather than later.

\*\*\*

Wesley Haversham had been up since the cock crowed at four that morning. Knowing that Father George was dead, Wesley knew there wouldn't be any call for him to dress in his Sunday Best, which just happened to consist of the only shirt and tie he owned; his father had a shirt and tie, too, just one of each, like his son, and those were (you guessed it) Pa's Sunday Best.

Wesley fed the chickens and milked three of their five cows all before Pa came out to join him in the barn.

"You eat breakfast?" Pa asked.

"Yessir. Had a slice of that ham you smoked the other day."

Pa nodded. "That all you have?"

"Yessir."

"Go inside and grab you a hunk of bread and a glass of milk. I'll finish with the cows."

"Yessir."

Wesley jogged from the open barn, across what amounted to his backyard, where a clothesline and smoker sat cloaked in morning mist, and up the back stairs. He ripped a healthy portion of bread from the loaf on the counter and poured a glass of milk. He dunked the bread in the milk and savored every bite. When he was done, he washed the glass and brushed the crumbs off the table and into his hand. He dropped the crumbs, what few they were, into the pig trough. Miniscule additions to the slop, but his father had always told him, *waste not, want not,* and Wesley did everything his Pa told him to do.

He returned to the barn only for Pa to send him out to the road to weed at the front of their property, where the scrub met the road, between the hedgerow and the tarmac.

He was yanking dandelions out by their roots when the fat kid shuffled over the crest of Highway 607 and into view. Wesley made note of the kid but kept right on ripping weeds from their beds. He imagined he could hear them screaming, which excited him. He wondered if the dead returning to life and clawing themselves from their graves would sound something like the soundtrack playing in his head.

When the fat kid shuffled near enough, Wesley dusted his hands on his overalls and waved.

The fat kid waved back.

"Don't you go to my school?" Wesley said when the fat kid was close enough.

"You're Wesley Haversham. You sit right in front of me in Science."

"Right. I don't reckon I ever paid attention to your name."

"Nobody ever does. I'm Pete Blackwood."

"Hiya, Pete," Wesley said with a grin.

"Hi." Pete did not return Wesley's joviality.

"You okay?"

"Yes."

"You sure?"

"Yes."

"Um. Okay."

"Okay."

And then Pete started walking again, as if he'd never shared a single word with Wesley. Everything about the fat kid—*Pete, his name is Pete*—said that he wanted to be left alone. But everything inside Wesley told him not to leave Pete alone. Something about the way Pete walked, with his head down and feet all cocked outwards like a duck, made Wesley think that Pete needed someone to talk to.

Wesley called to Pete's back, "You want to hang around? Maybe help me with my chores? Then we can swim in the creek, or take a ride on my tractor."

Pete's head snapped around. "You got a tractor? One we can ride on?"

"Well, it ain't mine. It's my Pa's, but he lets me drive it, so I don't see why we couldn't drive it around for a piece."

"For a piece? Like a piece of ass?"

Wesley blinked and shook his head as if he'd just been slapped. "Do what?"

"Nothing. Sorry. Just thought that—never mind. You sure your old man won't mind?"

"Positive."

"Why so positive if you haven't asked him yet?"

"'Cause I don't plan to ask him."

Pete laughed. "You aren't worried you'll get in trouble?"

"Nah. Pa don't really get mad. Besides, haven't you realized that it's easier to ask for forgiveness than it is to ask for permission?"

"Never thought of it like that."

"Well, now you can think about it like that. Me? I don't choose to think too much. Ruins all the fun when you overthink something. Just better do it and suffer the consequences once it's done. Saves you a load of worries, is what I say."

"That sounds dangerous."

"What does?"

"Doing things without thinking. Sounds like someone could get hurt doing that."

"Sure you gonna get hurt sometimes, but that's life—right? I mean, weren't nothing discovered worth discovering that didn't wind up killing a whole mess of folks. You heard 'bout all those who died on the Mayflower and whatnot. Those people, they took the ultimate chance for a better life and gave their all for a chance to live without kings and stuff. Best we can do is follow in their footsteps, and maybe we find a better life too."

"That's an odd way of thinking. We aren't settlers. Shoot, I'm not even much of an explorer."

Wesley shrugged. "No time like the present to start."

"What do you suggest we explore?"

"Anything we ain't never seen."

"Anything we *haven't* seen."

"That's what I said. Anything we ain't never seen."

"*Ain't never* is a double negative. It's not proper grammar."

"Ain't nothin proper about me, I don't reckon," Wesley said with a laugh. He liked this kid. He hated that he'd never talked to him before.

"Do I have to get on my knees?" Pete asked.

Wesley frowned. "To do what?"

Pete hitched his chins at the pile of evicted dandelions sitting by the Haversham mailbox. "To weed. You wanted me to help, right?"

"Oh. Yeah. Sure. If you wanna."

"I don't mind as long as I can sit. All this walking has worn out my knees."

"All right. Yeah. I suppose you can sit down anywhere there's weeds and rip 'em out just fine. Want some gloves?"

"You aren't using any," Pete said.

"'Cause I got farmers' hands. You should see Pa's hands. You couldn't cut through them things with a table saw. His hands are tougher than most metal."

"That him?" Pete pointed back toward the barn. "That your Pa?"

Wesley glanced over his shoulder. Pa was standing in the open doors of the barn, wiping his hands on a towel he'd draped over his shoulder. When Pa saw Wesley looking, he waved. Wesley waved back and Pa disappeared back inside the shadows of the barn.

"Yessir, that's him."

"He's a good guy?"

"I guess so. I don't have any complaints, lest he's hollerin about a ball game or somethin, then he can get kinda annoyin."

"I don't watch ball games," Pete said.

"Me neither. I'd rather play em instead of watch em."

"I don't like playing ball games, either. I don't do much of anything, I don't suppose."

"You walk, don't'cha?"

"Well... today I did. But only 'cause I didn't want to go to church."

Wesley said, "I don't suppose there's gonna be church today, what with all that happened yesterday."

Pete frowned with confusion. "What happened?"

"You ain't heard?" Wesley said. "Shoot, I done thought everyone would've heard by now."

"Well, go on. What happened?"

"Father George, do ya know him?"

Pete nodded.

"He killed his wife and baby girl and then shot himself. I saw the whole thing. Well, not him killing the baby and Molly, but I seen him shoot himself. What come out of him, it looked like blackberry preserves my momma used to make. She's dead, too, my momma is."

Pete's jaw dropped. Wesley looked into that mouth and saw nary a cavity in sight. He subconsciously covered his mouth with the back of his hand to hide his own teeth, which he knew were nowhere near as clean as they could, or should be.

"You saw him kill himself?"

Wesley nodded. He didn't think anything more needed to be said on the subject, but Pete obviously thought differently.

"How'd he do it?"

"You really want to know?"

"Oh, yes. Please."

"Kinda morbid talk, isn't? I mean, don't'cha think?"

"Well, sure, but I'd still like to know." Pete seemed to think for a minute, and then blurted, "I bet that's what all the phone calls were for yesterday! My grandmother was on the phone nearly all day yesterday, gossiping with her friends. I didn't much listen. Boy, do I regret that now!"

"Why you so interested in Father George killin his-own-self? I mean, I don't think someone should look as excited as you look right now. I don't reckon it's, well, I don't reckon it's proper."

"Oh. Sorry." All the excitement drained from Pete's face. "I'll leave then. Sorry again."

Pete turned to go.

Wesley hollered, "Hol' up! Where ya goin?"

Pete faced Wesley. "I didn't think you'd want to hang out anymore, seeing as how I'm not proper enough for you." Pete's version of what Wesley had said sounded harsher than Wesley had intended.

"I never said you weren't—just, I don't know, just that I wouldn't react that way, s'all I'm sayin. I mean, I saw him do it, and it wasn't nothing to get excited over. It was pretty bad, him killin himself, but what he looked like, boy-hoo, that was even worse."

"What do you mean what he looked like?" Pete asked, his eyes shining with expectation.

"Well, he looked like there weren't nothing inside him. His eyes were all wrong. They were just, I don't know, they was emptier than a bear's butthole come springtime."

Pete laughed. "I like that. *Emptier than a bear's butthole come springtime.* Oh, boy, that's funny."

Wesley smiled but did not laugh. "I guess it were funny, but had you seen Father George, you wouldn't be laughing. Bet you'd run screaming, had you seen him."

Pete's face grew somber. "I've seen someone empty. I know what you mean."

"You have? Where?"

"The man who killed my folks, he were—I mean, he was empty. His eyes were the only thing I could see of him. He wore a mask. Something that covered the whole of his head."

"What kinda mask?"

"A babydoll mask. All shiny like. Like it was made out of rubber."

"Wow. So he killed your folks?"

Pete nodded.

"Where were you, you know… when it happened?"

"I was right there."

"No way!"

"Yes way."

"And you just sat there and watched?"

"I didn't know what else to do."

"Wow," Wesley repeated. "Wowzers!"

"Could we change the subject? If you don't wanna tell me about Father George that's fine. You don't have to. But I really don't wanna talk about…" Pete's voice trailed off as he glanced at his watch.

"Yeah. Sure. Sorry. I can tell you what I saw, if you want, but we ain't gotta talk about none of it, if'n ya don't want to."

"I'd like to hear about Father George, if you don't mind."

"You sure?"

"Yeah, I'm sure. I guess I wanna know because it's nice to know that I'm not alone. Nice to know that I'm not the only one my age who's seen something terrible."

"Everything is horrible now," Wesley said.

"Yeah. I guess you could say that. After seeing—"

"No. That's what Father George said before he shot himself with his shotgun. *Everything is horrible now.* Creeped me out."

"Whoa. Why do you think he said that?"

"Pa says that we might never know, and I'm inclined to believe him. He says that sometimes bad stuff, it just happens, and worrying on it too long will only drive you crazy. At the very least, it'll keep you sad, so I try not to dwell."

"I don't blame you. Wow. *Everything is horrible now*, you say he said?"

"Yep."

And with that, the boys started weeding. By the time they were done, they'd created a friendship that would, for one of them, last a lifetime.

\*\*\*

Hap knew that not everyone in town would have heard about Father George's death. He could think of well over a dozen folks in town who didn't have phone service yet, nor did they subscribe to the paper. When they showed up to the End's only house of worship to find there would be no worshipping done today, things were bound to get interesting. Because those out-of-touch sorts, those without telephones and newspaper subscriptions and ties to the outside world, well, those were the sort of folks who caused a fuss. They already didn't like this world of flesh they inhabited, not to mention the unclean sorts who populated it, so any deviation from their weekly ritual and routine could be seen as utterly catastrophic. Swinging by the church might be best.

Chastity Baptist sat in the center of town. Not downtown, but the geographical center of Bay's End. The brick-and-mortar structure had a steepled roof and white shutters on windows that were never closed on a sunny day. Hap had only attended church twice in his entire life, and both of those times had been to attend weddings to which he'd been unfortunately invited. Not that he didn't believe in God. Just the opposite. He believed someone was watching out for him up there in the great blue wonder. Hap just didn't like church. There were better things to do on a Sunday morning. Like fucking.

The first two rows of Chastity Baptist's parking lot had been overtaken by vehicles that looked held together by nothing more than their owners' thoughts and prayers. One Ford pickup in particular no longer had a bed. Two struts jutted from the rear of the truck like the legs of a rust-brown grasshopper. A station wagon that had pulled in directly ahead of Hap towed a hay cart behind it. Three dirty children in overalls and no shoes dangled their filthy legs over the sides of the cart, each one's smile the color of fresh butter. The station wagon pulled through, taking up two spots, front and back, and Hap pulled in beside it.

The way the church was situated, the parking lot came right up to the front doors. Main Street ran off to the right. Nothing but trees on the left, some of what the town called Marietta Wood.

Hap got out.

Two people were already at the front doors of the church. One guy dressed in a white button down with a brown stain on the front that looked as if it had come from either coffee or chewing tobacco was watching him as Hap approached the steps. A woman without any front teeth, top or bottom, and a greenish-brown bruise around her left eye smiled at Hap when he walked past. Her appearance unsettled him. It was the bruise. Not that he didn't think a woman shouldn't be put in her place from time to time

(after all, hadn't he just put Janice Larson in her place last night?);
it had nothing to do with that. He was disturbed by the look of the
bruise. It looked as if someone had taken a seed from an avocado
and replaced it with an eyeball. He shivered at the thought.

"No one's home, boys," Hap said as he clopped up the front
steps.

"Whatchoo mean ain't no one home?" Coffee Stain said. The
guy was so tanned Hap thought he wasn't a shade paler than a
Negro. Why any white man would wanna let his skin get that dark
was an oddity to the sheriff's way of thinking.

Hap cleared his throat. "Hate to be the bearer of bad news,
fellas, but Father George passed away yesterday morning."

"He didn't!" the one yanking on the door howled. "That
woman come by here spittin those lies earlier, and we told her—we
told her we wasn't gonna fall for the devil in her. Father George
ain't dead. Cain't be! He'll be here. And these doors best be open
when he gets here!"

*We got ourselves a live one, ladies and gentlemen.*

The Live One had on a red flannel shirt with a hole in the
middle of the back and its sleeves were rolled to the elbow. His
jeans weren't anything to write home to mother about, either, what
with the quarter-sized hole in the seat advertising how much
money this guy saved on underwear.

The smell coming off these two could have driven away the
devil.

"What's your name, son?" Hap asked the Live One, who
continued to tug on the door.

"I ain't none of your kin, lawman," the Live One growled,
still not looking at Hap. And if he wasn't looking at Hap, how the

hell did he know that Hap was a *lawman*? Maybe he'd seen Hap pull in. That had to be it.

And who said Lawman? When had he stepped into a fuckin western?

"Listen, fella, I think you need to stop pullin on that door and look at me when I'm talking to you."

To Hap's surprise, the Live One quit tugging and turned to face him. Hap had looked into the eyes of many a drunken sort—when you were the only law in town, everybody's domestic business eventually ended up your business, and folks in the End loved to drink—but this aimless bastard had all of them beat. His blood-red eyes seemed cracked, as if the sclera had hardened and fissured along red fault lines. The wrinkles between the Live One's eyes had actually cracked on the horizontal, giving Hap the impression of a tic-tac-toe board. A spot on the Live One's cheek had the look of raw, red meat. The guy's arms were dotted with dead and rotting flesh, yet his hands looked strong as vice grips, powerful and callused.

Hap wouldn't have been surprised if the Live One had said he'd just gotten back from a vacation in Hell itself. Had the guy said that, Hap felt he'd be inclined to believe every word of the story.

"What's your name?" Hap managed to say, mainly because it was the only thing he could think to say. The Live One and his horrible skin had shaken him far more than he'd ever want to let on, even to trusted company.

"Jerimiah!" the Live One yelled. Spittle flew from his mouth and dotted the concrete steps. Hap thanked that omniscient presence he believed in that none of that spit had touched his bare skin.

"Listen, Jerimiah, you're gonna end up succeeding in your mission to rip that door off its hinges, and then I'm gonna have to take you in for destruction of property. Now, I don't wanna do that, and I'm sure you don't want me to have to do something I don't wanna do."

"Fuck what you want, lawman!"

"Jer, Jer, brother, calm down," said Coffee Stain.

"Listen to your brother, Jer."

Jerimiah didn't seem to take too kindly to Hap calling him Jer.

"What? You think you know me? Don't call me Jer, lawdog. Don't you call me nothing but *sir*, ya hear me?"

Hap laid a hand on the Colt revolver in the rawhide holster on his hip.

"I don't want to have to ask you again, Jerimiah. Stop your tuggin on that door." Truth be told, Jerimiah had stopped tugging on that door a few seconds ago. Now Hap and Jer the Live One were face to face, albeit about five feet apart. Hap remained impressed at how badly these guys stunk. The fecal-and-body-odor mélange about brought Hap to tears.

"Or, what? You gonna shoot me with yer pistol, *lawman*?" Jerimiah said the epithet in a sing-song voice that ground Hap's gears. He hated dealing with crazy. He didn't care to deal with anyone as unpredictable as himself.

Hap took a single step toward Jerimiah before a voice stopped him.

"Sheriff?"

Hap turned to find a woman with silver hair down to her knees standing in the parking lot, between the first row of cars and the church steps.

"Don't touch my boy, sheriff. He's sick, sir. Jerimiah's just sick, is all."

"What's wrong with him?" Hap paused and looked the woman over. Everywhere skin was on displayed so were the gray-rimmed cracks in the flesh. And, while her face was unblemished, the woman's neck looked as if a wild animal had been at her. She swooped a darned shawl around her neck when she saw him staring. Hap added, "What's wrong with the both of you?"

"We're sick, is all."

"So you said. Mind telling me why you threatened me?"

"Threatened you?" the woman asked. He had to give it to her, she looked honestly confused.

"You said I shouldn't touch him, as if there would be consequences if I did."

"Oh, yessir," she said. "There most definitely would be consequences."

"That right?" Hap said, unbuttoning the strap over the gun on his hip.

"Yessir. We's a cursed peoples, we is, sir. We got the leprosy. And whatever touches us, gets sick with it."

Hap buttoned the latch on his gun.

He said, "Your skin's dyin?"

"Yessir. This why we come here, here where God lives. This is why we've come to worship the only one who can save us."

*Because he's done such a good job so far, right?* Hap thought with an inward smile. He'd let these people have their antiquated superstitions. Wasn't any healing going on here, and Hap thought he knew why. If there was an Almighty up there, Hap assumed he was partial to worshippers who bathed and wore underwear. You know, decent-like folks.

Jerimiah giggled. "Wan' I should caress your cheek, lawdog?"

"Jer'll behave, sir," said Coffee Stain. It was odd, seeing the shift in attitude with this one in the presence of the silver-haired woman. Even his facial muscles were calmer. His eyes had a dull sheen now, too, like that of someone in a trance. "He's just shaken by that woman what done come by here spoutin her lies."

Hap regretfully took his eyes off the silver-haired woman and focused once more on the two at the head of the steps.

"Who come by?" Hap asked.

"That *witch*!" Jerimiah raged.

"I said. Calm. Down." Hap hadn't said that, but who was really paying attention to words at this point?

"Her name's Blackwood. She's *injin*." Coffee Stain's nose curled up as he said it, as if he'd finally gotten a whiff of himself.

"Beulah Blackwood?" Hap said, confused.

"Yessuh," said the woman behind him. "That's her name. She's been... *unkind* to me and my boys. When my husband lost his battle with the leprosy, she said *Good riddance*, and that he shouldn't have a Christian burial. O' course, Father George, bein the good Man of God that he is—"

*Was*, Hap thought. *The good Man of God that he was...*

"—did my Henrik's soul right, he did. He laid him to rest with beautiful words and blessing the likes none o' us ever heard!" She dropped to her knees and genuflected at the bottom of the steps. Then she kissed the concrete beneath her as if it were a long-lost lover.

*Oh boy, here we go.*

"What's your name, ma'am?" Hap said.

"Gertrude," said Coffee Stain.

Hap wished these sons of bitches would pick a spokesperson and stick with them. All this turning back and forth was making him dizzy.

"Gertrude what?"

"We Fulgores, *lawman*," Jerimiah growled.

Hap said, "Gertrude Fulgore. That right, ma'am?"

Although her lips and nose were flush with the concrete, Gertrude nodded.

"All right, Mrs. Fulgore, ma'am, I'm going to have to ask you and your boys to leave. Everybody gonna have to leave."

"Why come?" Coffee Stain said.

"Why come? Well, for one, Beulah, that is, Ms. Blackwood, wasn't lying to you folks. As hard as it is to believe, Father George is dead and gone. Ain't no lie in that. I'm sorry for your loss, and that the news was brought to you unkindly by someone who you don't rightly like, but it is the God's honest truth. Father George took his own life yesterday morning."

"Liar," Gertrude spoke to the concrete. "You're a liar, jus' like that Blackwood woman. You're a liar like the Devil hisself."

Her not looking at him when she talked—well, it unsettled him, is what it did. He didn't like the feeling. Anything that disrupted his usually calm demeanor upset Hap on a visceral level.

*Look at me when you're talking to me, you old bitch*, thought Hap.

But what he said was, "Ma'am, get up."

To his shock, she shoved herself up to one knee then fully erect.

"You can live in your den of lies, sheriff, but the Lord's reckoning is upon us. This town will burn, and your fat will sizzle on the hot plate that is its bedrock."

*Damn woman's* Looney Toons.

"Come on, boys," Gertrude Fulgore said and her boys listened. Jerimiah and Coffee Stain strode past Hap, leaving him in the wake of their unseemly body odor. When he was done here, he'd need to cauterize his nose hairs to burn the stench out of them.

"Y'all have a good day," Hap said with a wave. None of the three Fulgores returned his goodbye or his wave as they headed for a shit-brown pickup truck.

Jerimiah, for all his faults, opened the passengers side door for his mother before jumping behind the wheel. Coffee Stain, whatever his real name was, leaped into the bed. The Fulgores backed out of their spot and headed for the Main Street exit.

After the nuts were gone, several people who'd been hiding in their cars got out and approached Hap. He knew the lot of them. They were his people. His tribe. They were Enders.

"Good to see you, sheriff," Martin Opinsky held out his hand and shook it.

"Feeling's mutual, Marty. Where's the missus and the boy?"

"She's sick with a head cold, and Doug, well, he's stubborn. Didn't feel like fighting to get him out of bed this morning, so I left him with his mother."

"I don't blame you. Nothing worse than going to church with someone who don't wanna be there."

Martin Opinsky smiled. "That why we don't see you here on Sunday, sheriff?"

"I work Sundays, Marty. You know that," Hap said with a wink.

A crowd gathered around Hap, each person's face a mixture of gratitude and concern, that weird middle ground where indecision and fear copulates and multiplies. They all wanted to ask. He could feel the curiosity and genuine concern emanating off them. Had Beulah Blackwood not stopped and talked with everyone? Or had she arrived before them all, only to be chased off by the appearance of the Fulgores?

"Y'all wantin to know why the church is locked, I reckon?"

Heads nodded, and some even murmured *yeses* and *that's rights*.

Hap sighed, as if it pained him to say the words he said next, when in honesty, saying them didn't bother him whatsoever.

"Father George took his own life yesterday morning."

Gasps throughout the crowd.

"What seems to have happened is that he murdered his wife and baby girl before killing himself. I'm sorry. I know how much they all meant to you."

"He killed Georgina?" asked a woman in the back. Sheryl Carter was her name. She owned the town laundromat.

"And Molly?" asked Frank Sikes, father of Ralphie Sikes, the kid who'd caught rabies a few years back. Hap would never forget that incident because he'd had to shoot the dog himself. He liked dogs.

Hap didn't answer either question vocally; he only nodded his head.

"Oh my God," said Nancy Wanamaker, who worked in the jewelry store from which every married person in attendance had purchased their engagement and eventual wedding rings.

"I know it's rough news but—"

Then something shifted. Hap could feel something in the air, something tangible enough to stop him from finishing his sentence. A powerful sense of doom came over him, and he wouldn't have been a bit surprised to look to the sky to find it falling down on top of his head.

*This town will burn...*

A woman in the middle of the group turned her head first. Nancy Wanamaker followed suit. Martin Opinsky and Hap himself were the last two to look and see the blood-drenched teenager shambling toward them like a creature in a horror film.

Kirby Johnson. Hap would have recognized the kid anywhere, even soaked in blood like he was now. Kirby wasn't what you'd call popular, not in the End anyway. Infamous was likely a better word for what Kirby was. Rumor had it that his mother had sent him away for a time due to some deviant behavior on the boy's part, but Hap didn't know how true that had been.

Kirby collapsed several feet from the group and began crawling toward the steps of the church.

"Gottfried! Gottfried!" the boy wailed.

Gottfried was Father George's first name. Hearing the boy howl the dead man's name froze Hap's spine.

"Kirby," Hap said. "Kirby Johnson. Hey, buddy. What happened?"

"Gottfried!" the boy lamented.

Hap watched in stunned silence as the boy crawled up the half-dozen steps to the front door.

Kirby grabbed the handles on the doors and hefted himself to his feet, wailing all the while, screaming Father George's first name as if it were an incantation that could summon the pastor from the grave.

"Kirby, I'm gonna need you to calm down, son," Hap said. He still hadn't moved toward the church steps though. Something about this situation felt more than wrong. Something far more dangerous than what appeared on the surface alone. Hap's head rattled with the cacophony of a dozen alarms: the blood, the repeated name, the stunned-silent crowd, the clouds overhead. Where had those clouds come from? Hap could've sworn the sky had been clear just a moment ago, when he'd been dealing with the Fulgores.

"*GOTTFRIED!*" The boy's screams hurt Hap's heart. No one would ever accuse him of being a sentimental man, but suddenly he wanted to crawl into bed and cry the day away.

*What the fuck is going on here?*

Hap broke the spell he'd been under by moving. He stormed up the steps like an angry father who's come home from work to find out his child's been bad at school. Maybe it was this disciplinarian attitude, this storming after Kirby that caused Martin Opinsky to call Hap's name in warning, as if to tell Hap to watch himself, as if Martin were the mother in this situation. *Don't hurt the boy, Hap, just teach him a lesson and be done with it.* But when Martin Opinsky said Hap's name, Hap didn't turn around.

Kirby did.

Several women in the crowd screamed.

Martin Opinsky muttered, "My God."

Nancy Wanamaker fainted and cracked her head on the parking lot's asphalt. She'd need four stitches before the afternoon was over.

What Hap saw couldn't have been. It wasn't logically possible.

Charlie Marchesini and Mary Robichaux stood at the doors of the church, arm in arm like a couple just married, their charred bodies smoking, their blackened faces smiling, white eyes glaring.

"What the hell," Hap murmured and took a step backward.

And then they were gone. Just like that. The only person standing at the head of the church steps was the blood-drenched and sorrowful Kirby Johnson.

Kirby met Hap's terrified gaze.

*Those eyes*, Hap thought.

But he said, "My God, son, what happened to you?"

Weeping, Kirby Johnson said, "Everything is horrible now."

\*\*\*

After the incident with the Coat Men the night prior, Kirby had slept fitfully, his mother warmly tucked in next to him, there to keep him safe and comforted. But, upon waking, Kirby found she was gone. Her lavender scent lingered on his sheets, which was pleasant to wake up to but disconcerting because there was another odor accompanying it: the smell of ozone, of the earth before a hard rain, the metallic scent of spent adrenaline.

Kirby swung out of bed and rushed into the hallway. Noises came from the kitchen. Maybe the scraping of pots and pans? Kirby sniffed the air and found no lingering aromas of cooking food. Unhurried, slowed by the thought of a possible threat present somewhere in the house, Kirby crept toward the kitchen.

He exited the hallway and turned left into the open kitchen.

His mother was arranging dishes on the dining room table. A frying pan was on the stove, the burner set to medium heat. A bowl of whole eggs yet to be cracked sat on the counter, beside the sink. Shredded potatoes lay on a plate beside the stove. The grater's handle jutted from the sink. Thin pieces of starchy potato clung to the stainless steel.

Everything seemed all right. Yet that feeling of impending disaster haunted him.

"Good morning," Kirby said, his voice meek and mild.

"Good morning, Kirby," his mother said with a smile. Donna Johnson was lovely this morning in a blue dress, her hair recently curled. Had she come into his room in curlers? He couldn't remember. How long had she been up? What time was it? And, speaking of time, why did it feel like he was running out of it?

His mother said, "I only have eggs and bacon this morning. Shouldn't take long to cook both. I'll go to the store this afternoon, if you'll be okay alone."

"Yes, ma'am."

Kirby took a seat at the table, facing the stove, and lay his hands flat on the treated-wood surface. He stared down at the knots and swirls in the wood while his mother fried bacon. He heard her drain the pan into a coffee can when the bacon was done, and then the sizzle of cold eggs as she poured them into the leftover drippings.

There was a face in the wood of the table, one that had stolen his attention: an old man with a long beard and severe countenance. This was the face of a man who'd lived a rough life. A man who had become as hard and gnarled as the tree that had imprisoned his likeness until some woodsman chopped him from his cage. Or perhaps the tree hadn't been a prison. Maybe the bearded man had been hiding.

Kirby knew a bit about hiding. He'd hid parts of himself for so long. Then, when he'd finally shared his secrets with another human being, that person had betrayed him. For his trust, Kirby had been taken away from the comfortable, secretive life he'd lived and hidden away from the prying eyes of the public. Hidden again, but this time in the literal sense.

*Humble Hill.*

A seething anger filled him. His fingernails clawed at the face of the bearded man in the table. His jaw clenched, cheeks bulging with strained muscle. There came a feeling of increased tightness throughout his body; every inch of tendon and cartilage hardening to bone. It all felt so familiar. Not in any comfortable way, but in such a way as to strike a sense of knowing. Knowing that this rigid state had happened before. And often, too.

He trembled from head to foot. The floor quaked beneath him.

"Kirby?" His mother's voice cut through the fog of his fit and dragged him smoothly back into the moment.

"Yeah?" Kirby said, smiled tentatively. She'd been through so much. She didn't need to worry anymore. There was nothing wrong. Look at him. Would he be smiling if something were wrong?

She grinned nervously and lay a plate of dry, rubbery scrambled eggs and half-cooked bacon in front of him. Mother wasn't a very good cook. The bacon would no doubt give him the runs, like it always did, but even with that knowledge, Kirby would still eat the underdone strips of glistening pink meat. He'd do just about anything not to upset his mother. She'd been upset enough since he'd come home, not to mention all the drama she'd faced before shipping him off to Humble Hill. She'd suffered so much: the stares, the gossips, the alienation. All because of him. He'd done this to her. Only he was to blame. He'd caused her all this pain and anguish with his selfish attitude and unclean desires.

Donna Johnson sat across from her son, her own steaming plate of food on the table before her. When had she put her plate down? Kirby couldn't remember her doing that. He'd drifted again. Time to focus and lockdown the moment. Here we go...

*Say something.*

"This looks delicious."

"Are you okay?" she asked, worry creasing her face.

*Reassure her.*

"Yes, ma'am. I'm fine."

*Smile.*

He smiled.

"Any more episodes after you fell asleep? Any more dreams?"

"No, ma'am."

"That's good, then. Isn't it?" Her eyes were painfully hopeful.

*Answer her.*

"Yes, ma'am."

She frowned. "Are you sure—"

"I'm fine!" He slammed his palms on the man in the wood. Kirby could have sworn he heard the old bearded guy groan.

Kirby's eyes drifted up to meet his mother's. Her eyes were wide with terror, but she, somehow, remained seated and still.

*Apologize. Now.*

"I'm... I'm sorry."

"No, no, it's all right," she stammered. "I know how much strain you're under. I just wanted to make sure—"

Mom kept right on talking but Kirby stopped listening because something was happening behind her and he had no idea how such a thing could be occurring.

The oven door was slowly and steadily opening itself. Kirby knew it wasn't really happening, that he was imagining everything. It was all in his head.

But it looked so damn real.

The oven door banged fully open. Kirby jumped. He glanced at his mother. She hadn't heard it. She went on talking.

Flames crackled in the open oven like a raging fireplace. He could feel the heat from across the kitchen and around his mother. He could feel the outline she made in the heat, it was so intense, as if the heat were coming off her instead of around her.

An impossibly long arm covered in red flesh reached through the flames. The fire affected the flesh of the arm not at all. A hand with too many fingers with too many knuckles grasped the edge of the oven door.

Mom continued talking.

The arm from the fiery oven flexed and a Coat Man pulled himself from the flames. Number Fourteen crawled out of the fire and onto the kitchen tile. The Coat Man unfolded to its full height;

it was so tall that it had to cock its featureless crimson head in order to stand upright. How tall was the ceiling here? Eight feet? Ten? More?

*This. Is not. Happening.*

Mom talked and talked and talked...

Number Fourteen's face split. It opened a mouth full of nine-inch ivory nails.

Kirby began to whimper.

"Kirby? Kirby, what's wrong?" The fear in his mother's voice was palpable. "Talk to me."

The Coat Man behind his mother bent forward at the waist. Its impossible mouth grew and grew. With a sharp downward jerk, it enveloped the entirety of Donna Johnson's head. Only when it bit did Mom react. Her hands flew up, grabbing at the glistening red orb that was Number Fourteen's head. With her own head vanished inside the Coat Man's mouth, Mom resembled a cherry lollipop. She mumbled something that sounded like a question before the Coat Man bit and gnashed and twisted, tearing her head off, like meat from a drumstick. Her headless body, arms still raised above her shoulders in a defensive pose, slumped forward. Blood spurted from severed carotids, painting Kirby from belly button to face in gore. When he tried to scream, he caught a mouthful of blood that tasted of oysters. He shoved backward, simply wanting to be gone, to be far, far away, and his chair toppled, with him in it. The back of his head hit the floor. Teeth clicked.

He was lucky he hadn't bitten off his tongue—

—like the Coat Man had bitten off his mother's head.

From where he lay on the kitchen floor, Kirby saw the Coat Man slither off the edge of the table like a snake with arms. Gravity didn't seem to affect the thing. It dangled over him, like a cast fishing rod over a lake, smiling its ivory-nail smile.

*Run.*

Kirby rolled out from under the Coat Man, attempted to get to his knees but slipped on the gory kitchen floor and went sprawling into the warm blood that had fallen from the side of the table like a red waterfall. He scrambled for the carpet in the living room, his gory hands slapping down on clean tile, leaving bloody handprints in his wake.

Once he hit the carpet, he climbed the arm of the couch, pulling himself to his feet. Out of breath, pulse hammering in his temples, he refused to look behind him or so much as think about whether or not the Coat Man intended on pursuing him.

The front door. He had to get to the front door.

He rushed in that direction. Grabbed the brass knob. His blood-slick hand slid uselessly on the metal. No grip. Tears and snot and flop sweat poured down his face, his back, his armpits, in torrents. He screamed for the door to open but it wasn't listening.

A red hand with too many fingers and too many knuckles reached around him. The many-jointed fingers lay themselves on top of his own hands, which were still sliding about on the brass door knob, and squeezed. Kirby squealed and tore his hands away from under the abomination. He dove into the corner of the foyer, where the wall met the front door. There he cowered, waiting for the end.

But the end didn't come.

The door lay open, trapping him in the triangle of door, jam, and foyer wall.

Tentatively, Kirby pushed the door away, hinges whining, shoving ever so gently with trembling fingertips, just enough to extract himself from his triangular prison.

All three Coat Men stood in the space where the kitchen tile met the living room carpet. Number Three, its face once more Father George's face, held Kirby's mother against itself, her back to its front. The thing lifted his mother's hand by one limp wrist. Donna Johnson's headless corpse waved at her son.

"Time to go, Kirby," the face of Father George said. The voice was light, playful even. "We're just getting started here. But you can run. If you like. Run and tell them all. Tell them something's coming. Something's coming, and it's gonna be swell. Just you wait." Father George's face twisted in rage. "**JUST YOU WAIT!**"

Kirby cut around the open front door and ran. He had no idea where he was going. He simply ran for his life. All the while he felt chased. Chased by something incomprehensibly huge; something far bigger in size and mass than all three Coat Men combined. He felt its footfalls in his chest, could feel its hot, rancid breath tickling his nape. He knew that whatever was behind him could swallow the world whole if it so desired. He knew this like a baby knows how to breathe. And this thing, whatever it was, would eventually catch him.

Eventually.

And wasn't that it, really? The feeling of eventuality? Of not being able to escape that which chased you? Wasn't that the worst thing of all; knowing that no matter how quick you were, running would be futile?

And if this presence at his back was as powerful as he felt, only one question remained.

What was stopping it from devouring all of creation?

\*\*\*

A total of nineteen residents of Bay's End saw a blood-drenched Kirby Johnson running through town that morning. Twelve of them knew the sixteen-year-old, and, of those twelve, only three gave a damn about his wellbeing. The other nine all thought the exact same thing in the exact same words:

"Serves him right."

The three who cared all thought varying things. But only one of them was of any importance.

Janice Larson, still sore and feeling violated and unclean after four showers, was staring out one of her two front-facing bay windows. She was watching squirrels scavenging and playing in the tree out front and wondering who she could tell, if anyone, about what Hap had done to her last night. Just thinking about the act made her sick to her stomach, that morning's coffee churning in her gut like molten iron.

*He raped you*, she thought. *Say it aloud. Make it real.*

"He—"

And that's as far as she got. The next instant the blood-soaked figure of Kirby Johnson dashed by on the street. Somehow, even though his features were hidden under a mask of brownish-red, Janice Larson knew exactly who he was.

Would she run after him? Chase him down and make sure he was all right? Of course not. But she thought kindly of Kirby. No judgment for what he might have done to become covered in blood like he was. She knew a victim when she saw one.

Behind glass, in her own little world, she said, "Whatever you're running from must be awful."

And then she checked behind her. Because, just for a moment, she could have sworn she was no longer alone.

"Hap?" she asked her house; the home that no longer felt like a home.

"Eric?" A part of her said that, had it really been her husband, or anyone else for that matter, her having called out Hap's name first had certainly let the cat out of the bag. Luckily— or unluckily, given the ominous feeling pressing on her back and shoulders like a deviant's stare—she seemed to be alone.

Janice Larson closed her curtains and headed to the bathroom to take her fifth shower in sixteen hours.

# 5. A Cross to Bear

Beulah Blackwood was one of the few who remained in Bay's End after the burning.

She was a younger woman then, a woman ten years from marriage and thirteen from motherhood, in a time when Bay's End was simply called the Unincorporated. She would be widowed by thirty, and would mourn the death of her only child by age forty-five. What kept her sane through every tragedy, all the premature death, was a strong faith and love for God Almighty, and the fact that she felt justifiably punished for what she had done to that poor man and woman.

The first child to fall sick was Clark Grissom, aged five. The blemishes that would turn into festering sores by autumn's end showed up on his skin the day after Thanksgiving. At first, his mother treated it by cleaning the lesions in stream water and wrapping them in bandages. In those days, the nearest doctor was over forty miles away, in Chestnut, and only three people in town out of a hundred owned an automobile. In those days, Enders were people of the land, and the land had been good to them. They were a strong, healthy people. But something changed the day Clark Grissom fell ill, and a superstitious people will reach for any explanation when faced with the unknown.

The town's founder, Francis Bay, had just married a woman twenty years his junior on November 12. Marietta Bay was a sight to behold, and no one questioned Francis's motivations. Francis himself was an attractive man: broad-shouldered and thin in the hips; he carried himself with an air of superiority that did not crossover into his attitude. For Francis Bay was a humble, happy man.

Francis had been a field medic in the army during the Great War and had seen battle on numerous occasions. He'd saved some lives, but he had saved far less than he'd lost. Sometimes, at town hall meetings, he'd tell stories of how men had fought and died in trenches, in the mud. Beulah had been fascinated by Bay's storytelling ability. She could listen to him talk for hours. And she did.

When it was proper, she'd call on Francis to hear his stories. In those days, Beulah had fancied herself the next Mary Shelley, although Beulah's tastes deviated from the morbid quite drastically. She intended to write down all of Francis's stories with literary aplomb and sell them to fancy publishers in New York and Chicago. In the end, she never got the chance to write her book on Francis Bay's time in the US Army. If she had, it would have been more memoir than biography.

His new bride, Marietta, was inviting, a perfectly pleasant host at all times, but Beulah always sensed an air of jealousy coming from the woman, a feeling of competition, which was silly. Everyone knew how dedicated Francis was to Marietta. You couldn't have pulled him off her had she been on fire.

On a sunny but frigid day in December, Francis told Beulah about how he'd amputated a man's leg after a bullet had shattered the kneecap, completely destroying the leg. Had he not sawn off the ruined leg, the man surely would have become septic and died.

"What's septic?" Beulah said.

"It's an infection. In the blood. Nasty stuff. No coming back from it, I'm afraid." Francis had always spoken so well, something he said he'd gotten from the British soldiers beside who he'd fought and risked his life.

"How does it get in the blood?" she said, wide-eyed with interest.

"Through the wound, Beulah. Where else?" He laughed as if her question had been the silliest thing then patted her on the knee. A sharp jolt of electricity ran from his touch and up her inner thigh. She felt an ache in her belly, almost like a cramp. She swallowed and exhaled at length, said a silent prayer for strength, and asked Francis to continue his story.

"I had to make the incision well above the knee, you see. Right here." He placed his index finger on her leg, at mid-thigh, and applied enough pressure so that she could feel him through the heavy fabric of her dress. "The knee, of course, was a disaster. And because I didn't have the talent, nor the tools, for invasive surgery, I had to cut far above the wound, lest I miss some shrapnel and bone fragment. Things like that can fester. That's how one gets sepsis."

"And sepsis is the same as septic? What I mean to say is, are they plural and singular, like in grammar, or do they—Why are you laughing at me?"

"No, no, nothing like that, my dear Beulah. Not like grammar. Septic is the state of being. Sepsis is the disease."

"Oh."

"Oh, indeed." Francis chortled and let his hand relax on her thigh.

Marietta appeared in the doorway to the study with a tray of cookies and two cups of strong black coffee. If she saw Francis's hand upon Beulah's thigh that day, she made no mention of it. Nor had she reacted in any physical way. Beulah wrote it all off to confidence. Francis doted on his new bride. No way could Marietta ever believe that Francis would stray from his marriage bed.

Marietta was just sitting down the tray of cookies and coffee when there came a hammering on the front door. Francis stood, an air of concern fogging his features, and took long, elegant strides out of the room to answer the door.

Beulah and Marietta locked eyes, and in that moment Beulah felt herself come to like Marietta. No one with eyes as kind as hers could ever wish, much less cause, anyone any harm. Beulah doubted that the woman would swat at an irritating fly. She'd likely just shoo it away.

Marietta smiled. "I wonder who that could be?"

"Whoever they are," said Beulah, "they're insistent."

"Shall we see?" Marietta's eyes gleamed with mischievous intent.

"Should we?" said Beulah.

"Oh, I don't see why not."

How could anyone deny that smile?

"Well... if you're sure."

Marietta held out her hand for Beulah to take. Beulah accepted it.

"Come, before they've gone."

Both women rushed into the main hallway of the Bay's lavish home like little girls dashing to the tree on Christmas morning. Their girlish joviality did not last.

A woman was at the door, a young boy in her arms. Francis stood off to the side of the door, allowing the woman entrance to his home.

She said, "His hands are all seized up. He can't walk no more. I didn't know where else to take him, Mr. Bay. Swear 'fore God, I didn't."

"Calm down Bonnie. Take him into the study so that I may have a look at him."

Beulah and Marietta pushed themselves up against the hall wall in order to let the woman and, assumingly, her son pass by. The woman was thick in the hips and thin in the torso. She had no chest to speak of, but her collarbones jutted like pubescent breasts, even through her ratty and sweat-stained white blouse. Her pants were made of some kind of coarse material, like a potato sack, but not quite. The woman's hair was long and oily, stringy as a wet mop. Her cheeks were flushed, but the rest of her was decidedly pale. This was a woman who'd lived a hard life.

Beulah caught only a passing glimpse of the shirtless boy, but even so she could tell he was very sick indeed. She could only see him from the waist up because his lower half was wrapped in a quilt, but what she could see of him was covered in gray or raw flesh. His fingers were hooked and stiff, like an eagle's claws as it descends upon its prey. His arms were clenched to his sides so severely that the skin had blanched from lack of circulation.

The woman sped past Beulah yet stopped in front of Marietta. Marietta looked down on the boy. The boy looked up at her. Marietta gasped in what could only have been horror and spun away. Beulah could only see the top of the boy's head now.

Whatever Marietta had seen, Beulah had been spared as the boy's mother shoved his face into her shirt.

Mother and child disappeared around the corner and into the study.

Francis approached Marietta, gently grasped her chin, and turned her head to face him.

"Get control of yourself. She's upset as it is."

"Yes, my love," Marietta said with a bow of her head.

"Beulah, a hand, please?"

"Yes, Francis."

Beulah followed him into the study, and it was only then that she realized that the woman had known where Bay's study had been, as if she had been here before. Should she ask Francis if he was acquainted with the woman? Then again, if he was, what would it matter, really?

"Lay him on the couch, just there," Francis told the woman. "Beulah, this is Harmony Grissom, and the boy there is Clark."

Harmony Grissom lay her son on the claw-footed couch. The woman never took her eyes off her son. Not for a moment. When Beulah managed to pry her gaze from the mother, she saw quite clearly what had frightened Marietta so.

The boy had no nose. Instead of the usual cute button most children are born with, this boy had an open cavity rimmed in gray flesh. His nasal passages flexed and waned as he wetly breathed. Beulah fought to keep her breakfast down. She was suddenly very glad she'd not had the chance to sample Marietta's cookies and coffee.

"My God, what's wrong with him?" Beulah asked before she could stop herself.

"I've no idea. Now quiet. I need quiet. Stay at hand, though. Marietta will be useless to me at this point. She's so sensitive to such things as this that it renders her immobile."

"Yes, Francis, I understand."

Beulah rubbed her hands together until they were warm and red all while listening to Francis question the woman.

"Has he been in contact with anything new? A new plant or animal, maybe?"

"No. Not that I know of. But he's a boy, Mr. Bay. I don't always got eyes on 'im!"

"Right, right. Sorry. Just remain calm and think. Have you used any new soaps or—" He stopped there, as if he'd realized that it had been some while since either mother or child had bathed. Beulah watched with stunned awe as he deftly changed his course of questioning. "Is there anyone else in the household affected by this?"

"My Gertrude has the patches, but she feelin fine."

"The patches?" Francis asked.

"Them gray spots on 'im. Gerty got them too, but hers is more subtle-like. They ain't even gray right yet. They a more red color."

"And they haven't been into anything?"

"I don't know!" Harmony cried. It seemed to Beulah the cry was more in frustration than anger.

"Right. Sorry. So, just so I am perfectly clear, neither he nor Gertrude have been into anything new to them?"

Harmony nodded so quickly that Beulah expected the woman's head to pop from its socket.

"And his nose? How long has it been like this?"

"Just this morning. He were bawling like a newborn. That's what woke me. I come into his room and he was just a twitchin. Like he was being shaken by demons. That's when I first noticed his nose. It weren't bleedin or nothing like that. It was just like you see it now. Just gone, like someone erased it."

Beulah's gorge rose. She chewed it back. She couldn't lose it now, not when Francis depended on her the most.

"And his hands? Were they like this yesterday?"

"No, sir, they weren't. They was fine. The nose and the hands, all that just happened this morning. He's not talking to me, either, Mr. Bay. He's not said a word since I found him in the state he was in."

"Ease on back, Harmony. Let me see him up close."

Harmony did as she was told without protest, or so much as another word spoken. Francis retreated to his desk to grab instruments Beulah could no better assume the purpose of had they been an engine block or printing press. One was a metal cone on a metal stick. It shone in the sun coming through the windows, casting fleeting rays of light across the walls and ceiling. The other instrument seemed to be tongs of some sort, but with more a likening to an alligator's mouth than she was comfortable with. No doubt about it, the tools looked more dangerous than helpful.

Francis sat on the edge of the middle cushion, placed the conical instrument to his eye, and leaned in to view more closely the cavity that had once been Clark Grissom's nose. He used the alligator pinchers to poke and prod the gaping wound. Although the boy's eyes were wide and frightened, he didn't seem to mind Francis's exploration. In fact, he looked as if he couldn't feel a thing Francis was doing.

"Does this hurt?" Francis said.

The boy remained silent.

"What have you been into, Clark?"

The boy refused to answer. Whether he had a choice in the matter, Beulah hadn't a clue.

"Clark, please, if you can talk to me, I need to know what you might have been into. It could save your life. Otherwise..." Francis's voice trailed off and he glanced at the boy's mother. Harmony crossed her arms over her breasts and rubbed at her exposed forearms as if she were freezing. The day certainly had a chill to it, but Francis's home was wonderfully toasty thanks to a fire in the hearth.

"Clark, I need to—"

The boy sneezed. Blood and mucus splattered Francis's face. He fell from the couch in his attempt to reel away. He got to his hands and knees and spat onto the plush Persian rug beneath him. What a shame, a part of Beulah thought, for surely the carpet would be ruined.

"Towel!" Francis gagged. "Fetch me a towel!"

Beulah, nodding like a simpleton, rushed into the hall to find Marietta and ask her where they kept their towels, but Marietta was no longer standing in wait. The front door had been closed, and soft music played from an upstairs room.

Beulah grabbed her dress, hiked it up and over her feet, and dashed up the stairs. She followed the music to the end of a long hallway on the second floor, where she knocked on one of the bedroom doors.

Marietta answered. She seemed nonplussed, as if Beulah had caught her doing something indecent.

"Where are your towels?"

"Why, in the linen closet. Where else would they be?"

"Where is the linen closet?" Beulah asked, bordering on frustration.

"Oh, I'm sorry, dear. Down in the main hallway. There's a closet between the kitchen and the study. You'll find everything you need there." And with that, Marietta closed the door on Beulah's face.

Bay's wife had seemed a different woman, but Beulah didn't have time to think about Marietta's sudden change in character.

She rushed back downstairs and found the hall closet easily.

"Beulah!" Francis called.

"Coming!"

She tore towels that smelled of the outdoors from the cabinet and returned with haste to the study. Instead of handing Francis the towels, Beulah began to wipe clean his face. He snatched the towels from her grasp, as if she were doing it all wrong. He dabbed at his eyes and wiped the mess from his cheeks. Scrubbed his chin and brushed at his neck. There was a bit on his shirt, as well, but he seemed not to notice.

Where was Harmony? Beulah hadn't seen her leave, but she was nowhere in sight. Beulah moved about the room, calling her name, and soon found the woman passed out behind the couch.

"Oh my," Beulah said. She wondered if Harmony had fainted. Beulah knew she'd had to steel herself in the face of the boy's sneezing on Francis, but that was only to redirect a tide of nausea. She'd never felt faint in all her days. She surely didn't feel that way now.

What kind of mother fainted when faced with her own sick child? Beulah liked to think that, in this woman's shoes, she would have reacted stoically. People without children judge parents quite often, having no idea the trials and tribulations of parenthood. As Beulah got older and finally had kids of her own, she would look back on this moment and feel ashamed.

Funny how one's constitution can change so drastically when faced with tumultuous times. Compassion can turn to disgust, and empathy to apathy, all within the flutter of a hummingbird's wings. Beulah's shift might have occurred due to her close proximity to a dying child, but one can never know what causes such a quick and lasting change of heart and mind.

From upstairs there came the rhythmic thumping of tribal drums.

No. Couldn't be.

Someone was singing.

But surely they were not. Why would Marietta be singing while Francis and Beulah were downstairs and dealing with a sick child and overwrought mother?

Why, indeed, Beulah thought.

"Beulah," Francis said.

She turned to face him.

"Where's the boy's mother?"

Beulah pointed to the floor. Francis rounded the couch. After what seemed no more than a cursory glance at the unconscious woman, he spun and headed for the hall.

"Francis, where are you going? What about the boy?"

What she wanted to do was scream, *Don't leave me alone with him!* but somehow managed to keep her emotions in check.

"The boy is beyond my help." Francis left without another word.

Beulah looked over the back of the couch and into the boy's staring eyes. She watched him for some time. It was a long while before she realized he was no longer breathing.

Clark Grissom was dead.

He was the first of many.

In the coming weeks, more children in town took ill. But not adults. Nine girls and four boys, all with graying patches on their skin. Some on their arms and legs, others out of sight under clothing. But you knew they were there. You'd see people crossing the street to get away from the poor souls. Which begged the question: who was telling who which children were ill?

The children who caught the disease did not live long. All aside from one.

Gertrude Grissom.

Harmony's little girl Gerty would live a long, if not full, life. She'd even come to have kids of her own one day: three boys named Jerimiah, Malakai, and Henrik. But Gerty Grissom, being only six at the time, was too young to remember what happened in Bay's End that fall.

Beulah walked everywhere in those days. The soles of her feet were thick and callused from her near-constant trips into town, and the errands she ran for her aging father, whose memory was not what it used to be. She went to church, religiously, attending every service the pastor caught the whim to have, as well as the standard twice on Sunday. It was on her way to an evening service one night, three months after the death of Clark Grissom, that she ran into Francis and Marietta Bay.

The couple's atheism was well known around town, an atheism that, Pastor Wallace said, stemmed from being too well-educated for their own good. When Beulah had asked the pastor if being well-educated was truly such an awful thing in the eyes of the Lord, Pastor Wallace had assured her that the only education one needed in this unholy world was a healthy fear of God. The Almighty would take care of the rest.

It was the couple's views against religion that caused Beulah to question why they'd be at church that evening.

"We've come to pay our respects and maybe calm some nerves, my dear Beulah," Francis said, Marietta at his side. Her soft smile could be taken as genuine if one had a good imagination. "We've spoken with your man Wallace," —not *Pastor* Wallace, Beulah noted— "and he thinks church would be the best time to speak to everyone in one place."

Marietta slapped playfully at Francis's arm. "Don't be modest. *You* went to *him*. It was his idea, dear."

Beulah nodded in acknowledgment, but she wasn't really listening. All she could hear when Marietta spoke were those tribal drums and that hauntingly sorrowful singing.

"Fine. Have it your way," said Francis. "I told Wallace I'd like to speak to the town at one of his services. He wouldn't give up Sunday morning, but he said that Sunday evenings were just as good. Stubborn old—"

"What will you be speaking on?" Beulah said.

Francis did not like being interrupted, she could see that much in how stiff he'd become when she'd cut into his insult of Pastor Wallace.

Francis cleared his throat. "I wish to offer my services, is all."

"Couldn't *Pastor* Wallace tell the flock? I mean, it could have saved you the trouble of coming across town." Beulah blinked too many times, giving the impression that she was batting her eyelashes at Francis. Marietta scowled.

*Serves you right,* Beulah thought, and was instantly taken aback by the unkind thought. She'd grown harder in countenance since the day of Clark Grissom's death. There was no doubt about that. But she harbored no ill will toward the woman. Right?

*Those drums...*

*That singing...*

Francis said, "Is Sunday evening services so very long, Beulah, dear?"

"Same as any service, I suppose."

Marietta and Francis shared a look and a smile then looked back to Beulah. Their tandem movements felt unnatural to her.

Francis began, "Dearest Beulah, I'm sorry, but we've—"

"—never been to church," Marietta finished.

Beulah gawped. "Not ever?"

"No, dear," Francis said with a broad smile. "Never was inclined."

Beulah met Marietta's eyes. "Not even once? Not even before marrying Francis?"

"Not once," Marietta said.

"Well," Beulah said because she didn't know what else to say.

"Shall we go inside?" Francis said, sweeping his arm out to direct the two ladies in his presence toward the church door.

Marietta's gaze locked onto Beulah but she was speaking to Francis when she said, "Oh, yes, my love. Wouldn't miss it for the world."

Most of Bay's End attended service that evening. Residents packed the pews, ten to a row, five rows deep. A few latecomers were forced to stand at the rear of the church. Francis and Marietta sat with the choir, together at the end. The two ladies whose seats they'd taken, stood off to the side, against the wall.

Pastor Geoffrey Wallace clopped from the rear of the church to his podium, his heavy footfalls felt all the way at the back of the room, where the latecomers lingered. Wallace was a huge man, in both size and presence, and he had a great shaggy beard of coarse brown hair spotted with gray, which he rarely ever combed, and a bald head that he shaved twice a week with a straight razor. Beulah always wondered how he cleaned up the back of his head and neck. To think he reached around blindly, or used a hand mirror, with a leather-sharpened razor—well, if she were honest, the thought scared her silly and raised goosebumps on her scalp and shoulders.

Pastor Wallace addressed his flock. "Ladies and gentlemen, the Devil's come to Bay's End in the form of a sickness that only targets our very young. We've prayed, but the Good Lord, in his infinite wisdom, has yet to answer our prayers. Everything in the Lord's time, I say, but I cannot refuse an offer of goodwill. Our gracious town's founder, Mr. Francis Bay—accompanied tonight by his lovely wife, Marietta—will now speak to you. While Bay is not—" Pastor Wallace cleared his throat. His heavy, bearded jowls jounced gelatinously. "—not a *religious* man, he is a man of science, and such a man might, I must admit, be sent by God to help our good town. So, far be it from me to turn him away, as the innkeepers did to Mary and Joseph in their time of need. Thus I shall allow him to speak to you, briefly, and then we will carry on with our service."

Francis, seemingly unbothered by the pastor's ungrateful introduction, approached the podium. "Good evening, ladies and gentlemen. I will make this brief so that I will not take up the entirety of your evening. But first, I would like to address something your pastor said."

Pastor Wallace, who'd taken a seat in a chair to the left of the podium, glanced at Bay with a look of obvious curiosity. Beulah was sure that this part of Bay's speech had not been approved by Pastor Wallace. She was also sure that Pastor Wallace had not run by Bay what he'd intended to say about him, so all was fair, she supposed.

"Your man Wallace is right. I am most decidedly *not* a religious man. Guilty as charged." Bay smiled greatly, the brilliance of his beaming face shining on all in attendance like a searchlight—or, perhaps, the finger of God. "Wallace got another thing right, my dear people. I *am* a man of science. Unfortunately, science does not have all the answers."

"You ain't kiddin!" called someone from the back of the building. A few people laughed, but their tittering was short-lived. Pastor Wallace shot daggers in their directions. The room quieted.

"All I can offer at this time is support to those of you who have sickly children. I will do my best for them in their time of need. I do not have a cure for this disease, as of yet. I have a call in to some colleagues of mine in New York who might be able to help, but as of right now, we're alone in this. I can, however, offer your children comfort."

"Did you offer my son comfort?"

Beulah cast her gaze to the side but did not find the source of the outburst. She craned her neck and saw a man coming up the aisle between the pews. His affect was troubled, his eyes on fire. He looked awfully familiar, too, but she couldn't put a name with the face.

Pastor Wallace stood and said, "Martin, please. He's trying to help."

"Damn his help and damn him, too!" this man named Martin said. Even with the knowledge of his name, Beulah could not place his face.

"You let my boy die!" Martin roared, his voice booming inside this house of God.

*That's why he's familiar. He looks just like the boy. Just like Clark Grissom.*

"I did everything I—"

"You did nothing! And that's what he will do for the rest of you. Nothing!"

"Please, Martin," Pastor Wallace begged.

"Fuck you!"

The crowd gasped, as such language was rarely heard outside of taverns and shipyards.

Francis did not respond.

Martin spat on the church floorboards as he continued toward Francis. "I spit on your damned science. And I'll spit on you if you let me close enough, Bay. I swear 'fore God, I will!"

Francis took the hint. He retreated from the podium and around the side of the choir pit, where he lurked in shadow while Martin Grissom spoke to the church. Martin turned and placed his back to the podium. Tears cuts clean paths through his grimy cheeks. Beulah hadn't thought him filthy, only dark, but now she saw that what she'd taken for tanned skin was really a layer of unmentionable nastiness.

"There's something wrong with these two," Martin told the congregation. "You ain't seen it yet, have you? Ain't none of you put two and two together? Think real hard. Wrack them uppity brains of yours. Did any child get sick before he married that woman? Huh? Was there a single one of your children got sick before that devil bitch come to our town?"

There were no gasps at Martin's language. Not this time. Every churchgoer sat rapt. Beulah could nearly hear them all thinking the same thing, the same thing she herself was thinking: *he's got a point.* She glanced at Bay in the shadows of the choir pit to judge his expression. It was grim, that of a man charged with a crime he was most assuredly guilty of.

"No," Beulah breathed, not wanting to believe it. She snapped her head to the left, hunted Marietta.

Marietta Bay smiled in the face of the accusation. If Beulah had been asked, she would've said Marietta looked almost... proud. Beulah was sure others garnered the same information from Marietta's smile and took it as boastful. In the end, Beulah thought that was what did it. That smile. All the accusations and hearsay in the world might not have convinced the congregation as a whole that evening, but Marietta's smile was damning.

Of course, no one could have been sure. The residents of Bay's End, including Beulah, were not mind readers. What they were, however, was a scared people collected together in a house of worship. How many things could be attributed to the events of that night? The End might never know.

"Burn her!" cried a woman in the front row. Beulah thought the woman was Deborah Smith, the owner of the town's bakery, but Beulah couldn't tell from the back of the woman's head alone, and she never found out later, either. Later, everyone would deny what happened. Even Martin, the man who'd started the whole mess.

Now, a cry of "Burn her!" might not have been enough to set the average adult on a course of murderous intent, but these were deeply religious people with a mind and heart for God and the Word. The Bible was their map, a series of guideposts directing them how to live their lives. And in this good book of theirs, there is a line that reads, *Thou shalt not suffer a witch to live.* When seen from this perspective, poor Marietta was a witch in league with the Devil himself and not as a human being created by God and his infinite wisdom, it's no wonder the congregation reacted the way they did. They weren't murderers. They were the Hand of God. Thy will be done, and all that.

Another contributing factor might have been how alien Marietta Bay seemed to the congregation. She'd never been to their church. They didn't know her from Adam. Where had Bay met her? Where had she come from? The unknown can be a frightening thing. And fear can lead good-hearted people to do evil.

At the holler of "Burn her!" the smile melted from Marietta's face. A dozen people rose from their pews and headed for the stage. Marietta leapt from her chair, but she had nowhere to go. Being unfamiliar with the church, she had no way of knowing that there was an exit behind the pit. The door was hidden from view by the men and women of the choir.

Bay, his eyes full of panic and terror, rushed forward, his hands waving frantically.

"No, no, you don't understand!"

He grabbed ahold of Martin's arm.

Martin raged, "Hands off me, devil!"

Martin punched Bay in the face. Bay's nose exploded in a splash of blood. He grabbed at his busted nose, reeling backward, and sat down hard on his butt.

Beulah almost went to him then. Almost. The only thing keeping her from seeing about Francis was what was happening to his dear wife.

Marietta was cowering in the corner. Churchgoers en masse, like a pack of wild dogs on a rare sirloin, dragged her down the center aisle by the arms, her legs sliding behind her, toes scraping the floorboards—what happened to her shoes?—and out the double doors of the church.

The church in those days had been built on Fairchild Farm, a piece of property claimed by Waverly Fairchild. When his son went mad and stabbed himself in the eye with a fork, Waverly had the boy committed to the Pointvilla Home for the Criminally Insane, which had closed down after several of the staff were murdered by a man dressed like a baby doll. Those that survived refused to return to work. Even the doctors abandoned their patients, and the institute was torn down. Fairchild was long gone from Bay's End by that time. With Fairchild gone and the site abandoned, the town reclaimed the property and built the church. Pastor Wallace took over services, and the rest, as they say, is history.

Like any church worth its salt, there was a cross out front. A great big cross, twelve feet high with a crossbar seven feet wide. Plenty big enough to crucify someone, even someone as tall and lanky as Marietta Bay.

A hammer was procured from the bed of someone's truck. The railroad spikes from the trunk of someone's car. A ladder, which had been used in the painting of the church eaves two weeks prior to this night of death, was taken from the rear of the church. By the time everything was collected, and the deed started, Marietta Bay was unconscious. Whether she'd fainted or had been knocked out, Beulah didn't know. She could barely see what was going on from the back of the crowd.

Bay would shove his way into the mass of bodies and then be expelled like a baby newly birthed—spat out onto the concrete as easily as Martin Grissom had spat on the floor of the church.

The night was alive with the roars and screams of a mob fueled by blind madness. These people were not the townspeople she knew. The few faces Beulah saw that night, during the time leading up until the burning, were those of a people possessed—of capering demons hellbent on doing the Devil's work.

Martin Grissom carried the unconscious Marietta over his shoulder and up the ladder. The crossbar was seven feet off the ground, and two men Beulah knew all too well as David and James Marchesini, David riding James's shoulders, helped nail the woman to the cross. The first nail going in did not arouse Marietta. But the second one did. She came awake screaming like a banshee.

"Marietta!" cried Francis Bay.

"Help me!" Marietta shrieked from the cross.

Once the second nail was in, Martin let her loose. Her weight dropped, dislocating one of her shoulders. The joint bulged under the flesh of her clavicle like a baby's head crowning. If Marietta had been screaming before, it was nothing in the face of this new sound escaping her. Beulah covered her ears and backed away, shaking her head with incomprehension.

What was she allowing to happen?

Could she even stop them at this point?

Did she want to put forth the effort?

*Serves her right*, came the whispered words of a voice she did not recognize as her own thoughts.

Something in the depths of her soul laughed the deep, throaty chuckle of devilish glee.

"Stop," Beulah muttered. Her voice was so low she couldn't hear herself over the roar of the raging crowd. "Please, stop."

*Forgive them, father, for they know not what they do.*

Throaty laughter faded into the nothingness.

It wasn't too late. Marietta, whatever her crimes, did not deserve this. No human being deserved to die like this. Beulah cast her gaze around, seeking help, searching for someone, anyone, who might help her, and found Pastor Wallace standing in the church doors, his dark figure outlined in the soft lights coming from the interior of the building. She ran to him.

"Help her!" Beulah begged. "They're going to kill her!"

"The Lord's will be done, child." Wallace's voice did not sound like his own. If she didn't know any better, Beulah would have said that she was hearing the throaty voice from her own thoughts.

"This isn't of the Lord," Beulah cried, her voice cracking under the strain of her emotions. "This is evil. Pure evil. Did the Roman's do the Lord's work in killing Jesus?"

Pastor Wallace cut his eyes at her. "They ushered Christ unto us, child. Without their nails and their spear and their crown of thorns, we'd burn forever. The Romans—Herod—Pilate, their actions were good in the eyes of the Lord. Do not question His will, Beulah. For His will be done, whether you approve of it or not."

Pastor Wallace's eyes drifted back to the scene unfolding at the cross. The unmistakable odor of kerosene filled the air. Although Beulah couldn't see through the crowd, she knew their intent; their horrible, monstrous intent.

"Thou shalt not suffer a witch to live," Pastor Wallace said. He smiled. "It could have only ended this way, Beulah. You do see that, don't you? This was preordained. Set up by the highest of powers. Called down from the highest of thrones. His *WILL— BE—DONE!*"

A thought struck Beulah's chest like a fist of stone and she saw. For the first time that night, all of her assumptions, all her rationalizations, vanished in a puff of smoke: the speedy call to action at the request of "Burn her!"; the railroad spikes on hand; the ladder; the kerosene. This night, this horrible, unforgiveable night had been planned from the outset.

"You set a trap for them," Beulah said, but her voice was much too low to be heard over the cacophony of the vengeful mob. She grabbed Pastor Wallace by his shirt front and bunched her fists. "You planned this!"

"Your tongue betrays you, Beulah. Mine will not betray me."

"How could you? Bay came to you to *help*, and this is how you repay him?"

He snatched away from her. "How does one help when one is the source of the suffering? Answer me that?" he growled. "*She* did this to herself. *She* summoned Satan into our midst. Would you have every child in town fall down dead? Would you see every mother weeping over their unbreathing child? Would you?"

"You have no proof. None of you do!"

"We have the will of the Lord behind us." Pastor Wallace adjusted his shirtfront. "And His will be done."

"STOP SAYING THAT!"

A great whoosh and the night brightened. Beulah spun as Marietta's screams lanced her ears. The crowd backed away, the ring of people surrounding Marietta on the cross expanding like an artery filling with blood. The throng pulsed. Swayed. Sang. Their hymnal lifted high on the wind, easily drowning out the burning woman's agonized wailing.

Marietta caught fire a little at a time. At least at first. The fire tickled her toes. Played at her calves. Licked her thighs. Caressed her hips. And then, in a blink, she was fully engulfed. Her hair vanished in a puff of wispy black smoke before the flames engulfed the head entirely. Beulah didn't want to see but she couldn't pry away her eyes.

Besides, even if she turned away, she'd still be able to smell the woman cooking. Her hungry stomach growled. It was unconscionable how much a human burning smelled like a pig cooking.

Francis, who had up until now been denied access to his bride, was finally allowed to break through. The mob parted and Bay rushed forward, seemingly mindless and uncaring of his own safety.

"NO!" Beulah wailed. "FRANCIS!"

She dashed forward but was pulled instantly back by a hand on her collar. She stumbled backward, sat down hard, and lost track of Bay as the crowd came together around Francis like a wound around a knife.

Pastor Wallace bent and whispered in her ear. "You cannot save him, child. No one can. He harbored a witch. He is culpable."

The crowd ceased their hymn. In their quietude, she could hear the lamentations of Francis as he screamed for his now-silent wife. Beulah climbed to her feet in time to see a dark figure attempting to climb the burning cross.

Francis.

Francis now aflame.

Marietta silent.

Now it was her love that screamed.

Francis's flaming form dropped from the cross and fell silent. Someone in the crowd—a woman—cried out. The mob parted once more and a fiery creature burst from captivity. The stumbling beast raced toward the church.

Toward Beulah.

No.

117

Toward Pastor Wallace.

This was no mindless comet. This was a missile with a purpose.

The heat coming off the figure as it dashed past Beulah was intense enough to scorch the hair on that side of her head. She slapped at her smoldering locks but did not remove her eyes from the flaming figure.

Francis Bay, engulfed in flames and driven by hatred, tackled Pastor Wallace into the church. The men wrestled only briefly before Wallace was still. Impossibly, horrifically, Francis Bay shoved himself to his feet. Beulah watched as Francis tore his arm free from the pastor's gaping mouth like a man pulling a foot from a sock.

Crying, terrified and confused and disgusted, Beulah reached for him. He ignored her. She squinted against the heat as Francis shambled past her, back toward the crowd.

The ring of people had straightened out. They now stood in a straight line, facing the church. Beulah thought they were watching Francis as he returned to his bride on the cross, but their gaze did not shift when he climbed up Marietta's charred corpse, like a fly up a wall, and clung to her—a child seeking comfort at its mother's breast. But the crowd wasn't watching Francis Bay. They seemed to be watching Beulah, but that wasn't right either. They were, all of them, looking at something past her. Behind her.

They were watching their beloved house of God burn.

Beulah had missed the part where the fire from the burning corpse of Pastor Wallace spread to the floor, the pews, the walls. In the short time that she'd been hypnotized by the impossibility of a man on fire moving about as if being on fire was nothing more than a minor inconvenience, the entire building had caught. She hadn't even felt the heat until she saw how close she was to the inferno. Now she realized that sweat had drenched her but was now rapidly drying to a shellac, baking on under the intense heat.

How had the church gone up so fast?

How had Francis survived as long as he had?

How had everything gone so horrible so quickly?

*His will be done.*

Beulah faced the crowd. Martin Grissom stood at the front, his blank face orange with firelight. Beulah stormed toward him. When she was close enough, she hauled off and slapped the tar out of him. His head jerked slightly to the side, just a hitch of the chin really, before his eyes settled back on her.

"You're a monster." She spat in his face.

He seemed unbothered by her or the surrounding scene. The crowd behind him stared at the burning church with cow-like dullness. They were indifferent, the lot of them. Not one of them moved, as if the throng were under some spell.

"You're supposed to be men and women of *God*!"

No answer from the glassy-eyed mob.

"You murdered them!" she sobbed. "You're killers. All of you!"

A bone-deep exhaustion weakened her. She dropped to her knees, her body wracked with emotion. She buried her face in her hands and cried. There she stayed for what seemed like hours. When she finally did look up, the crowd was dispersing. Each one of them seemed to come back to reality at different times. The life seeped back into them, and they would walk away with no more urgency or purpose than a flock of geese around a familiar pond.

Somehow, she managed to find her way home that night. Had she crawled some of the way? She seemed to remember doing so. Her memory was blurry in spots. Some part of her said that everything had been a terrible coincidence; that the churchgoers having nails and kerosene and murder in their heart hadn't been pre-planned. That Pastor Wallace had not organized the deaths of the Bays. Then the truth would flood back in and she would be driven to her knees and forced to crawl.

Or at least that's what she recalled.

The next morning, she returned to the church grounds, to Fairchild Farm and the reek of smoldering evil.

The church fire had burned out. Nothing resembling a house of worship was left. Only a pile of charred ruin, like logs in a long-dead fire, lay in the middle of Fairchild Farm. Not so much as a thread of smoke reached skyward. Beulah knew that was impossible. She knew a fire like that did not devour itself so quickly. Something like that should have taken days to smolder and die. But no. The scorched wood was cool to the touch. Cool enough to send an icy shiver up her arm and down her spine.

A blackened hole where the cross had been was the only proof of what had happened to Francis and Marietta. If they'd been taken down and given a Christian burial, Beulah didn't know. Suffice it to say, she didn't think that was the case. Of one thing she was entirely certain—she didn't want to find out. Her hands were dirty enough as it was.

She smelled them, though: the reek of cooking flesh, so much like roasting pork. And she would continue to smell them, her stomach churning with hunger and revulsion, until the day she died.

\*\*\*

The morning after Father George died, Beulah got up and dressed for church as she would have any other Sunday morning. It wasn't until she cracked and dropped an egg into a cast-iron skillet sizzling with lard that she remembered that, like Pastor Wallace of thirty years ago, Father George was dead. And at his own hand, at that.

She cried for Father George then as she hadn't cried for Pastor Wallace. The egg blacked in the pan. She turned off the burner and moved the pan to the sink. She ran cold water into the hot skillet and blackened egg and let the stream wash away her sorrow.

Thinking he'd just have to eat cold cereal this morning, Beulah went to wake Petey up.

She opened his door, looked in, and sighed. His bed was slept in but empty. She moved back down the hall and into the living room, where she picked up the phone and dialed the sheriff. His deputy answered. She didn't much mind Ronnie Short. Good kid, that one. At least he went to church, unlike Harold Carringer, the old coot. She asked for the sheriff and Ronnie put her on hold. A minute or so passed before Harold answered. She relayed that Pete was, once more, missing. She tried to sound angrier than she felt so that he'd take her seriously, but Harold was a stubborn man. Still, she had faith either he or his deputy would check on her grandson.

*He's your* son *now.*

This was true. Her daughter—his mother—was dead. The boy had her last name now. He was, for all intents and purposes, her son. She needed to start thinking of him as such at all times.

Boys need mothers. Boys without mothers, well, they didn't ever grow up. At least that had been her experience.

She stood in her living room, looking down at the phone, wondering what on Earth she was going to do with the rest of her day.

Then it hit her, like a thought suddenly remembered, and she grabbed her car keys up from the bowl on the table in the foyer and headed out to her car. The old station wagon took some time starting. It always did in cold weather, and this morning was a nippy one.

She drove to church, singing softly, barely above a whisper, the entire way.

*So I'll cherish the old rugged Cross…*
*Till my trophies at last I lay down…*
*I will cling to the old rugged Cross…*
*And exchange it some day for a crown.*

# 6. A Handful of Visitations

Certainty comes pre-installed with boyhood. The male of the species is never as sure of himself as he is before the sprouting of hair in strange places and the deepening of voice. A prepubescent boy is clever, brave, and unstoppable. Immortal in the sense that Death is not in his lexicon. Of course he knows Fear. Fear is that niggling inner voice that reminds him there might be consequences to his actions. But, for boys, all consequences are temporary inconveniences.

Along with his everyday certainty, Wesley Haversham was quite sure he liked Pete Blackwood more than just passing fair. The tubby pre-teen had an air of mystery about him, an unmistakable siren's call that Wesley would've followed anywhere. That Pete would lead him knowingly into danger never crossed Wesley's mind. He was certain. And certain people do uncertain things.

"You really saw Father George kill himself?" Pete asked as they walked through the cornfields located in the rear of the property. After they'd finished weeding, Pete had asked about the cross in the middle of the corn, and Wesley, instead of telling, decided to show his new friend what exactly was on the cross.

"Yeah." Wesley balled a fist, brought it to the side of his head, and made an explosion sound with his mouth as his fingers came open. "You should've seen the stuff that came out of him."

"Blackberry preserves." Pete whistled.

Wesley had almost forgotten that's how'd he'd described the contents of Father George's head to Pete. "Yessir."

"And he said what again? Just before he shot himself, I mean."

"*Everything is horrible now.*"

"What's that mean, do you think?"

"That things was bad?" Wesley shrugged. "I don't know."

"Wow." It was the third time Pete had said as much in ten minutes. "Say, do you read at all?"

Wesley stopped. Pete walked on for another five steps before he realized Wesley was no longer beside him. He turned and asked Wesley what was wrong.

Wesley said, "You think I don't know how to read?"

"I didn't mean it that way. I was just wondering if you liked to read. Guess I should've said it differently. How about—do you like to read?"

"Oh. All right. Um. I don't know. Never thought much on it."

"You own any books?"

Wesley shrugged.

"Comic books, even?"

Wesley shook his head. "Them's expensive. My allowance don't cover that kinda thing."

"I have a few my parents bought me. I got a Wonder Woman before the run was cancelled in fifty-three. Some Green Arrow, too. Wonder Woman's better than Green Arrow, I think, but don't tell no one I said so—okay?"

"Why not?"

"Because I asked you not to?" Pete's eyes pleaded with Wesley.

"No, I mean, why don't you want no one to know you like Wonder Woman over Green Arrow?"

"Oh. Because they'll think I'm a sissy. Bad enough as it is, me being fat. I don't need to be a fat sissy."

"What makes you a sissy for liking Wonder Woman?"

Pete raised his shoulders, held them there as if in thought, then let them drop.

"I guess because she's a woman superhero."

"What's that got to do with anything?" Wesley said, confused.

"I don't think it does have anything to do with anything, but some boys, well, they think that women can't be superheroes."

"Like who?"

"Some kids in the school I used to go to. Before coming here. Before, you know."

"I know?"

"Yeah. Before what happened in Columbus."

"Your parents getting killed?"

Pete nodded. Wesley wasn't a bright kid, but he knew when someone was uncomfortable, and Pete's discomfort was coming off him like stink off sunbaked roadkill.

"Come on," Wesley changed the subject, "It's just over here."

Pete smiled and the two boys went to see about a scarecrow.

\*\*\*

"What the hell happened in here," Hap muttered as he looked over Donna Johnson's blood-drenched kitchen. Donna Johnson—what was left of her—sat in a chair at the kitchen table, her headless corpse slumped over the tabletop. Coagulated blood dangled from the table's edge like stalactites in a cave.

Eric Larson, Janice Larson's cuckolded husband and one of Hap's deputies, stood on the other side of the table looking ill. The man was working overtime; he'd been on shift since eleven last night, and should've been off by eleven this morning, but Hap had asked him to stay over when he, Hap, had brought in a gore-covered Kirby Johnson for questioning. Right now, Kirby was cooling his heels in one of the two cells the sheriff's office had. And if Ronnie had listened, the teenager was currently being cleaned up and looked over for injuries. Given the scene here at the Johnson house, though, Hap doubted any of the blood was Kirby's.

"Where's her head?" Hap figured Eric would know, seeing as how the deputy had already been here for a good hour.

Hap had sent Eric out to the Johnson house as soon as he got back to the station. He'd get out there eventually, Hap had said, but first he needed to clean the blood out of his car. Priorities—Hap didn't much have them. Had he thought well enough on the subject, he might've driven out to the Johnson's with Kirby in the back seat to make sure Donna wasn't in need of assistance. He hadn't, though, and now he hoped that no one made mention of his error in judgment, or lack thereof.

His only excuse was that something had pressed on him as soon as he'd seen Kirby; the urgent need to get this kid in a cell, locked away from the public. That, if asked, was what Hap would have said had been his number one priority at the time. Now, thinking about the sixteen-year-old sitting in lockup made Hap feel like a scared and irrational old man, even if he wasn't yet forty.

"What do you mean, *where's her head?*" Eric Larson asked, his brow furrowed. The deputy looked much younger than he actually was, which was not much younger than Hap himself. Eric had a full head of wavy brown hair of which Hap had to admit he was jealous. Eric was, however, a little soft around the middle, and short in the pants, or so that's how Janice told it. She'd informed Hap her husband's dick wasn't much bigger than her own thumb, in both length and girth, and Hap had chuckled in amusement and sympathy for the poor bastard.

"What else could I mean, Eric? What's a person normally mean when they ask where something is? Means that something's missin, don't it?"

"Oh. Uh, yeah, I 'spose. I, um, don't rightly know, Hap. Haven't found it."

Hap glanced around the kitchen. Other than an open oven door and blood splatter damn-near everywhere, there was nothing out of place. Nothing that caught his eye, anyway. Some dirty pans in the sink. An open cabinet full of canned goods. A toaster surrounded by a ring of breadcrumbs. But no head.

"Her head's missing." Hap said. It was not a question.

Eric nodded dumbly. "Yessir."

"What would someone want with her head?"

"Don't know, sir."

"Kirby didn't have it with him. Must've hid it before leaving the house."

"You think the boy done did this?"

"Ain't a doubt in my mind, Eric. Not a single, solitary one."

"Huh."

"What's *Huh*?"

"Well, you wouldn't think the kid had it in 'im, sir. I mean, what with him being... you know?"

"What do I know, Eric? Stop playing fuckin word games and spit it out."

"Sorry. Thought you knew. Just 'bout everybody knows, I thought."

"*What*, Eric? *What* does everyone know?"

"Oh. Yeah. Well, he's a sissy, sir."

"A sissy."

"Yessir."

"He likes boys?"

"I reckon. That's what I heard, anyway."

Hap sighed at length.

Eric said, "You think that's why he killed her? Being unbalanced like he is?"

"Check the rooms and the bathrooms for the head. Then I want you to write up a report on exactly how you found this place before I got here. *Exactly* how it was when you first arrived. I knew I should've come out here myself, right off," Hap lied.

"Sorry, sir."

"What's done is done. Find that head, Eric. It didn't run off to Mexico, or nothin. It's here, by damn, and you're gonna find it."

"Yessir."

"In the meantime, I'm going back to the station to question the kid."

"The kid, sir?"

"Kirby, Eric. I'm going to question Kirby Johnson to see why he killed his mother."

"Oh. Right. Sorry."

"Find that head, deputy."

"Yessir."

\*\*\*

"How long's this been up there?" Pete gazed up at the scarecrow with squinted eyes. The sun was high in the sky and behind the scarecrow. Pete stepped into the straw man's shadow. There. That was better.

The scarecrow was maybe five feet tall, and two feet off the ground, so that it looked down on the boy with its black-stitched Xs for eyes from a good seven feet in the air; a decent three feet taller than Pete. Had Pete said the scarecrow wasn't intimidating, he'd have been lying through his teeth. The scarecrow wore a red flannel button-down shirt and jean coveralls, not much different from how Wesley was dressed today, Pete noted. Had his father been dressed the same way? Pete couldn't recall.

"I call him Frank."

"Frank?"

"Yep."

"Frank's a swell name."

"I thought so."

"Does he do a good job? Of scaring crows, I mean?"

"Don't get many crows out this way. He scares more sparrows than crows, I 'spect. I guess you could call him a—I don't know, a scaresparrow?"

"Yeah."

"Yeah," Wesley echoed.

"That rolls off the tongue nicely."

"What does?"

"Scaresparrow, scaresparrow, scaresparrow," Pete stumbled on the fourth iteration of the name and giggled. "Never mind. Say it enough and it's kind of hard to say."

Wesley looked up at the scaresparrow. "How 'bout that, Frank? You a scaresparrow? Don't mind if we call you that, do ya?"

"I don't reckon," Pete said in a deep voice, out the side of his mouth. He was shocked at how much he sounded like his father. He cleared his throat to get rid of rising emotions. Last thing he wanted was to cry in front of his friend. Especially not right now, when they were having so much fun.

This was fun, Pete realized with a jolt. For the first time in months, he was actually enjoying himself.

Wesley said, "So, Frank, now that you can talk, how's the air up there?"

"Smells like corn," Pete said in his father's voice, which was now Frank the Scaresparrow's to use as Pete deemed necessary.

"Well, you are in a cornfield, I reckon."

"I reckon, so."

"How'd you get up there?" Wesley said, obviously holding back laughter.

"I reckon I don't know. I was just minding my own business, and then suddenly I had this stick up my ass."

Both boys burst into laughter. Tears filled Pete's eyes, the happiest kind, and he swiped at his face with a hand that was still dirty and raw from weeding.

Wesley patted him on the shoulder. "That was a good one."

"Thanks." Pete lifted the bottom of his shirt, exposing his chubby belly, and blew his nose on the fabric. He didn't even consider that Wesley might make fun of his fat stomach, and Wesley didn't betray Pete's blind trust.

"How long can you stay today?" Wesley asked once he'd stopped laughing.

"I don't know. I guess as long as I want. Mama doesn't know I'm gone."

"Mama? Thought she was your grandmother."

Pete shrugged. "She says I should call her Mama, so I do."

"But what about your real mother?"

"What about her?"

Wesley frowned. "I guess I think it's disrespectful to your mom, seeing as how she's dead and all. You'd think your grandmother would want you to remember your mom as your mama."

"Oh. I hadn't thought about it that way."

"Why you think she would want to erase your mama?"

"I—I don't *think* that's what she wants. She just—she, uh—well, I don't suppose I know."

"Strange," Wesley said and gazed back up at Frank the Scaresparrow. "Should I ask him if he wants to stay for lunch, Franky Boy?"

"Yeah," Pete said in his own voice. "Yeah, you should."

Wesley smiled at Pete and threw an easy arm over his new friend's shoulder.

"I like you, Pete."

"Same," Pete said. "I mean, I like you too."

"Come on. I wanna introduce you to Pop and see what he says about you staying for lunch."

"What if he asks if my grandmother knows I'm here?"

"Pop won't care. Pop barely knows to check on me, much less someone else's kid."

\*\*\*

Ronnie Short thought Kirby Johnson was the creepiest thing he'd seen in all his days.

*You stay on that side of the bars, you queer freak.*

Ronnie didn't know if the rumors about the teenager were true, but he was of the opinion that homos were no better than kiddy diddlers and those who copulated with animals. *Bestiaries*, or whatever they were called. He didn't know the proper name and didn't care to know it. If it were up to him, the death penalty would be broadened to include folks like Kirby Johnson, and the world would be a better place for it, too.

"You get done with that bucket and you pour it down the toilet, you understand?"

Kirby nodded as he washed the caked blood from his face and neck. The boy was down to nothing but his skivvies. Boxers, to be exact. *Real men wear briefs*, Ronnie thought. The deputy kept glancing at the pinched-open pee-hole in Kirby's shorts to make sure the kid wasn't getting turned on by him standing there. First sign of an erection and Ronnie would kick it inverted, he swore before God he would. Wasn't no queer gonna get turned on by him. No, sir. No way. No how.

Kirby had probably had something to do with Father George, too, from what Hap had said. Something about how the kid had said something in line with what the Haversham boy told him Father George had said before blowing his own fool head off. Ronnie couldn't rightly remember what that was though. Didn't matter too much, he didn't reckon.

"Don't you be looking at me, neither. Just clean yourself off and dump that bucket, and if you need to, run you some more water. I'll be in the next room. You holler when you're done."

Kirby nodded.

*Creepy fucker.*

Ronnie headed back up front to the station desk. He poured his third cup of joe of the day and sat down to type up the report Hap had written yesterday, pencil scratchings to the tune of Father George's suicide. Ronnie had just started typing when something walked by the desk.

Ronnie looked up.

Nothing there.

He went back to work. He'd transcribed no more than fifty words from the handwritten report to the typewritten document when something moved in his peripheral vision. Whoever it was, they'd moved into Hap's office before he'd gotten a good look at them.

"Who's there?" he called.

No answer.

*Course not, you dumb bastard. If someone were playing hide and go seek with you, like this someone obviously is, they ain't gonna say "I'm over here", now are they?*

"You know who you're messin with, fella?" Ronnie knew it was a man. Wasn't no woman on the face of the earth bold enough to play games with a sheriff's deputy.

Ronnie got up. A breeze, like exhaled breath, played across the back of his neck. He spun, fists up, and swung at empty air, like a punch-drunk boxer.

There was no one there.

"What the hell is wrong with me?" he said aloud, placing a nervous laugh at the end of his sentence to assure himself of how funny all this was. A grown man jumping at shadows and breezes. What a riot. Never mind that he was alone. Don't even mention how there was nowhere from where a breeze could have issued. Just a wall, and a corkboard poster with papers pinned with brass thumbtacks. No windows. But never mind that, ladies and gentlemen. Just never you mind it.

*"Ronnie..."*

Ronnie twisted this way and that, seeking the origin of the voice. Wasn't nobody here. He swore before God, wasn't nobody here.

"Goddamn it, you're gonna stop messin with me, or you're liable to get shot. You hear me?"

*"Ronnie..."*

The sound was snake-like and playful, soft and sibilant. Someone was playing with him and he didn't like it. Not one bit. He almost pulled out his gun, but thought better of it. The culprit was probably some kid who'd snuck in while he'd been seeing about Kirby Johnson in the back, and the last thing Ronnie needed was to plug some wily tike who lacked adult sense. That's why he hadn't found anyone in the office, because they were just a kid, and small enough to hide in tight places. Sure. That was why. No other logical explanation for it.

"*Ronnie...*"

"Listen, kid. You need to stop playing around before someone, namely you, gets hurt real bad. If you jump out at me, I can't say how I'll respond. I'm serious now. You could get hurt real bad-like. Possibly even die. You don't wanna die, now, do you? What would your parents—"

There was a hand on his shoulder. Gooseflesh rushed up his arms, over his shoulders, and down his shoulder blades. Wasn't no kid on the planet tall enough to place a leisurely hand on his shoulder. Ronnie Short was far from his namesake, every bit of six-feet tall. A kid small enough to hide in Hap's office wouldn't be tall enough to put a hand on him up there. No way. No how.

"*No, sir...*"

He could feel their breath on the back of his neck. He swallowed a lump roughly the size and sharpness of a cinder block. It landed in his stomach with a thud.

He slowly—ever so slowly—placed a hand on the revolver in his holster. Began to draw it. A second hand, warm and moist, lay upon Ronnie's own hand, the one drawing the gun, and gently—ever so gently—shoved, pushing the gun back into its holster.

He wanted to tell whoever was behind him what kind of trouble they'd started, how big was the dilemma they'd stepped into, but he could no longer form words.

"*Wuz the matter, wittle Wonnie Short? Are you scared? Where's the big man who'd kill a homo, if given the chance?*"

"K-k-Kirby?"

"*Shhh, that is none of your concern.*"

"Puh-please don't hurt me," Ronnie whimpered, for he was very scared now. Wittle Wonnie Short was very, very scared, indeed.

"*We won't hurt you, Wittle Wonnie. We promise, you won't feel a thing.*"

"What are you gonna d-d-do to m-me?" Snot bubbles burst in his nose. Tears streamed. His body hitched with sobs.

"*Hush Wittle Wonnie, don't say a word...*"

\*\*\*

In his cell, Kirby Johnson heard the deputy scream. There was a sharp thud, and then all was quiet.

He dipped the crimson rag, which had once been white, back into the murky red water of the bucket and scrubbed at his temples. Kirby found that blood was nearly impossible to get out of a hairline.

He dumped the filthy water into the toilet and flushed. Refilled the bucket in the sink. Dumped the second batch. Refilled it again. He did this a total of nine times before he gave up. In all that time, he never did hear another peep from the deputy who'd been so cruel to him.

He wondered how long he'd sit here before someone came along. Couldn't be too long. He simply hoped the sheriff—or anyone, really—came back before nightfall. He didn't want to be here alone overnight. He didn't want to be anywhere alone overnight. Not with Mommy gone. Despite what little comfort she had been. Kirby felt that even a modicum of comfort was better than none at all.

He lay back on the bed and stared at the ceiling.

The ceiling undulated, as if a great worm writhed beneath the paint.

Kirby rolled onto his side so he didn't have to see the thing. Whatever it was.

He closed his eyes.

The Coat Man bit off his mother's head.

He opened his eyes.

Carved into the wall, inches from his face, were four words:

*Everything is horrible now.*

Had he written them? If so, he didn't recall doing so. Besides, how could he have? They looked to have been etched into the wall with something sharper than he had in his possession. Like nails. The kind of nails you hammer into wood. Not the kind on his fingers. He ran a hand over the letters and the words disappeared.

Nothing but his imagination.

Maybe what had happened to Mommy had been all in his head too? Maybe? He didn't think so. Just look at all the blood he'd washed from himself. Some of it was still caked in his hair. He'd need a shower to get it out, he was sure.

He curled into a fetal position and began to hum a quiet song.

*So I'll cherish the old rugged Cross…*

*Till my trophies at last I lay down…*

*I will cling to the old rugged Cross…*

*And exchange it some day for a crown.*

It was a long time before someone came to check on him.

\*\*\*

Hap had too much crap to deal with for him to have time to sit in front of the Larson house, but he had to make sure everything was copacetic. He'd been awfully hard on Janice last night and thought he should apologize, you know, to keep her quiet-like. He didn't think she would tell anyone. Especially not Eric. But one never knows what goes on in the hearts and minds of women. They were as alien to him as a conscience.

He got out and headed across the lawn, adjusting his belt as he walked. Nothing wrong with the way it sat on his hips. It was just force of habit.

He knocked three times, loud, like the officer of the law he was, and the door swayed open on well-oiled hinges.

"Janice?" Hap called into the house.

She didn't answer. He remained on the front step for a count of three before calling her name again and stepping inside. He left the door open.

The living room was empty. So was the kitchen. The hallway floor was hardwood. Pink picture frames hung on pastel blue walls with bright yellow baseboards. He recalled the first time he'd seen the hallway after Janice and Eric had stripped the wallpaper and applied fresh paint. What a plum monstrosity.

When Janice had first shown Hap the freshly painted hallway, he'd said, "Looks like the Easter bunny had a hard night of drinking and puked all over the place."

"Oh, hush," she'd said, hugging him close. "I like it."

She'd kissed him then.

He'd broken the kiss and looked her in the eye.

"Looks queer."

"Stop it." She'd slapped him playfully on the chest as she pulled away. "Eric approved."

"He would."

"What's that supposed to mean?" Her brow had furrowed in confusion.

"I mean, there's a reason you're fucking me instead of him."

Now, Hap stood in the hallway, considering what he'd said in a time far removed from the present. What had it been? Five months since he started screwing Eric's old lady? Maybe more. He couldn't be certain.

Now he felt even worse for going off on her last night. Seems that, at some point, he had considered the idea that she'd stopped making love to her husband when she'd started making love to him. He didn't like being wrong. The feeling didn't gel with his mindset whatsoever.

"Janice? I come to apologize for last night."

No response.

He checked the bedroom, the guest bedroom, the bathroom, and the laundry room. He searched the garage by way of the connecting door in the kitchen, and found not a sign of her.

He didn't like where this was going. When he put two and two together—what happened last night plus the now-empty Larson abode—he got an answer he didn't appreciate in the least.

Maybe she was out shopping. Yeah. That could be it. The Larson's only had the one car, but Hap couldn't remember if the couple's Ford Fairlane had been parked at the station or not. The pastel blue car—the same blue as those godawful walls in the hallway—was kind of hard to miss, but there was no way for Hap to be sure. He'd had no reason to look for the car, so it all came down to a bad case of out of sight, out of mind.

He walked back into the house, closing the connecting door as he went. He picked up the phone in the living room and dialed the station. The phone rang a dozen times before Hap hung up.

Without much thought, he picked the handset up again, dialed information, and asked for Donna Johnson's residence. The operator put him through. The phone rang five times before Eric Larson answered.

"Hullo?" said the dunderhead.

"Eric. It's Hap. Did you drive your car to work last night?"

"Yessir." Then: "Why?"

"Oh, no reason. Thanks."

"Uh, okay. Bye."

Hap would thank his lucky stars for many years to come that he'd hired an idiot the likes of Eric Larson. If it weren't for that man's stupidity, things might have gone much differently than they did.

Okay. So either Janice had walked somewhere, or someone had come to pick her up. Or—

"What are you doing here?"

"Jesus Christ!" Hap hollered. He spun around on one foot, tottered, almost went over, but caught himself at the last minute on the wall.

Janice stood in the hallway, her arms crossed, staring at him like he was a cockroach in her egg salad.

"I just come to check in on you. I was awful to you last night, and I wanted to apologize."

"I'd like for you to leave, Hap." Her gaze cut into him. He'd seen plenty of hate in his life, and this bitch was full of it.

"Listen, Jan, I—"

"I told you to leave."

Hap sighed. "Where the hell were you just now? I checked everywhere and—"

"You didn't check the backyard. Please, leave."

Hap had had just about enough of her bullshit.

He took a step toward her and said, "Look—"

Her arms dropped away from her chest. He took this as her dropping her guard and stepped forward again. She reached behind her back and pulled a revolver as long as his dick—which was quite long, if he did say so himself—from her pants. The barrel of the gun was as wide and deep as a tunnel in a mountain.

"Goddamn it, woman!" Hap cried. He took several steps backward until he thudded against front door.

"I told you to leave."

"You shoot me and you're gonna be in a word of shit!"

"I shoot you and I'll be a vindicated woman. I can't believe I ever let you between my legs. Now get!"

"You better—"

She thumbed back the hammer.

"I better what?"

Hap swallowed a goose egg.

"Nothin. I'm leaving."

"Damn right you are. I don't *never* wanna see you around here again. I don't care if my husband invites you over for a barbeque. You come up with some excuse not to come, or I swear

141

'fore Christ, I'll blast a hole so big in you, you'll have to decide which hole to shit from."

"Jan—"

"I said, GET OUT!"

The rage in her eyes and voice were enough to get him moving. He quick-stepped out the front door, across the grass and street, and dropped behind the wheel of his squad car with a grunt.

"Fuck!" he roared and punched the steering wheel. The horn gave a short blat. He punched it four more times, for good measure. Hap glanced back toward the Larson house in enough time to see the front door close. He wanted nothing more than to storm back inside and teach that cock-tease what for. How *dare* she? No one treated Harold Carringer like that and lived.

*NOBODY!*

He'd show that sloppy cunt. One way or another, he'd show her good.

Hap started the engine and tore a good centimeter of tread off his tires peeling out. He was mad and not thinking and had already forgotten that no one had answered when he'd called the station.

\*\*\*

Janice Larson shut the door and slumped against it. She sat the .357 on the table in the foyer, atop the telephone book, and took several deep, shuddering breaths. Her nerves were shot.

She'd been at the kitchen sink when Hap pulled up at the curb. When he'd gotten out of his squad car, she had rushed to the front door, fully intent on locking it and barring his entrance and pretending not to be home.

Then an idea had occurred to her. She cracked the door, just so, just enough so that, when Hap knocked, it would come open. Being first and foremost an officer of the law, Hap would feel the need to investigate. And when he did, he would find her in the backyard. Holding a gun. She would have then shot him in the face, in his stupid, hateful, rapist face, and claimed that she had thought he was an intruder.

*Why were you in the backyard of your house at this time?* she imagined a judge asking.

*I was gardening, Your Honor.*

*And why were you carrying a gun while gardening?*

*Have you seen the size of the squirrels in my neighborhood?*

That wouldn't have gone over well at all, and she'd reconsidered shooting Hap in his stupid, hateful, rapist face. After the realization that killing Hap would not have been in her best interest, she'd waited until she'd thought he'd gone, until all was quiet on the Western Front, as it were, and had headed back inside. That's when she'd found him on the phone.

For a moment that seemed to last for hours, she'd aimed the .357 at the back of Hap's head, her finger resting on the trigger. She felt she could have killed him in that moment. Had this been last night and her wounds—emotional and physical—freshly carved, she would have blown the entirety of his head off and then danced a Mexican Hat Dance on his corpse.

*Ariba!*

In the end, she'd lowered the gun before he'd turned around. To keep herself from automatically shooting him upon seeing his stupid, hateful, rapist face again, she'd tucked the .357 in the back of her pants and hoped she wouldn't—quite literally—blow her own ass off.

She couldn't believe she had actually scared him off. Then again, there was no one on Earth Hap Carringer loved more than himself. No matter how much he'd wanted to course-correct her actions and teach her a lasting lesson, he'd never have risked his life to do so.

However, she knew this wasn't over. As long as she and Hap lived in Bay's End, there would be the threat of violence and the need for her to protect herself. There was no way she could tell Eric about what had happened today for fear that he'd find out the rest of the story. If she told Eric about Hap's threats Eric was bound to confront the sheriff—his boss—and lose their livelihood in the process. She'd already betrayed Eric's trust; she didn't wish to emasculate him further.

A baby cried from down the hall.

From where she stood, back against the front door, she could easily see all the way down the hall: past the bathroom and guestroom, respectively, on the left side, then along to the hall closet and master bedroom on the right. The wall heater stared at her from the end of the hall, the dual rows of stacked and slatted vents looking like a judgmental gaze.

*Waaaaah*, the baby squalled.

Janice Larson didn't have a baby. And, by her knowledge, there were no new infants on the block either, so the sound wasn't carrying from another house on her street. Of course, that was false logic, and she knew it. Any one of her neighbors could have had visitors this morning, and one of those hypothetical visitors could have brought a baby along with them.

But something told her that the crying was not coming from anywhere other than her own room.

Worse yet, the crying seemed to be getting closer.

Something thudded to the floor in the master bedroom and Janice jumped. She shoved against the door, as if she could escape through the wood, by osmosis.

The crying stopped. An eerie quietude settled upon her like a vast weight; she felt its presence crushing her into the floor like a stubbed-out cigarette.

She both wanted and did not want to rush down the hall, gun drawn, and face whatever might lie in wait for her in her bedroom.

What if it *were* a baby? That was madness. But *what if?* What harm could it do to her? How much danger could she actually be in? None, that's how much. She could shoot it before it so much as crawled too close to her.

*Listen at you, talking about shooting a baby. Why you're no better than...*

*Oh, no...*

"Georgina?" Janice whispered to the quiet house.

A shadow, rounded at the top and about a foot long, jutted from the open door of her room.

Every fiber of her being told her that she was imagining things. There had been no baby crying. There was no baby's head casting a shadow on her hallway floor. There was absolutely nothing to fear.

There was nothing in her room.

Nothing there.

Nothing at all.

The baby cooed.

Janice Larson spun, yanked open her door, and ran.

\*\*\*

Hap's motto had always been: one could never be too prepared. A Boy Scout through and through, Hap headed home. Once there, he removed the unregistered .38 from the safe in his closet and strapped its ankle holster just above his right shoe. He considered the .45 lying on the top shelf of the waist-tall safe, but figured it would be too bulky for concealed carry.

Besides, the .45 was registered. Not to him, mind you. It was registered to a gentleman named Bruce Patterson. Bruce had run a moonshine dispensary out of his barn. Once word got around to Hap that the still was an active one and Bruce seemingly didn't care about being caught, Hap had busted up the operation. He didn't mind Bruce making some money off illegal 'shine. It was the blatant disrespect of the office of the Sheriff that had finally done it. Same as Hap believed that screwing another man's wife was perfectly acceptable as long as you didn't brag about it. Bragging was plain and simple disrespectful. And while Bruce Patterson had not bragged about his profitable bootlegging operation—at least not that Hap had heard—Hap could not ignore the gossip floating around his town. A still right under Hap's nose? He'd be damned if he was going to let that rumor float around untended.

So he'd busted Bruce and confiscated about seventy-five percent of the man's product. The other twenty-five percent, along with a .45 Hap had found under the man's pillow, had changed hands from Bruce Patterson to Harold Carringer. Hap knew the benefit of owning an unregistered firearm. But one that was registered to some other unlucky bastard? That was just the universe smiling down on him.

But the .45 would remain in the safe for now. The .38 was coming with him. He didn't know when he'd next run into Janice Larson, but when he did, he was going to teach her a very valuable lesson. One she would never forget.

You didn't fuck with Hap. No, ma'am.

He tugged the .38 from the ankle holster and checked the load. Six brass casings gleamed at him. Fully stocked. And did one of these pretty little bullets have Janice's name on it? Oh, he thought it did. He thought it did, indeed.

Armed to his liking, Hap headed back to the station to question Kirby Johnson.

Something was wrong in his town and he planned to get to the bottom of it.

*Everything is horrible now, my ass*, Hap thought. *Everything goes back to normal today, or my name isn't Sheriff Harold Goddamn Carringer—that's two R's, if it do ya fine.*

\*\*\*

"Why do you keep looking at me like that?" Pete asked Wesley.

The two boys sat on the front porch, eating bologna and cheese sandwiches, legs dangling off the top step, Wesley with his back to the banister, facing Pete, and Pete facing the road. Every time Pete glanced over, Wesley's eyes were studying him. Pete never would have found the looks suspect, but Wesley kept skittering away. It was painfully obvious that the other boy didn't want to be caught staring.

"I was just wondering about—well. About your parents, I reckon. I don't wanna ask, but it's got me curious something fierce."

Pete took a bite of his sandwich, chewed briefly and swallowed. He didn't care much for chewing. It slowed down the eating process. He only chewed enough so that he wouldn't choke on what he swallowed.

"What do you want to know?"

"What happened to them?"

"I told you. They were killed. By a guy in a mask."

"What kinda mask?"

"A baby doll mask."

"*Really?*"

Pete nodded.

"Wowzers."

"Yeah."

"So why'd he leave you alive?" Wesley took a massive bite of his sandwich. Watching Wesley chew it down into manageable pieces made Pete's jaw throb.

"I don't know. He never said anything to me. He just ignored me."

"He didn't say nothin at all?"

"He said…some things, but he never said anything to me."

"What kind of things did he say?"

"I don't know. It was too low to hear him well," Pete lied.

"Wowzers."

Again Pete nodded, but only because he didn't know what else to say.

Wesley said, "Ain't nothing like that ever happened around here. Not that I know of, anyway."

Something surfaced in Pete's mind. Something he hadn't thought about in ages.

"Is it true the town burned its founder alive?"

"Oh. Well, I guess so, but I don't know much about it. Just some rumors. Don't reckon I had any reason to ask after it. Just something that happened long 'fore I was born. I don't normally think much about history and whatnot. Been that way all my life," Wesley said, as if he'd already lived a long and fruitful life. Pete almost laughed but refrained when he saw that Wesley was serious.

Pete said, "My mother told me about it, but she didn't go into detail. It was kind of a cautionary tale."

"*Caw-shun-airy*? That's like that word what means you burned something to stop it from bleeding, right?"

"What? No. At least I don't think that's one of its meanings." For all his book learning, Pete was unfamiliar with the word *cauterize* at that point in his life. "But a cautionary tale is a warning, like a fable."

Wesley frowned. "What's a fable?"

"Aesop?"

"*Who* sop?"

Pete laughed. He couldn't help it. Wesley chuckled, too, waylaying any fear Pete might have had due to laughing at his friend. In his opinion, it was always preferable to laugh with someone instead of at them.

"Aesop was a guy—least I think he was a guy—who wrote fables. Fables are stories that teach a lesson." Pete had perked up.

149

He loved talking about stories. He thought that, one day, he might even become a writer. "Ever heard the story about the lion and the mouse?"

"The lion's got a thorn in his paw in that one, don't he?"

"Yeah. That's the one. It was written by this fella Aesop. It teaches the lesson that even the biggest, meanest King of the Jungle needs help sometimes."

"I thought it was about doing to others what you want done to you. Least that's what Pop says. He used to tell me a lot of stories, at bedtime. He don't do it no more though." Wesley seemed to think really hard about something but said nothing more.

"Well, I suppose it can be seen that way, too. But the way I was taught is that it has to do with strength and weakness. About how we can all be weak and strong in our own way. No matter our size."

"All right," Wesley said. "So what about these fables? What's your point?" Though Wesley's words seemed harsh, Pete didn't take offense.

"Some of them are cautionary tales. Like the frog and the scorpion. You heard that one?"

Wesley shook his head. "You can tell me if you like."

"Okay," Pete said. Wesley seemed to be eagerly awaiting the beginning, so he started without further ado. "Once there was this frog who hung around this one river. The river was long and wide and not easy to cross unless you were a fish or alligator. Or a frog, like he was. So one day a scorpion came along and asked the frog for a ride across the river. The frog said no because the scorpion would sting him. And the scorpion said no I won't sting you. They went back and forth for a while. But the frog was a good guy, and he finally let the scorpion crawl onto his back."

"That one dumb frog."

Pete laughed. "He wasn't really dumb as much as he was kind."

"Sometimes that's the same thing," Wesley said.

Pete couldn't find a counter argument, so he continued.

"Anyway, so they're halfway across the river when the scorpion stings the frog on the back."

"See. Told ya he was dumb. Nice or not, that frog was denser than a bucket of cement and half as bright."

Pete laughed and went on. "The frog, as he's dying, asks why the scorpion stung him. Now they're both going to die. And the scorpion says he had no other choice because that's his nature. He's a scorpion."

"Right," Wesley agreed. "And the lesson is you don't trust people."

"Well, no. It's that you should always do what's right."

"Huh?"

"Yeah. The right thing to do in this situation was to trust his instincts and not get into bed with a scorpion."

"He got in the scorpion's bed? I thought they both drowned."

"No. I mean—shoot. Okay. What I meant by that was that he helped the scorpion when he knew better. He, um—uh—He went against his better judgment! That's what I mean."

"Fables are confusing. Did E-Stop write that one, too?"

"*Ae*-sop. And I don't think so. He might have, but I don't know for sure."

"Okay. But what's all this got to do with your mother?"

151

"What?"

"Sheesh, Pete, you're the one who started this!" Wesley slapped his thighs. "You done said at the very beginning that your mother told you a *caw-shun-airy* tale, or some such thing. That's what got you off on this rip you're on."

"Oh. Sorry."

"Don't apologize. Get to your point. Jeez, Louise."

"Okay. Well." Pete thought about the road he'd been going down when he'd detoured and backtracked the best he could. "Fables...cautionary tales... Oh. Right. What I was saying was, my mother told me about how the town burned Francis Bay at the stake. She said it was the reason she didn't believe."

"Believe in what?" said Wesley.

"In Religion. In God, and such."

"*She didn't believe in God?*" Wesley looked truly and utterly taken aback. Shock stretched the skin of his face and widened his eyes to a laughable extent.

Pete chuckled.

"What's so funny?" Wesley asked. His face had melted from shock to distrust in an instant.

"Nothing."

"No. Tell me. What are you laughing at?"

"Well, I guess I just think like my mother. Religion is, I don't know, kinda silly."

"You wanna go to hell, or somethin?" Wesley screeched.

"I can't go someplace that doesn't exist."

"*Hell doesn't exist?*" Wesley wailed. "*What's wrong with you?*"

"Nothing's wrong with me."

"You don't believe in God and say that Hell ain't real. Boy, there's a whole bunch of something wrong with you."

Pete dropped his head and said, "I'm sorry."

"Don't apologize to me. Apologize to God. Sheesh. I should get off this porch 'fore lightning strikes you dead, and me along with ya."

"All right." Pete put the last uneaten bit of sandwich on the porch boards and got up. He headed for the street.

"Hey," Wesley called. "Where ya goin?"

Pete turned. "Home, I guess. Don't want you getting struck by lightning, or whatever."

"I didn't mean you should leave."

Pete said nothing in return.

Wesley said, "I didn't. I just don't like hearing stuff like that."

Pete waited.

"Come on back here. Tell me another story. Something that don't got nothin to do with not believing in God and Hell."

"That's the point of the story," Pete said. "My mother told me the story about Bay to warn me off religion and... religious people."

"Oh."

"Yeah. Oh."

"You ain't got any other stories?" Wesley's eyes pleaded.

Pete thought for a moment.

He'd had no idea how religious Wesley was, nor did he think he would've hung around this long had he known. Mom had been adamant about not keeping company with religious types, much less conversing with them.

*There's no room in an intelligent person's mind for superstitious nonsense, Pete. None. Intelligent people do not believe in things. They trust that science will find answers. Faith shuts down thought and asks you to have faith in one answer, whereas science is a tool with which to find answers. There's no arguing, much less conversing, with religious people.*

"No. No other stories. I really should go. I'm sure my grandmother's having a cow."

"But—I thought we was having fun? Don't'cha wanna play no more?"

"Maybe some other time," Pete said, but meant, *There won't be a some other time.*

"Okay then," Wesley said.

"Okay. Bye."

Not, *See you later.*

Not, *Bye for now.*

Just, *Bye.*

Pete, mourning the loss of a friendship newly made, headed home.

How does one gain and lose the same friend in a single day? When we're young, we suspect every relationship will be lifelong. Pete had some experience with the fact that such a definitive statement is not always true. His parents had been taken from him early on in life, and their absence hurt more than he could bear. Wesley he'd only known for several hours, but the pain he felt on his walk home was deep and significant. Why that was so, Pete Blackwood could not say. He was certain of only one simple truth. He already missed Wesley Haversham very much.

# 7. You Must've Been a Beautiful Baby

Pete Rothsberger weighed eleven pounds, eight ounces when he was cut from his struggling mother's stomach. Joyce Rothsberger spent eight days recovering in the hospital before she returned home with her—hospital staff agreed—amazingly large, bouncing baby boy. Pete's size stemmed from gestational diabetes, an odd reaction that occurs in a pregnant woman's body, like toxicity—a dangerously elevated blood pressure—due to the body's refusal to carry what it considers a foreign body to term. So it was that his mother's body had been the first to reject him.

Even though the family lived in Columbus, Pete's father—Patrick—commuted to and from Bay's End on a daily basis, Monday through Friday, to Humble Hill, the rehabilitation facility where he'd been employed for, at the time of his death, fifteen years. Patrick worked as a technician, or so his wife believed. Truth be told, he didn't have a solid name for what he did. That he

155

worked with electronics of some sort was enough information for his wife, a self-proclaimed layman on the subject of "electronic doo-dads." When Joyce would giggle and say she didn't so much as understand how a television set worked, Patrick would smile and say, "Neither do I, hon. I doubt anyone knows for sure."

What Patrick did for Humble Hill was his concern and the concern of those who employed him. The bills were paid monthly, and there was food on the table every night, so there was no need for anyone to inquire further into the nature of his employment.

Pete was a happy boy. Having two intellectuals as parents and role models, the boy grew up precocious to a fault and lived a rather uneventful life, for the most part. The Rothsbergers' Thanksgivings were plentiful, and their Christmases bountiful, and the family took regular vacations to distant parts of the country at least twice a year. Vacations that were, unbeknownst to anyone but Patrick, paid for by Humble Hill. By the age of nine, Pete and his parents had been to the Grand Canyon, Niagara Falls (the far more aesthetically pleasing Canadian side), and had visited lesser known attractions such as: the World's Largest Ball of String, the National Hubcap Society, and Wingnuts Emporium!, which in reality had absolutely nothing to do with wingnuts.

But Pete's favorite vacation had been to Nevada, to a little place in the middle of nowhere, based entirely on a cartoon show named *The Flintstones*. Several domed structures that resembled hollowed out boulders but were more than likely some kind of fiberglass and/or clay construction, dotted the landscape desert. A car with two great stone cylinders for wheels sat in the middle of it all. Pete had sat behind the wheel, his hands on the smooth surface of what was supposed to be a stone tablet for a steering wheel but was in all likelihood just wood painted a glossy gray, while his mother snapped a picture of him attempting to drive the stone-age conveyance. One hut... or dome... or house—or whatever one should have called the multi-colored domes—even had a little television built right into the wall. This TV aired a constant stream of the animated show. Pete and his parents sat watching the show for an hour before finally leaving. They talked about the show the entire way to California, their final destination being Hollywood and an up-close look of its famous mountain-top sign, and part of that conversation concerned the hows and whys of them having missed, up until that point in their lives, watching a single episode of the admittedly cute cartoon show, *The Flintstones*.

It wasn't until 1960 that Pete would realize that *The Flintstones* and the theme park he remembered so clearly hadn't existed before that year, 1960, and that his memories were impossibilities.

He was a teenager by this time and walking the streets of New York, where he'd come to live after leaving Bay's End, when he came across a furniture store with brand-new television sets proudly displayed in its storefront windows. He stood watching the show, reminiscing about childhood—the good years, before his parents had been murdered—when a mother and who he assumed was the woman's black-haired son stopped to watch alongside him. Although the sound was off, Pete understood the context of the episode, for he'd seen this one. Pebbles was teething, and Wilma was at her wit's end. As was the case in most episodes, BamBam over at the Rubbles' was suffering the same issues with his own incoming teeth.

Pete said to the woman, "This show has had a run, hasn't it?"

"Beg your pardon?" the mother asked, her face lit with a pleasant albeit slightly confused expression.

"It's been on the air forever. I remember, this one time—"

"Sorry, son, but I don't follow. What is it you mean?"

"*The Flintstones*." Pete pointed to the television on display and the cartoon on its screen. "The show's been on television for an age. I remember going to a theme park when I was a kid and watching this very episode on a television they'd somehow built into a wall. It was nifty. Just a sight to see, I tell you. Way ahead of its time."

The woman frowned and moved along. At the time, he'd not thought anything more about it. After all, this was the Big Apple, and while New Yorkers were generally inviting of conversation, they were also usually in quite the hurry.

A week later, Pete read in *TV Guide* about the new Hanna-Barbera cartoon, *The Flintstones*, and spat his coffee all over the paperback booklet.

"What the hell?" he muttered as he read more about how the flagship season, which had first aired on September 30th of 1960— *this year!*—had been a massive success with children, and "some adults, too!" *The Flintstones* came on at 8:30pm, just after *Harrigon and Sons*, and was followed-up by *77 Sunset Strip.* So far this year, *The Flintstones* were in the top twenty shows for that season. Amazing.

*The Flintstones* were not the oddest thing to have happened to Pete in his life, for his time in Bay's End seemed as impossible as having seen a cartoon and having visited a themed park modeled after said cartoon show almost a decade before it had originally aired on television. However, it was definitely up there with the strangest occurrences of his life.

But, admittedly, what the strange realization reminded Pete of most of all was his parents, and the time he'd spent with them up until their deaths. Those would always be the happiest days of his life.

The summer he lost his parents had been cooler than most. He spent every day outside between June and August, relishing the oddity in climate. Usually the asphalt would be spongy this time of year, the tar heat-softened to the texture of wet clay, but not this summer. No. The ground was just as cold and hard as it was in fall and equally unforgiving. Pete crashed his bike one sunny day, and skinned both hands—he would come to say—*"all the way down to the bone."* That, of course, was not the case, but the imaginations and over-exaggerations of boys are not for anyone to question. He ran inside, squalling, hands dripping blood, and his mother washed the grit and dirt from his scarlet palms; he danced by the sink as she did so, performing a jig on par with any trained Irish performer. When the blood and detritus was significantly washed away, his mother said, "See? It isn't so bad." And it wasn't. Sure, his skin was dotted and indented like a junkyard fender, but the cuts were small, miniscule, really, and some were even too fine to see, invisible until they once more started to bleed.

"Hands and faces bleed an awful lot, Pete. Wounds here" — she tapped his forehead— "and here" —his ruddy palm— "always bleed terribly. But it's not so bad, is it?" Pete nodded in agreement and watched as the tiny lacerations began once more to bleed. Joyce put his hand under the cold water falling from the faucet and Pete grew mesmerized by the swirling pink blood as it thinned in the water and disappeared entirely in the waterfall that poured from his cupped hand.

If only all wounds were better than they appeared on the surface.

That night, Pete lay in bed, on his back, staring into darkness, listening to his parents make love in the room next to his. He was ten and had no idea what the soft squeak of springs and subtle moans meant, but he somehow knew it was a pleasant sound. His parents were happier than ever, and so was he. Life, as they say, was good.

There came a crack in the night, a shattering of glass, which was followed by a quiet so still it only served to further enhance the sound that had come before it.

In his parents' room, the bedsprings squeaked one last time, and his father's heavy footfalls moved across the master bedroom and into the hallway. Patrick Rothsberger stuck his head into his son's room and said, "Stay in bed."

"Yessir," Pete said, cloaked by comforter.

Pete listened to his father's footsteps change from the whisper of carpeted steps to the slap of bare feet on tile. Dad was in the kitchen. Likely at the backdoor. Where an intruder had obviously entered. A tinkle of glass projected an image into Pete's over-active imagination:

*His father standing by the backdoor, picking at the broken window set in the upper third of the door. A piece comes loose. Pete watches it fall in a slow descent and shatter on the floor. Dad takes a step back. A shadow looms behind him... an arm raises... comes down... buries a hatchet in the back of his father's head.*

If only it had been that simple.

If only it had been that quick.

In later years, Pete's memory would skip somewhere around this point and he would forget several key elements. As is the case with children and trauma victims alike, Pete's recollections were not to be trusted.

Here is what happened that night, in the summer of his eleventh year, every detail, especially those he locked away.

A thud followed immediately by the rattle of ceramic and creak of wood. Pete knew this sound well, for he had either tripped and fell or clumsily slid into the curio cabinet in the kitchen more than half a dozen times since his parents had purchased it when he was four. Then came a brief struggle wherein men grunted and flesh slapped before the bark and squeak of the dining room table skating across the tile caused Pete to cringe. The repeated slamming of cabinet doors—the ones under the sink with the warped hinges that wouldn't stay shut unless you used more than a modicum of force.

His father cried out. This Pete had only heard once before when his father had been changing a tire and the lug nut had been stubborn. Dad had been shoving on the crowbar, giving the tire tool all of his strength, when the thread on the nut gave and he'd barked his knuckles on the asphalt. Blood and tears came, although the tears were far fewer in quantity.

It was the first time he'd seen his father bleed.

It was the last time he'd seen his father cry.

More noises of varying volumes and intensities came and went, but Dad made no further sounds. Heavy footfalls moved down the hallway, and Pete hoped a child's hope that his father would pop in to tell him the coast was clear, that there was no more danger, boy, you can relax in the knowledge that I have bested my adversary.

But, no, that wasn't in the cards this night.

The heavy footfalls passed Pete's door and moved into his parents' room. His mother said, "Patr—" before the word morphed into a hideous scream.

In retrospect, Pete would imagine springing from his bed and escaping into the night. He would run to the neighbor's house and awaken Tom and Mary Meredith from their peaceful slumber with a cacophony of screams. Mary would comfort Pete while Thomas called the authorities.

In another version of this same make-believe scenario, Pete is a grown man when the intruder bursts into his home and is able to make mincemeat of the man.

Sadly—tragically—none of this happened.

His mother was dragged, pleading for her life, down the hallway. Her hands and feet thudded against the carpet and walls as she struggled for freedom. Pictures fell and thunked on soft carpet. Mom continued to fight. He listened in agony as she begged for her life as well as the life of her husband and child. And then, when they reached the kitchen, she cried at the state of her husband.

All of this is lost to Pete's long-term memory. In his adult years—and even during his short time in the End—Pete's mind skips from his father's struggle with the intruder to the man in the baby doll mask bursting into his room.

The streetlights through his windows painted the intruder orange, but Pete color-corrected this in his memories of that night. In his version, the doll's face was grease-paint white, like a clown's makeup, bright and seemingly metallic. Its cheeks were dotted with solid circles of pink that served as blush. The lips were colorless; its mouth a straight and emotionless line. Blue eyes twitched inside the eyeholes of the mask. Whoever hid behind the mask was a white man. Of that much Pete was certain. The man wouldn't stop blinking, as if he were staring into studio lights. The doll-faced madman wore all black, from head to foot. The mask and eyes peeked from the hood of a sweatshirt.

Pete scrambled off the bed. Thudded to the floor. Blood pounded in his ears. Sweat popped on his forehead. He crawled for his closed closet door, as if sanctuary lay on the other side.

A hand snatched the back of his pajama shirt. The top two buttons popped off and disappeared forever. He was all but strangled on the third button as the intruder dragged him to the door. Pete grabbed the frame on his way out but was only able to maintain his grip for the briefest of seconds before he was yanked free. Down the hall and into the kitchen he went, in reverse, his heels dragging painfully across rough carpet; those same heels would be raw and rug-burned for weeks to come.

Then he was lifted, tossed, and for a time knew nothing at all.

Here is where Pete's mind skips ahead for a second time. What happened during this time is this:

Pete was thrown into the cabinetry over the kitchen counter. He banged his head against the door and lost time. With the boy out of the picture for a moment, the doll-faced man sat down at the kitchen table, where he'd lain Pete's mother. Pete's father was in the corner, where the kitchen wall met the back door, the spring on the baseboard that kept the backdoor from crashing against the wall when it was open dug into Patrick's hip. A few minutes passed. Patrick's eyes fluttered like butterfly wings. He gazed murkily upon the massive doll and thought he was dreaming.

"Hello, Patrick," said a muffled yet familiar voice that was anything but the voice of a baby doll. No *Mama* or silly cooing. Just a strong male voice that Patrick knew but could not place.

Patrick's own voice was groggy and confused. "Wha—what do you want?"

"I think you know what I want, Patrick. Let's not waste time. You've made a terrible decision and broken numerous rules. For that you must be punished. But, first, you have a choice to make. Unfortunately, whether or not you choose to talk, I will have to kill you." The man behind the mask sighed. "The choice you have is a simple one. You tell me what I want to know and I'll kill you quickly and refrain from hurting your wife and child any more than I already have. If you don't, well—I'll make you watch me kill them both before I cut off your head and show you your own decapitated body."

Patrick glanced from the table to the counter—from wife to child.

"You won't get away with this."

"I think you know better than that. Stop stalling and tell me what I want to know."

"Fuck you."

"Such language is not required, Pat." The man in the mask stood and went to the drawer next to the sink. He pulled it open and rummaged inside. Metal and wood clinked and clacked. The doll pulled a cleaver from the drawer and returned to the table.

Patrick raised a hand, as if he could ward off the man in the mask with nothing more than the power of his mind.

He got out one word.

"Don't."

The doll-faced man said, "You silly shit. You know that doesn't work on me."

The intruder's arm jerked up, came down. Simple as that. The cleaver sliced into Joyce's chest with a wet chop. Her arms jerked upward, and for a moment, she looked like Frankenstein's Monster shambling away with arms raised.

"No," Patrick sobbed. "You bastard."

It was in that moment that Patrick realized he couldn't move from the waist down. Something in his back had snapped when he'd been thrown into the corner. He knew without a shadow of a doubt that, even if he lived through tonight, he'd never walk again.

"So weak and powerless. What makes a man so pitiful, Pat? What makes a man such a failure?"

Through tear-filled eyes, Patrick noticed his son's eyes were open and staring.

Staring at his mother.

Staring at the cleaver lodged in her chest.

Pete stared at the cleaver buried in his mother's chest but did not move. Did not utter a sound. He did not so much as breathe.

"What's the phrasing, Patrick," the doll-faced killer asked Pete's father.

Patrick looked from Pete and back at the doll.

"I can't say it in front of him."

The doll's face swung in Pete's direction.

Pete squeezed closed his eyes.

His father barked, "I know—I know he's asleep, but it might still affect him."

"Fine." Three thuds as the doll moved from tableside to where Patrick sat in the corner.

Pete opened his eyes. He didn't want to, but he felt that he needed to.

The man in the mask dropped into a catcher's stance in front of his father.

The doll-faced man said, "Whisper it."

"It might affect—"

"Tell me the phrasing or I turn the fat little shit into slabs of bacon."

"Okay. Come closer."

For the briefest of moments, Pete thought his father was baiting the killer, but such was not the case. The doll leaned closer and Pete's father whispered in his ear. Pete heard little more than the smack of his father's lips. Not a peep of the actual words. Not so much as the hiss of exhaled breath.

The doll stood.

"Well," the man in the mask said, "isn't that fitting. It was nice knowing you, Patrick."

The man in the mask swung up then down. The cleaver bit into the top of Patrick's skull. Patrick's left eye snapped inward to look at his nose. His right eye remained focused forward, directed at his son, although Pete knew that his father no longer saw anything. Nothing living resided in that gaze.

The doll tugged the cleaver out of Patrick's head and took another swing.

And another.

And another.

Five chops in all until Patrick's head was bisected all the way down to his upper lip.

The doll didn't face Pete again, but he spoke as if he knew Pete was watching.

"Everything's fine, kiddo. Everything's just swell now. I've got what I came for and I've no intention of harming you. Your dad would have wanted you to live a full and happy life, and I intend to give you that chance."

The doll walked into the living room and disappeared into the night.

Pete remained on the counter for some time. Anytime he tried to move, his vision swam and his head pounded. Twice he drifted out of consciousness. He'd later find out that he'd suffered a concussion, but for now he simply knew he shouldn't move until the world stopped moving first.

At some point before dawn, Pete managed to roll off the counter and onto unsteady feet. He used the phone in the living room to call the police.

He sat in his father's chair until they arrived.

What came next was not for Pete to know, nor was it worth discussing. Investigators investigated, and the process failed to find the killer in the doll mask. The world, as they say, moved on, and Pete was sent to live with his grandmother.

Having no other family, Pete had no one else to claim him. His parents, as intelligent and forward-thinking as they'd been, had not drawn up a will, much less stated a person whom they would like Pete to live with should anything ever happen to them. Patrick and Joyce had been young and carefree and well-off. Death was the furthest thing from their minds.

So it was that Pete transferred from the care of a loving atheist couple to an overbearing religious woman literally overnight. New rules were laid down before him: he must drop beside his bed every night before bed, place his palms together, fingers to the ceiling, squeeze shut his eyes, and pray for forgiveness.

"What am I asking forgiveness for?" he would ask.

"For your sins," Mama, as she liked to be called, would say.

"But I've done nothing wrong."

"You're sinful in the eyes of the Lord, Pete."

"But I didn't do anything wrong."

"Hush now," she'd say in a voice that suggested this was just how things were. But Pete knew better. This was not just how things were. His grandmother was crazy, blaming him for the sins of a couple of apple-stealing fictional characters. The worst part, however, is that Pete's parents had tried to warn him. But words of warning aren't necessarily preparation, because Pete was anything but prepared to live under Beulah Blackwood's roof.

Mama and he prayed twice a day: on waking, and before bed. They attended church three times a week: once on Wednesday night, and twice on Sunday. Sunday was the worst day of the trio, for Sunday began at the crack of dawn. No matter the weather—blowing rain or scalding heat—they'd arrive at Chastity Baptist to hear Father George's sermon before the sun had gotten a decent start to its day. Those gray Sundays, when the sun didn't shine at all, those mornings that existed somewhere between daytime and evening, were unbearable. Those were the Sundays that Pete remembered his parents the most because those were the days when his mother would have put on a pot of soup and made hot chocolate and snuggled with him on the couch until his father came home from work.

Because Patrick Rothsberger worked seven days a week. Because Humble Hill could not do without him. Because it would take an impossibility like time travel to allow Patrick a day off.

In those early, happier days, Pete never questioned his father's dedication to the job because Patrick was a good father; a father who spent time with and cherished his son. After work, in the months before his murder, Patrick would play cards with his boy, or they'd toss a ball around in the backyard. He taught Pete how to grill a hamburger, and how to peel a potato with a paring knife, because those pesky peelers wasted too much flesh. He ran and played with Pete as if he were a child himself. The time before all the eventual heartache was what made the time after so horrible.

The worst part wasn't that Pete had come to live with Beulah; it was that, now, he had to live without his father. That time in his life, the time spent with his dad, had been the best time in the world.

Mama—his real mother—was simply the icing on the cake.

One Sunday morning while they were in line, waiting to walk into church, Pete asked his grandmother, "Why do they call him Father George?"

"Because he's our pastor. He's our leader. The head of our church."

"But he's not anyone's father."

This was before Georgina's birth. Molly was pregnant, but Georgina was still a few weeks shy of the world.

Beulah smiled. "He will soon be a father to his own child. But that's not the kind of father he is to us. He's a father to us like a shepherd is like a father to his flock."

"So you're like sheep?"

"In a way, yes."

"But don't sheep only follow because they don't know any better?"

"I wouldn't say that, no," Beulah said with a frown. "Sheep know that the shepherd only has good intentions. They trust him because they know he will not lead them into danger. He keeps them away from wolves and other predators. That's what Father George does."

"But isn't the shepherd only using the flock for his own benefit? For wool and skin and meat?"

Her frown became a forced smile. Pete thought this new smile made her ugly.

"It's not our place to question the Lord, Petey."

"Why not?"

"You're treading into blasphemy, Petey. Best not to ask too many questions." She ruffled his hair, an action that had come to mean that she was no longer going to humor his inquiries, which only made Pete want to ask even more.

His father had once told him, "Questions are good, Pete. Whenever you're unsure, it's always best to ask a question than to assume you know the answer. Sometimes, the answer cannot be found without asking the right questions. That's the very basis of science."

In line for church that morning, Pete had said, "It all seems too good to be true."

"What does?" Beulah asked. She no longer looked at him; she was gazing over the shoulders of those ahead of them in line.

"Heaven, I guess. It seems, I don't know, like the perfect scam."

"Petey!" she hissed at him. He had her attention now, but he wasn't sure that was a good thing.

He steeled himself and continued: "I mean, you spend all this time at church, you tithe your hard-earned money, and you don't get any return on your investment" —his father's words, not his— "until after you die. And no one knows what's after you die because no one's ever—"

She slapped him so hard that, in the days to come, his cheek would bruise to a shade of greenish-brown, like that of a gangrenous limb.

"You shut your mouth!" she stage-whispered as Pete massaged his hurt cheek. "I will not have any child of mine questioning the Lord or the Lord's Kingdom. Do you *want* to go to Hell? Do you?"

He could hear his father's words answer his grandmother's question for him.

*Hell's an even bigger scam, Pete. A place created to control people. It's the religious equivalent of telling a child they better behave, lest they want a spanking. Be good, little churchgoer, for if you don't, Hell awaits.*

*Hell awaits...*

Surely living with Beulah Blackwood was a certain kind of Hell. Sure as hell seemed that way to Pete.

Once inside, Pete suffered the projected voice of Father George as the man warned against—you guessed it—the fires of Hell.

"And it was the Lord God that cast Lucifer into the fiery pit for the crime of challenging the throne, thus proving that you should not question the Lord and his right to the Kingdom of Heaven!"

Shouts of "Amen!" answered Father George.

Beulah Blackwood shouted, "Praise Jesus!"

Pete remained silent.

He looked upon the flock of sheep and wondered what had gone wrong in their lives. How could one believe in such a thing as God after leaving childhood behind? He'd stopped believing in Santa Claus when he was six; mainly because Mama and Daddy had told him the truth—that Santa Claus, like Jesus before him, had been a real person who'd been deified by a superstitious people. There was no doubt that Santa Claus and Jesus had existed, but they certainly were not the magical beings the faithful believed them to be. "That's something you must remember as you go through life, Pete," Dad had said, "The line between myth and truth can be a fine one, and only questioning which side of the line you stand on can keep you cemented in reality."

"Are religious people crazy?"

He'd considered this for a moment and then said, "In a way, yes. There's something called *Mob Mentality*. Do you know what that means?"

"No, sir."

"Well, it means that if you get enough soft-minded people together, they can do terrible things. It can result in a form of hypnosis. And that's what happens in church. They congregate—that means *gather together*—in buildings without any outside influences, and only one person is allowed to speak at a time. They get to nodding their heads and finding sense in the senseless and are told that questioning is wrong and a slight against God, when in reality they don't want you to question anything because, if you look too closely, their doctrine falls apart. These stories—the Bible, the Quran, the Book of Mormon, all of them—are make-believe, Pete. Like Hansel and Gretel, or the Scorpion and the Frog. And like any piece of fiction, good or bad, these books have plot holes."

"Like when Rocket Man escapes the car as it goes over the cliff, even though he's handcuffed to the wheel?"

"Yep. Exactly like that. If you think too hard about any religion, you see the man behind the curtain."

"Like in *The Wizard of Oz*?"

"Exactly like that. Pulling back the curtain and finding a man standing there can be deeply disturbing to a religious mind."

"So they just pretend there is no curtain to pull back?"

Patrick Rothsberger beamed with pride. "How'd you get so smart?"

"Just lucky, I guess."

They'd laughed, and then Dad had kissed him on the forehead and wished him pleasant dreams.

But, before leaving him to the insistent pull of sleep, his father had said, "All that being said, Pete, you gotta remember that these people mean well. They do a great deal for their communities. They are not, by default, bad people. Meaning, their religion doesn't automatically make them bad people. They're just

173

gullible. Yet there are some of them who believe that good deeds are not capable without the motivation of their respective gods. You have to remember that decency precedes religion. Always remember that. Being religious does not make you a good person. Being a decent human being makes you a good person. Nothing else. Plenty of terrible things are done in the name of God."

"Why are so many people Christian? Why is that one religion so... *big?*"

Patrick sighed. "A lot of people died so that Christianity could reign supreme, Pete. The Crusades. The Spanish Inquisition. The Salem Witch Trials. Numerous bloody wars. Had Muslims or Jews or even Buddhists killed as many people as Christians have in the name of Jesus, their religion would likely be—how can I put it?—*king of the hill*. Americans are a scared people because we're still such a young country. We're on top of the world right now because we've won so much. And some people give the credit of those wins to God. Basically what I'm saying is—"

"They killed their way to the top."

"Exactly. Now, enough talk of killing and such. Go to sleep, son."

"Goodnight, Dad."

Another week had passed before his mother sat him down and told Pete the true story behind the name of her hometown, the tale her mother had told her, the horrific truth of what had become of Francis and Marietta Bay. Joyce had thought her ten-year-old son could handle it because he was so mature for his age, when, in fact, the tale had terrified him. That same night he'd dreamt of the charred couple: Marietta nailed to the cross, and Francis clinging to her middle, like a child seeking comfort.

Marietta's blackened eyelids had creaked open like a coffin lid in a vampire movie. Her eyes were not eyes but two pinpoints of yellow light as tiny and sharp as the tips of sharpened pencils. The lights from her eyes widened into citron cones, like spotlights, to bathe Pete in their cold fire.

Francis Bay craned his fire-cracked neck and gazed over his blackened shoulder at the boy standing below them.

"Everything is horrible now," Francis Bay had said. "Everything is horrible now."

Marietta joined in her husband's chant and their words followed Pete up and out of sleep.

Pete's eyes came open and he sat up.

"Everything is horrible now," he muttered in the dark of his room.

And it was. He sat in the confusing aftermath of his dream and trembled like a bush in a hurricane. When and where he was didn't seem to matter. He knew his folks were dead. He knew he'd recently gone to church. He knew that his new Mama was asleep down the hall.

Pete swung his legs from under the covers and off the bed. He stood on sleep-weakened legs and shambled to the window. He was in his new bedroom in his grandmother's house but the view outside the window was not of his grandmother's backyard. Through the glass he saw a cornfield unlike any he'd ever seen. It stretched on forever, bathed in the light of a full moon. In the distance, the field rose, continued up a hill and out of sight.

Two crosses jutted from the field and loomed tall over the corn. Only one cross cast a shadow on the stalks.

Pete blinked and the vision was gone. Only his grandmother's backyard lay outside the window: the shed where she kept her gardening tools; his dead grandfather's domed barbeque grill; a picnic table with peeling red paint. The grass needed a trim. It wasn't bad yet, but it could use a cut before the next rain.

In a shadowy corner of the backyard, two yellow eyes peered from the darkness.

"Everything is horrible now," Pete whispered.

He went back to bed. His sleep was peaceful and dreamless.

That had been a week ago. Before Father George had killed himself. Before Pete had met Wesley. Before Pete had decided, uncharacteristically, that he was somehow above his new friend.

Now, halfway between the Haversham farm and home, Pete Blackwood stopped on the side of the road and gazed skyward.

He wasn't looking toward Heaven, or even the sky above. What he saw instead of fluffy grayish-white clouds floating across a pristine blue background was Wesley's property and the cornfield inside which he'd stood earlier that day, admiring Wesley's buddy, the Scaresparrow.

Hadn't the Scaresparrow been rooted to a cross? Maybe a crucifixion was not the intended result, but hadn't that been the case? The final effect of placing a humanoid figure on a post with a crossbar certainly brought to mind a crucifixion. At least for Pete it did.

The boy shuddered.

In his mind's eye, he saw not one but two Scaresparrows in Wesley Haversham's cornfield, just like the two crosses in his dream.

Goosebumps crawled across his flesh.

Pete continued on, toward home. Along the way, he passed a house with its windows open. Music drifted from inside. Long after he left the house behind, Pete found himself singing along with the dulcet tones of Bing Crosby crooning Johnny Mercer lyrics, the music of Harry Warren following him all the way home.

"*You must've been a beautiful bay-bee… 'cause, Baby, look at you now.*"

# 8. All Over the Place

Hap pulled up in front of the sheriff's office at a quarter to noon. He locked his squad car and crunched across the gravel parking lot to the side door—the employee entrance, if you will. He wanted to talk to Kirby without a million questions from Ronnie Short about what he'd found at the Johnson house and going through the side door was the only way to achieve such.

The employee entrance led into a short hallway. The hallway was lined with shelves stocked with office supplies, boxes of ammunition, and toiletries to restock the restroom located in the front of the building, across from the station desk. Hap unlocked the door at the end of the hall and stepped through into the holding cells.

The station's two cells sat on the left. Bare walls to the right. Everything, even the bars on the cells, had been painted gunmetal gray. The walls back here were cinderblock and sweated with condensation in the winter months.

Kirby's cell was the one closest to the door that connected the front of the sheriff's station to the rear. Hap stepped up to the bars and looked in and down at the teenager on the cot.

"Get up, Kirby. We need to talk."

Kirby craned his head to see who was speaking to him then swung up and sideways to dangle his legs over the edge of the metal cot.

"Yessir," Kirby said in a meek voice.

*Goddamn sissy,* Hap thought. In his head, his words didn't sound unkind. More sympathetic. Truth be told, he felt sorry for any queer, male or female, and didn't understand why anyone would choose to live such a lifestyle. Had to be hard, hiding all the time. Hap recalled how rough it had been during that short period of uncertainty between killing Charlie Marchesini and Mary Robichaux on Saturday and finding the cover-up in the paper on Monday. Hap didn't wish that feeling on anybody.

"We found your mother."

Kirby nodded, as if to say, *It was eventually gonna happen, yes.*

"Care to tell me what the hell happened?"

"He killed her."

Now this was unexpected.

"*He* killed her? He *who*, Kirby?"

"The Coat Man."

"A man in a coat killed your mother?"

"Yessir."

"You're the one covered in blood, son. We found no sign of a struggle, either."

"He bit her head off."

"Oh," was all Hap could think to say. He was obviously dealing with a crazy person. He had no idea why he should be so surprised at the revelation. He should've known. Any man who found other men sexually attractive couldn't be right in the head.

"You wanna tell me what really happened, son? The courts will go a lot easier on you if you're honest. You lie and you're bound to end up dying in the 'lectric chair. You understand that?"

"I didn't kill her," Kirby said, very plainly, and lay back down, facing the wall.

"Damn it, Kirby, I'm trying to help you. You need to tell me what happened in that house this morning. If nothing else, you need to tell me where her head is. She deserves a Christian burial." Of course, Hap didn't give shit-one about giving Donna Johnson a Christian burial. He simply wanted to know where her head was. Call it morbid curiosity. Call it whatever you want, but the fact of the matter was that Hap didn't like not knowing things. It made him feel like a failure at his job, and such a feeling could not be accepted.

"Kirby, if you tell me where the head is, I might be able to save you from riding the lightning. You gettin me? They're gonna fry you, son. *Bzzzt!* Over and done with. Overdone, even."

Kirby remained silent.

"Don't say ol' Hap didn't try to save you." Hap headed for the adjoining door when a thought surfaced. He turned back to Kirby. "You recall what you said to me at the church, right before I arrested you?"

Kirby didn't so much as look at the sheriff.

"You said, *Everything is horrible now*. Why'd you say that?"

"Some things are better left unknown, sheriff."

Kirby's voice was different. Hap couldn't place exactly what the change was though. Maybe the teen's voice was deeper all of a sudden. Perhaps there was a doubled quality to it. Like two people on either side of your head whispering the same phrase, the pitch of their voices varying slightly, just enough that you know you're not hearing the same voice in each ear.

"Do you know what happened at Father George's house yesterday, Kirby?"

Silence.

"Kirby, I need to know if you have any information regarding—"

One second Kirby Johnson was laid out on the metal cot and the next he was standing inches away from Hap, the only thing separating the two men the gunmetal-gray bars of the holding cell. Kirby's arms shot through the space between the bars and grabbed Hap's shirt. The teen yanked Hap flush with the bars, close enough to kiss. Hap went for his gun but it was gone. His fucking holster was empty.

What the shit was happening?

"Everything is horrible now, Hap. A tsunami of change is headed this way, and it will drown your Podunk little town. The chaos of the Void will swallow whole the sins of this damned place. The Bastard will rise. And you're all going to die."

"Let go of—"

In a blink, Kirby was back on his cot, as if he'd never moved, and Hap's gun was back in its holster, as if it, too, had never moved. Yet Hap could still feel Kirby's grip on his shirt. He patted down his shirtfront even though it didn't need to be smoothed out.

"What the fuck just happened?" Hap said, hating the tremor in his voice.

"It's only gonna get worse from here," Kirby Johnson said from the cot. "It's all coming to an end because there is no end. No end to any of this. Because everything is horrible now."

"What the fuck just happened, Kirby?"

"She's coming," Kirby repeated.

Icy spiders scurried over Hap's shoulders and down his back.

"Who's coming?" he asked.

"Joy."

The name didn't strike a chord with Hap.

"Joy is coming. And there's nothing any of us can do about it."

"What does that mean, son? You're not making any sense. Is Joy someone's name? What's her last name? Does she know what happened with your mother? Hell, does this Joy lady have your mom's head? Answer me, Kirb. I'm only trying to help."

"Best see about your deputy, sheriff," Kirby said in that subtly doubled voice. "I don't think Wittle Wonnie Short is doing so well."

Hap glanced at the connecting door and then back to Kirby.

"What'd you do to my deputy, Kirby?"

Not *How did you get out*, but *What did you do*, because Hap was all of a sudden certain that Kirby had somehow gotten out of his cell and harmed—

*Wittle Wonnie Short*

—Ronnie Short. There was no doubt in Hap's mind that this was the case. Kirby had left his cell and done something awful to Ronnie. The only question in Hap's mind was, what had Kirby done to Ronnie. Well, maybe there were two questions in Hap's mind.

What had Kirby done to Ronnie?

And did Hap really want to find out?

Hap moved, as if through refrigerated molasses, toward the adjoining door. Ronnie's name sat on the tip of his tongue, unmoving, like a dead fish on a plate, but he couldn't bring himself to call out his deputy's name. Hap's fist closed around the brass doorknob. His wrist twisted. The door eased out of its frame. Hap swung the door wide and stepped into a slaughterhouse.

Blood streaked the floor, the walls, the ceiling, as if someone had been dragged, injured and leaking, up and down and all around. There was a gory handprint in the upper-right-hand corner of the room. The impossibility of the scene mattered not to Hap, for he was assured in his heart that everything he was seeing was reality, because seeing, to Harold Carringer, was believing.

"Ronnie?" Hap managed. "Ronnie, where are you? Come on and tell me you're all right. Tell me I ain't seein what it is I'm seein."

"I told you, sheriff," came the doubled voice of Kirby Johnson; that voice that sounded like two people speaking in different ears; that singular voice that was actually two. "Wittle Wonnie Short isn't doing so well."

"Ronnie!" Hap hollered. He couldn't stand how terrified he sounded. Sheriff Hap did not frighten easily. Shit, he didn't frighten at all. Nothing in the world was bigger and meaner than he was. It was time to man the fuck up.

He swallowed his fear and bellowed, "Ronnie! You come out here, and you come out here—Right—Now!"

Hap's office door creaked open, but stopped long before it hit the inner wall. Three chewed up fingers peeked from under the door: a middle and ring finger, plus a pinkie. A gnarled, bony stump was all that was left of the index finger.

The pinkie twitched, breaking the spell that had come over Hap, the one that had, up until now, rooted him in place. He got moving, being careful not to slip and fall in the blood that seemed to coat every surface in sight. He squeezed through the space between the jam and the door and into his office.

He peered around the door, expecting to find Ronnie laid out, arm extended, gnawed fingers blocking the inward swing of the door, but that wasn't what he found.

The arm had been chewed off at the elbow. Hap could see the teeth marks in the ravaged flesh. Whatever had been at Ronnie hadn't been human. This was obviously the work of some kind of wild animal. Possibly a rabid one. But even as his logical mind was cycling through the possible four-legged culprits—mountain lion, wolf, grizzly—his subconscious was considering the possibility that whatever had done this to Ronnie was not of this world. Or, at the very least, nothing Hap had ever seen or dealt with in all his days.

"You ever wonder what they did with the bodies, sheriff?" said Kirby's doubled voice. Even though there were now two doorways between the teenager and the sheriff, Hap could hear the teenager in his head, as if Kirby were right next to him; the doubled speech coming from a mouth that sounded close enough to kiss Hap on the cheek.

"Who the fuck are you talking about? Whose bodies?"

"Never mind," said the doubled voice of Kirby Johnson. "I should be asking that Blackwood woman. She'd know."
\*\*\*

Beulah Blackwood was reading her bible when her grandson finally decided to come home. She could have been angry with him, but it was her opinion that you attracted more flies with honey, so when he walked through the door, she simply said hello and asked him how his morning had gone.

"I almost made a new friend." He wouldn't meet her eyes. She couldn't tell if he was sad, or concerned that he might be in trouble. She'd be glad when enough time had passed and his parents had receded far enough from his memory so that she wouldn't feel terrible about disciplining him. She couldn't be hard on the boy in his current state of mourning. Doing so would be unchristian of her.

"Almost, you say? How does one *almost* make a new friend? I would assume you either do or do not make a friend. Pray tell, what happened?" Her voice was sugary sweet, and she thought maybe she should tone it down before he realized that her concerns were false. Because, no, she didn't care about whether or not he made friends. The Good Lord Jesus was the only friend a boy needed. Besides maybe his mother, of course.

"He, um, didn't like the same things as me. I thought he did, but he didn't. May I be excused?"

"Excused to do what?" she said. "We've just begun talking."

"I'd like to go to my room and read."

That the boy read so much, and everything *but* the Bible, bothered Beulah, but she wouldn't raise a stink. Not this morning. Soon, though. When the time was right.

"That's fine by me," she said. "Would you like to borrow this?"

Beulah held out her Bible. Petey frowned at the book. Her heart cracked to see such a frown. If she couldn't save him, he'd burn in Hell for all eternity, she was sure. Those parents of his— her daughter Joyce and son-in-law Patrick—had done near-irreparable damage to the boy, and it was everything Beulah had in her to keep from tackling Petey to the hardwood and attempting an exorcism right then and there. She could see the demons in her grandson's eyes. She shivered, as if she stood in the path of glacial winds.

"No, thank you." Petey met her eyes. "May I be excused... Mama?"

Oh, he already knew her so well. Knew just what to say to get his way. She sighed and nodded and watched as he shuffled past her to the hallway and down to his room, where the walls were blue with white ships and anchors, because every boy loves boats, and Beulah was a grandmother who aimed to please. She thought that boats and baseball were to young boys what honey was to bees. She considered how odd that comparison was and if there wasn't a better one hidden in her brain as she cracked open her Bible and read of Samson and Delilah.

The phone rang a little while later. Beulah sat down her bible and picked up the handset from its base on the table beside her chair.

"Hello?" she said into the phone.

"Beulah?"

"This is she? Harold, is that you?"

"Yes, ma'am, it's me. Hap. Mind coming down to the station for me?"

Beulah frowned, looking not unlike Petey had when he'd scowled at the Bible in her hand before he left the room. The thought of heading down to Hap's dirty den of deviance turned her stomach. She didn't want to imagine what kind of evil had left its mark on that place, what with all the deplorable criminals who'd haunted its halls on a near-regular basis; least that's what she thought happened there. Truth be told, she had no idea what happened in a sheriff's office. She only knew the place couldn't be worth visiting, not when one took into consideration the fact that the place was run by a heathen like Harold Carringer.

"Come to the sheriff's station? Whatever for?"

Sheriff Carringer cleared his throat. "I have some questions to ask you."

"Then I would suggest you ask me over the phone."

"I can't do that, Beulah."

"Well, I certainly am not—"

"Beulah, get your old ass down here before I come over to your house and arrest you."

"Well, I never!"

"I'm sure you haven't. Fact remains, you're coming, so come on."

"You can't just threat—"

"I'm not in the goddamn mood, Beulah. You have thirty minutes before I come over and slap these fuckin handcuffs on you."

"Such lang—"

"I don't fucking care about any fucking language, you old bitch! Get your ass down here. It's about the Bays—Francis and Marietta Bay!"

"Okay," was all Beulah could think to say. What the sheriff had said certainly changed things. Changed things quite a bit, in her opinion. "Fine then, Harold. I'll be—I'll be right over."

"Thank you. And leave the fat boy at home, okay? You ain't gonna want him here."

"Yes, Harold."

The sheriff hung up. Beulah placed the handset on its base and sat for a moment, staring at a wall, seeing through the wallpaper and into the past, where a cross burned under a starry sky, and a woman's screams floated hauntingly above the roar and crackle of a fire.

"Petey? Petey, dear?"

"Coming!" he called from his room.

"No, no. No need to come here. Mama's gotta run down to the sheriff's office, you hear? I'll be back shortly."

"Yes, ma'am."

"Be—Be home soon." Then, "I love you, Petey."

"Yes, ma'am."

She waited for Petey to say he loved her back.

He never did.

And he never would.

Beulah took the Buick into town. She still had her dead husband's old Chevy pickup, the one with the shit-brown paint job and chrome bumpers, but she'd always prefer the Buick to his Chevy. The truck, however, came in handy in the winter months, when she needed to haul firewood home from Carringer and Sons Logging. They always had the best prices on logs come colder weather. Anyway, carting around firewood was the only reason she kept the truck. If it weren't for that, she'd have sold it ages ago.

She arrived at the sheriff's office a little after one that afternoon and parked in the front lot. She could see the sheriff's car, along with two civilian vehicles—a blue station wagon, and a white pickup—alongside the building. She assumed this meant that

Harold wasn't alone. That was good. She didn't care too much for being alone with the godless heathen.

Her shoes crunched gravel on her way to the entrance. She pulled the door open and stepped inside.

Seeing the blood streaked all over the walls stopped her breathing in the midst of an inhalation. She choked on nothing but air, barking like an angry mutt protecting a patch of sacred land.

Sheriff Harold Carringer appeared in the doorway of his office, gun drawn, its massive barrel pointed directly at her face. His wide eyes deflated a bit at the realization that Beulah posed no threat to him. He sighed and stuffed his gun into the holster on his right hip.

"For Christ's sake, what are you doing here?" he said.

"What am I—" she stammered. "What do you mean, what am I doing here?"

"Exactly what I said, woman. What the hell are you doing here?"

"*You* called *me*, you crazy fool."

"I didn't call nobody. I've been busy handling—dealing with all this." He gestured to the bloody walls and gore-splattered ceiling.

"My God, what happened here?" Beulah said. She would confront him further about his phone call luring her to the station in a moment. For now, her curiosity was piqued, and once her curiosity was piqued, it was answers or nothing. In that regard, Beulah Blackwood was more feline than human.

Hap exhaled at length. "Shit if I know."

"You mean to say you don't know where all this blood came from?"

"That's exactly what I mean. I think Ronnie's dead, but I ain't got no body. I got an arm. But no body."

"An *arm*?"

"That's what I said, Beulah. For fuck's sake, keep up."

"I will not have you cussing me, Harold. Bad enough you cursed me out on the phone—"

His tense figure softened a bit, as if someone were letting the air from a tire. "I *said* I didn't call you, Beulah. Get off it already."

"Well, I certainly didn't imagine you calling me. You said you needed me up here. Something about"—she considered whether or not it was a good idea to mention the Bays, given how the sheriff was currently swearing he hadn't called her. She supposed it could have been anyone on the phone. Harold's voice wasn't all that unique; your typical gruff male voice, was all. She'd seen a guy on Ed Sullivan who could do ladies' voices so well he fooled his own mother into thinking he was a woman on the phone, so someone impersonating the sheriff wasn't beyond the realm of possibilities. But if it hadn't been Harold Carringer on the phone earlier, who had it been? Not knowing who wanted to talk about what had happened to Francis and Marietta Bay way back in the Back When had her unsettled. "You promise you didn't call me?"

"I ain't got no reason to lie to you, Beulah. Besides, I kinda got my hands full here, wouldn't you agree?"

She sniffed. "Why's it smell like oysters?"

"Does it?"

"Yes, it does."

"Fuck if I know."

"If you do nothing else to show me respect, please, for the love of God, do watch your language around me. You can run off to Hell, if you so desire, but I'd appreciate it if you saved me the displeasure of joining you on your journey."

Harold laughed at her. The nerve of this man…

He said, "You've always been a wordy so-and-so, I swear."

Beulah felt sick all of a sudden. The longer she smelled the salty, metallic sea-stench of fresh blood the sicker she was going to become.

"I need some air."

"You can head on home, if you like. I honestly don't need the distraction."

"She can't go home yet," came a voice from the back of the building.

"Shut up in there!" the sheriff hollered. "Nobody asked you."

"Who's that?" Beulah whispered.

"Donna Johnson's son."

"Kirk?"

"Close. Kirby."

"What on Earth is Donna Johnson's boy doin here?"

"I'm pretty sure he killed his mother."

"Donna Johnson's dead too?" Beulah gaped at the sheriff like a large-mouth bass going after food.

"Yes, Beulah, Donna Johnson is dead. I think we should step outside now."

"I don't," said Kirby Johnson. "I would really like to talk to her, sheriff."

"Why's he want to talk to me?" Beulah hissed.

"No clue."

"I want to talk to you about the Bays."

Beulah's breath caught in her chest.

"Does he have a phone in there?" she asked the sheriff.

Harold seemed to consider this. After a brief second of inner thought, he said, "Definitely not."

"The person who called me, the one who said they were you, said they wanted to talk about the Bays. Now he's saying he wants to talk about them, too. I don't think that's a coincidence, Harold."

"What could the town's founders have to do with anything?"

"I don't know, but maybe it's all connected somehow."

"What's all connected? What the shit are you going on about?"

"I don't know, Harold. All of it. All of this."

"All of *what*?" Harold was obviously exasperated with her, but she couldn't help that.

"If I had any answers, sheriff, I sure wouldn't be so vague. Thing is, we don't know what happened out there at Father George's yesterday, and if what you say is true about all this blood, you have no idea what's happening here, either. Am I right?"

"I don't see how any of this could have anything to do with Francis Bay."

"Neither do I, which is why I think I should talk to the boy." She hitched her chin to the rear hallway. "To Kirby."

Harold sighed for the third time since she arrived. It was getting to be annoying.

"Listen, woman. I've seen some things. I saw some things when I picked him up this morning, and I just saw some more things when I was back there with him. You're a god-botherer, so you better not so much as crack a smile at me when I say this, but what I saw just weren't possible. Not in a sane world. So, as long as you know what you're getting yourself into, I suppose you can talk to the kid all you want. But, should anything happen back there, I ain't responsible for you. I want that to be clear. Are we clear?"

"Crystal clear, Harold." She raised a palm to the ceiling. "Hand 'fore God, I swear I won't blame you."

"All right then. Let's make this quick."

\*\*\*

Wesley Haversham was understandably upset. With what had happened between him and his new friend Pete still fresh in his mind, he went to find his father. He needed someone he could talk to about the whole thing, and he felt Pop was the only logical respite from his current internal struggle.

He found Pop hunched over, neck-deep in the engine compartment of the old tractor that had broken down last season. Luckily the aged workhorse had waited until the final week of last year's harvest before kicking the bucket, but harvest was once again upon them and things did not look good for the tractor, or Pop's patience. Wesley hated to bother Pop right now, but he truly didn't see any other way around it. He had to talk to *someone.*

Wesley waited at a distance of ten feet or so, so as not to startle his father. When roughly five minutes had passed, by Wesley's estimation, he very softly said, "Pop?"

If Pop heard him, he made no movement or sound to acknowledge Wesley.

Wesley repeated himself, a little louder the second time.

Pop eased out of the engine compartment and looked around. He did a double take on Wesley before settling on his son.

"You alone? Where's your friend?"

"He went home. I don't—I don't think we're friends no more."

Pop frowned. He pulled a stained hand cloth from the back pocket of his coveralls and rubbed his palms and fingers with it. No way was he going to get his hands clean that way, but the towel was more his father's thinking aid than it was cleaning implement.

"Somethin upset him?" Pop asked.

"I don't rightly know. That's why I come see you. I'm not sure I wanna be friends with someone like him, but it hurts that he might feel the same way about me."

"You're not making any sense, son."

"I know. That's how come I wanna talk to you. I don't like botherin you none. I know you're busy, but I'm all busted up over it and I ain't got no idea why. So can we talk? Just for a little bit?"

"Sure. Grab a bale."

Pop took a seat on one of the hay bales stacked on the western wall of the barn. Wesley said he preferred to stand. Standing helped him think.

Pop said, "I think better when I'm sitting. I think it shoves my brains out my ass and back into my head so I can think properly."

Wesley laughed and Pop smiled. If Pop wasn't good for anything else, he was good for a joke. Best of all, Pop's jokes usually had a sprinkle of cursing in them that made Wesley feel like a grownup to hear, mainly because Pop didn't talk that way around women and children. If Pop cussed around you that meant he respected you as an equal. Least that's how Wesley saw it. But Wesley understood not everybody felt that way. Some people found foul language disrespectful on principle and principle alone.

Wesley supposed he could understand that, but he also knew without a shadow of a doubt that Pop meant absolutely zero disrespect when he cursed.

"All right. I'm comfy. Go ahead on with your story."

Wesley told his tale as best he could, trying to remember word for word what transpired between him and Pete, all the way up to the part where Pete had shocked the fire out of him by saying God and the Bible were make-believe.

That's what he'd said, right? Even if that hadn't been it, word for word, that had certainly been the gist.

When Wesley finished his story, he stood before his father and waited for his response.

"You say Pete doesn't believe in God and doesn't want to hang around with you no more because *you* believe in God?"

"Yessir."

"Well, I don't guess you have any say in the matter."

"Huh? Whataya mean?"

"Remember last night, when I told you that no one might never know why Father George did what he did?"

"Yessir, I do."

"Well, just like we might never find out about Father George's motivations, you can't never control how someone else feels about you. Do you understand?"

"Nossir, I don't guess so."

"I'm probably not sayin it right, no way." Pop took a deep breath and let it out at length. "Son, other people's minds is gonna act however they act, and trying to make sense of what someone else says or does is only gonna drive you batshit crazy."

The corner of Wesley's mouth twitched into a smile for just a second at the sound of *batshit* then he stopped smiling because it didn't feel appropriate to the conversation.

Pop said, "If that boy—"

"Pete. His name's Pete."

Pop nodded. "If Pete Blackwood doesn't want to be your friend because of how you believe in God, there ain't a single thing you or I can do about that."

"But isn't it good to testify your love of Christ and do good works, and such?"

"Yessir, it is. But some people don't believe in the words of the Bible, and while it is possible to save those people—that's for God to change their heart, not you. If you find a friend who don't believe what you believe, don't push the issue. You boys are too young to be disliking each other over religion and politics and grownup stuff like that. You should be boys, is all. Have fun while you can, because this world is a meat grinder, Wes. It eventually chews us all up. The trick is to stay whole—to stay young and intact—as long as possible."

Wesley cringed at the idea of being shoved into a meat grinder and spat out the other end. He knew his father wasn't being literal, but that didn't stop his imagination from running wild.

"What should I do about Pete?"

"Maybe you could apologize? That's where I'd start."

"Apologize? For what? Believing in God?"

"Nossir. Not for believing in God. I'd apologize for letting the talk of God come between you."

"But I didn't let it come between us. He did."

"Did he?"

"Yessir."

"The way you tell it, he mentioned that he didn't believe in God and the Bible, and you reacted like he was stone-cold crazy."

"'Cause he is!"

Pop laughed. "See what I mean?"

Wesley swallowed. "Oh."

"Yeah. *Oh.*" Pop stood and wrapped his arms around his boy. Wesley hugged him back. "This world ain't about being right or wrong, Wesley. I know you want to save your friend from Hell, and I respect that, Lord knows I do, but you also gotta respect his feelings. You gotta be what they call *the Bigger Man.*"

"The Bigger Man?"

"Yessir. That's when you know you're right but you don't act like you do. Because what does it really matter if you're right? God knows how you feel in your heart. And his judgment is the only judgment that matters. Right?"

"Yessir. Judge not lest you be judged your-own-self."

"That's exactly right. You save the judging for God, and do good works throughout your life, and maybe you lead people to the Pearly Gates by example and not force." Pop let Wesley loose so he could meet his boy's eyes. "Wouldn't that be something?"

"Yessir."

"You gonna apologize to Pete?"

"Yessir."

"You gonna mean it?"

"Yessir. Most definitely I will."

"Good boy. Nah, you're a good *man*? Yeah. Good man." He ruffled Wesley's hair, and Wesley Haversham could not have loved his father any more than he did in that moment. His heart felt as if it would explode under the strain of all that love. And there was only one thing to do when a heart is so very full of love.

You have to share the overflow.

Wesley told Pop his plans and Pop gave him his blessings.

Then Wesley Haversham hit the road.

He had a friend to apologize to.

Yes, Jesus, he sure did.

\*\*\*

"Hello, Beulah. It's been such a very long time since we last saw each other." Kirby Johnson shot a knowing smile through the bars of his cell and Beulah Blackwood's blood ran cold.

Beulah mustered her courage and said, "What do you want, Kirby?"

A blood-streaked metal bucket sat in the corner beside a toilet with pink smears on its seat. Beulah had dripped on toilet seats enough times during her menstrual cycle to know half-cleaned-up blood when she saw it.

"Were you the one who called Beulah, Kirby?" Harold asked.

Kirby didn't answer the sheriff. He only stared at Beulah. She felt uncomfortable under his gaze, crushed, as if his eyes gave off a tangible weight.

"Am I the one who called you, Beulah?" Kirby asked in Harold's voice.

"Fuckin hell," Harold muttered. "How'd you do that?"

"Say what you have to say, Kirby," Beulah pushed.

Harold said, "I wanna know how the hell you got a phone in there. Did Ronnie bring you one before he—just—did he bring you one? Yes or no?"

Kirby looked at Harold and blinked once before returning his gaze to Beulah.

"I don't want to talk in front of him," said Kirby.

"I don't give a rat's ass what you want, kid."

"Give us a minute, Harold."

"Beulah, I don't think—"

"I didn't ask you to think. I asked you to give us some privacy. Please, Harold. You can stand on the other side of the door, for all I care. Just give us some space. Is that all right, Kirby?"

"Yes," Kirby said. "That will be fine."

"For fuck's sake—"

"Your language, Harold."

"This isn't a good idea, Beulah. I can feel it in my bones. This ain't going to end well."

"Duly noted, sheriff."

"If you hurt her, son, I'll shove the barrel of my gun so far up inside you you'll have a shiny new set of lead dentures. You hear me?"

"Please, spare us the vulgarity, Harold."

"Fine. Don't say I didn't warn you."

Harold left. When the door closed him, Beulah said, "So what is it you wanted to tell me, Kirby?"

"Stop calling me that."

"Stop calling you what? Kirby?"

"Kirby isn't my name, child."

*Child?*

"Then what *is* your name?"

"We'll get to that."

"I think I should know who I'm talking to from the get go—don't you?"

"Who I am is of no concern at the present. You should concern yourself with who's coming, not those which have already arrived."

"Okay." Beulah said a quick and silent prayer for strength and guidance before pressing on. "Who should I be concerned with? Who's coming?"

"We'll get there. But, first, a story."

"A story?"

"Oh, yes. I have such a story to tell."

"I'm listening."

The teenager before Beulah who claimed not to be Kirby Johnson smiled an impossible smile; a smile so big and wide, Beulah half expected his cheeks to split.

"Once upon a time," the thing that was not Kirby Johnson said, "there was a boy named Kirby. Kirby was in love. He loved this person so very, very much that he'd risk everything to be with them. And he did. Risk everything, that is. He risked it all, and all he got was shunned and hated and hid away. He was sent up a hill, a very humble hill, never to return again..."

# 9. It Happened on a Hill

Kirby Johnson fell in love for the first time on a Sunday. He fell in love in church, of all places, and with a man of God, no less.

He fell.

In love.

He *fell* in *love*.

*Fell.*

*Love.*

Were there two scarier words in the entirety of the English language? Maybe, but Kirby Johnson couldn't imagine what they might be.

Sixteen years old was an advanced age for a first love, but when your sexual attractions were better left hidden from the public eye, love at first sight was a dangerous concept. Mooning over the one you adore could cause all kinds of drama, and in some circles even bring you physical harm.

This wasn't Hollywood or New York City. Kirby had been born and raised in Bay's End, Ohio, and Bay's End, Ohio, was not in possession of anything that could be even remotely mistaken for a gay community. Were there homosexuals in the End? Certainly. But their identities were as much a mystery to Kirby Johnson as his own sexuality was.

Before he fell in love, Kirby had never had even a passing sexual attraction. Maybe he was a late bloomer in that regard, but no man before that day in church had given him—well, if we're being vulgar—no man before Father George had given him a rise. Kirby had lain his Bible over his crotch to cover up the issue, and his mother, Donna Johnson, had gone unaware.

To think that Father George would ever return Kirby's feelings was a thought that never crossed his mind. Kirby had heard the boys in school call each other queers and faggots and cocksuckers and turd attendants (the latter made even Kirby giggle) and he knew that none of those things were acceptable. He knew that he'd somehow taken on the role of villain by simply existing.

All of his erections before that day in church had been spontaneous incidents: sitting in class doing math work; swinging on a swing set; boiling eggs for egg salad sandwiches. These had been the things that had previously given him erections, and to think he found egg salad sandwiches attractive was beyond silly. Although we will not discuss whether or not he tried to make love to a bowl of the creamy yellow goodness. Such things are not topics for casual acquaintances to discuss.

On that day in the summer before Father George's death, Kirby Johnson sat with his erection secure behind the binding of his personal Bible. Written on the inside of this Bible, on the very first page, was a list of names, starting with his great-great-grandfather and working down to his father, and then his own name. In his mother's Bible, the same was true, but the names were women's names instead of men's names: from great-great-grandmother down to Donna herself. Their Bibles chronicled the Johnson Family from the point they left Germany and settled in New Hampshire, by way of New York immigration. In Germany, the family name had not been Johnson, but it had been decided on the boat to America that the family would change their name— Miser, it had been—and never reference their old surname again. So the family's original name died and the Johnson Family was born.

On the opposite side of page one, where the names had been written, there was a family tree that explained who had married whom and from whom each new addition had come. While all of this was fascinating to Kirby, he found it hilarious beyond measure that his ancestors were, in a way, holding back his erection from view.

Father George spoke about the evils of the flesh, and that might have been what did it. The straw that raised the camel's erection, so to speak. Hearing such a handsome man talk about the sins of the flesh, of wanton desire and cardinal pleasures, drove Kirby Johnson mad with teenage lust. He imagined stripping the clothes from Father George and bending him over the pulpit and having his way with the pastor, utilizing every orifice, sliding in and out of him, massaging his—

"Kirby," his mother hissed. "You're drooling. Clean yourself up."

"Sorry, Momma."

Kirby wiped a line of saliva from the corner of his mouth and chin. Donna Johnson kept an eye on him for the rest of the service. Kirby tried not to slip off into dreamland again, a feat that took considerable effort to pull off.

When he got home that afternoon, he excused himself and took a shower. His second shower of the day, seeing as how he'd showered before church. He masturbated furiously under a stream of near-scalding water and ejaculated like a shotgun blast against the shower curtain. He hunched forward and rested his forearm against the cool tile, his forehead stuffed into the crook of his elbow. Hot water dribbled down his back as he attempted to relax his breathing. After a few moments considering what he had done and who he'd imagined while doing it, he cleaned himself thoroughly—the shower curtain, too—and cut off the shower. He was in the middle of toweling off when he heard his mother's voice from the hallway.

"I'd like to speak to you when you're done in there."

She sounded as if she were right outside the bathroom door, right there, on the other side of the wood. As if she'd been waiting. Listening.

Dread built inside Kirby, and he spent the rest of his time drying off sick with worry. For a time, he stared at his reflection in the foggy mirror before sliding a hand across the cool glass and wiping away the steam. He looked like a different person. What had once been cloudy was now clear.

For the first time in his life, Kirby Johnson knew who he was. And he didn't hate himself for it. He'd always known he was different, that his tastes were unlike anyone else's, at least those who he knew, but he'd also been trained by society that being different was not good. If you were different in any way, you were expected to conform. But conformity was not Kirby's style. And, he decided, if no one else would respect him, he would respect himself.

He dressed and joined his mother in the living room.

She was on the couch, sipping tea. Kirby sat on the opposite end. Both mother and son twisted, so that they were facing one another. Donna put her cup down on its matching saucer and smiled.

"Did you have a nice shower?"

"Yes'm."

"That's good. Did you enjoy yourself at church?"

"Yes'm."

"Fine. Just fine." She swallowed and Kirby thought the action looked unbearably painful. "Is there any—Is there anything you'd like to tell me?"

"No, ma'am."

"Are you sure?"

"Yes'm."

"Because—"

"No, ma'am, there is nothing I'd like to tell you. May I be excused?"

"Not just yet."

Donna Johnson picked up her cup and slurped tea into her mouth. She winced, blew steam, and took another sip. This second sip seemed to go down easier.

Kirby's pulse pounded in his head. Had she somehow seen him in the shower? Had she read his thoughts in church? Did she know? For the love of God, how much did she know?

"I've always been able to—able to sense things, Kirby. Do you understand what I mean?"

*Oh, God. Oh, no. Please, God, no.*

"Yes'm," he said.

"I think you've been born with some of the same gift. A knowing, a sense of certainty of thought. Do you understand?"

No matter how much Kirby forced himself to speak, there was no doing it. He couldn't so much as part his lips. There was no forming words. Not now. Seemingly not ever again. So he simply nodded. It was everything he could do just to get his neck to move.

"Maybe it's skipped you, but I somehow doubt that. It's not anything magical, nothing like mind reading. Don't think that. It's more like what I said. A *certainty*. Do you know what I am certain of, Kirby?"

"Yes'm." It seemed he wasn't mute after all.

"You do?"

"Yes'm."

"Good. Then you're not going to lie to me and tell me you're not having unclean thoughts—are you?"

"No, ma'am."

"Good." She lay a hand on his knee. She was shaking as badly as he was. Somehow, that knowledge, that she herself was terrified, soothed Kirby's nerves. How someone could be so frightened and so frightening at the same time Kirby hadn't a clue.

"You do realize that what you've been thinking—what you've been thinking is *wrong*, Kirby. It's not—well, it's not *natural*."

"Yes'm."

"I think we should go to see Father George."

"W-why?" Kirby squeaked in a tiny voice.

"Because he's a man who is close to God, Kirby. He'll know what to do. He'll know what to say, and how to pray this—he'll know how to pray it all away. Do you have faith in God, Kirby?"

"Yes'm."

"Then I need you to have faith that God is pointing me in the right direction. I believe he's given me this gift of certainty for this very purpose—so that I might guide my child away from his sinful thoughts and ways. So that I can direct you to a more righteous path."

"Yes'm."

"That's all I want. I love you and care about you, and I only wish to spend eternity with you in Heaven. You understand that—don't you?"

"Yes'm."

"Then you may now be excused."

Kirby shot to his feet and walked stiff-legged toward the hallway. When he was halfway to his room, his mother's voice called from the living room.

"And Kirby?"

Kirby stopped mid-step and said, "Yes'm?"

"Please do not—don't do what you did in the shower. Never again. You're not the only one who lives in this house. Thank you for respecting my wishes."

Kirby closed himself in his room, where he lay down on his bed and quietly cried for a solid hour while listening to his mother, in the bathroom, singing hymns and scrubbing the shower spotless.
\*\*\*

Donna Johnson didn't know what to do with her son. It was everything she had in her just to sleep under the same roof as him her disgust was so strong. To think that one could be so disgusted by their own child, their own flesh and blood, was a thought that rocked her faith. She prayed more frequently than ever before that God would cleanse her child's mind and correct his sinful ways.

She'd given birth to this boy. Kirby had come from her, but this person he'd become was not of her. She might have given him life, but something had perverted his soul. Never in her days could she have believed her son capable of such lewd thoughts and actions. There was only one place to turn. The boy needed God, and she intended to introduce Kirby to the Lord even if he hated her for it.

They met with Father George that next Wednesday, in the hours before evening services. Molly George made the trio tea and shuffled from their presence, to parts unknown. Father George drank his tea with cream only while Donna and Kirby accepted two lumps each from a covered glass bowl on the pastor's desk.

"So, what can I do for you two today?"

Looking at him now, Donna could understand the draw. Father George was a handsome man, and if it weren't for her respect and Christian affection for him, she might have been, like her son, physically attracted to the man. To imagine him between her thighs was a dangerous, but not unpleasant, notion.

Father George gave her a knowing smile then looked to Kirby.

"Perhaps you should start?" said the pastor.

"I've been having unclean thoughts," Kirby blurted. Donna placed a hand on Kirby's knee to give the boy strength.

"Oh?" asked Father George. "What might those thoughts be, Kirby?"

"I touched myself in the shower while thinking about you."

Kirby's words struck Father George like a slap in the face. Donna saw the pastor flinch from the contact. The pastor's Adam's apple bobbed. For a second she thought he'd swallowed it, but then it popped back up and settled into its rightful place in the center of his neck.

"Oh my. Okay. So you're having homosexual leanings? Toward—involving—involving me?"

"Yessir," Kirby said. For all his faults, the boy was brave. Donna had to give him that. Kirby looked straight ahead, right into the pastor's eyes, and didn't once break contact, not even when Father George looked away. Donna was certain this was because Kirby knew that if he looked somewhere else, he'd never be able to look in a mirror again.

She grasped his hand and gave it a squeeze. He squeezed back.

He wanted to be better. She was certain of that much. But she was also certain that, even now, he was warring with himself over his feelings for Father George. This certainty hurt Kirby and Donna alike: him because he knew she hated to see him this way, and her because she was certain he didn't want to change. Nobody liked change. That was human nature. That was why God had to tear some people down to their foundations before he could begin to rebuild them. In Kirby's case, such a thing might be the only hope for him.

"Well," Father George said, "I suppose we should start by praying. Does that sound like a good idea, Donna?"

"Oh, yes, it most certainly does."

The three of them held hands, and Father George led them in prayer.

When the praying concluded, Father George asked to speak privately with Kirby.

"There are things he might tell me that he might not tell you. And if we're going to tear this demon inside him out by the root, we must dig as deeply as possible."

"Okay, but—"

And then a certainty hit Donna. She sucked in a deep breath and took a step back, away from Father George.

"You don't want to *talk* to him," she said, shocked stretching her features.

Father George shook his head, as if to clear it.

"Don't be silly, Donna, of course I do."

"You want to—you want to—" She couldn't say it. The picture her certainty had painted in her mind appalled her.

She had to be mistaken. For the first time in her life, her certainty had to be questioned. This was a test of faith and nothing more. She was Job. She was Lot's wife, turning, turning, turning to look upon Gomorrah, back to oblivion. But, no. She would not allow herself to become a pillar of salt, for Kirby relied on her. He depended on her to do the right thing, and the right thing in this moment was for her to allow Father George to have private counsel with her troubled son. Yes. That was what was right.

"Never mind. I'm weak in my faith, Father. Forgive me."

"You need never ask me for forgiveness, Donna."

"Yes. Of course. Tell Kirby I'll be just outside."

"Do you plan on hanging around for services tonight?"

"Yes, Father."

"Then you may wait in the church itself. Deacon Henry might even be there, readying verses. He'll keep you company until I'm finished with Kirby."

There was that knowing smile again, that smile that said he knew something she didn't know. Or something she wouldn't accept.

Her certainty niggled her. But for the first time in her life, she ignored what had up until that point been her better judgment, and went to see if Deacon Henry were in the church, as Father George had said he might be.

\*\*\*

Kirby looked up when Father George reentered the room. Something had changed in the pastor's eyes. No longer did he look like the calm, helpful soul he'd been when he left. Now he seemed darker. But not in an unattractive way. His eyes were smoky and beckoning. His posture loose and welcoming. God, but Kirby would give anything to have this man.

Seeing that thoughts such as these were what landed him here in the first place, he tried to wipe them from his mind. Father George, though, was having none of it.

"So," Father George said as he sat on the edge of his desk and spread his legs, his crotch level with Kirby's eyes.

Kirby licked his lips.

Father George grabbed his own thighs and squeezed, as if massaging his legs. His hands went up and down the length of his thighs, both thumbs trailing from knee to crotch, crotch to knee.

Was it just Kirby's imagination, or was the bulge in Father George's pants becoming more pronounced. Was the fabric rising, a little at a time? Was the man achieving an erection in his presence? Surely Kirby was only imagining all this.

"So," Father George repeated, "What is it you'd like to do to me?"

Kirby swallowed.

"Everything."

"*Everything*, you say?"

"Yes."

Father George came to him. He held out his hands for Kirby's and Kirby obliged. Father George pulled Kirby gently from his chair.

Father George kissed him. Kirby kissed him back. He wasn't a very good kisser, but Father George was a patient lover. He eased the boy through the paces: when to open his mouth, where to lick, what to suck, what went into where.

In the quiet sanctity of the rear corner office of Chastity Baptist Church, Kirby Johnson lost his virginity to the man of his dreams. If Heaven truly did exist, it existed in that microcosm of time, those few seconds before Father George climaxed inside of him, and then once more when Father George ushered Kirby into his own orgasm.

Their clothes left in a pile in the locked office, Father George cleaned Kirby and himself in the restroom that could be accessed from the inside of his office. Warm water and a wash cloth cleansed any evidence of their sin. Kirby lovingly cleaned the brown evidence from Father George's penis. He felt it was the least he could do. After all, it was his own mess. Father George then rinsed the wash cloth and cleaned Kirby where Kirby was raw and sore. They toweled off together and redressed.

For a moment, they stared into each other's eyes. Father George petted Kirby's cheek.

"You can't tell anyone, Kirby."

Kirby only nodded, his eyes full of adoration and gratitude.

"Thank you," Kirby whispered.

"No, son, thank you."

Father George corrected the boy's collar, and they, together, went to find Kirby's mother.

\*\*\*

That next Sunday, Father George pulled Kirby to the side before church, speaking to him once again in the office where'd they made love for the first time.

"I'm going to request that your mother send you to Humble Hill for evaluation. Is that okay with you?"

"For—for what?" Kirby didn't understand. Didn't they love each other? Wasn't Father George just like him? Why would the pastor want to send him away?

"I work there, Kirby. I'm one of the new councilors."

"I don't understand. I thought—"

"We can see each other. Every day but Saturday and Sunday, Kirby. It's the only safe way for us to be together. Don't you want to be together?"

Kirby's heart filled with a joy so profound that he expected love to blast from his heart in brilliant spears of light.

"You want to be with me?" Kirby said, tears of happiness dripping from his eyes.

"Of course, Kirby. I'd never abandon you. Not now. Not now that I know."

Kirby embraced Father George. Father George's hand drifted down to Kirby's butt cheek and Kirby felt the pastor give him a firm squeeze followed by a pat.

"Now go on, back to your mother. And remember, not a word."

"Yes, Father," Kirby said with a giggle.

Kirby was so very in love.

Everything was perfect.

Nothing could ever be wrong again.

In the days to come, Father George would speak to Donna Johnson about Humble Hill and assure Donna that the facility was Kirby's best bet for a cure. With thoughts such as Kirby was having, there was no simple fix, no definitive procedure, no overnight successes; the road to normalcy would be a difficult one, fraught with failure. The teenager would have to be, in Father George's own words, *retrained* and *reprogrammed*. Kirby would be put into certain situations with female subjects. Was that all right with her? Donna said that it was. Maybe he'd even find a girlfriend, someone to bring home to meet dear old Mom? That was certainly a possibility, Father George said.

All the while, Donna Johnson ignored her niggling certainty that all of this was wrong. Satan was pulling out all stops, really doing a number on her. She could no longer trust herself or her innermost feelings. She prayed nightly that God would return her certainty to its once true form, but that only strengthened her certainty that something was wrong with the whole mess. Father George was up to something and Kirby was in terrible danger.

*Stop it*, she chided herself, *You have faith in God and that's all that matters. He'd never put you and Kirby in harm's way, not unless there was a Christian lesson to be learned. All things in time—all things in* His *time.*

On a sunny Monday morning, Kirby and Donna Johnson met Father George at Chastity Baptist. Kirby removed his suitcase from the trunk of his mother's car and moved it to Father George's car. He kissed his mother goodbye, and she crushed him in a hug.

"You behave yourself and do everything Father George asks of you. Hear?"

Kirby smiled a smile not unlike Father George's knowing smile.

"Yes'm. I will do everything he says, no matter what."

She caressed his cheek.

"My beautiful baby boy. I know they'll help you. I just know it. I'm certain of it."

"Yes'm."

"Go on now. And I'll see you again. When you're better."

"Looking forward to it," Kirby said, and he really did look ready to be cured. He seemed so excited at the possibility that he was heading off to a new and bright future, a future bereft of sinful thoughts.

Donna somehow managed to smile as she waved goodbye to Kirby. Father George pulled out of the church's parking lot, and she kept right on waving. Then she somehow managed to get in her car and drive home. She somehow cooked dinner and washed dishes and lay down for bed. And, somehow, she slept.

All the while, her certainty sang like a shrill alarm keening in the back of her mind.

Somehow, she ignored it.

*Somehow.*

\*\*\*

Why hadn't Donna taken Kirby to Humble Hill herself? Well, Father George had said that wasn't a sound idea. The rehabilitation facility was home to some thirty men and women, young adults included, and each one had their own neuroses and psychoses that could be exasperated by the arrival and departure of outsiders. For instance, Father George had said that there was a young man who stayed by the window in the day room during social hours, and that same young man would pitch a fit anytime a vehicle arrived on the property because he swore up and down that it was his mother and father come to rescue him from the horrors of Humble Hill. This young man was very, *very* sick, or so Father George had said, but on the way to Humble Hill, Father George had admitted to Kirby that this boy who stood by the window was nothing more than a figment of his, Father George's, imagination.

Kirby watched trees scroll by outside his window. "I don't like lying to my mother."

"Neither do I, but I think it would be best if she didn't know where the grounds are."

"Can't she find out? I mean, isn't Humble Hill in the phone book?"

"Actually, no it is not. It's not in any directory."

"Why's that?"

Father George glanced at Kirby then back to the road.

"Don't you trust me, Kirby?"

"Yessir."

"Then trust me. Stop asking so many questions. It's... unattractive."

"Oh. Okay." Kirby lay his hands in his lap and stayed quiet for the rest of the drive. The last thing he wanted was for Father George to think him unattractive.

Humble Hill was, for all intents and purposes, a gated community located between Bay's End and its closest neighboring town, Chestnut. Technically, the land was owned by the United States government, but Humble Hill itself was a private venture that had no ties to the government. Something had been arranged so that this could happen, although Father George told Kirby he knew not what that might have been.

Somewhere in the woods beyond the hospital's property lay the massive sinkhole in the earth known locally as Waverly Chasm, named so after Waverly Fairchild. Tours were given of the location, once a week, on Saturdays, but the site was otherwise off limits to the public.

Kirby said, "I think I've heard the poem that goes along with that place."

Father George nodded. "It's a pretty famous poem around these parts, I'd say."

They pulled up to the guard shack at the entrance to Humble Hill and Father George lowered his window. He passed a placard to the black man in the booth. The guard dipped low to look Kirby over then passed the placard back to Father George without a word. The gate grumbled to life and skated slowly open. Kirby felt like an eternity had passed before the space in the fence was wide enough to allow them entrance.

Father George pulled through and followed a curving road into a dense wood.

"This still Marietta Wood?" Kirby asked.

"Sure is. Of course, that's not what the government folks call it, but it's all the same forest."

"I guess at some point everything was the same forest."

Father George glanced at Kirby.

"I guess that might be a valid theory. The Pangea theory supports that, anyway."

"Pangea?"

"Yeah. There is a theory surfacing and gaining traction that once, way back before humans walked the earth, all the continents were connected. Some scientists and geological types have matched rocks and such from the coasts of America to the coasts of Britain and the like. So, at one point in history, you could've walked from Canada to Russia, or Florida to Africa, without ever crossing water wider than a river. Pretty neat, huh?"

Father George's hand found its way onto Kirby's thigh and squeezed. Kirby lay a cold hand atop Father George's warm one and traced the pastor's fingernails with the tips of his fingers.

Kirby smiled. "This is going to be great. I can feel it."

"Oh, yes, everything will be just fine. You're safe here. Completely safe."

Kirby ignored his own certainty that something was off here and trusted his new love wholeheartedly.

Around another curve, the woods thinned and then disappeared altogether. They entered a community that looked very much like a suburb, with tract houses on either side, complete with their own mailboxes. Not a single car sat in any of the driveways. In the distance sat Humble Hill itself, a great cube of steel and glass that looked as if one could see right through it if not for the reflection of the sun and surrounding forest in each pane of glass.

Humble Hill had been built, quite literally, on a hill, so that the building looked down on the small community of houses below. Kirby thought that was where they were headed and was thus shocked when Father George pulled into the driveway of the second to last home on the strip.

The blue bungalow was quaint, with flower boxes below both of the front windows and no porch to speak of. Two concrete steps that had been painted a bright yellow led up to the front door. The eaves of the house were a vibrant green to match the flourishing bushes that separated one front yard from the next. The front door, however, was a solid black door. A gilded number one and nine hand been nailed to the door. Obviously this house was Number Nineteen. Even the mailbox said so.

"This is your new home."

Kirby gawked.

"I get my own home? All to myself?"

"You won't be living here alone, no. You'll have a roommate, as it were. A female, Kirby. A woman like you. A woman who likes the same sex. You two will be put into a domestic relationship and expected to act like a married couple. Do you understand?"

"Are we supposed to have sex?"

"Eventually, yes. It's the only way to prove to the doctors that you're training has taken. I need you to understand something though. This is all about perception. If they perceive you are cured, you are cured. You may go through life loving and making love to whoever you choose, especially me" —Father George smiled lovingly— "but you must keep it a secret. Moreso than anything else that's what this place is for. The doctors want to fix you, but I know you're not broken. If we can assure them that you are cured, then you can go back home with their approval and maybe your mother doesn't have to worry so much."

Kirby frowned. "But she'll know. She has a way of knowing. I mean, I didn't even tell her about how I felt about you. She just *knew*."

"Don't be silly. She didn't know anything. She caught on to a signal you gave off, is all. It's a parent thing. It's how cops get criminals to confess. They say things with certainty, like, *We know you bumped off your wife*, and the criminal thinks they have more information than they actually do, so he spills his guts and ends up riding the lightning."

"Riding the lightning?"

"Sorry. It's slang for being electrocuted."

"How horrible."

"The people who are electrocuted are horrible people, Kirby. They deserve to die."

Kirby shivered. "That's not very Christian to say."

"The same thing could be said of our relationship, Kirby. That it is not very Christian. But is it a bad thing, do you think? Do you think that love could ever be wrong in the eyes of the Lord?"

"I don't suppose so."

"And doesn't it say in the Bible, *An eye for an eye*?"

"I guess so."

"Well, I will say, it does say exactly that. No one who murders someone else in cold blood can be allowed to live."

"What about police, and soldiers at war?"

"They only kill bad people, Kirby."

Kirby nodded, but knew that that was not necessarily true. Not everyone in Hiroshima and Nagasaki had been a bad person when the bombs were dropped on them. How could they have been? There had to have been children, maybe even infants, who died in the surprise blast. Surely that couldn't be explained away as anything other than evil. Surely that was the very opposite of Christianity. What Kirby thought was this: all too often people made excuses for their actions by saying they were acting out God's plan, when in reality they were simply bending the doctrine to fit their own agenda.

Father George carried Kirby's luggage to the front door and Kirby followed him inside.

The living room was colorful to the point of annoyance. The couch was made of neon-pink leather; the recliner a garish red. The chandelier over the dining room table, which had a yellow-and-purple checkered lacquer surface, shone like tinsel in a lit Christmas tree. The cabinets in the kitchen were an alternating blue-brown, and all the appliances were silver: the fridge, stove, dishwasher, washer and dryer. That was another thing altogether: everything was new or in pristine condition. The amount of money put into this place had to be exorbitant, but Kirby wasn't complaining. He'd love every minute that he would live here, he was sure, for the place was as bold and cheerful as he felt life should be. It was a happy place meant for happy people. The word *gay* never fit as well as it fit here.

"It's wonderful."

"Yes, it is," said a soft voice from the hallway.

Kirby found a young woman of maybe twenty years standing in the middle of the hall, her hands clasped in front of her, palms wringing.

She said, "I'm Sadie Brouchard. You are?"

Father George said, "This will be your new husband, Sadie. His name's Kirby Johnson."

She drifted down the hallway toward Kirby. When she was within reach, she hugged him close and kissed his cheek.

"Then I am to be Sadie Johnson. How lovely that sounds."

Kirby glanced uncertainly to Father George.

Father George nodded.

Kirby looked back at his new wife and said, "Nice to meet you, Sadie."

"Lovely to meet you, too, Kirby. Should we consummate the marriage now or later?"

Father George said, "Later, Sadie. Let Kirby get settled first."

"Sounds wonderful. Here, husband, let me show you your new home."

She held out both hands for Kirby to take. Kirby looked back and forth several times, from her hands to Father George.

"Go on, Kirby. I'm leaving you with Sadie for now. I have some paperwork to do. Admittance stuff, is all. You two get to know each other while I'm gone, and I'll come by to see you before I head back to the End. Sound good?"

"If you're sure."

"I am," Father George said with that knowing smile of his. "I'm more than sure. Sadie here is a terrific hostess. She throws the best parties I've ever attended."

She beamed. "Why thank you, Father George."

Kirby accepted her hands and cemented his fate all in one movement.

\*\*\*

Sadie was a terrific cook. For lunch she made him pasta salad with a mayonnaise base and pimento cheese sandwiches that were to die for. He washed it all down with ice-cold whole milk and sat contented on the neon-pink couch watching a news report about the possibility of the Russians launching a probe into space as early as November.

"Silly Russians. There's no way they're advanced enough as a country to do such a thing," Sadie said as she sat down beside Kirby. She crossed and tucked her legs to elevate herself so that, when compared to Kirby, they were the same height.

"You don't think they'll do it?"

"Lordy no. They're Russians. If they were Americans, maybe I could see it. No foreign power could ever be more technologically advanced than we are. We're the greatest country in the world!"

She spoke kinda funny, and Kirby thought she would take some getting used to. All of this—his new community, the house, a *wife*—would take quite a bit of getting used to indeed.

"So," Sadie said, "what do you like to do for fun, Kirby?"

He shrugged. "I don't know."

"Surely you know what you like to do for fun," she said with a giggle of girlish glee. He couldn't place her age. He'd assumed when he'd first met her that she was around twenty, but maybe that had been wrong. She was definitely older than him, but no older than twenty-five, at least Kirby didn't think so. Still, there wasn't a doubt in his mind that the woman sitting beside him was no teenager.

Although he didn't find Sadie attractive, he could admit that she was classically pretty. Wide in the hips, almost motherly in shape. Someone his grandmother would've said was *perfect from the neck up*. He supposed a man with normal sexual attractions—

225

or whatever you want to call a man who didn't like men like he did—might say that Sadie's breasts were on the small side. Having no dog in that fight, Kirby thought her breasts were adequate enough for feeding a baby, should she ever have one, and wasn't that their only purpose? To feed an infant? Kirby thought so. Sexualizing a woman's chest was, to him, as strange as trying to feed a baby with a penis. It seemed all wrong. Backward thinking, even.

"Do you like to play cards? Bridge? Canasta? Maybe dominoes?"

"What are dominoes?"

Sadie gasped. "You've never played dominoes?"

Kirby couldn't help but to laugh.

"No. I've never played dominoes. But I could learn, I'm sure."

"True, true. All right. Let's teach you how to play dominoes."

Sadie spent the better part of thirty minutes going over the rules of the game, and then they played a practice run that she said wouldn't count for anything. She wouldn't even keep score. They'd simply play until each of them ran out of dominoes. Then they'd start over, for real this time.

Had she been keeping score that first practice round, Kirby would've won, by a landslide. The second hand, the one that mattered, went to Sadie. As did the third. And the fourth. By his fifth defeat, Sadie couldn't stop giggling as Kirby fake-raged over his defeat. He bellowed in anger, but all the while there lay a smile on his face, and it was clear that she shouldn't take his shenanigans seriously.

"You're funny," she said between titters. "You're fun *and* funny, Kirby. Any girl would be lucky to have you."

That brought back the reason he was here. All of a sudden Kirby was no longer having fun. The smile died on his face and he cleared his throat.

"This is fun and all, Sadie, but I think we should talk about why I'm here."

"Oh, Kirby, dear, I know why you're here. Same reason we're all here."

"Same reason we're all here? There's more than just you and I?" Deep down, Kirby knew this was the case, but to hear it spoken made it real and Kirby had always been uncomfortable with anything real.

"Oh, yes. All of us are here for the same reason."

"How many is *all of us*?"

"Total? All the patients of Humble Hill, or just us on Lord's Way?"

"Lord's Way?"

She nodded. "It's on the street sign as you come in. Didn't you see it? It's the name of this street. All of our mail is addressed to Lord's Way, and then the house number. We're Nineteen Lord's Way, in case you missed it on the door."

"I saw it on the door, but I missed the street sign. Lord's Way, huh? Seems a bit, I don't know, cryptic, doesn't it?"

She frowned. "How so?"

"Never mind. Tell me more about why you're here. How'd you come to live here?"

"Well, as you've likely figured out, I had some issues with women before I came to Lord's Way and Humble Hill. My mother walked in on me kissing the neighbor girl. We said we were just practicing, you know, for when we got boyfriends, but my mother saw right through me. Mothers always know. I think it has something to do with pregnancy. It gives them a kind of—"

"Certainty," said Kirby. It wasn't a question.

"Yes. That's it exactly. A certainty. I remember, when I was a little bit of a thing, that my mother seemed to always know when I was goofing off. Even when I was out of sight, I wasn't out of mind. She'd show up a step before I went too far to stop me from doing irreparable damage to myself, or someone else. And she'd always say the same thing, too. *One of these days, Sadie May, I won't be here to save you. Then what are you going to do?* Well, here I am, as far away from her as I've ever been, and I guess I'm doing all right for myself. Sure showed her, didn't I?" She gave Kirby a meek smile.

"You liked girls? Like, as in that way?"

"Sexually, you mean?"

"Yes. I guess I do."

"You can say it. *Sexually*. It's not a dirty word. Sex is natural, as long as it's between a man and a woman. Between, say, you and me."

Kirby nodded.

He said, "So, you liked girls sexually?"

"Yes. Yes, I did." Sadie patted down her fluffy skirt "If my mother hadn't walked in on me and the neighbor girl—"

"Didn't she have a name?"

"A name?" Sadie looked honestly confused.

"Yeah. This neighbor girl. Surely she had a name?"

"Why, I don't know what you mean. A name?"

"Yes. Like your name is *Sadie* and my name is *Kirby*. Surely you knew this girl's name. This girl you were kissing?"

Sadie's bottom lip began to tremble as if she were about to cry.

"Her name?" Sadie whimpered.

"Sadie? Sadie, are you okay?"

"Her name was..."

Sadie's fingernails bit into the neon-pink upholstery. The material tore. Her fingers wormed into the guts of the cushion and started tugging out tufts of cotton. Tears streamed down her face, running her mascara, carving through foundation.

"Her name was...was...was—"

"Sadie? My God, Sadie, it's okay. Forget I said anything. Please, just forget I brought it up."

Sadie slackened, as if every muscle in her had given up the ghost at the same time. She remained cross-legged and upright, but every inch of her flesh sagged. She looked deflated, was the best way Kirby could describe it. Like a balloon with only a quarter of its air left inside.

"Sadie? Oh God, Sadie, are you all right?"

The corner of her mouth twitched once, twice, a third time, but she didn't answer. She only stared at him. Through him, really.

"Everything is horrible now," she murmured.

"It's not. It's not horrible at all," he tried to assure her. "It's fine. I won't bring the neighbor girl up again. Okay? She doesn't even exist."

"She doesn't even exist," Sadie echoed.

"You'll never hear me ask about her again."

"I'll never hear you ask about her again."

"Sadie? Sadie, you're really scaring me."

"I'm scaring you."

Kirby grabbed her shoulders and shook her.

"Stop it!"

Her neck flopped and her head bounced.

Someone knocked at the door.

"Oh, thank, God," Kirby said as he bounded from the couch and answered the door.

A bald man in a red coat with the number three sewn into his lapel stood on the front step. His smile was so large his face seemed to be nothing but teeth.

"Is your wife okay?"

"I... I don't know," Kirby stammered.

"May I come in?"

"Yes, yes. Please do. Something's wrong with Sadie."

The man in the red coat entered. He walked so stiffly that Kirby assumed a hard breeze would knock him over. Like a domino, if you will. The man rounded the couch and plopped onto the couch beside Sadie. He slipped a hand around her neck, under her hair, and said three words.

"It gets better."

Sadie's head snapped around to face the man in the red coat.

"It gets better." She smiled, and just like that, Sadie was back. Her eyes fluttered as she looked about the room. "Where's my husband? Where's Kirby?"

"He's just there. Over at the door."

"Oh," she said and stood up. She faced Kirby, her face filled with a joyous expression. "There you are!"

She rushed around the couch and hugged Kirby. Her grip was a fierce one. He felt like a life preserver on the Titanic.

"Are you okay now?" he said as he hugged her back.

"Whatever do you mean?" she asked, still hugging him.

Her hair smelled of the calm before the storm; the scent of lightning and coming rain.

"Never mind," Kirby said, looking to the man on the couch.

The man in the red coat, still smiling his gargantuan smile, stood and came around the couch. He nodded once to Kirby and squeezed by them, out the front door. Kirby loosed Sadie and stepped out onto the first concrete step. He watched the man in the red coat walk down the pathway that led through the center of their front yard, to the sidewalk, make a left on the sidewalk, and continue down to what Kirby assumed, by simple math, to be Number Three Lord's Way.

"His coat matches his address?"

"Whose does what?" Sadie asked from the doorway behind him.

"The man in the coat. The number on his label said three. If I've counted right, I believe he's gone into Number Three Lord's Way."

"Man in a coat? What are you talking about, husband?"

Kirby faced Sadie. "The man who told you, *It gets better.* The man in the red coat."

Sadie's ever-present smile vanished. "I think you should come inside, Kirby. It's not safe out there."

"Not safe? What do you mean? What's going on?"

"Come inside, dear, and I'll make you dinner."

"I've just had lunch. Don't you remember? You made me pimento cheese sandwiches and... and—and I don't know what else. Doesn't matter. I want to know who the man in the coat was!"

Sadie slammed the door in his face.

"Sadie!" Kirby hollered. He knocked three times. When she didn't answer, he knocked harder. Ten times he pounded. Still no answer. He backed away from the gilded number nineteen that held pride of place on the solid black door. A door that looked like a starless night; that looked like a void. He backed down the concrete path to the sidewalk. The curtains had been drawn. He couldn't see inside the house. The curtains, like the front door, were black, giving the house the appearance of a face with empty sockets and a dark, gaping maw.

"Help ya?" said a pleasant voice to Kirby's right. He snapped his head in that direction. Another man in a red coat stood on the sidewalk, this one had hair, unlike the guy with the number three on his lapel. This man with the head full of bushy brown hair had a black fourteen stitched onto the breast pocket of his red coat.

"Yeah, my wife—Sadie—she's acting strangely."

"We all act strangely from time to time, partner. That's why we're here. To learn how to act normally."

"I know. I mean—I mean, she's not letting me in. She's—she's not letting me into my own house."

Number Fourteen frowned. "Well, then, that is troubling, isn't it?"

"Yes," Kirby huffed. "Yes, it is."

"Let me see what I can do."

Kirby watched Number Fourteen move down the concrete path to the front door. The man in the coat knocked three times, paused, knocked twice more, paused, then knocked one last time. The door came open. Sadie stood backlit by light from the kitchen.

If Number Fourteen said anything, Kirby couldn't hear it. But, after a moment, the man in the coat stepped aside, and there she was, Kirby's beautiful wife of several hours, beaming once more at him as if he were God's gift unto her.

"Kirby! Kirby, honey, what are you doing outside?" Her giggle had returned. Kirby no longer thought it sounded so innocent.

Father George's white Park Avenue pulled into the driveway. Kirby hadn't heard it coming down the road from the main hospital. Father George stepped out of the car, looked at Number Fourteen and Sadie, to Kirby, and then back to Number Fourteen.

Father George said, "Everything all right, Greg?"

"Oh, everything is just fine, Father George. Just a bit of a misunderstanding between husband and wife. I'm sure things will be far less bumpy from here on out. In fact, I'd give a lifetime guarantee on the topic."

"Very good." Father George turned to address Kirby. "Mind if I speak with you for a minute?"

Kirby jogged to Father George's side.

"Something's wrong here."

"Nothing's wrong, Kirby. You just have to get used to the way things are done here."

"What's with the men in the coats?"

"They work here. They also live here. They're staff. Nothing more."

"There's something wrong with Sadie. She was acting...strangely."

"She's fine now, it seems."

Kirby took a step back. "What is this? What's going on?"

Father George laughed. "Nothing's wrong, Kirby. I know all this is gonna be hard to get used to, but you have to trust me. You *do* trust me, don't you?"

"I don't know what I trust right now."

"Well, if you're gonna get better, you're gonna have to trust that I know what I'm doing?"

"Get better? What do you mean if I'm going to *get better*?"

Father George quickstepped toward Kirby and grabbed his shirtfront. He yanked the teenager close until they were nose to nose.

"You're here to get better, remember?" Father George hissed. "You said you understood why you were here. Don't do this to me."

"Oh," Kirby whispered. "Oh, I'm sorry. Yes. Yes, I do remember why I'm here. I'm here to get better so that I can return home. Yes. I'm sorry, Father George. I will try to do better from here on out."

Father George released him. "Good. Now I have to be going for the night. Sorry I can't stay longer, Kirby, but I promise you, I will be back tomorrow, and every day after that. Except—"

"Every day except weekends," Kirby finished for him.

"Right," Father George made to reach for Kirby but drew his hand back at the last minute. Kirby saw and appreciated the gesture. A gesture that said, without a single word, that Father George wanted nothing more than to touch and comfort him.

Kirby's heart filled to overflowing with love for the man in front of him.

"I'll see you tomorrow, Kirby."

"Yes, Father George. Goodnight."

"Goodnight," Father George said, but left unsaid between them hung the words, *I love you.*

*I love you, too, you dear man. Until tomorrow.*

*Until tomorrow...*

\*\*\*

They came for Kirby the next morning.

He hadn't slept a wink up until that point, having spent the majority of the night staring at the blackness above him that might have been ceiling, or the ever-present crushing void of the universe. You know, either or.

The sun wasn't even properly up yet when he heard the front door come open. No knock. No "Hey, anybody awake?" Just the jingle of a turning knob, the slight creak of hinges, followed by footsteps thudding down the hallway.

Three of them in all: men in red coats, every last one of them. Three, Fourteen, and the only one Kirby had yet to meet, Number Nine. Number Nine, to Kirby's shock, was a black man with a face like an Easter Island head. The guy was handsome in a rough and rugged sort of way, but now was not the time to be appreciating someone's physical attributes.

As they poured into his room, one after the other, Kirby screamed and tried to roll away. Sadie, who lay next to him in bed, barely stirred when he crashed into her. She'd taken something to sleep the night before—he'd seen her pop the pill and chase it with tonic water from the fridge—and hadn't moved a lick all night.

Even now she remained blissfully asleep and unaware that he was, apparently, being kidnapped.

"Now, now, Little Birdie," the new one, Number Nine, said. "Be a good little birdie and hold still. Hold still for Drake. Just you hold still." All the while Number Fourteen—Drake—was grabbing and slapping at Kirby, trying to get a handhold on the slithering, writhing teenager.

"Help! Help me!" Kirby cried. But it was no use. No one was coming. Somewhere deep down inside him, or perhaps tucked away in the attic of his mind, he'd known this was going to happen. Father George had done a fantastic job of lulling him into a sense of false security, of seducing him and, in turn, lowering his guard, setting him up for an easy betrayal.

But had Kirby actually been seduced. Could you seduce someone who was already, at a base level, attracted to you? Likely not. But to think that Father George had only made love to him in order to convince him to come here was insane. Wasn't it? Surely Father George knew that all that would have been required was for Kirby's mother to insist that he go. Kirby was only a teenager, having turned sixteen this summer, and had no other choice but to do as his mother wished. Why the subterfuge? Why the sex? Why the lies about coming here so they could be together? None of it made any sense.

Number Fourteen—Greg; Father George had called the man Greg last night—stepped in to help Drake—Number Nine—and the two of them had little trouble wrestling Kirby from the bed. They each grabbed him under an arm and dragged him out of his bedroom and down the hallway, his toes skating across the floor the entire way. Out into the purple morning they took him, screaming and crying and begging for his life. He had no idea where they were taking him or what they had planned once he arrived, but he knew that, whatever it was, it couldn't be good. No one kidnapped someone and took them to the movies, or out for dinner. Only bad things happened to kidnapped people.

A white van sat on the street, at the curb, in front of his house. Number Three—whose name was as yet unknown to him— came around the two Coat Men who held him to open the rear doors. In he was tossed, like an unwanted ragdoll into a waste bin. Number Three crawled in after him, his bulk big enough to block the only exit out of the van. The doors slammed shut behind him. Kirby scrambled into a corner, behind the driver's seat, and cowered there, whimpering.

Number Three hadn't spoken as yet, but Kirby remembered him now. This was the same bald-headed guy who had shown up last night to comfort Sadie after she'd said—

—what had she said?

*Everything is horrible now.*

And what had Number Three said to her?

*It gets better.*

Yes. That was it.

*It gets better.*

For some reason, Kirby decided to try it out.

"It gets better," he told Number Three as Drake and Greg climbed into the driver and passenger seats, respectively.

"It does, it does," Number Three said, nodding with every other word. Up on *It*, down on *does*. "Oh, it most certainly does."

"Hold 'im, Percy!" Drake hollered from the driver's seat. "Hold 'im still. Don't let 'im bounce around back there. Lagotti's gon' be mad if he's bruised up when we get there."

"Oh, I got him. Don't you worry none 'bout us. I got him good, I does."

Three—or Percy, if you please—reached for him with fingers like claws and fingernails caked with dark matter.

"Don't touch me!" Kirby squealed.

"I won't touch you unkindly, son. I promise. All the touching I do is from the heart. All the touching I do is with *love*." Percy tittered madly as he fell upon Kirby. He tugged the teenager to the floor and lay his entire weight on top of him as the van started and pulled away from the curb.

"You settled back there?" Drake asked.

"Oh, yes, we are plenty comfortable, Drake, sir."

"Good. Here we go."

The ride to the hospital was short and smooth and uneventful. Kirby, having Percy laid out on top of him like he was, decided fighting was not in his best interest. He was outnumbered three to one, and he felt it was in his best interest to go along for the ride, to see what they had in store for him. If his life truly was in danger, he would fight. But only if a threat presented itself. All of this could be some kind of unfortunate misunderstanding. Sure. Why not? He was new to Humble Hill and somebody must've gotten their wires crossed. Some idiot had labeled him a danger to himself and others and sent these three goons after him. Something like that was entirely possible. At least Kirby convinced himself that such a thing was entirely possible. It was better to convince himself that this was all some kind of horrible mistake rather than worrying over whether or not he was about to be murdered in cold blood by a trio of men in numbered red coats.

"We appreciate your cooperation, son," Percy whispered in his ear. "It's for the best, I assure you."

Percy's mouth was so close to his ear, Kirby could hear the man's lips stretch into a smile. They cracked like knuckles popping.

The quality of the light in the van changed from early-morning-purple to artificial-white. The van jerked to a stop. Drake and Greg got out. Seconds later the back door opened and even more artificial light poured in. Percy pushed off Kirby and backed out of the van. The trio of coat men stood in a line, seemingly waiting for Kirby to remove himself from the van. When he didn't move, Drake grabbed Kirby's ankle and tugged.

"Come on, Little Birdie. You got a date with Dr. Lagotti."

Tug, tug.

Kirby scooted out on his butt.

They were in some kind of garage set up. Another white van was parked next to the one he'd rode in on. There was a bloody handprint on the back door.

"What are you going to do to me?"

"We ain't gon' do anything to you, Little Birdie." Drake put a hand in the small of Kirby's back and directed him toward the only entrance Kirby could see: a steel door set into the wall with a nautical wheel set into the middle; the kind of door one might find inside a submarine, not a hospital.

"Where are we?"

"Humble Hill. Where else?" Drake spun the wheel and pulled the heavy door open on squealing hinges. Kirby noted the four heavy cylinders set into the edge of the door. The cylinders likely served as the door's locking mechanism. Once the door was closed and the wheel spun those cylinders would slam into place and nothing short of a tank would be able to get through. Once Kirby, Greg, and Percy were through, Drake pulled the door closed by way of a steel ring. Kirby noticed with a shock of terror that there was no wheel on this side of the door. Meaning, the door served one purpose and one purpose only: all entrance, no escape.

But what could be inside here that would require a door with such a secure and impenetrable locking system? If they were dealing with the mentally ill, as Father George had assured Kirby was Humble Hill's purpose, surely a normal door and dead bolt would suffice—wouldn't it? Maybe a crossbar would be in order, but certainly not a door one would normally find installed on a bank vault.

Drake's hand in the middle of Kirby's back shoved and Kirby got moving again. The corridor he found himself in had beige walls, white baseboards and white crown molding. Simple. Clinical, even. The door at the end of this corridor was white and made of wood. Greg opened the door and the four of them moved through into what looked to Kirby like any other waiting room inside any other hospital.

"Have a seat, Little Birdie," Drake said, and pointed to one of a dozen chairs that sat on the perimeter of the otherwise-open floorplan. Kirby sat in the corner and hunted an alternative exit. Should things go bad (or worse than they already had), he wanted an escape route. There was the door they'd come through, a glass window behind which sat a fat woman with glasses and a gray beehive hairdo in a blue blouse and a name tag Kirby couldn't read from where he sat, and one other door. This other door seemed perfectly normal. No locks. Only a brass handle that showed his warped reflection. If things got bad (or worse), he'd try that door first.

"I've brought you a little birdie, Harriet. Aren't you proud of me?" Drake told the woman behind the glass.

"Oh, yes, you've followed directions just perfectly. What a pleasant surprise." Harriet's words dripped sarcasm.

"I do love it when you flirt wit' me."

"Sign him in and have a seat."

"You want we should stay?" Drake glanced back at his two partners. Greg shrugged.

"Just one of you. I don't need all three of you."

Drake turned to the other Coat Men.

"Which one of you wants to stay?"

"Why can't you stay?" Greg asked.

"'Cause I don't want to. I stayed with the last one."

"I don't even like the kid," Percy said. "I had to reboot the dyke in nineteen last night because of this one. First fuckin day here and he's already causin' problems."

"Fair enough," Drake said. "Greg?"

"Not me, Tank."

*Tank?* Kirby thought. *Must be a nickname.*

Greg added, "I had to deal with him last night, too. This one's on you."

Kirby considered telling Drake—or Tank, or Nine, or whatever his name was—that Greg didn't do much last night. He only had to leave his house for a few minutes before Father George arrived. In the end, Kirby decided to keep his mouth clamped. Last thing he needed to do was upset any one of these weirdos. No telling what they'd do, if pressed too hard.

Drake sighed and Kirby could smell his breath from across the room: a mixture of old milk and onions. "Fine. But you two owe me lunch."

"Deal," Greg said and headed for the door Kirby hadn't seen the other side of yet.

"Be careful. I think he likes ya." Percy laughed and slapped Drake on one thick bicep before following Greg to the door. Before walking out, Percy bent down and whispered in Kirby's ear. "Don't fight it, kid. It hurts like hell if you fight it."

"Fight what?" Kirby whimpered.

Percy didn't answer. He chuckled and left out the same door Greg had. Kirby tried to bend forward and catch a glimpse of what lay on the other side of the mystery door, but it swung closed before he could catch anything other than a blur of blue as bright as a cloudless sky.

Drake dropped into a chair halfway down the wall from Kirby and studied his fingernails. Nothing left to do but wait and worry.

An unknown amount of time, which Kirby felt was close to an hour but was actually more like fifteen minutes, passed before the door by which Greg and Percy had exited opened and a wide-hipped woman with a thin torso in a white nurse's uniform and canoe-like hat stepped in to address Kirby.

"The doctor will see you now." She smiled with gray teeth Kirby could almost see through. To Drake she said, "You can stay out here."

"Have fun, Little Birdie," Drake said, punctuating his sentence with a throaty chuckle.

Kirby followed the woman into a corridor the color of unpolluted waters. The walls were so brightly painted blue that they hurt his eyes to look upon them directly. He stared at the brown carpet but still had to squint to keep from being blinded by the glare off the walls. Because he had to squint so severely he didn't get a good look at this new corridor. He kept his pinched eyes trained on the backs of the nurse's heels, where a stocking had run on her left leg, until she turned left into a room that didn't feel so bright.

This new room's walls were white with red baseboards. A painting of a sunset hung on the far wall. A wooden cross on the wall adjacent the sunset. In the center of the room was a chair not unlike the kind you'd find in a dentist's office. The nurse gestured to the chair and Kirby scooted sideways into it.

He was no less nervous than when he'd first arrived, but having walked into this plain room and having sat down in this familiar type of chair instead of some kind of medieval torture chamber filled with racks and stocks and iron maidens had done something to calm his pulse rate. No longer did his heart race; it beat hard yet evenly in his chest. He took a deep breath and saw stars. He tried to blink them away but to no avail.

"The doctor will be in to see you in just a moment." The nurse headed for the door.

"How long?" Kirby asked, as if this were nothing more than a routine checkup. Odd how familiar surroundings can calm one as easily as unfamiliar surroundings can disorient and disturb. He didn't know what he'd been expecting, but it certainly had not been this completely ordinary examination room.

"You're his first patient of the day, so I'd say not long at all." With a smile, she closed the door between them.

The chair he sat in faced the cross on the wall. He said a quick prayer for his own safety and sat back. He closed his eyes, tried to figure out what he should expect of this as-yet-unseen doctor. The style of the room spoke to a simple general practice, but Kirby knew that this place was anything but simple, and whoever walked through that door would be anything but a general practitioner. Perhaps this was just a routine checkup; an appointment to judge the quality of his health before moving on to whatever curatives they'd invented to deal with his sexuality. Father George's assurances that all Kirby would have to do is fake being cured settled Kirby's nerves even further. Surely there was no way for this doctor to know what and who he was attracted to. Kirby decided he'd give it three or four appointments before proclaiming, "Yes, Jesus! I can't describe how badly I want to insert my penis into a normal, everyday vagina right now!" Maybe that would be a little much. But something like that would be the order of the day, certainly.

Kirby had just about convinced himself there was nothing whatsoever to be afraid of, that he'd not been essentially kidnapped and dragged from his home to a place with doors that allowed passage in, but not out, when a tall, dark, and unbearably handsome man came traipsing into the room.

"Hello, Kirby." The doctor—Kirby assumed that's who he was anyway—wore a red lab coat over a black turtleneck and gray khakis. Other than the color of his coat, the doctor looked like any other doctor: pens and scopes and other doctor-related ephemera in his coat's breast pocket; a stethoscope dangling from his neck. "My name's Dr. Lagotti. Pleased to meet you."

Kirby shook the outstretched hand. The doctor's palm was cool and dry and soft, his smile straight and white. His olive skin shone in the fluorescent lights overhead. Dark half-moons hung below the man's eyes; deep pools of darkness that spoke more to a possible Arab ethnicity than it did lack of sleep.

He was gorgeous. Kirby hadn't yet thought about what his *type* was, but Dr. Lagotti was surely it. If Kirby was honest with himself, he found Father George ugly by comparison.

"Hello," Kirby managed.

"You're looking healthy today."

*What an odd thing to say*, Kirby thought.

"Care to tell me, in your own words, why you've been brought before me today?" Dr. Lagotti spoke so oddly. His words were not accented, as Kirby in his ignorance of other cultures might have expected them to be, but they were strangely mechanical. Perhaps, Kirby thought, *clinical* was a better word for it.

"I'm a homosexual."

"No, you're not." Dr. Lagotti seemed proud of his statement. "No one is homosexual. Sometimes people are confused, or their minds are sick, but you're no more homosexual than someone who has the flu is a virus. Do you understand?"

"I guess so."

"You do not *guess so*, Kirby. We do not speak in maybes here at Humble Hill. We speak in definites. Speaking in definites will allow you to see the fleeting nature of your disease. Right now, you are confused. Say that for me. *I am confused.*"

"I am confused."

"Good." The doctor, who'd been at his side, stepped around so that he stood at Kirby's feet. "Now, I want you to tell me why you are confused."

"I'm sorry, I don't—I don't understand the question."

"What are you feeling right now? Do you want to have sexual intercourse with me?"

"I—I, um—Well—"

"Definites, Kirby. Speak only in definites, my boy. Am I attractive to you? Would you like to have sexual intercourse with me?"

"Y-yes. I suppose—"

Doctor Lagotti slapped Kirby hard across the face with a hand as forgiving as solid stone. Kirby squealed. His hand shot up to grab at his affected cheek but Dr. Lagotti snatched Kirby's arm away before his hand could reach his face.

"No. Do not comfort yourself. Accept the pain. Acknowledge the pain and associate it with your sexual dysfunction. You considered, for a moment, that you wanted to have sexual intercourse with me, and because of that, your cheek now hurts. Is that correct?"

"Yes," Kirby whimpered. He tongued a throbbing molar. The tooth wiggled in the gum.

"Good. Now we'll go a bit further." Dr. Lagotti walked to the door and pulled it open. A stainless-steel cart rolled inside on squeaky casters. The nurse from earlier stepped in behind it, pushing the cart farther into the room. She trundled the cart up beside Kirby's chair. Then she left the room.

Atop the cart was a square metal box that slightly resembled a ham radio. Two curly wires extended from plugs set in the face of the device and ended in two rubber-handled paddles whose tips looked like the metal pole inside of a tesla coil Kirby had once seen at a carnival. A white tube with a blue rectangle inside which lay a white K and Y lay beside the device; the tube looked like it might have been toothpaste. Kirby had never seen the product before.

"Now we're going to try to reprogram your brain, Kirby. This device reorders your brainwaves and allows them to pulse in the proper order. That's the easiest way to explain it, anyway. You look confused. Here. Let's try this tactic. Are you a car guy at all?"

"A car guy?"

"Do you like cars?"

"They're—they're all right, I guess."

"Definites, Kirby."

"Yes. Okay. I like cars."

"Then think of your brain as an engine. Your brain has jumped time, and now we need to fix that error. Do you understand now?"

Kirby was even more confused now than he was before, but he nodded, sure, he understood just fine, thank you very much.

"Good. Now we can proceed."

The doctor grabbed each of the metal poles from the cart, held them both in one hand while he picked up the tube of what looked to be toothpaste, and then proceeded to squirt a clear, goopy substance from the tube onto the ball of each paddle. Dr.

Lagotti lay the paddles down once again and reached under the top shelf of the cart. His hand came back into view holding piece of red rubber shaped into a horseshoe. He handed it to Kirby and Kirby asked what it was for.

"It's to protect your teeth. The device can cause them to grind together, and this saves you the headache."

His teeth grinding together sounded painful beyond words, so Kirby popped the mouthpiece in and awaited the next step.

Doctor Lagotti flipped a switch on the front of the machine and it hummed to life. Something screamed inside Kirby; a keening that begged him to run, run far, far away.

Dr. Lagotti placed a paddle to each of Kirby's temples, and Kirby Johnson went away.

\*\*\*

*Shockingly blue light. Blinding. A racing feeling, of heart and body and mind.*

*Kirby's standing in a valley. There's a path ahead. A stone path that, upon closer inspection, Kirby sees is made not of stones but human teeth. There's a cabin by a stream. A giant of a man steps from the cabin, sees Kirby, and frowns.*

*Light flashes. Lightning strikes behind his eyes.*

*Kirby stands on the front porch of an old antebellum mansion. Two black women, one decades older than the other, the younger one barely a teenager, sit in front of him, in rocking chairs, discussing something called the Roaming. The older woman sees Kirby and frowns.*

*"He not 'spose to be here, he not. Go on ahead, you. Go on."*

*"Who you talkin' to, Mia?"*

248

*"Never you mind, child. Ain't no one you should be bothered with, seen?"*

*"Yessum."*

*Lightning cleaves his brain.*

*A doll in the night. A massive doll. A sense of harmful intent, of cruelty, emanates from the great lumbering thing as it tosses a leg out and moves down the road with an old rolling gait.*

*"Ma-Ma," the doll coos.*

*One last flash of shocking blue and Kirby is standing in a child's room. There are white anchors on blue wallpaper. A young man lies on his bed, masturbating feverishly, and Kirby, disgusted, looks away. A ghost stands in one dark corner. Or what looks to be a ghost, anyway. It's a child-sized person with a sheet draped over them. No eyeholes in the sheet, nothing like some kids will cut into their mother's good bedding to create a Halloween costume.*

*The boy on the bed screams, rolls, cracks his head on the nightstand, and falls to the floor, bleeding from one temple. The ghost drifts over and reaches for the boy's wound with a tentacle made of sheet. The length of sheet suckles at the boy's laceration and red threads of blood are drawn up the fabric like blood flowing through veins.*

Someplace, *Kirby thinks.* This is the Someplace. *He thinks this, but at the same time has no idea where the thought has come from or what* the Someplace *actually is. All he knows for certain is that he is unwelcome here.*

\*\*\*

Kirby awoke unable to breathe, fighting restraints that were not there, tugging spider webs that did not exist from his creeping, crawling flesh. All over, ants were marching. His blood seemed to have been replaced by lava. Every inch of him burned.

"Medicate him," said a distant if familiar voice.

Kirby slept.

When he awoke for the second time, Father George sat beside his bed in a yellow-leather armchair.

"Good morning, handsome," Father George said, petting Kirby's hair.

Kirby snatched away from the man.

"Hey, now. It's okay. It's over."

"Where am I?" Kirby yelled, his head snapping back and forth, looking every which way but taking in absolutely nothing but blurry surroundings.

"You're home."

"Mom?" Kirby called.

"No, Kirby. You're not in the End. You're at your house. With Sadie. She's in the kitchen, cooking your supper. And I'm here. At your bedside."

"What the hell is going on?"

"Nothing, Kirby. Nothing is going on. You've just been asleep."

"The Coat Men—Dr. Lagotti—the ghost in the sheet—the Roaming."

"What?" Father George looked painfully confused. "What are you talking about?"

"They took me. The Coat Men. Three, Nine, and Four—Fourteen. But that wasn't their names. They were Drake and John and Percy. No. Not John. Greg. *Greg*! His named was Greg!"

Sadie appeared in the door to the bedroom. She looked terrified.

"Is he all right, Father?"

"I—I honestly don't know, Sadie."

"They took me!" Kirby raged. He tossed off his covers and fell from the mattress onto the floor. His legs weren't working. Why weren't his legs working?

"My God, Kirby, be careful," Father George said as he came into view around the bed. "Here, here. Lemme help you up."

Father George grabbed Kirby under the armpits and dragged him to his feet. Kirby stood on his own. His legs worked just fine. What had happened to him on the floor? Why hadn't they worked? What the hell was going on?

"Breathe, Kirby. Please. I don't wanna call an ambulance but I will."

"No! No ambulances! No hospitals!" Kirby screamed as he tore himself from Father George's grasp and raced past Sadie out into the hall. He crashed into the wall in the hallway, bounced off, and dashed into the living room. He spun, hunting an exit. He raced for the front door. Out and down the concrete path. Into the street. Screaming the entire way.

"Kirby?" said a man who was standing in the front lawn of the house across the street, watering his grass. "Kirby, you okay, buddy?"

"I don't know you. Who are you?"

"It's Tater, Kirby. You know me. William Tate? Everybody calls me Tater. *You* even call me Tater. We play Bridge on Friday nights. Gin Rummy on Saturday. Penny poker on Wednesday. Our wives have Tupperware parties for Christ's sake, Kirb. You *know* me."

"No," Kirby whimpered. "I don't know you. What the fuck is going on?"

"Hey, watch the language, Champ. I don't like to hear such things."

Kirby felt the Coat Man coming before he actually saw him. Kirby reeled on him. Drake—Number Nine, Tank, whoever—was approaching him from farther down the street. The tall muscular dark-skinned man froze in his tracks and held up his hands in a placating gesture.

"Careful now, Kirby. I don't mean no harm."

"You left me there. You left me with *him!*"

"*Who*, Kirby? I don't know who you're talking about."

"You called me *Little Birdie* and you *took me to him!*"

"Whoa, now, Kirby. Ain't no one—"

Kirby saw it before it happened—he saw Drake's head swelling, his skull filling with blood and expanding to an impossible size, and then *POP!* Drake's head exploded on his neck. The man's legs folded and the headless body collapsed.

Sadie screamed from the home they had shared. William Tate—*Everybody calls me Tater*—vomited into his freshly watered front lawn. Someone a few houses down shrieked. Up and down the block, people were hollering and squealing and coming out to see the mess Drake had made.

"My God, Kirby," Father George said from where he stood on the curb at Kirby's side. "My heavens, what have you done?"

"I didn't—I didn't *do* anything. How could I do that? It's not—it's not possible."

Father George held out his hands in a defensive pose and backed away from Kirby, into the grass of Kirby's front yard.

"I didn't do anything!" Kirby cried. Hot tears rolled down his cheeks. "I didn't do anything to anyone!"

A hiss and a thud and something jutted from Kirby's neck. He tried to look down to see what it was, but he was already dizzy.

*What a pretty feather.*

*Pretty feather?*

*Red and green and blue and gold.*

*Pretty, pretty feather, fly away.*

*Fly away.*

*Gone.*

Kirby collapsed in the middle of the street…

\*\*\*

"And what happened then?" Beulah Blackwood asked from where she stood on the other side of the bars.

"What?" Kirby asked, confused.

"What happened next? When you woke up again?"

"When? I" —Kirby glanced around— "I don't understand."

"You were just telling me about how you collapsed in the street. What happened next?"

"I don't know. I have no idea what you're talking about."

"Kirby, you *just* told me how you woke up and walked outside and exploded someone's head. You *just* told me that."

"No I didn't. Where am I? Why am I in jail?"

"Oh, good God, this ain't funny, kid."

"I'm not kidding."

"Kirby, I—"

"Where's my mother? I want to see my mother."

"Quit playin with me, Kirby."

"I want my mother." He grabbed the bars and pushed his face between them. "I want—to see—my mother!"

"Harold!" Beulah Blackwood hollered as she backed away from Kirby's face where it poked through the bars of his cell. "Harold, you might wanna come in here!"

Feeling no resistance at all, Kirby kept pushing and pushed right on through to the other side of the bars. Just like that. One moment he was in the cell, and the next, he was standing in the hallway, inches from where Beulah Blackwood cowered against the wall in front of him.

He looked down at himself, his intact self, and smiled.

"Well, now, isn't that just wonderful."

He looked back to Beulah.

"I wonder what else I could do, if I put my mind to it?"

"Harold!" Beulah screamed. "Harold, get in here now!"

A crack of lightning and Kirby was sitting back on the cot, in his cell, behind bars. He shook his head, as if to clear it, and looked back to where he had been, a second prior, on the outside of this prison.

He half expected to see Beulah Blackwood standing at the bars as if nothing had occurred between them. But, instead of that, she cowered against the wall, hands up to her face, trembling like a popcorn kernel in hot oil.

"Beulah?" Kirby's mind stroked lazily across a sea of confusion.

Beulah slowly lowered her hands and gazed with shock and terror at the boy inside the cell.

"How?" was all she asked.

"I—I don't know."

"I'm going to get Harold. The sheriff. I'm going to get the sheriff. You—you wait here."

He might've said, *where else would I go?* but thought better of it. Somehow he knew he wasn't imprisoned behind these bars, but how he could escape was beyond him.

Had he really traveled outside of the bars to terrorize Beulah? Sure as hell seemed like it. Look at how scared she'd been, how surprised she had been to drop her hands and see him, once again, out of reach, inside this cage.

Beulah scurried from sight. A second later he heard the door open and close at the end of the hallway. She was gone. For now.

A voice whispered inside his head, words so removed from this plain of existence they seemed another language altogether.

*I wish to speak to you.*

"Who is this?" Kirby asked an empty cell.

# 10. One Man's Religion is Another Man's Superstition

It was a quarter to three by the time Wesley Haversham found Pete Blackwood's house. Luckily, the clerk at the 76 station knew who Beulah Blackwood was and where she lived (very few people in Bay's End didn't know who Beulah Blackwood was, her being one of the oldest Enders still living in the End), or else Wesley might've spent the day reading mailboxes.

Wesley knocked on the door to the third house down on the right—if you enter Lime Street from Hibiscus, that is—and waited for someone to answer the door. Heavy footfalls on hardwood floors preceded Pete opening the front door.

"Oh. It's you." Pete didn't seem upset to see Wesley. Just indifferent.

"Hi. Look, I wanna apologize, in person, for upsettin you. It wasn't a nice thing to do, I reckon, shovin my religion down your throat like I done. I talked to Pop, and he gave things prospectin."

"*Prospectin?*" Pete frowned. "Oh! You mean *perspective*."

"Yeah. That word. Anyway, if'n you ever wanna come by the farm and play, or just talk, it's fine by me. I mean that. Pop didn't make me come, or nothin. He just put things into... into..."

"Perspective." Pete smiled.

Wesley smiled in return.

"You want to come in and read comics?"

"Sure."

Pete stepped aside to allow Wesley entrance and Wesley moved through the foyer and into the living room.

Wesley said, "Place smells like moth balls."

"That'd be Mama. She stinks because she's old. Ever realize how odd old people smell for no reason at all?"

"Always. Even Pop is startin to smell somethin strange. Like he bathes himself in dust, or somethin."

"Exactly. That's what it smells like. Like an old shut-up house. Dusty-like. Makes my nose itch. But I try not to sneeze around Mama because then she'll think I'm sick and I'll never get to leave the house. I already don't get to leave much."

Wesley surveyed the house some more, not really paying Pete much attention; just enough to answer his friend's questions when they came. Wesley had never been inside Beulah Blackwood's house, nor anyone else's house in the End. Like Pete, he didn't get out much. He went to school and came home and did his chores and homework and went to bed. Then he got up the next day and did it all over again.

Wesley never had any downtime with which to consider how uneventful his life was. Maybe *uneventful* wasn't even the right word. Perhaps *monotonous* fit better. But *monotonous* wasn't a word Wesley Haversham was aware of. He'd go to his grave not knowing plenty of interesting words that he might have used to help people understand more clearly what he was attempting to say, because farming didn't take much more education than math skills and hard labor, and a farmer could go through life just fine, thank you very much, without a lick of English training beyond the basic skills of reading: knowing what sounds letters made; context clues for words that didn't sound like themselves, like *through* and *cough* and *though*; and sight words like *the* and *and*. Wesley would never be a reader, no matter how much influence his buddy Pete had on him, and Wesley was okay with that. The world needed laborers just as much as they needed thinkers, and he was perfectly fine with working until his back ached and his heart raced and the want of a cold beer or six to get to sleep at night grew from a want to a feverish need. Such a life had treated Pop well, and it was Wesley's opinion that Pop would make a swell role model for any kid.

"You coming?" Pete asked from the hallway.

"Oh. Yeah. Right. Coming." Wesley followed his friend down the short hall and into a room with white anchors on blue wallpaper. "Um, nice room."

"Don't laugh. Please don't laugh."

Wesley laughed. After all, what are friends for?

Pete sighed, and then he laughed too, because he had to admit, the room was a funny place for an eleven-year-old to sleep.

Pete said, "She had the wallpaper put up just for me, too, which makes it even worse."

"You mean, she meant to do this?"

"Oh yeah. She was proud of it, too." Pete did his best impersonation of an old lady, but ended up sounding like a wicked witch. "*I put this wallpaper up just for you, Sweetums! Isn't it lovely?*"

"Stop!" Wesley cried gleefully. "I'm gonna pee myself."

"Bathroom's across the hall," Pete said in between laughs.

Wesley rushed out of Pete's room and into the bathroom, where he peed forcibly in the toilet. He'd left the door open because he was used to living with his father and rarely had to use the toilets at school. As he was zipping up, he glanced out of the bathroom and into Pete's room to find Pete staring at him.

Down there.

Wesley didn't feel ashamed, or even disgusted. Truth be told, he was curious about such things, too. Was his penis like other guys' penises? Was his big or small or average? Did other guys' penises look like anteaters?

Pete saw Wesley had caught him staring and adverted his gaze. Wesley shook off and zipped up and not another word was said about the matter.

Wesley said, "So, you wanna tell me what you were gonna tell me before I cut you off?"

Pete dropped down onto the edge of the bed. "About what?"

"About what happened to the Bay's."

"Oh. That. Yeah, sure."

Over the course of the next half hour, Pete relayed the tale his mother had told him, a tale his grandmother—Beulah—had told her, piece by piece, bit by bit, in its entirety. When Pete was done, Wesley whistled a long, tonally challenged toot.

"I heard a bit differently, that Bay chopped up some guys with an axe before they threw him on the pile, but other than that the rest of the story is the same as what I heard. That must've been terrible, burning up like that."

"See why I don't go for religion?"

"Naw, I don't. Weren't like God did those things. Men are evil. We're sinful beings, and whatnot, and only through his love and light can we seek to be good enough for Heaven."

Pete said, "You really believe in all that? That there's some magic place where everything is perfect?" There was no derision in his voice. The question seemed honest and posed with no malicious intent intended.

"Yeah, I do. I mean, it's a nice thought, even if I didn't believe. What's wrong with a little faith? A li'l faith never hurt nobody."

"I think the Bays might disagree."

"See, there you go again. People did that, Pete. Not God. The will o' man is his business and his alone. Ain't nothin God can do about what we do, 'side from punish us after we die by sending us to Hell."

"But what if you're wrong? You waste your life following this belief and having all this faith, and then come to find out it was all a lie and there isn't a Heaven. What then?"

"Guess it don't matter. I'll be gone, I s'pose. If what you say is true, and we just die and that's it, then I don't see a problem in believing in God while I'm alive."

"But you'd have wasted your whole life on something that's not real."

"Me and you got different ideas of what's waste and what's not. I don't see any problem with serving God and being the best person I can be and spending a few hours in church every week. Because it's not about what if I'm wrong. It about what if I'm right. You wanna chance Hell? I sure as certain don't."

Pete seemed to think about this.

Wesley added, "Besides, I don't think there's gonna be church for a good long while, not with what done happened to Father George and his family. I think the town's gonna be mighty upset for a while."

"Yeah," Pete agreed.

"That does bother me a good bit. I can say that without lyin none. He was supposed to be a man of God, but what he done to himself weren't godly at all. Suicide is against the pact God made with man, or so's I've been told. I really think Father George is in Hell."

"You ever wonder if there's, I don't know, something else other than Heaven and Hell? You ever wonder if some other religion got it right and not yours? Stuff like that is what gets me. There are so many possibilities, even ones we haven't considered, ones we might never come to our attention. For instance," Pete shifted his weight on the bed to face Wesley better, "what if there's something else, but it's not God or Satan or whatever. What if it's something our minds can't even understand? I read this book my father had, by this guy named Lovecraft, and Lovecraft wrote that there might be something bigger than our minds out there. Something bigger than our comprehension. How do you think we'd handle that?"

Wesley shrugged. "I don't rightly know. I only know what I believe, and I believe there's nothing bigger or scarier than God."

"You think God's scary?" Pete looked perplexed.

"Not in any dangerous way. Well, maybe. But not in a way that I need to worry about. It's like he's a parent. You can go against your mom and pop, but do you really wanna find out how mad they can get? With God, though, you don't have to worry about a spanking, you gotta worry about eternal damnation. So it's that kind of fear."

"Okay. I can see that." Pete paused and added. "I like talking to you, Wes."

"Thanks. I like talking to you, too. You don't talk like no kid I ever met. I like that."

Pete grinned. "Thanks."

"You're welcome. So now whataya wanna do?"

"Comics?"

Wesley shrugged. "Sure."

\*\*\*

Gertrude Fulgore bounced around in the passenger seat of their beat-up pickup truck as her son, Jerimiah, took the rutted country roads seemingly without a care in the world.

"Slow down," she requested without a shred of authority in her voice.

"Yes, ma'am." Jerimiah applied the brakes.

"Take the next left."

"Yes, ma'am."

"Here, 'tween them trees."

Jerimiah aimed the rusty pickup at a section of woods that was little more than cleared of trees. Detritus littered the forest floor here, where no dirt road existed. In the wake of the truck, piles of dead leaves exploded; shot off in all directions like grenade shrapnel. They were traveling long-untraveled territory. Gertrude could smell the fear coming off Jerimiah, a smell more powerful than even his rotting flesh.

The boy was, at this point, held together by little more than prayer. How he'd survived this long with the blood curse was anyone's guess. She certainly had no idea how he'd lasted so long. Same as she had no idea why she'd been spared these last five decades. She should've been dead long ago. Like her little brother had died on Francis Bay's couch.

The woods peeled away and Waverly Chasm crept toward them. A small oval of clearing sat at the lip of the chasm where the State Men started their tours for foolish travelers. Those who went in rarely came out, and those who never exited were soon forgotten, as if they'd never existed in the first place. The magic of this place lay in the memories of those it swallowed. All of creation worked this way, but Gertrude was only one of a handful of living persons who knew this simple truth.

Jerimiah pulled up to the lip of the chasm and thrust the gear selector into park. He reached for the door handle. Gertrude lay an unsteady and liver-spotted hand on his shoulder.

"No. I go alone this time."

"You sure?" her son asked. His decaying nose twitched. She saw red in there.

"I am. Stay in the truck. Do not get out. No matter what you hear. If this is how the Lord wishes I should go, then this is how I shall go."

"Yes, ma'am."

Gertrude said a silent prayer, pulled the handle, and stepped from the truck. Gravel crunched underfoot as she rounded the bed of the truck and headed for the natural stairs that served as an ingress to the touring trail. She pulled her knitted shawl close about her, for there lay a chill in her bones that could not be entirely blamed on autumnal climes, or the whispered breath of the surrounding forest.

She descended.

Long ago, when the state's parks and recreation department bought this property from the city of Bay's End, there had been a guy wire installed: a 200 foot long length of steel cable strung through eyelets at the end of iron spikes set deep into the rock of the trail. Her fingers glided effortlessly along the chilled metal like fingertips on a lover's skin.

The trail curved to the right, around an outcropping of rock. Gertrude Fulgore followed the stony path past the bend and out of our reality.

Her ears popped, painfully, and her head swam. She smelled ozone and something akin to the carrion reek of the long-dead.

She pressed onward, seeking answers.

\*\*\*

Beulah Blackwood found Sheriff Harold Carringer posted up against the outer wall of the sheriff's office, next to the entrance, smoking an unfiltered cigarette.

"Where the hell *were* you?" the old woman growled.

"I needed a smoke." Hap flicked ash and refused to meet Beulah's glare.

"I could've been killed in there." She willed herself to remain calm. She was a seventy-year-old woman. If she had a heart attack, who would take care of Pete? She took a deep breath to calm her pounding chest.

Harold said, "He's locked up, Beulah, what more do you want me to do with him?"

"There's...there's something not right about him."

"Yeah? No shit." Harold finally looked at her. "Again, what more do you want me to do with him? He's locked up. He's not going anywhere."

"You sure about that?"

"What do you mean?" Hap said. Did his eyes belie knowledge beyond what he would admit to? Beulah thought so. No use in fighting a man. They were all unbearably stubborn.

She shook her head in exasperation.

"You're useless."

"Now you listen here." Harold jabbed at her with the two fingers holding his cigarette. "I got a woman missing a head, an arm missing a body, a dead pastor, and a nutty old woman to contend with. I'm halfway to being fed up with all this weird shit, so just back off me. I come out here to think, so lemme think, goddamn it."

"I think the boy has—" Beulah struggled with how she wanted to say what she'd seen, or thought she had seen, moments prior in the cellblock. "I think he's got the Devil in him."

"Fuck off," Hap laughed impatiently. "I ain't got time for your supernatural mumbo jumbo, Beulah."

"There are powers in this world that you don't understand. God and Satan are at constant war for our—"

"Stop it. You just stop it right there. Ain't no gods or devils influencing that boy. He's unstable and dangerous, yes. But there ain't nothin supernatural at work here."

"What about your deputy? Think something human did that?"

"I seen a lot of accidents and murders in my day, both in this town and outside of it, and I know it don't take spooks and specters to kill nobody. Ever seen the aftermath of a really bad car accident? That shit can look like someone stuck a whole pig in a blender and set that sumbitch on high. Ain't nothin supernatural about that. Nothin *paranormal*. Ain't no *devil* in death. Just blood and bone and meat."

"That in there ain't no car accident, neither."

"The devil—ain't—real."

Anger rippled through her. "I ain't gonna stand around here and listen to you dig yourself to Hell Eternal. You gonna repent before this is over. Believe me you."

"Go on somewhere, Beulah." Hap pulled at his cigarette and loosed a cloud of bluish smoke.

"You mark my words, sheriff. You just mark 'em."

She turned to leave.

Hap said, "What did he say to you?"

She whipped back around.

"What do you care? You ain't gonna do nothin about it, and I ain't got the mind to tell you."

Harold shrugged, the smug bastard.

"We can work together, Beulah, or you can keep ranting and raving about devils. Which is it gonna be?"

Beulah saw for the first time what lay behind the sheriff's nonplussed eyes.

"You're scared," she said.

Hap crossed the short distance between them in two quick strides. Nose to nose with her, he growled, "I ain't scared of nothin. Simple fact of the matter is, I have several murders and a suicide to deal with and not a single fuckin lead. If you know

267

something, you damn well better tell me before you leave, or else I'll lock you up right next to that crazy motherfucker in there."

"He come out the bars at me." Beulah spat the sentence out in one burst of breath, fear wafting from her as only true terror can. "He come *through* the bars at me."

"He's out? Christ's sake, Beulah!" Harold rounded her and made for the door to the sheriff's office. She grabbed him by the bicep and tugged. She wasn't anywhere near strong enough to stop him, but he stopped anyway, of his own accord.

"He ain't out. Not anymore. He—he went back in, is the best way I can explain it."

Hap scratched at his neck. "How'd he get out in the first place?"

That he didn't immediately discount her testimony was telling.

Beulah squinted at him. "You know something."

"The hell you preach. I don't know the first thing about what's going on. All's I know is that some weird shit is happening and I need some answers. So, you tell me, what—did—he—say?"

Beulah sighed. "He—he told me a story. One you ain't likely to believe. One that, if I'm honest, I don't rightly believe. But then he done that thing, walking through the bars, like he done, and I'm starting to believe him. You say his momma's head was missing, right?"

Harold nodded.

"Well, he told me he done something like that once before, to some Negro that worked at a hospital he was taken to."

"Where?"

"I don't know, but that's where he's been for the past couple months. His mother sent him out there for—for having impure thoughts."

Harold shook his head. "I don't wanna hear about that unless it's got something to do with all this that's going on right now. Does it?"

"Not really. That's just why she sent him out there." Beulah took a deep breath. This next part was going to be hard to say. It tested her very mettle. "He did say that he and Father George were lovers."

"For Christ's sake, I told you I didn't want to hear any of that nonsense." Harold spat brown phlegm onto the concrete. "It does make a kind of sense, though. Father George didn't kill himself for no reason. I kinda figured he was cheatin on Molly. Just didn't think it was—well, you know."

Beulah nodded. "You say you don't want to believe in gods and devils and their influence on this world? Well, Harold Carringer, I don't believe Father George was that kind of man. Just can't picture it, nor do I want to. But I do know that professed men of God can do evil. I seen it with my own eyes. So, as much as I don't wanna admit that Father George was some kind of pre-vert,"—just like that, *pre*-vert—"I'm gonna go along with what the boy said, because I want you to also consider the very real possibility that what's happening here is the doings of something unnatural."

"Easier said than done, Beulah. Me believing in your hoodoo with a snap o' my fingers would be like getting you to believe that your Bible book is only stories written by drunks and madmen."

"Please don't mock my faith, Harold."

Harold eyed her strangely and tongued the inside of one cheek. She thought this meant he was thinking.

"Okay. Let's say that that boy in there's got something freaky going on with him. Say he's possessed, or some shit. What do we do?"

"I only know one course of action in a situation like this."

"And that would be?"

"We pray."

Harold laughed in her face.

"I *asked* you not to mock me."

"I'm sorry, Beulah, but I need some other course of action. Somethin that's gonna get me results *right now*. I ain't never seen no one pray and get blessed that instant. Neither have you. Be honest."

"God's will takes time, yes. But do you have a better idea?"

"You say you only have one course of action. Well, so do I."

Hap lay a hand on the overlarge handgun at his hip.

"You can't just kill the boy. He's a pawn here, Harold, not the perpetrator."

"And how do you know that?"

"Because that's not how the Devil works. He doesn't have any power here, so He uses people."

"Why? You explain that to me. You tell me why your devil man can't just pop his fork-tailed ass out the ground and suck us all down to Hell. Go on. I'm listening."

"Because God gave us freewill, and Satan has no dominion over that. Satan cannot make us do evil, just as God cannot force us to be good. Sweet gospel, Harold, ain't you ever read the Bible?"

The sheriff smiled. "That's like me asking you if you've ever taken a dick in the ass, Beulah."

Her gorge rose.

"You *filthy*, *foul* little man."

Harold chuckled. "Ain't nothin little about me, Beulah. But cool your engine. I said what I said just now to give you context—all right? You ain't never done anything uncouth and I ain't never read your storybook. We understand each other."

"Heavenly days," she said with a great expulsion of breath. "I suppose so. But please refrain from that godawful speak of yours. Have a little respect. If God's going to help us out with this, he ain't gonna wanna hear your mouth."

"Deal. Now, shall we go question Mr. Johnson?"

"Thought you wanted to kill him?" said Beulah.

"Why you assume such things about me, Beulah? Deep down, I'm a decent human being, I assure you."

*I doubt that*, Beulah Blackwood thought but did not say.

\*\*\*

Gertrude Fulgore couldn't have said how it happened. Only that it did happen.

One moment she was walking along Waverly Chasm's rocky trail, and the next she stood before a fire, warming her hands. She looked up, expecting a mantelpiece and found a man's head mounted on the wall above the fireplace as if it were a ten-point buck. She screamed and reeled but moving was like struggling in molasses. Her arms wind-milled in slow, fluid motions. Her mouth creaked open to birth a scream that blasted from her not in a high-pitched shriek but in the *sotto voce* of a muted bassoon. Twirling like a ballerina in quicksand, Gertrude kicked out a leg, prepared to run, and was frozen solid in mid-pirouette.

From where she'd stalled she could see a claw-footed couch, not unlike the one her brother had died on. But this wasn't Francis Bay's house. Whose house it was, she didn't know. She was only certain that it was not Bay's.

She could also see an archway that led to what looked to be a foyer and front door. Lush Persian rugs dotted the hardwood in the room where she currently stood frozen, but the foyer and hall were carpeted. Somehow she knew that if she could see around the corner there would be an elegant staircase leading up to a second floor.

Something breathed just out of sight. Something massive. Something that smelled of death. The metallic taste of adrenaline flooded her mouth.

"What do you want?" asked the small voice of a child. To say the least, she had not expected such a timid voice to come from the direction of the feral breathing.

She couldn't talk. Her jaw and throat simply wouldn't follow her directions. So she thought and was heard.

*Where am I?*

"I asked you what you want."

*I'm seeking the Bastard*

"Do you have any idea how poor of a decision that is?"

*I am in need of truth.*

"The Bastard is a liar. *I* am truth. Ask what you will of me."

*Who are you?*

"I am time eternal. I am Joy, for I did swallow Her. I am the Lord. I am the Creator."

*You're... God?*

"I am the closest you're gonna get, Gerty."

*Let me see you*, she demanded.

"You're in no position to be demanding anything."

*My God is merciful.*

"Your God is dead. I ate her."

*Blasphemy.*

"Reality. Now ask your questions before I eat you too."

*I wish to speak with Father George.*

"He cannot come to the phone right now. Please leave a message after the beep. Beeeep."

*What are these riddles?*

"Gerty, I suggest you ask your questions before you upset me. I have all of eternity to look forward to, and this is not how I want to spend it. Ya dig?"

*I wish—to speak—with—Father—George.*

"My, my, aren't we in a pissy mood? Fine. But I must warn you. You're not going to be talking to him. Not in the way you think. He's nothing more than your memory of him. While I don't expect someone as small-minded as yourself to understand what I mean, you should know that he'll only be able to speak to you in loops of pre-expressed patterns. Basically, Gerty, you're talking to a recording."

*What's this recording?*

"It's what you're about to speak to. Have fun. Holler if you need me."

Whatever held her in stasis, floating in the middle of this strange house, released her, and she collapsed to the floor. When she raised her head, she was back on the rocky trail of Waverly

Chasm. There was no need to stand up. She was already standing. Confused, she turned in a full circle and came face to face with Father George.

He wore his Sunday best: the clerical collar, the pressed black shirt, creased pants, shoes polished so they shone like lava rock. His famous smile sat on his face, and he looked honestly happy to see her.

"Hello, Gertrude. Lovely to see you today."

"Father George. Oh, my Lord, I knew you weren't dead. I just knew it!"

She rushed the man and walked right through him. She tripped and went down to her knees, skinning them through the fabric of her skirt. Growling in the face of the pain, she used the rock wall to brace herself so she could stand once more. When she was up, she did a one-eighty.

Father George stood several feet away, his hand extended as if awaiting her own.

"Glad to see you at services this morning, Gertrude. I have been blessed with a wonderful sermon."

"Father George?"

Father George beamed. "Why, yes, ma'am, I do know how good God is."

"Father?"

"I'm sorry to hear that, Gertrude. I wish him a speedy recovery."

"What are you talking about? Why won't you talk to me?" she begged.

"All things in the Lord's time, Gertrude."

Had she heard all this before? Hadn't he said these things to her, once upon a time? She thought he had. What was it the child, the one that claimed to be the Creator, had said back at the house?

*Basically, Gerty, you're talking to a recording...*

Gertrude thought that maybe a recording was a repeating of a kind. She also thought that this wasn't Father George at all. This was dark magick, the kind devils used. Perhaps not devils. Just one. Singular. *The* Devil.

"You ain't Father George."

"Oh, Gertrude, don't cry. I'm sure he'll be fine."

"You're false!" she hollered, spittle flying. "You're not Father George. I want to talk to Father George."

In a blink, Father George was replaced with a small boy, maybe ten years old, with an eyepatch over one eye. The boy's good eye twinkled redly before becoming blue.

"I told you he was only a memory, Gerty. And a memory is the best I can do."

"Lies! You speak lies!" she screamed at him, her old vocal cords mangling her words, her voice cracking under the pressure of her anger.

The boy child sighed. "Gerty, I wish I could make you understand. This isn't pleasant for me. I don't want to be here, with you, right now. I would much rather be off in France, or Istanbul, of even Toyland. Anywhere but here."

"Stop speaking in riddles. I demand you speak the truth, in the name of the Lord!"

"In the name of the Lord." The boy exhaled at length. "Listen, Gerty, unless you start paying attention, I'm going to leave you here on this trail to deal with whatever might come along. I've stepped in to help where I've not been invited, and I expect you to have a little respect for my presence. So, if you please, get to the point. What is it you'd like to ask Father George? Even if he can't answer you, I might be able to."

Gertrude eyed the child suspiciously. "Why should I talk to you, devil?"

"Devil? Now that's just rude. I'm the furthest thing from a devil and the closest thing you're going to get to God, at least in this place. But you don't have to believe me and I can't make you believe me, so ask your question or don't. But if you don't, I'm leaving you to the Bastard."

"Yes. Yes, do that. He is who I came to speak with."

"You have no idea what you're asking. I'm *trying* to help you. Don't you get that?"

"I wish to speak to the Bastard!"

"Fine, fine. Make your deal with the real devil. I'm done here. Don't come crawling back to me, begging for forgiveness. I won't hear you. To be clear as glass, all lines will be permanently closed to you. Is that really what you want?"

"Go away!"

"He will do no more for you than I could."

"He will explain to me what he has done with Father George. He will, *in the name of the Lord*, answer for his actions."

"You silly, silly woman. Your will be done."

The boy vanished and reappeared inches in front of her in a flash. He shoved with seemingly little effort, but the connection was more powerful than Gertrude could have ever expected.

Over the guy wire she went, into Waverly Chasm, and beyond.

276

\*\*\*

Janice Larson didn't know where she was going until she got there.

Chastity Baptist Church sat like a symbol of normalcy in a world of chaos and strife. She strode up the stairs and tugged on the front doors. No luck. They were locked. She ran around to the back of the building where she found the rear doors locked as well. Cellar doors, equally secure. As far as she could tell there was no way into the church without breaking and entering.

She grabbed a rock from the curbside and used it to smash one of the windows near the back of the building, out of sight of any passing traffic, or surrounding neighbors' windows.

She used the rock to knock all the shards of glass from the frame that she could, but still managed to scrape up her forearms climbing in. Her legs were protected by her pants, her feet by her shoes, but her hands were a bloody mess by the time she'd gotten inside.

An eerie silence possessed the church. She could feel the quiet like a tangible weight pressing ever downward. Churches and religious symbols freaked her out at the best of times. But to experience this place without another human present was to experience an overwhelming sensation of wrongness. She felt nothing holy here. Only absence. She thought that maybe what made a church a church was not the building but the congregation.

The people.

The humanity.

She'd never been much for religion, although she did believe that there must have been something that created the universe. There was, in her opinion, absolutely no way for all of this to have been created by accident. But could any one religion have gotten the origins of everything correct? She didn't think so. So she remained agnostic, amen.

She approached the two stairs that led up to the stage. She climbed the steps and moved behind the pulpit, looked out over everything—a shepherd assessing her flock.

Why was she here? The answer to that question seemed obvious and elusive at the same time. She was here because she had nowhere else to go. But she also didn't fully understand why she didn't feel at home in her own house.

The baby.

The baby crying in her room.

A shiver electrified her. She trembled behind the pulpit as if the very ground at her feet were quaking. Blood dripped from her lacerated hands to plop onto the hardwood of the stage.

She could, even now, hear that baby's insistent wail.

Her stomach churned, and she realized with mounting dread that she had to pee. Did she dare hunt out a restroom in this empty building and drop her pants to do her business? Dare she allow such vulnerability?

It was either cop a squat in a creepy church devoid of parishioners, or piss all down her legs.

She chose the restroom option.

Janice found the ladies' room in the foyer with little trouble. Her bloody hands slicked the door knob, but she was finally able to turn it. The door opened with a coffin-like creak. She stepped inside.

The restroom smelled of lemon-scented chemicals. The sinks were on the right wall; the stalls on the left. Off-white tile floors and ugly yellow wallpaper. Gooseflesh rippled up her arms—the skin of a freshly plucked chicken. She ran hot water in the sink and did her best to wash the cuts on her hands. Bladder bursting at the sound of the tap, she entered the first of the two stalls. It was cold beyond belief inside. Teeth chattering, she tried the second one, as if she expected it to be warmer. Surprise, surprise—it wasn't.

Not able to hold her water another second, she thumbed down her pants and dropped onto the frigid toilet seat. The sounds of her stream and spatter echoed dully in the small space. She expected at any moment for the ladies' room door to creak open. To hear a baby's mournful cry, the crackling wail of an infant in need.

No such thing happened.

Instead, she heard a voice, soft and sibilant:

"*I wish to speak to you.*"

"Hello?" she asked and felt her IQ drop. She was so stupid. Why had she done such a thing?

The voice did not, however, respond.

Janice bent forward, squeezing the last of the urine from her bladder. In her haste to be fully-clothed again, she forgot to wipe. Up went her pants. Open came the door. Out of the stall she dashed.

She tripped over something and went sprawling. Her blood-wet palms slid across smooth tile. She crashed nose first into the floor. Something crunched. Pain exploded behind her eyes and radiated out, across her cheeks and into her temples. She clutched at her face and flopped like a fish in agony. The pressure and pounding in her head was unlike anything she'd ever known. Blood trickled into the back of her throat and she gagged, spewing half-digested egg and rancid milk onto the tile.

Something heavy and soft climbed onto the back of her leg. She kicked, but whatever was back there clung tightly to her calf. Sharp spikes dug into the skin of her calf and ankles, several on each side of her right leg. She rolled onto her back and repeatedly slammed her leg onto the floor of the restroom.

Her vision blurred. She tried to sit up, to reach for the thing clinging to the back of her leg, but she didn't have the strength. The pounding pain, the blood cascading from her nose, the sheer terror of the situation, was all too much to bear. All she wanted to do was give up and give in. It felt so right, to just let go. To stop fighting.

To succumb.

Something scurried up the back of her thigh, lifting her slightly as it moved between body and floor, and tore into the ass of her jeans. The seat of the denim split and something icy pressed itself against her crotch. The lips of her vagina parted.

Something entered her.

Janice Larson loosed a scream of anguish and violation.

She would not die this way.

Her bloody hands shot to her crotch, where she ripped the slimy thing from where it had bedded itself in her womanhood. She yanked the ghastly, bloodied thing into view.

It was a child. A baby. Nothing more. Nothing less. A boy child, at that. The pudgy baby boy squinted, as if he were a puppy whose eyes had yet to open.

She held the infant under the arms and looked him over. The situation was odd yet familiar. A heaviness settled on her—a tremendous, crushing sorrow.

"Who are you?" she asked the infant.

He did not answer.

The pain in her nose was gone and her fear had retreated. Faced with this beautiful child, Janice Larson felt only joy flow through her; a sense of completion.

She brought the boy to her chest and caressed the back of his gory head.

"Shhh," she hissed. "There, there. Mommy's here. Mommy's got you."

Her ears popped.

And then she was alone, laying on the bathroom floor in a puddle of her own blood and vomit, hugging herself.

Such a loss she had never known.

# 11. The Importance of Being Gertrude

The Fulgores came to America somewhere halfway between the nineteenth and twentieth centuries. But, like their children's birthdays—Gertrude Fulgore's included—dates were of no importance to the clan. Only survival was.

Rome had been a hellscape for the Fulgores, and while America during the Civil War was no paradise, it was, for the family, far safer environs, for the Fulgores had a religion that the Catholic Church did not abide. A religion whose focal point was emotions instead of gods; or, more accurately, where emotion was god. Where the Catholics feared and mourned their god, the Fulgores worshipped Joy and Sorrow. Their god was the Bastard, the first fatherless deity to exist in the Void, amen.

In Rome, they were persecuted. In America, they could believe what they wanted without risk of punishment. Or so they were led to believe.

Yet, as time passed, so did the devout nature of their beliefs. The former generation failed to instill in the next generation a proper respect for the Bastard. Now that they were knee-deep in the American dream, now that anything was possible, emotions were of a lesser consequence; nothing but feelings that got in the way of rational decisions. Love and Hatred, the basest human emotions, became fleeting. Affections devolved into meaningless utterances of "I love you." Anger lacked passion. Regret meant nothing if "I'm sorry" was not accompanied by sincerity.

Then Mother and Father Fulgore passed on, and their daughter Harmony married a man of Christian faith named Martin Grissom. Overnight, the Bastard's religion was forgotten, and Harmony Grissom accepted Jesus Christ as her Lord and Savior.

Gertrude Grissom was born at home, in the middle of the night, after a rough labor of five and a half hours. She fought her way out of her mother like a demon digging itself from Hell, and for this reason alone, Harmony would show Gertrude less love and affection than she did her son Clark.

When Clark became ill with what would be referred to by the Grissoms as the Blood Curse little Gerty was all but forgotten. Gerty washed and cleaned the house, and did the laundry in the creek that ran alongside the property, all while her mother Harmony comforted the sickly Clark. It didn't matter that Gerty had, like Clark, begun showing signs of rot. Even so, Gerty took the burden of her raising upon her own shoulders.

It was on one of the days she spent washing at the creek that she met the thing in the woods. It came to her like Gethsemane would one day come to Wesley Haversham—creeping from the trees to ruin everything.

She had knelt beside the creek, was rubbing a bar of lye soap up and down one of her father's shirts, which was draped over the rutted washboard, when something caught her attention out of the corner of her eye.

She looked up.

A fog boiled from the tree line, and in that fog stood a figure of shadow. A single red eye twinkled in the center of the humanoid-shape's forehead.

The day had been bright and warm, but now it seemed as if the sun had retreated behind cloud cover. The temperature dipped twenty degrees. The little girl hugged herself and rubbed at her arms.

"Hello?" she said to the man made of midnight. She asked in her uneducated vernacular, "Who you?"

"Gerty, child, how nice to meet you," said the Midnight Man. "How are you this morning?"

"I'm fine," she murmured.

"That's good, that's good. Doing some wash, I see."

She nodded.

She felt so tiny in his presence. Even smaller than her three-and-a-half feet. And was the Midnight Man growing? She thought that he was. Or perhaps he was just coming closer. No. The tree line was approaching. Or she was approaching the tree line. She didn't know what from where anymore. She simply went along with wherever her body seemed intent on taking her.

"Come, child, I've got something to show you," whispered the Midnight Man in a voice no louder than little Gerty's own thoughts. Little Gerty Grissom fell in behind the shadowy figure and followed wherever he led.

She cleaved swirling fog as she moved through a now-dark wood. The sun vanished completely, and a bone-deep cold settled within, yet she was not uncomfortable. In fact, the more her young brain processed the feeling, the more it felt like a lack of heat than any coldness she'd experienced. This temperature simply felt right, as if this were the climate in which she'd been meant to exist all her life.

"Where goin?" she asked the Midnight Man. She couldn't so much see him as she could feel his presence moving through the dark and fog. He slid along, like butter in a warm tilted skillet.

"Oh, some place. Keep up, though. Don't dilly-dally."

"Okay," she said in a tiny dreamlike voice.

The trees thinned and the Midnight Man drifted into the center of a clearing. All this time she thought he'd been facing away, but it seemed his red eye had never left her, for the shadow did not turn. He only glared.

"Who you?" she asked again, because it felt to her like the right thing to say, when in all actuality, it was more like she'd been meant to ask. Everything, for all of time, seemed to have led up to this one moment, and little Gerty Grissom was only playing a role she'd been destined to play from birth.

"Once upon a time, Gerty, there was nothing. In that nothing, a shape was born. I am that shape."

"You God?"

"In a way."

"You devils?"

"You could say that."

Gerty chewed at her thumb. "Why for I'm here?"

"Because you must see. For the purposes of what happens next, I need you to understand that you are no longer outside looking in, but inside looking out."

"Out what?"

"Time immemorial."

"Im-em-who?"

"No matter, child. Listen—" The Midnight Man drifted closer. "I am the Bastard. I am the first of my kind, the first of the fatherless. I am thought. I am memory."

"Mem-wee?"

The Bastard's eye flashed and Gerty pictured in her mind a scene of pain and blood, of suffering and wailing, and saw herself come into this world. She was spat red and slick from her mother like a discarded thing, and for a moment, loneliness polluted the child. Sickness churned in her guts, and she thought she might vomit.

"No worries, child, you cannot be sick here because you are not here. Your body, I mean. Do you see?"

"I'm in my head."

"Yes. Exactly. Such a bright girl you are."

Gerty—or perhaps only the thought of Gerty—smiled.

The Bastard continued, "I was born of Man like you were born of your mother but I did not exit any body. I still reside in one, and always will, for my creator—*the* Creator—is eternal. Do you know what that means, Gerty, my dear?"

"You dunt die?"

"Again, you are right. Good, good. I see church has taught you just enough. Glory be to God." Although she couldn't see any features on that midnight face, she did, however, feel the Bastard smile. "Now, come. I've something to show you beyond even this place."

The shadow of a man reached out to her, and the effect was such that the darkness held shape beyond the second dimension. The oddity of a three-dimensional shadow intrigued Gerty. There was something not right about darkness with substance.

She reached out to touch it and found her own arm gone, replaced by an appendage made of shadow. No fear cycled through her. Nor a moment of hesitation. Her shadow-hand grabbed the Bastard's own.

When they connected, Gertrude Grissom felt whole, complete, sated and fulfilled. She grew in that moment, from child to woman, surpassing the anti-knowledge of childhood and stepping wholly into adulthood. The shock to her system was such that her mind compressed the information and tucked it into a space no bigger than the memory of her birth, a memory so painful and traumatic that most people, as a defense mechanism, forget it entirely.

And as with birth did her advancement into maturity shove her into light; a light brilliant and spectral and white against the background of the Void. A presence of light that defeated all shadow, even the Bastard, and Gertrude Grissom stood alone in a desolate land of gray withered trees and blood-red sky. Ash, thick as snow covered the earth. Her shadow legs left twin trails through the fallen soot as a cartoon rabbit might through snow.

A disembodied voice came from all around her.

"I am not welcome here, child. This is your place, and yours alone. You should know it and cherish it and maintain it beyond your death. This is the Roaming, where you will reside until such a time that the Creator no longer exists. Here, you will keep things of import until such a time as you need them. Here, you will be safe from the world. This is your Heaven, dear one. In the Creator's name, amen."

"So pretty," she said in a small voice.

"I would think so, dear child. After all, you made it."

She walked for a time, through the skeletal trees and drifts of ash, until she came to a house not unlike her own, the one she'd left back in what she thought of as the Real World, for surely this place, wherever and whenever it was, couldn't be reality.

The house in the Roaming was a flatter shade of green than the glossy paint on the outside of her house, the house her grandfather had built. The porch's banisters were a softer white, more of an eggshell than she recalled, and the shutters were brown instead of beige. The front door, which had been swung inward, was the same eggshell as the banister, yet in the Real World it had been solid oak. Grandpa Fulgore's vine-like engravings were present upon the door as well, although they seemed less defined, blurry, as if seen through a fogged lens.

She glided up the stairs and through the door and into a foyer with hardwood floors. The boards were rougher in this version of her house. Jagged splinters jutted, and Gerty was grateful that she was not in her body. Stepping on any of those exposed wooden daggers would be painful beyond belief.

A trilling came from the living room area, where not a spot of furniture sat. She followed the noise into the empty space where so many of her after-dinner memories, those just before bedtime, had been created.

In the Real World there would have been Father's wooden rocking chair and Momma's darning chair and Brother's cot, which had been set up under the only window in the room so the boy could get some sun. The room she shared with her brother had no access to natural light. Not a single window. "*Winders* was *spensive* back then," Father had told her. "And besides, it was a lot of work to add a *winder* to a room. Prolly more work than your grandpappy wanted to do."

Here in the Roaming she found only a small object sitting on the bare floor, in a corner. The black object was a texture and material of which she was unfamiliar. Shiny and hard, the body of the thing reminded her of a beetle. Written on its slanted face were numbers, zero at the bottom, then around in a three-quarter circle to the number nine. The thing, whatever it was, seemed to have ears, and from one of these ears grew a coiled rope of the same shiny black material as the body had.

The ringing was definitely coming from this thing. There wasn't anything else in the room.

The ears lifted from the base and floated up toward her. On the bottom of each ear were dots: a circle of six on one side, and a square of thirty-six on the other. The closer the ears got to her the better she could see that the dots were not dots at all but holes.

And from these holes came a soft male voice.

"Hello?"

"Hello?" she echoed.

"Who may I ask is calling?"

"I'm Gerty."

"Gertrude?" the voice sounded terribly confused. "Gertrude Fulgore?"

"Nossuh. Gerty Grissom."

"Sorry, little girl, but I think you have the wrong number."

"Wrong nummah?"

"Yes. Sorry about that. Maybe you should have your mother help you with your call next time. Have a blessed day."

The man was gone with a click and Gerty, perplexed, floated away from the odd object in the corner. She glided from the sitting room, the man's voice already fading from her memory.

In the kitchen, which was likewise devoid of her home's Real-World furnishings, she found a knife stabbed into the pantry door. Hanging from the knife was a pencil drawing of a cross. Black swirls came off the graphite-colored cross like billowing smoke.

She floated down the hallway and into the room she shared with Clark. The walls here were strange; unlike they were in the Real World. On the walls were paintings of white anchors on a blue background. No, not paintings. Paper. Like canvases. Canvases that covered all four walls. She only knew this because the bare walls underneath were showing through in places. Who draped paper on walls? Such a thing seemed silly to her. Why not just paint over the wood? That seemed much easier and far more permanent than hanging paper.

Back out into the hallway Gerty drifted. She saw her parents' room at the end of the hall, but what was this new door on the left? The door was closed so that she couldn't see in. There was no doorknob, nor did she have hands with which to turn a knob had there been one. But as she glided toward it, the door came open and she was allowed entrance.

She stepped through.

She stood in a green field. Gray tombstones dotted the grass. Here, words written on a grave marker looked familiar. Although she lacked the book-learning to read the words, they came unbidden into her mind.

*Harold Carringer.*

She drifted on, through the gray slabs jutting from the earth, looking upon the face of each tombstone and hearing the names spoken in her mind.

*Eddie Treemont.*

*Lei Duncan.*

*Walter Scott.*

*Brent Cummings.*

These names meant nothing to her, but somewhere in her mind she knew they had been important people. Maybe not good people. But important.

A simple truth flooded her—sometimes, bad people do good things. And, every so often, good people commit atrocities.

A hill rose ahead, as if the very earth was pregnant and close to giving birth. Atop the hill stood a child, a brunette boy with an eye patch. He was dressed like the fancy folk Gerty sometimes saw in church, the people Daddy said were *holier than thou.*

The boy waved at Gerty and vanished—there one moment, gone the next. She climbed the hill, which took not a bit of effort in her ethereal form, and stood at the crest of the hill as the boy had done. She could see everything. All of creation lay before her. Everywhere her gaze fell, people were roaming. One bounced off the other, this place was so crowded. The land curved downward at the horizon, and she couldn't see beyond, but somehow she knew that this sea of humanity continued, around and around, in perpetuity.

She only vaguely noticed that the graveyard with the important people's names written on the stones was gone. Perhaps those people of import were not meant to reside here, in the Roaming. In Heaven.

For that's what this place was to Gerty. Or, should it be said, that is how she perceived it. If Heaven ever did exist, surely it was this feeling of togetherness for all time. This feeling of an eternity spent among those you loved. This feeling that things went on forever. Because the finality of death was terrifying to the most stable mind, and something is always better than nothing.

In the span of ages that lasted mere seconds, Gertrude Grissom came to know the truth of the universe. That mankind was not alone, but no one religion had gotten it right. Heaven was being remembered and coexisting with your fond memories, while Hell was being trapped in the bad ones. These truths came to her through a stream of consciousness. The idea that the afterlife was memory, and that emotions were the true gods, gave Gerty a grasp on reality no other human before her had latched onto.

Church and religion and congregating and tithing and hymnals, none of this was of any importance. The true meaning of life was existence. To exist. And, beyond that, experience was the only religious doctrine one should follow.

But there were those that roamed who did not belong. These souls, these remnants, were dragged along into the Roaming by those who kept fond memories of them. In this way, the Roaming was replete with what some would consider evil. These roaming memories were of a different substance than those who remembered them—misty and intangible, although Gerty would have guessed that everyone here was intangible, even if she didn't know what the word meant. The explanation her mind allowed was this:

Most of the Roaming was populated by a thicker type of people, people with presence, but following those people were thinner souls, for lack of a better word, who expressed no emotion beyond the emotions their carriers recalled.

Here was a beautiful woman in a pretty white dress and veil, dragging behind her a man with an angry expression on his face. The bride could no longer remember what her husband had once looked like when he smiled, long ago before she entered his life and made it a living hell. But she was happy, and therefore welcome in the Roaming. Gerty wished she could look into the other place, whatever it was called, and see how the groom remembered life. Would it only be the beautiful bride? Would the bride still be beautiful? Oh, to know the extremity of the universe and everything that rested on this side of the Void.

Here was a child of no more than three, toddling around, seeking balance, dragging behind him a bloated dog, its corpse infested with flies, foam caked around its mouth, and the name Hagrid sewn into its collar. The dog's death had been a happy occasion for the toddler, for the mangy cur had been nothing but a nuisance: getting into things the boy was then blamed for; chewing and destroying binkies; pooping in the child's bed. Yet when the boy retaliated by twisting the dog's ear or biting a paw, the parents would chastise the child. Why did the doggy get to be mean and bad? Why should the bad doggy get away with being horrible while the boy got punished? Gerty thought back to how Clark was more beloved than she was in her mother's eyes. She thought about how she might end up carrying Clark into the Roaming along with her when she died. She thought it would be best if she stopped being concerned with him and live her own life.

Here was a man who had dragged an entire group of people into the Roaming with him. These sad sorts were all noticeably dead. Each one of them wore clothing with black-and-white stripes. They were, all of them, skinny beyond belief. The man wore a uniform with a symbol on one arm, a great many angles, like conjoined capital Ls, which in turn created a circle of a fashion. The terrible thoughts roaming this man's mind were disgusting to Gerty, but she found the dichotomy of his existence here cause for concern. He was obviously an evil man who had done terrible things in his life, but these terrible things of which he was guilty had brought him great joy, and that joy had led him here, to the Roaming, where he could frolic to his heart's content. Again Gerty wondered what the other side would look like, if there wasn't a part of this uniformed devil who resided there, as well. Surely someone kept memories of his crimes close to their heart. But why should that damn them while he experienced joy everlasting?

Did he, though? Did he really experience joy everlasting? Or was this simply how he remembered it? Could it be that, in life, he'd created this bubble of happiness in which to reside, a place of shelter from the travesty of his existence?

Was he still alive? Were all of these people still alive?

Gerty saw the Roaming as entirely different from what she had first perceived.

The Roaming was each individual's creation. Her own Roaming was a gray wasteland covered in ash where she felt the most comfortable, but what would happen to her Roaming once she died? Dead, she would no longer have emotions. She'd simply cease to exist.

She would only live on in other people's memories of her.

For some reason, and rightly so, this thought terrified her.

The Roaming wasn't Heaven.

The Roaming was a lie. A place built solely on the imaginings of one's self-worth.

And if you only lived on in other people's memories, then the afterlife was also a lie. There was no *after*life. There was only the Void.

Because, after all, what did you carry with you when you died?

Nothing.

Absolutely nothing at all.

Gerty loosed a soul-rending scream. The denizens of the Roaming did not acknowledge her, nor did they stumble on their preordained paths. For they were not truly here. They were all going about their lives, living the best they could, while they could, each one hoping to be remembered positively because that was all that mattered, that people carried fond memories with them. If people loved you, you could live forever.

Of course, if they hated you, you could live forever as well.

"I wan' gone!" she wailed and received no answer. "I don' wan' be here!"

Her ears popped.

And then she was kneeling beside the creek once more, grinding Daddy's shirt against the washboard, as if she'd not just witnessed the truth of the universe.

She was a child again. A child who no longer felt like an adult. A child who was five years from her first menstrual cycle, and a decade from maturity.

She left the wash by the creekside and headed home. She had to tell someone about everything she'd seen, all she'd witnessed, the true meaning of the universe, and the actuality of the afterlife.

But when she arrived home, no one was there. The house, while furnished, was just as empty as it had been in that other place—that *Someplace*. The other version of her house had not resided in the Roaming, she knew that much. That had been before the Bastard had showed her the Roaming. So what had the *Someplace* been? Where had it been? Had that been the other side? The Hell to the Roaming's Heaven?

Gerty, unable to think of anything else to do, lay down for a nap. Hopefully it would kill enough time, and then when everyone returned, she would tell them about all the sights she had seen, all the places she had been.

When Momma and Daddy returned home that evening, it was without Clark. Clark, they told her, was dead. The Blood Curse had finally taken him, and it was a man's fault. A man named Francis Bay. A man who Daddy said would *pay for his crimes*. That Bay would *pay for not saving my son!*

Gerty attended her brother's funeral: a small event only her immediate family attended. Clark Grissom's remains were buried in Eternity's Gate cemetery. Pastor Wallace read from the Bible as Clark's simple pine coffin was lowered into the ground.

Time passed and Bay, along with his witch of a wife, paid for their crimes. Pastor Wallace died, too, by Bay's hand, no less.

The night of the burning, Daddy burst through the front door ranting and raving about how he needed help, about how something had to be done about the cross.

Gerty eavesdropped from the door of her bedroom, the room she no longer shared with Clark because Clark was dead.

"This damned night is gonna end us all!" Martin Grissom raged.

"Calm down, Martin," Harmony begged her husband. "What are you talking about?"

"They burned that witch! The Bay woman. The town burned her alive!"

Although Gerty could not see her mother, she could see Momma clearly in her mind's eye: Momma chewing at her fist, like she always did when presented with a troubling situation.

"They did it, Harmony. My God, they actually done it. I didn't think they had it in 'em. Now I gotta do something about that cross."

"What are you gonna do?"

"I don't know, but I gotta do something. Get Gerty. Go on! Get!"

Gerty, hearing all of this, dove into her bed and pulled the covers flush with her chin. In came Momma, hollering for her to *get up, get dressed*. They had to go into town, right now. *Hurry, honey. Hurry!*

They took Gerty along not because they were afraid to leave the girl alone—they always left her alone—but because they needed her strength, even the little strength she could provide.

The scene was something out of a nightmare. The church had burned to the ground, was still on fire in these early morning hours, and the smell coming off everything reminded Gerty of the cookouts her family sometimes had after a big hunt, when they had too much meat and no way of storing it.

In the foreground of it all was a smoldering cross, upon which hung something almost human—a fetal, charred husk of a thing clutching what seemed to be another humanoid shape. The pyre below the cross had all but burned itself out. Only red coals were left behind.

She watched in silence as Daddy lassoed a length of chain over the top of the cross and anchored the other end to a nut and bolt attached to the heavy bumper of his truck. Daddy got in and eased the truck forward. The chain pulled tight, and the fire-weakened cross snapped at the bottom. The whole thing, charred corpses and all, went over, crashing down into a smoking ruin. Pieces of wood and scorched human remains exploded everywhere. Smoking briquettes littered the gravel.

Martin exited the truck cursing; such foul words Gerty had never heard come from his mouth. Momma cowered at the bed of the truck looking scared and lost. Gerty went to her side and Momma clutched her to one hip.

"Martin," Momma said, her voice small in the big, empty night.

Daddy didn't respond. He cursed and kicked at the smoldering debris and scratched at his short hair.

"Martin?" Momma repeated.

"What, Harmony?" Daddy growled. Gerty didn't know this man with the scary voice. This man was not her father. He was not Daddy.

"Maybe we should leave."

"*Maybe we should leave*," Martin mocked. "Do you hear yourself?"

"I just don't think there's anything left to do."

"I'll tell you what's left to do, woman," the man who was not Daddy said, his back thankfully to them, because Gerty thought that maybe she didn't want to see his eyes. She thought that— maybe, just maybe—they would be her father's eyes, Daddy's eyes, and that was something she would never be able to live with. Let this man be someone different forever and always, amen.

"What's left to do is to clean up this mess. All this went poorly, and it must be cleaned up. It must be fixed."

"But you wanted this, Martin. This is what you set out to do," Momma said, and Gerty, even with her lacking an adult's life experience, thought her mother a fool for uttering those words.

Daddy spun and faced them. Gerty closed her eyes, squeezed them tight, didn't want to see Daddy's eyes, or what might have become of her father.

Daddy's presence was suddenly close, closer than Gerty was comfortable with, and Momma squealed. Something—or someone—thudded against the truck. Momma had loosed Gerty at some point, although the girl had no idea when, and Gerty could hear Momma squeaking, like a tiny, asthmatic mouse.

"You and that little girl are gonna help me clean this up if it takes us all night. Do you understand me?"

"Ye-yes. Yes, Martin," Momma muttered in a winded voice. "Yes, dear. We'll—we'll do whatever's necessary. Whatever you want. Yes, yes."

"Good." Another thud and Daddy's presence drifted away.

Gerty opened her eyes and watched Daddy walk away from them. Momma had sat down with her back against one of the truck's rear tires. She sobbed quietly. When she noticed Gerty was looking, she somehow managed to compose herself.

"We gotta help your daddy, Gerty. Gotta help him clean up."

"Yessum," little Gerty Grissom said. "Yessum, I udder'tand."

The trio of father, mother, and daughter spent the next hour stomping out coals and shoveling the remains of the cross—and those who had died on it—into the back of the truck. Martin used the chain technique again to tear the remaining stump from the ground, and then used a spade to toss it on top of everything else.

The family drove out to Waverly Chasm and repeated the cleanup process, only this time in reverse. By the time the final shovelful was thrown over the lip of the chasm, the sun had peeked over the trees in the east.

On the way home, Gerty whispered to her mother, "What'd we do?"

"I don't know, honey. Now hesh up."

"We fixed things," Daddy said. "We fixed things and now the Bastard will see fit to spare us. Spare *you*, is most important."

"The Ba'tard?" Gerty asked, confused.

"Never ya mind. Do like your momma said and hesh up. Just know we done a good thing." And then again, as if Daddy needed to convince himself more than her, he said, "We done a good thing."

All the way home, little Gerty Grissom fought internally with something just out of reach. Something she'd meant to tell Momma and Daddy. Something that had seemed unforgettable. Something important.

Oh well. It would either come back to her, or it wouldn't. And if it didn't, obviously it hadn't been as important as she'd once believed. Whatever it was.

Years passed and Momma and Daddy died, but not before giving their blessing to Gerty's marriage. Gertrude Grissom wed a man named Terrence Hilton. She would have two children with a man she would come to call Terry before his death of a heart attack ten years after the birth of Jerimiah. Terry had been a relatively stupid man. A man who had accepted Gertrude for all her faults, the biggest of which had been, in her eyes, the missing patches of flesh that dotted the landscape of her body. The Blood Curse had taken little from her, just a bit of skin here and there, but the worst of the damage had been to her face. Terry hadn't minded so much. He seemed mostly interested in what lay between her legs instead of what resided above her neck. If for no other reason than because he didn't recoil from her in disgust or terror, she loved him back. She was a good wife and a better mother, and no one could say differently about her unless they were lying.

Time progressed and the world along with it. Gertrude came to know telephones and wallpaper, and all sorts of intriguing things she hadn't known as a child, but the thing that did it, the thing that truly struck a chord with her, was meeting a man she'd only heard before. His words were kind, and he seemed a gentle giant. Not that he was tall, but his presence was as big as all of creation.

Father George seemed bigger than God and twice as glorious to Gertrude Fulgore, who had, in the years after Terry Hilton's passing, reverted to her ancestor's name. Her boys were Fulgores now, too, and would be until the day they died. Because in reality, Terry had been unimportant; nothing more than a sperm donor, really. He'd served his purpose, though. She had three lovely boys—Henrik, Malakai, and Jerimiah—thanks to Terry, and that was all that mattered.

Life, for a time, was good. But, history, like mankind, is doomed to repeat itself.

Henrik and Jerimiah got sick with the Blood Curse shortly after Gertrude met the new pastor. Father George was a devout man of God, a Baptist man of God who preferred the Catholic prefix *Father* over the Baptist *Pastor*. For a while there, at the beginning, people frowned at Father George when he politely corrected them.

"Nice to meet you, Pastor George."

"Please, call me Father George."

Frown. "Okay."

In time, it became second nature to the congregation, and Father George's name stuck, like Christ on a cross. Services were held Wednesday nights, and twice on Sunday, and the town seemed to come together like never before. The mood around the End changed from one of indifference for their fellow man to a true feeling of community. Church groups were started: a youth group, a ladies' club, and one for the guys, a Men-of-God group, which Father George led. Molly ran the ladies' club. Although there were few women of a geriatric age living in Bay's End at the time, they got their own group, one ran by Beulah Blackwood, called the Amazing Grays. Beulah was quite proud of that name and told everyone who smiled at the word play that she had come up with it. People joked that she took more pride in naming the Amazing Grays than she did in her own child and grandchild, who no one at church had ever met. "They live out of town," she'd say, and Gertrude would knowingly grin and nod, because *They live out of town* was code for *They can't be bothered to visit me.*

The mystery of Father George and Chastity Baptist Church was that both had popped up in town seemingly overnight. Construction on the church started before the Georges moved to the End, and when nosey townsfolk inquired about the new construction on Main Street, the men tasked with building the house of God would shrug and say that such information was above their paygrade. Rumor had it that the building was a new restaurant. Deep rumor, which is usually ill-informed or downright fallacy created by gossips, had it on bad authority that the restaurant would serve Cajun food, including alligator and beaver. How such rumors get started is anyone's guess, but some people talk simply to have something to say, and when there's nothing to be said, they manufacture conversation out of the ether.

That the new building was a church became obvious late in the year. Construction had begun in March, and was completed in November, but no one had a clue it was a church until August. As summer drew to an end, the steepled roof was placed like a hat atop the skeletal structure, and even the blind could see that the building was more house of worship than dining establishment. During September and October, construction halted, for reasons unknown, and then in November, just before Thanksgiving, the roof was put on the building. Menfolk could be heard around town saying that the place had been, in their professional opinion, built as *backward as a tail-faced cat*, and that the architect had to be *denser than a bucket of cement and half as bright*, because what if it rained? *What if it rained!*

It didn't rain. Not a drop during the entire nine months the church took to build. But once the roof was on, the End saw record downfall. A full month of rain flooded Haversham Lake and the surrounding properties. Fairchild Farm became a lake, and residents joked that if the rain didn't stop soon *God would owe the world another rainbow*. Such was a popular saying, but Gertrude, if no one else, knew that the rainbow of Noah's time had been God's promise to never restart the world again.

The rain ended, and the church opened. Mind, there hadn't been a church in the End since Pastor Wallace's church had burned down, so people were admittedly skeptical of this new house of God. Yet the first Sunday morning Chastity Baptist opened its doors, nine people stood on the steps, awaiting the word of God. Gertrude was one of the first nine.

Beulah Blackwood attended the grand opening, as well, although Beulah seemed the most skeptical of all. Gertrude had no idea what kind of gossip Beulah was because Gertrude didn't associate with too many people in town. What her family didn't grow on their own property they purchased from Peaton's Grocery, and what they couldn't find at the store, they did without, but shopping in town had made her and her boys passing acquaintances with a number of townsfolk: Sheriff Carringer, Al Sarafino (manager of Peaton's Grocery during this time), and a checkout girl whose name Gertrude always forgot. Other than those three people, Gertrude only spoke with one other person in town: Father George.

So when Henrik and Jerimiah got sick, the pastor was the first person she went to see.

"Is it leprosy, you think?" Father George asked on the day she'd brought in the boys in to be prayed over.

"Leprosy? Like what the leper in the Bible had?"

Father George nodded. "That's what I'm thinking. Might want to take them to see a doctor, Gertrude. I don't think there's anything I can do for them."

Gertrude took the boys into Chestnut the following day, to Mercy Medical, the first hospital anyone in her family had visited since arriving in America. Tests were done, and those tests came back negative for everything, including leprosy, except for, in the case of Henrik, a significantly low iron count. He was sent home with iron pills that would, as the doctor had said, *Sort him out.*

Gertrude returned to Father George the following afternoon. She found him in the main church, practicing a sermon, which she found odd to witness. She'd always believed that the words he said during Sunday service were given to him on the spot, from the lips of God to his ears, and seeing him reciting from written lines struck Gertrude as odd and, in a way, false. The revelation didn't quite shake her faith, but it did make her look at Father George differently. He was no longer the voice of God to her but a man playing a part, like an actor in a play. That Sundays were rehearsed bothered her. Not enough to stop her from attending service, but just enough to rattle her mettle.

Henrik had been too weak to come along with her to church this day, but Jerimiah lurked at her side, his tall, lanky teenager's body like a scarecrow attached to her hip to hip.

"Gertrude! Jerry! How goes it?" Father George called from the pulpit. He hopped down the steps and jogged toward them. He shook Jerimiah's hand, sores and all. "So nice to see you, son. You look better. Did the doctors find anything out?"

Gertrude shook her head.

Father George frowned.

"That's odd. God's assured me the boys would be fine. Did you want to pray, Gertrude? Jerry? I know you've likely been praying since the boys first showed symptoms, but it wouldn't hurt to pray some more. Never hurts to pray more." Father George beamed, and for a moment, Gertrude thought that everything might turn out all right in the end.

Father George, Gertrude, and Jerimiah knelt at the steps leading up to the pulpit and Father George led them in prayer, asking the Lord to cure and heal Henrik and Jerimiah. He went on to ask God and Jesus to *Heal Mother Gertrude's scars, and bless this family, in the name of Jesus and the Lord, amen.*

Gertrude thanked the pastor and sent Jerimiah out to the truck, for she wanted to speak to the pastor alone. Jermiah, looking—if possible—more morose than before prayer, dipped his head and took his leave from his mother and Father George. Father George sat in the front row of pews and patted the seat next to him. Gertrude took a seat next to the pastor and sighed deeply.

"I'm worried this has somethin to do with me, Father."

"You? How so?"

"I feel like I've somehow sinned and damned them to this illness."

Father George thought for a moment.

"Okay," he said, "let's imagine for a moment that you did something to call down the Lord's wrath, or for him to turn his back on you and allow the Devil to test you as, say, Jonah was tested. If that is the case, why hasn't Malakai been affected?"

"I hadn't thought about that."

"Now we must figure out why only your youngest and oldest are afflicted with this… whatever this is."

The duo sat in silence for several minutes. Father George picked at his slacks as if they were coated in lint Gertrude could not see.

If for no other reason than to break the silence, Gertrude asked a question that had long plagued her mind.

"Why do you ask to be called *Father*?"

The pastor smiled. "You're the first one to ask me that. Did you know that?"

Gertrude shook her head, her silver hair spilling across her shoulders and shimmering like strung tinsel. She'd washed her hair that morning, which was not something she usually did, seeing as how she had to use the creek to do so. Her home still didn't have indoor plumbing, and never would.

"Well," Father George continued, "the reason I request that people call me *Father* is because I'd like to think that I can be a father figure in lieu of our true father, God."

"But God is always with us," Gertrude said.

"Always?" Father George seemed skeptical.

"You don't believe that the Lord is always with us?" Gertrude said, flabbergasted.

"Oh, I believe that he is omnipresent. That means he's always around. I simply don't think he's always paying attention. Such would be a boring existence, don't you think?"

"I think you come devilishly close to blasphemy, Father."

Father George chuckled.

"What's so funny?" Gertrude tried to contain her sudden anger, but failed.

"I think I know a bit more about what constitutes blasphemy than someone like you might."

Gertrude stood and glared down at the pastor. "What's that 'spose to mean?"

"Calm down. It simply means that I speak with him daily, sometimes multiple times a day, and God hasn't once frowned down upon me. I do his will and his alone. I am a true child of God, Gertrude, and that means I am kin with the Lord."

She squinted at him. "I don't think I like what I'm hearing, Father."

"You don't have to like something, or even believe it, for it to be true. Look at God. He exists whether or not you believe in him. But not believing has consequences. So you have to look deep within yourself and ask one simple question. Do you believe in me?"

"I believe in God."

"And God believes in me." Father George once more patted the seat next to him. This time, Gertrude ignored the offer. He shrugged. "Have it your way. But I want you to consider that, even now, God is testing you. He's testing you by sickening some of your children and not others, and now he's testing your faith in your shepherd. Are you of my flock, or are you not?"

"I am of God's flock."

"But who leads you on Earth?"

"God does."

"Through me."

Gertrude shook her head. The more she heard the angrier she became.

"This is blasphemy, Father. I will not hear it." She strode for the aisle, and beyond that, the door.

But before she could get outside of hearing distance of the pastor, Father George said, "If you will not hear it, He will not save your children. Repent, Gertrude. Repent and let me help you and your children!"

With Father George's final words resounding in her head, Gertrude shuffled from the church.

Nine days passed, and in that time, Gertrude Fulgore watched her youngest child wither and die. Henrik, like her brother Clark, went slowly. The wounds in his flesh festered and putrefied. Two of his fingers fell off, as did most of the toes on one foot, leaving behind only the big toe, although it was nothing more than a rotten, grayish-purple nub.

His penis came off the day before he died, while she was giving him a bed bath. Gertrude screamed when it happened. Henrik didn't seem to notice. She doubted he would notice the end of the world, should it come before he died.

The day Henrik passed on was a hot one. Inside, the house was stifling, and Gertrude at first blamed the boy's labored breathing on the heat. As time went by and his breathing got worse and worse, she realized that this was it. She hadn't been there for Clark's passing, but both boys went the same way: hard and slow. Henrik's wheeze became a rattle, and an hour of rattling led to intermittent gasping. The boy's flesh—where it was intact, at least—was gray, the texture of damp leather and slick with cold perspiration. His eyes and cheeks sunk deeply into his face. His stomach an impact crater. He was emaciated; caved in and dented, as if someone had been at the boy with a large hammer.

In the final ten minutes of his life, Henrik gasped three times. Then it was over. Gertrude wept over his corpse until the sun came up, at which time her body failed her and she passed out in the bed beside her youngest son's dead body. Jerimiah woke her up for supper, a stew of beans and carrots and squash in a salty dishwater-gray broth. She ate with little vigor, and only because Jerimiah threatened to remove Henrik's body if she didn't eat. Malakai mourned in his own way, silent and forlorn. He didn't talk much as it was—Jerimiah was the talker. Still, Gertrude wanted noise. She wanted to hear screaming and howling and even cursing. Anything. Anything that would make real the sorrowful truth of the day: her child was dead. Dead of a disease that had spared her, one that threatened, even now, her firstborn.

But Jerimiah, aside from the open wounds dotting his skin, seemed unaffected. His energy level hadn't changed in the least since the Blood Curse had come calling.

Jerimiah had cooked dinner and cleaned the house while Gertrude had slept next to Henrik's corpse. She couldn't be entirely sure, but she also thought that the truck in the front yard— her father's truck—looked to have been washed as well. Had he really washed his granddaddy's truck? He didn't even like the old rattle trap. Why would he wash it?

The answer to that was obvious, though, and she knew it. This was all Jerimiah trying his best to stay busy. If you stayed busy you didn't have to focus on reality. You could be some place else. Some place safe.

*Someplace...*

Gertrude's eyes fluttered as her brain worked. Something important lingered just out of reach. Something she'd once thought too important to forget. The long-buried something pulsed, begging for release. She was exhausted after nine days of caring for Henrik's every need, and could feel old walls erected in her mind cracking and crumbling.

She went to the front door and pulled it open.

What lay outside wasn't the front yard with Daddy's truck parked in the tall grass but a whole new place.

No.

Not new.

This place was old and familiar.

She needed to roam.

So she did.

She stepped off the porch into knee-deep ash. She shoved through the snow-like accumulation and into a storm-dark wood. A red sky could be seen up through the boughs of overhanging trees, but none of the red colored the surface of this plane. Moving through this place—this *Someplace*—was like moving through a dream: languid, outside of time. A feeling possessed her, one which said that, here, in this place, anything was possible.

"Hello?" she called out but was given no response.

"Is there anyone here?"

Nothing.

On she walked, for what seemed like miles, until she came to the old house, the one that felt familiar and foreign, washed out and vibrant, all at the same time. She stepped inside.

In the time between visits to this old house, nothing had changed, aside from Gertrude herself, for she now knew what a telephone was. She found the once-alien object sitting in the corner. This time, though, it did not ring. She reached down with an unsteady hand and unbidden tears in her eyes and picked up the handset.

From the speaker came a soft trilling sound. She placed the phone to her ear and waited. After a while, someone answered.

A voice she knew all too well answered, "Georges' residence, how may I help you?"

"Everything," she stammered, "Everything is horrible now."

Silence crashed down. She could feel quiet bearing down on her, shoving her to the ground. She dropped to her knees, openly wailing.

"Everything is horrible now!" she screamed into the phone. Then a thought came to her, and she said, "Did He do this? Did God do this to me because I didn't believe in you, Father? Am I being punished? Is this what happens when you do not have faith?"

"Gertrude, you cannot—"

"Tell me! Tell me why! Why me? What is so goddamned important about me?"

"Gertrude, what are you talking about? Why is everything— what's wrong? What happened?"

"You said you like being called *Father* to remind people that even when God is absent, you'd be there. So why weren't you there for my son? Why weren't one of you there for Henrik?"

"Because you didn't ask."

"You devil. You charlatan!"

"Gert—"

"I know who you are!" And she felt that she truly did know. Memories hard and cold rolled into her mind like boulders down a hill. Long forgotten conversations fighting to the surface like a drowning man in concrete boots. "I know why you like being called *Father*. You're not fooling me. Not any longer. You're in league with the Bastard! You like being called *Father* because you never had one. You're... fatherless. I see you, pastor... devil! I *see* you, devil!"

She slammed the phone down and staggered away, punch-drunk with the moment. She had no idea if the nonsense she'd spouted had been the truth, but it felt like the truth. At the very least, it felt like it could be true.

"It could," she said to an empty room. "It *could* be true."

Even as confused and disorientated as she was, she knew she was being silly. The leap was a drastic one, connecting Father George and the Bastard like she had. Saying he preferred to be called *Father* because he was in league with the first fatherless one...

The *first* fatherless one...

What was it the Bastard had said about being the first?

*I am the Bastard. I am the first of the fatherless, and the first of my kind. I am thought. I am memory...*

And if he, the Bastard, was memory, surely he could affect memory. Could that be why she had forgotten the Midnight Man? Is that why, just now, she had remembered what she'd forgotten so long ago? Because he willed it?

What the hell was going on? What was happening to her, and why? What did she ever do to deserve this? Why her?

Gertrude felt him before she heard him. A deep cold leaked from her marrow. A cold so deeply rooted that her skin was the last to feel it. Gooseflesh popped up on every inch of her body. She shivered violently, teeth chattering.

"Leave me alone!" she cried. "I've done nothing to anyone!"

"The sins of the father will be revisited on the child."

"I am not my father!"

"We are all our fathers. Except for me. For I am—"

"Fatherless," she murmured.

"And thus, I am sinless. I am perfection. I am everything. God. The heavens. Hell. All of creation am I, and all of creation I will be until the end of time. As above, so below, forever and always."

"Amen," she said, breathless and trembling.

The disembodied voice of the Bastard chuckled as the room's only window screeched up and open. Through the open window fluttered a sheet of paper. The paper landed at Gertrude's feet. She bent to retrieve it.

Upon the sheet of paper was written eight lines of verse. She read them over in her mind:

> *The Dastardly Bastard of Waverly Chasm*
> *Does gleefully scheme of malevolent things*
> *Beware, child fair, of what you find there*
> *His lies how they hide in the shadows he wears*
> *`Cross wreckage of bridge, is where this man lives*
> *Counting his spoils, his eye how it digs*
> *Tread, if you dare, through his one-eyed stare*
> *This Dastardly Bastard is neither here, nor there*

"What's this suppose to mean? I don't understand."

"It's not for you to understand, Gerty. Neither is the universe, or the Creator's motives, or the Void beyond the known. The machinations of my brood are ours alone. You simply have a part to play. So fulfill your destiny. Play your part."

Gertrude thought back to walking in on Father George rehearsing his sermon, how fake it had all seemed to her. How false. Everything felt false now, the entirety of her beliefs: Heaven, Hell, Satan, God. How much of what she believed was a construct of Man, and how much was the creation of this creature? This Bastard.

"Everything I know is a lie," she said. Her tears had long dried on her face. No more would come. Not ever.

"You know nothing, Gerty. In many ways you're still the same bumbling, ignorant child you were when we first met. Nothing more. Nothing less. Poor little Gerty Grissom, lost in the woods, following shadows."

"Damn you," she said without any passion in her voice. She was suffused with a bone-deep exhaustion. She didn't want to live anymore, much less play her role in all of this. What was the point? It was all the very definition of useless. The only joy to be had now was the unknown.

So she refused to play along. Gertrude Fulgore ripped the poem in half and then in half again. She continued to tear and shred the paper until the remaining pieces were no larger postage stamp.

"Well, that was unexpected," said the Bastard.

"She's had enough of your shit, I believe," came the voice of a child: a boy child to be exact.

"I do believe you're right."

"Who are you? Really?" Gertrude asked the empty room.

A boy walked out of the corner of the room as if there was a doorway secreted in the wall that she couldn't see. He was small, and she guessed his age at between ten or twelve. Prepubescent, she believed. He wore a fancy, antiquated suit, the likes of which she hadn't seen since childhood. His shoes were polished to a mirror shine, and his smile glowed equally bright. A leather eye patch, with a red gem dead center, sat over his right eye.

"Fork," said the boy.

"Fork?" she asked him.

The boy made a gesture, as if stabbing himself in the face. "I did it with a fork. Stabbed myself in the eye. Owwie."

"What are you talking about?" she muttered.

"Gertrude, all of this is fun and all, but we really should be moving on. What's done is done, and what's coming cannot be undone. So, shall we?"

"I'm not going anywhere with you."

"Then you aren't going anywhere at all. I can keep you here forever, as a memory, as *my* memory. You've seen what happens to memories in this place. They roam. You don't want to roam, do you?"

"What's the other option?"

"To live and die like a normal woman. I can give you that gift. All you have to do is ask."

"Why should I ask anything of you?"

"Because I cannot make you do anything you do not wish to do. You have freewill, after all. I can only suggest and watch and wait for the results of your choice. Because every choice has consequences, both good and bad, but sometimes what is bad for one person is good for the other. Make your choice so that we can move on. We've been here far too long, and the spectators are growing bored."

"Spectators?"

"Those watching all this unfold. They're already asking themselves what is the point of all this? What does this have to do with anything? And I think it's finally time we end this chapter, don't you?"

Gertrude steeled herself and said, "I want my son back. I demand my son Henrik back, and then I will do what you want."

"I'm sorry, what?" The boy laughed. "Did you just *demand* something from me? I can't—are you hearing this shit?" the boy asked the ceiling. "She wants me to raise the dead." The boy met her gaze once again. He was close enough now that she could see his remaining eye was a beautiful shade of ice-blue. "I cannot raise the dead, Gertrude. Only you are capable of that."

"How?" she asked plainly.

"It's too late for your son, but you might be able to save someone else. Someone you might not think is worth saving. At least not now."

"Who?"

"Oh, who indeed. I'm sure you'll figure that out. But, for now, let me give you a hint. The Bastard told you everything you need to know, but you might have not been paying attention. Sometimes important information is hidden in the banal, and that's what you have to focus on now. Remember when the Bastard said that your Roaming was your place? That he could not enter your Roaming because it was yours?"

She nodded.

"Well, what else did he say?"

"I—I don't remember. That was forever ago."

"Oh, Gertrude, you don't know how accurate that statement is." The boy laughed. "Okay. Some more help. He said you could

318

place things in your Roaming that could not be touched by anyone else. Do you recall that?"

"Vaguely," she admitted.

"Well, when you find this person whom you deem worthy of saving, you can place them there, in your Roaming, and then, maybe, just maybe, you can call on them again. Do you understand?"

"No. No, I don't understand any of this."

"That really is too bad. Ta-ta for now."

With that, the boy was gone. Forever and ever, amen.

In the corner, the telephone began to ring.

Despite her better judgment, Gertrude Fulgore answered it.

"Hello?"

# 12. The Scaresparrow

The teenager in the cell, if Hap was honest with himself, creeped him out something fierce. Kirby Johnson's eyes seemed hollow and lifeless, as if Hap were looking at a corpse and not someone with a pulse. Hap kept wanting to shake the kid, slap him, wake him up, get a reaction, any reaction, just to prove that Kirby was alive and not some talking puppet bereft of an accompanying ventriloquist.

"What did you do with my deputy?" Hap asked the empty-eyed teenager.

"I didn't do anything to anyone. I don't even know why I'm in jail." The boy spoke with, if possible, even less emotion than his eyes displayed.

"You don't remember killing your mother?" Hap said.

"My mom's dead?"

"I don't have time for games, Kirby. We know you killed your mother, just like you somehow killed—who'd he kill?" This last part Hap whispered to Beulah, who stood out of sight of Kirby, in front of the uninhabited cell to left of the one inside which Kirby resided.

"I don't remember. All I remember is that he said he blew off the guy's head with his mind, or something like that."

"Who's that?" Kirby asked. "Who else is here?"

"Who that is is none of your concern, son. I need you to focus on what happened to your mother. She's missing a head, boy. Sound familiar?"

"What? No." A pause, and then, "I don't know."

"Kirby, you spoke with Beulah Blackwood earlier and told her that you blew off someone else's head. Just like your mother was missing a head. So you can see how I might see you more as a criminal than a victim."

"I didn't do anything." Kirby slumped back against the wall and studied the ceiling.

Hap didn't have the time or patience for this shit.

"Listen, kid, I need some answers, not all this playacting. You need to tell me, right now, how you're doing what you're doing. I need to know how you're doing these things you're doing, and what in tarnation you did to my deputy."

Kirby gazed at Hap with empty eyes.

"I don't know what's going on. You keep telling me I killed people, but I don't remember killing anyone. I don't remember much from the past week, period. I woke up last night to something outside my window, I think. Then I woke up here. That's all. That's it. Nothing more."

"Okay. Fine. Let's say you don't remember anything." Hap glanced at Beulah. "What about this morning? At the church? You showed up, covered in blood, and you said something to me. Do you remember what it was you said?"

Kirby shook his head.

"You said, *Everything is horrible now.*"

Kirby went dull-eyed. Whatever semblance of life had been there before was gone now. No one's home. Thank you, come again.

Hap cocked his head and his neck popped. The crack of adjusted vertebrae sounded like a gunshot in the enclosed space.

"Come here." He gestured for Beulah to approach. She did so, but with a tentative caution that fought with the smile on her face. How some people smiled when they were nervous had always gotten on Hap's nerves. Usually he got anxious grins from drunk drivers and guilty men whose beaten wives had finally called in, even if such a thing was rarer in Bay's End than a big-dicked turtle. Such nervous smiles normally made Hap angry to the point of violence. *Wipe the shit-eating grin off your face and get what's coming to you, ya idiot.* But in the case of Beulah, it didn't bother him near as bad. She had every right to be on edge, seeing as how—if Kirby was to be believed—the boy had the power to blow someone's head off with a single thought.

She leaned in and glanced at the glazed-over expression on Kirby's face, then quickly pulled away.

"That's it. That's what he looked like while he was telling his story. It's like he's two people or something."

"I think that's a little too on the nose for what we're dealing with."

"What do you mean?"

"Meaning, I think that's exactly what the kid wants us to think. That we're talking to more than one person. That he's possessed. Or that he has multiple personalities. Or some other nonsense like that. This all feels like... fuck, Beulah, it all feels like storytelling, you know? Like we're living some shit that ain't got no business being real. But staying on topic, he's trying to get out of trouble, is what I mean."

"You think he's faking?"

"In so many words, yeah."

"But," Beulah fought with the right words. Hap could damn-near see the gears turning in her skull as she ground a cog that hadn't been properly cast. "But that don't make any sense."

"Why not? Wouldn't you try to save your ass if your ass was caught in a crime?"

"No," Beulah said, and she seemed a hundred percent truthful. "I wouldn't never commit a crime in the first place. Second, if I did, I'd surely own up to it, because I wouldn't have intended to commit a crime. At least, one would hope. Would you not?"

"Would I not what?"

Beulah eyed him with a look he didn't much care for.

"Would you own up to any crime you happened to commit?"

Hap chuckled without humor.

"I don't have to worry about such a thing because I don't commit crimes."

"Well, then, stop asking me stupid questions. Of course I wouldn't lie to cover up a crime because I wouldn't commit a crime to begin with. No need to lie. What's done is done."

"Okay. Fine. But, for the sake of *this* argument, say you're not you. Say you're a scared kid who's capable of damaging things with your mind, or whatever it is this kid can do, and you get caught. Do you fess up? Or do you pretend to go all dead-faced when confronted with the facts of the matter?"

"Oh. I see. Well, I 'spose I would lie, maybe, in that situation. But we don't know if he's lying. I mean, why would he lie?"

"We just went over that, Beulah, for fuck's sake…"

"No. Listen, Harold. Why would he lie, seeing as how he can do what he can do?"

"Say again?"

"If he's truly capable of exploding people's heads, like he done to his mother and that man in his story, then why not just explode our heads and walk on out of here? If he killed your deputy, why not just leave right then? My view on this is, if he can explode a human head with his thoughts, surely he can get out of this cell."

Hap hadn't considered any of that, but he wasn't about to tell Beulah as much.

"Maybe he can't do all that. Maybe his powers only work on people, or whatnot. Maybe it has something to do with only being able to affect, you know, flesh and bone."

"Or brains," Beulah said, her eyes filled with star-gazing wonder. "What if that's it?"

"What if what's what?"

"What if he can only affect people and not objects because objects don't have brains and people do."

Hap raised both arms and let them drop in frustration. "That's what I meant. That's exactly what I've been trying to say this whole time," Hap lied. "Sheesh, women are dense."

"No need to be cruel, Harold. No need whatsoever to be cruel. I don't think this is the time or place for such things. I'm here to help you, is all, and you're making it difficult beyond belief to help you whatsoever."

"My apologies," Hap said but did not mean. "No more mockery from me. Promise."

"Thank you."

"You're welcome."

"Now," said Beulah, "if we're correct—if *you're* correct— then why doesn't he just kill me or you and threaten the other person with death if they don't let him out?"

Hap growled, "You really need to learn how to hush your dad-gum face, woman."

"What? What did I say?"

"Did it ever cross your mind that the kid hadn't thought of that yet?"

"Oh."

"Mind what you say, 'fore you give him any ideas. But, just for that, I'm hiding the keys. You hear that, you little bastard?" Hap growled into the cell. "I'm hiding the goddamned—sorry, Beulah—I'm hiding these here keys, so don't get any weird thoughts in your head. You," Hap nodded at Beulah, "watch him until I get back."

"Why? Why can't I come with you?"

"Because then you'll know where the keys are at."

"But how does that protect me?"

"Huh?" Hap asked, confused.

"And you say women are dense."

"Mind your words, Beulah. I ain't never been in less of a mood to deal with bullshit than I am right now."

"I mean, who's to stop him from killing me and threatening you with the same until you find the key."

"You really think I care enough about you for your death to affect me?"

"I said for you to stop being cruel. It's not funny."

*I wasn't trying to be funny*, Hap thought but didn't say.

Instead, he said, "It really won't matter if he kills you or not, and I mean that, Beulah." She opened her mouth to say something and Hap raised a hand to stop her. "Meaning, you'll be dead. You'll be done and over with, and Kirby here won't have no more bargaining chips. I think maybe he asked for you to come so he could have just that. A bargaining chip. With you dead, he'll have lost that. And only I will know where the key is, so he'll be— pardon my French, of course—shit out of luck."

"That's the dumbest thing you men say—that *pardon-my-French* crap. As if curse words were French. Just plain dumb."

Hap grinned. "Mighty cruel of you, Beulah, calling me dumb and all. Thought we were gonna be nice to each other, yet here you are, calling me dumb."

"Weren't you gon' to go hide something?"

"Yes, ma'am, I was. Watch him, and I'll be right back."

"Sir, yes, sir." She gave him a mock salute as he left the hallway.

Hap had somehow forgotten about the state of the sheriff's office's main room and grimaced at the bloody mess the station had become. To quell a lingering suspicion, he checked his office again for Ronnie Short's arm and found it where he'd last seen it.

Next, he opened the safe under his desk, where he kept important documents and bribe money he'd been paid over the years (sometimes drunks were given the choice between paying Hap a nominal fee or spending the night in jail, and rarely did the drunken goofballs take the overnight option), removed the cell keys from his keyring, and tossed it inside. He closed the safe, spun the dial, and returned to the front desk.

A man stood at the doors, looking outside; his body nothing more than a shadow against a wall of light. By the shape of him, Hap guessed the guy had his hands shoved in his pockets. Hap approached him, concerned by the state of his station and by this guy's obvious lack of care about such things.

"Can I help you?"

The man turned and Hap got a good look at the guy's face.

Eric Larson.

*Just what I need, the fucking cuckold of Pointvilla County.*

"Hap," Eric said, his hands still stuffed in his pockets. "It's been a long day, boss."

"You can say that again."

Eric looked around the bloody room: ceiling, floor, east, west.

"Is all this Ronnie?"

Hap found Eric's nonchalant attitude perplexing.

"I suppose it is. His arm's in my office. On the floor. On the floor of my office, I mean."

Eric nodded dumbly.

"You, uh, you okay, Eric?"

"Something happened at the Johnson house. Nuttiest thing I ever seen."

A cold chill rolled up Hap's spine. "What was that, Eric?"

"Well, I don't rightly know how to say this, Hap, but," the deputy cleared his throat, "first there was this baby crying. Strange, right? And then Father George showed up and told me something. He told me you been fucking my wife, Hap, and I'm apt to believe him because I can't find my wife and the neighbor lady said you was at my house earlier today. With Janice. Alone. She says you were there for some time, boss. Enough time to get up to no good, is what she reckoned."

Hap assumed Eric might take a swing at him, or he might even take out his sidearm and plug Hap in the forehead. Either or. Hap almost laid his hand on his own gun, but decided against it. He didn't want to antagonize the man.

"That's just nonsense," Hap said.

"Is it?" Eric cocked his head like a curious pup. "I don't think it is. Nossir. I think it's all true. Janice ain't been as welcoming as she once was, and you been different too."

"How so?"

With an utterly infuriating calm, Eric sighed. "You ain't yourself these days. You're nicer than you've been. I'm thinking that's 'cause you been sleeping with someone pretty regular. Ronnie thought so too." Once more, Eric glanced around the room. "And if this is the end result, well, I guess I don't want no part of it."

"I'm—I—what do you mean?" Hap stammered.

"If you can do all this, I ain't got no need in kicking a hornet's nest, as it were. Me and you is fine and dandy. And I don't see no reason why we can't share Janice."

Hap blinked several times.

"Can I go home and get some sleep, boss? I'm awfully tired."

"Wh-what about the Johnson woman?"

"Oh. Right." Eric cleared his throat and brushed a hand through his thick brown hair. "Coroner came and got her. Had all kinds of questions, but I told him we didn't know nothin. So she's in good hands, and I figure my job's done for the day, and maybe I can catch some Zs before I gotta be in to work tonight."

Hap couldn't believe his ears. All this and Eric Larson simply wanted to go home and sleep before his next shift.

*I'll be just goddamned...*

"Sure, Eric. Go get some rest. I'll take care of all this. Everything will be back to normal in a jiffy, just you wait."

"Nossir, I don't think they will. Nice thought, though. I hope all this" —Eric Larson gestured to the blood-soaked lobby— "is behind us. I like my life how it is, Hap. Or how it was. But how I look at it is, wasn't nothing wrong with all this when I didn't know what was happening, so I suppose ain't nothing wrong now. Maybe I can find me someone on the side, too. Whataya think?"

"I think you need some sleep, Eric."

"Yessir, I think you're right." Eric nodded and left.

To an empty sheriff's station, Hap said, "What the fuck just happened here?"

\*\*\*

Around suppertime, Wesley asked Pete what he wanted to do for dinner. When Pete shrugged and said he didn't care, Wesley suggested, "Wanna head back to my place? I know it's a long walk, but I'm sure Pa's got something waiting for me. Prolly enough for you, too."

330

Pete, having no idea when his grandmother would return, agreed, and off they went, walking through the End without a care in the world. Along the way, Wesley asked if Pete's grandmother would care if she came home and found him gone, and Pete told Wesley everything would be fine, which wasn't the entire truth on a good day, and a bold-faced lie on a bad one. The truth of the matter was that Mama would have several choice words for him upon his return, but he didn't care. He got to go out so little as it was, and only then because he was good at sneaking out. Who cared what Mama said, really? What was she going to do—ground him? He'd just sneak out again, and the snake would continue to eat itself.

Bay's End was quiet early in the afternoon, especially on a Sunday. Most of the End's residents either worked out of town, Monday through Friday, or they pulled odd hours in town. The only real jobs to be had—the only taxable jobs, anyway—were Peaton's Grocery or Carringer & Sons Logging. There were several other small shops and even a bookstore in town, but all of them were one-man or family-owned-and-operated operations. Today, the streets were near barren, and the boys saw only two cars during the thirty-minute walk, which led them out of town on Highway 607.

Along the way, they played at an end-of-the-world scenario. Pete constructed a dystopian future where Bay's End was the final town on Earth still populated by human beings. Everyone else had become undead lizard people with a taste for tree bark and human flesh.

"Why tree bark *and* human flesh?" Wesley asked as he pretended to fight off one of the decaying reptiles that had claimed man's previous spot at the top of the food chain.

"They just like skin, I guess."

Wesley laughed as he dealt a deathblow to a ten-foot-tall creature with half a tail and a horn jutting from the left side of its head; the thing had lost its other horn in an earlier battle with Pete, but obviously had not learned its lesson. You did not mess with an Ender!

"Bark ain't really tree skin, is it?" Wesley asked.

"Yup," Pete said and slayed a he-beast with a spiked tail.

"I ain't never thought of it like that, but I guess you're right."

Pete swung his stick/sword at a creepy-crawly lizard man who wore a kilt made of human flesh and beaded fringe, although the beads weren't beads—they were human teeth.

"I guess it's not really skin. I guess our skin is more like bark than bark is like skin."

Wesley scratched at his head. "My brain hurts when you talk like that."

Pete giggled and ducked, barely dodging an attack from a flying she-beast with ridiculously large and scaly breasts. This she-beast, her tits were armored and spiked, like great fleshy maces, and could be detached to swing from her undercarriage like deadly twin chandeliers. Pete told Wesley about the mace-chested she-beast and Wesley laughed so hard that he was overcome by a coughing fit. Pete had to stop and wait for his friend to catch his breath before their adventure could continue.

Overall, nine-hundred-seventy-five undead lizard men and women died this day. Pete held a moment of silence for the members of their party who did not make it: Batman, Ray Bradbury, and Ming the Merciless. Rest in Peace, men, and may Buddha have mercy on your souls.

"Buddha?" Wesley said, laughing.

"Why not?"

"How about God? I mean, none of this is real, so why not say God? Just for pretend? Just once?"

"Nope," Pete said with a smile. "Don't wanna start any weird habits."

"Oh, come on! You're a jerk!"

"Plus, Buddha is fat, like me. So I'm kinda partial to him."

"Liar."

"I'm not lying. Buddha is super fat. Big pudgy pudge pudding."

"Pudgy pudge pudding?" Wesley held his gut as he guffawed. "Say it again!"

"Big pudgy pudge pudding peddling pig parts!"

The friends died of laughter, both expiring in the grass along the side of the road. It was the spring of their youth, an eternal regeneration of the heart, where autumnal winds might blow but never chill them, not as long as their hearts were warmed by the fires of friendship. Such is the truth of boyhood companionship.

Somehow, they pulled themselves from the grass and continued on their journey, although neither had wanted to. They arrived at Wesley's house a little after four, and lo-and-behold, Pa had made Wesley supper after all. And, yes, there was plenty for Pete. They ate meatloaf, and cold, greasy fried potatoes that weren't at all bad, and drank milk that had been drawn from one of Wesley's dairy cows yesterday. While they ate, Pete told Wesley and his father a story about how two young warriors defeated a hoard of undead lizard men, and although Wesley had lived through the battle, he sat and listened to the tale as if someone else had lived through the tumult.

"And the good knight Wesley stabbed the scaly she-beast between her massive breasts and she fell dead at his feet. And so goes the tale of Peter and Wesley, killers of the Dragon Kin!"

"Wow. That was amazing!" Wesley cried. "Is that who they were? The Dragon Kin? Are they really kin of dragons? Do dragons exist?"

"Only," Pete said as he chewed a bite of sandwich, "in the form they live in now. There are no more dragons, per se—"

Pop leaned back his chair, stuck a match, and lit his pipe. He listened without saying a word, a smile ever-present at the corner of his mouth.

"*Per se?*"

"It means necessarily, or something like that. Or, better yet, it means, it's *like something* but not really. I wouldn't call your father a good friend of mine, *per se*. Like that."

Pop raised his eyebrows, let them drop, but remained silent.

"Ah. Okay. Swell." Wesley smiled.

"Do you make up a lot of stories?" Wesley asked, his eyes sparkling with curiosity and wonder. "Do you write them all down? Do you write any of them down? Will you write this one down?"

"Slow down," Pete said. "One question at a time. First off, I don't write them all down, no. I barely write any of them down nowadays because I don't have much paper and even fewer pencils and Mama won't buy me anymore since I keep sneaking out."

"Why did you sneak out?"

Pete shrugged. "I don't know. I guess because I live with my grandma. Living with her is… well, it's not very much fun. For those first couple of weeks I just went places. Even got to know the sheriff a little."

"Sheriff Hap?" Wesley said, more for clarification than in awe.

Pop scratched at his chin. His short-and-dirty farmer's nails on his salt-and-pepper stubble sounded like sandpaper on stone.

"Yeah. Hap. We're on a first name basis. It's neat."

"Swell. Does he ever let you ride around in his car?"

"Sometimes," Pete said, and for the first time in his life, he felt bad about lying to someone. Usually he'd chalk it up as nothing more than storytelling, but this felt different, wrong. Hearing the ease in which he was able to lie to someone he considered a friend bothered him. It bothered him so much that he decided to put an end to it.

"Hey, listen, Wes, I was lying. I don't know Sheriff Hap all that well and I have never, *ever*, ridden in his car."

Pop chewed on the inside of his cheek but did not speak.

Wesley frowned. "Why'd you lie?"

"Because I'm stupid. Sorry. I really mean that."

"But why?" Wesley didn't sound angry as much as he did curious. Pete loved that about his new friend, that innocent need for information, for the entire story. A true hunger to be part of the know. Wesley reminded Pete of himself in that regard.

"I guess I like telling stories so much that sometimes I forget when to stop?" It came out sounding like a question, and Pete thought that was because it likely was a question. As if he were asking if it were okay that sometimes he didn't know how to turn off the stories?

To see Wesley nodding in acknowledgment or agreement settled Pete's nerves a bit.

Pop stood and collected the plates from the table.

Wesley thought he knew just what Pete was talking about because sometimes he didn't know when not to talk. It was a real problem, how he ran his mouth at the most inappropriate times. He also hoped that by hanging out with Pete more he could learn when to speak and when not to. Pete was so smart that Wesley at times felt intimidated by his new friend, and that kept him from spouting off all the time, because he didn't want Pete to think him a fool.

"I talk too much," said Wesley.

"Really? I haven't noticed. If anything, I thought that I was talking too much. I thought maybe you would, I don't know, get tired of me jacking my jaw."

Wesley shook his head. "I like listening to you talk. Your stories are the best. Tell me another one."

"All right."

"Make it up right now. On the spot. Can you do that?" Wesley asked.

"Sure, I guess."

The boys shook on it and Pete dove into a whole new world.

\*\*\*

Gertrude Fulgore awoke in darkness, her heart pounding in her temples.

Where was she? What had happened to her?

She fought with a swirling mass of memory until the most recent one solidified in her mind. She saw the boy with the

336

eyepatch, the one claiming to be the Creator—whatever that meant. He'd shoved her and into Waverly Chasm she had fallen.

How had she survived the fall? How deep was this hole in the ground?

She tried to push herself to standing but couldn't. A familiar feeling of weightlessness overcame her. She knew this, this feeling that she was removed from her body. The closest experience she could compare it to was the feeling of being asleep and moving through a dream.

*Hello?*

No words sounded. Nothing echoed. Her voice was nonexistent, no more than thought.

A voice of many as one was a welcome intrusion in her mind.

*Gerty, dear, you've come.* She could hear the smile in the Bastard's voice. *What can I help you with?*

The boy who'd called himself the Creator, his words cycled through her mind—

*— He will do no more for you than I could.*

She steeled herself and projected her thoughts into the darkness.

*I need to speak with Father George. I need to know what happened to him.*

*He's dead, my dear.*

Her heart sank. So it was as the boy with the eyepatch had said. A despondent sense of dread drowned her emotions, killing all but one: sorrow.

*Is there no hope? None whatsoever?*

337

*I did not say that. I said he was dead. Out of your reach. All you have is—*

*The Roaming?*

*Yes, dear. Whatever you've maintained of him, anyway. Could be worse, I suppose. People enjoy music all the time, and that's nothing more than a recording. Here. See this.*

Her ears popped, and she was standing in the hallway of a house with a staircase running up the right wall. The off-smell of dirty dishwater clung to air like an aromatic stain. Ceramic, or perhaps glass, clinked behind her. She half-turned and found herself looking into a kitchen foreign to her. At the sink, Molly George was doing dishes.

"Molly?" Gertrude said, her voice snagging and tearing on a thorn of emotions. "Molly, honey?"

Molly did not turn, did not acknowledge Gertrude in the least. Dishes clacked together. Molly swayed but remained silent. Not so much as the hum of a merry tune floated from her.

A phone rang behind Gertrude.

"I got it!" Thudding footsteps followed the voice. Father George came into view on the stairs. He bounced as he approached, jovial and flushed. "I finally got her down, by the way."

"That's good, dear," Molly said from the kitchen. "She's a daddy's girl, just like I was."

Father George answered a telephone in the living room with a cheerful "George residence?"

Mirth died a horrific death on Father George's face. His smile did not melt. It dropped, as if someone had cut the strings holding up the corners of his mouth.

"You shouldn't call me here."

Gertrude, for all her ethereality, possessed no magical hearing abilities. She drifted closer in order to hear the voice on the other end of the phone. Even up close beside Father George, she couldn't hear the caller.

"Don't ever call here again. Do you understand me?" Father George whispered into the phone and hung up. He made it three steps from the phone before it rang again.

His face boiled with anger. Usually pale cheeks filled with blood. His fists balled at his sides. He spun and snatched the phone from the base, slammed it down with a grunt.

"Who is it, dear?" Molly sang.

"Wrong number. Must be stubborn, too."

"Be gentle, dear."

Father George didn't respond but Gertrude could see an unloosed roar building in his throat. She expected his mouth to come open and his words to blast her back into reality. Unconsciously, she floated back a foot.

The phone trilled once more.

"You—" Father George said but stayed his tongue before what Gertude thought might have been a pent up curse burst from his lips. He closed his eyes and his lips moved almost imperceptibly. Gertrude thought he might have been praying.

The phone rang twice more before Father George answered. He seemed calmer, collected, but did not speak into the phone. Instead of speaking, his face became a blank slate, emotionless. His eyes drifted to a place on the wall. Perhaps even beyond it.

What was happening on the other side of the line? What was being said? For all her knowledge on the subject, Gertrude thought

Father George looked like a man who'd just been given word that his child had died. She saw herself in that face and her heart broke for the second time since Henrik's death.

"Yes," Father George said. He seemed to listen for a moment longer, and then he hung up.

Things happened quickly from there. Flashes of images like a poorly cut together moving picture.

Flash:

*Father George on the edge of a bed, loading a shotgun.*

Flash:

*He stands behind Molly.*

Flash:

*The shotgun snicks closed and Molly turns. The gun goes off.*

Flash:

*He's looking down at a slumbering Baby Georgina and crying as he aims into the crib.*

Flash:

*Father George sitting on the porch, shotgun across his lap, as a boy-child walks into the yard and toward the steps.*

Flash:

*The shotgun under Father George's chin.*

Flash:

*A splash of gore on the wall.*

Gertrude tried to stop the flashes, attempted to pause time and space, but she was powerless here. Nothing more than a spectator.

*Que sera sera...*

\*\*\*

Beulah watched Kirby in his cell. His blank expression hadn't changed, nor had he spoken since Hap had left them alone together. A part of her feared the teenager. Another part, a deeper, motherly part of her, felt sorry for the poor child. There was obviously something wrong with him and she didn't fully believe that he was entirely to blame for his actions.

Of course none of this made her fear him any less. She kept expecting to explode at any moment. Far be it from her to know what such a thing would feel like, but she could only imagine that being reduced to pieces would be unpleasant. Then again, she'd likely not feel anything at all. Would she just wake up in Heaven? Was it as easy at that? One moment, feet on Earth. The next, head in the clouds? She sure hoped so. Amen.

A low humming came from the boy, a guttural moan like a musical growl. His head tilted back and his jaw fell open.

Beulah half expected something to slither from the teenager's throat like a snake from a prairie hole. Had someone asked her to explain what occurred next she would have said she'd done nothing more than blink her eyes. She hadn't blinked though. Nothing of the sort. Her eyelids didn't budge a centimeter. Nor did she lose consciousness, or anything else of the kind. She was simply there in the hallway of the sheriff's department cellblock. And then she wasn't. If the transition could be compared to anything, Beulah might have compared it to a dream: how one can go from falling into darkness directly into sitting up in bed without any of the dream's momentum carrying over into the real world. This transition, though, was the direct opposite. She'd gone from standing in that hallway, perfectly at rest, to speeding through a forest like a mindless rocket.

Not mindless, though. She certainly felt guided, even if she were not doing the guiding herself. Trees flashed by, brown and green blurs, and the dreamlike quality of this place faltered, for she could feel the wind on her face, in her hair, and she could smell something sickly sweet on the wind, something like death, but far more pleasant and inviting.

She dropped from what felt like hundreds of miles per hour down to a creeping crawl in another blink that wasn't a blink. She hovered over a clearing, shoes dangling, several feet off the ground, and saw before her a great grinning mouth carved into the very earth below. A yawning chasm rimmed with rocky teeth, and a throat as black as the interior of a cave. Lurking within that darkness were stars of a multitude of colors: red, gold, silver. Yet these stars gave off no ambient light, not like stars in the sky might. There was no corona of illumination, as one might find around a full moon. No. Because these stars weren't stars at all. They were eyes.

And they were watching her.

"She sees us."

"Does she now?"

"Look at her. She sees something, she does."

"What would you have me do?"

"Get rid of her."

"As you wish."

None of this made any sense, not in her mind. The Bible spoke of religious experiences where one felt outside of their body, or of oddities like speeches from burning bushes and the dead returning to life, but none of this felt like that kind of… was *magic* the word she was looking for? She didn't know, but what she truly meant was that none of this felt godly, not in the least, and in her mind, only God was capable of... well, of *magic*.

Beulah did the only thing she knew to do. She began to pray.

"No," said one of the many voices emanating from the chasm. "Such words have no power here, child."

"Child? *Child?* I'll have you know that I am sixt—"

"You're but a child to us, Beulah Blackwood. Nothing more substantial than a pinprick on the map of the cosmos. We could fit a trillion of your lifespans within our own."

Beulah considered the idea that she was indeed dreaming. Or perhaps she was dead? Maybe Kirby had finally succeeded in exploding her head.

"Who are you?"

"Your tiny mind could not view us without crumbling under the weight of our truth. You know what we are just as you know what you are. You're a child of Man, as are we children of Man. The only difference between us and you is that we exist entirely in the mind. In *your* mind."

"I'm dreaming?"

"Dreams are far more real than you could ever imagine. But no you are not dreaming. You're not even asleep."

"Then what am I?"

Laughter issued from the pit of eyes.

"Wouldn't we all like to know everything that we are? Wouldn't that be lovely? To know all the answers to the questions of our existences would be a kind of Heaven, would it not? Alas, we know even less of our origins than you know of yours. At least your Bible gives you a beginning point. Imagine how godless beings like us feel, not having so much as a god to pray to, much less a Bible to offer guidance."

"There is only one God, and he oversees all of Creation. If you are real, He is your god as well."

Laughter came once more from the chasm.

"There are a thousand gods on your planet alone. Each deity, from the logical to the illogical, exists: Christ, Muhammad, Buddha, Shiva, Thor, Odin, the list extends infinitely. One god is even a pile of noodles. Imagine that. Pasta. As a god. Heavenly days…"

Their soft chuckling dotted her arms with gooseflesh. Whatever these things were they were mocking her. That much was obvious. But underneath her anger at being made fun of resided a basic human fear, her lizard brain sounding an alarm that whatever lay within this pit meant her the greatest of harm. Harm far beyond that which mere words could convey.

"Can we stop for a moment and consider why she is here?" asked a decidedly female voice, one that sounded uncannily familiar to Beulah.

"Momma?" Beulah asked, her lip trembling.

"She's projecting," said a voice that sounded an awful lot like Sheriff Harold Carringer's voice.

"Let her project all she wants. It hurts us none."

Now all the voices coming from the chasm sounded like people she knew. Even the voices she couldn't place felt as if they came from people she dealt with on a daily basis: her friends, family, congregation.

"This is not what you think it is, child," said the voice of Father George. "You're looking for answers where there are none.

There are no explanations to be had here, for this is all in your mind. And when the mind is faced with impossibilities, it begins to attribute factual information to its own imaginings. You need an anchor to keep rooted to the real world so you are lending familiar qualities to the voices you are hearing. Nothing more. Nothing less."

"So who are you? Really?"

"We're you, Beulah. We're your thoughts and emotions. Pain. Anger. Regret. All of it. All of *you*. We are your collective consciousness. Pleased to meet you."

"Wait… what's this?" asked an unfamiliar voice. It might have been Beulah's own voice but for the male timbre. "We have an outlier."

"What do you mean?" said Father George's voice.

"A boy. Family. Her grandson."

"Pete?" murmured Beulah. Having no idea what any of this meant.

"He's been through, to the other side. The boy has been on the pretzel."

"Pretzel? What in the world are any of you talking about?" Beulah cut in.

"She doesn't know?"

"I don't think even the boy knows."

"How can that be? That he couldn't know he's travelled?"

"Because he's not the one who did the traveling."

"Should we look to him for my revenge?"

"Revenge?" Beulah cried. "What are you talking about? My boy's done nothing to you! Not to any of you, whoever you are!"

345

"Oh, child, I have someone here, in your deepest memories, who begs to differ."

The earth quaked. From the black of the chasm's maw flew a scream ripped from the depths of memory. And in that moment Beulah Blackwood knew everything but wished to know nothing at all.

\*\*\*

Hap opened the door leading to the cellblock and stopped on the threshold. Beulah hovered in the middle of the hallway, her feet inches from the floor, her hands dangling lifelessly at her sides. Kirby sat on his bunk, his head thrown back, as if screaming, his dead eyes gazing at the cinder block ceiling.

"Beulah?" Hap asked as he approached the woman. He lay a hand on her wrist. The skin was ice cold. He tugged at her arm. Beulah didn't respond. He pinched the tender flesh on the inside of her wrist. Still no response.

"What did you do to her?" the sheriff asked Kirby.

He hadn't expected a response from the boy, but words came from Kirby's mouth all the same.

"She's with us now, Harold. In here with all the rest of them. Charles...Mary...Eddy, all the lives you've taken, or will take. All the pain you've shared. It's all here. Do join us, Harold. Join us and see the end."

Beulah dropped to the floor. Her arms twitched at her sides. Her eyelids popped wide and her eyes rolled as if they had separated from the nerves to trundle loosely in her head like the wheels of a slot machine. A single word spluttered from her trembling, spit-slickened lips:

"P-p-pete!"

"Pete? Something's happened to Pete? Beulah? Beulah, has something happened to your grandson? Beulah!"

\*\*\*\*

It was time to say goodbye but Pete Blackwood didn't want to leave. He explained to Wes that he really needed to get home before Mama got there. If she had to go out searching for him her anger would be legendary. Getting home before nightfall would be best.

Wes walked Pete out, telling him, "I wish you didn't have to go. I was having so much fun listening to your stories."

"I wanna stay, too, but I don't wanna upset Mama."

"I understand."

The sun sat fat behind the trees, but the sky was still just as blue as could be. The world would go dark in an hour or so, and then Wesley would be alone. In the dark. Alone in the dark with the memory of having watched a man blow his own head off.

"Maybe you could ask your grandma when she gets home if you can spend the night?" Wes opened the gate and walked with Pete to the end of the drive, to the place where they had met for the first time this morning.

"I don't know. Maybe. I'll ask, but I don't expect her to say yes."

"Okay."

"Hey," Pete said, gazing at something just over Wesley's left shoulder. "I didn't know you had two scare—what did you call it?"

Wesley turned to see where Pete was now pointing.

"Scaresparrow?" Wesley said.

Sure enough, not one scaresparrow but two could be seen above the stalks of the cornfield. Both of them were cloaked in shadow, their details lost at this distance, and Wesley thought for a moment that what he was seeing was some kind of optical illusion brought on by distance and poor lighting.

"We only have one," Wesley assured his friend.

"Huh. Weird. Think your dad—Pop—you think maybe he put another one up today and you just didn't notice?"

"Maybe. But why so close? That new one ain't but a few feet from the old one."

"Good point." Pete glanced around, but was not entirely sure what he was hunting.

"Pop probably put it up. Maybe he's planning to take the other one down, or something." Wesley ran a hand through his kinky red hair. "I'll check it out after you leave."

"I could check it out with you. Won't take but a minute, right? So you won't be scared."

Wesley looked at Pete. "Why should I be scared? Should I be scared? Now I'm not sure if I wanna go out there."

"We can check it out together, or we could just ask your dad, I guess. That would probably be best, now that I think about it. Come on. Mama can wait a few more minutes."

Pop wasn't in the barn or the house, and he wouldn't respond to any of Wesley's calls. After ten minutes of searching and finding nothing, they came across Pop's battered and tattered dishwater-gray work hat at the edge of the cornfield.

"He in there, you think?" Wesley said, sounding uncertain but a bit hopeful nonetheless.

Pete said, "Maybe what we saw wasn't another scaresparrow but your dad working on the old one? Maybe that could've been it? Your dad on a ladder, or something?"

"Could be," Wesley said, but Pete could tell that Wesley didn't actually think his father was in there.

"Wait... has it gotten darker?" Pete said, because it did seem far less bright than it had mere seconds ago.

"The sun's going down," Wesley said, as if that explained the sudden increase in shadows.

"But it wasn't that far down a minute ago. It's like time sped up. Do you know what I mean?"

Wesley shook his head. He didn't know what Pete meant because he wasn't really listening to Pete. Wesley wanted to go into the cornfield but didn't entirely understand his motivation for doing so. Pete wanted very badly to run away. The stronger Pete's will to flee the stronger Wesley's need to enter the corn became. Neither boy spoke their warring feelings.

Pete took a step backwards while his friend stepped into the corn.

Wesley, like a blown-out flame on a candle, vanished in a puff of black smoke.

Pete, stunned beyond comprehension, his mouth agape, gazed dumbly into the corn. He knew he should move, go find some help, but his feet seemed bolted to the ground.

He glanced over his shoulder, fully expecting to see the Haversham farm and the house down by the highway, but he saw none of that. He only saw corn. Corn for as far as his eyes could see. And above the corn, a sky blacker than any he'd seen before it. The darkness was so complete, the corn seemed to glow a golden-brown against the ebon landscape.

The scene made Pete dizzy. Something had changed. He'd been knocked out, or something. Someone had sneaked up on him while Wesley and he were looking into the corn and bashed him on the back of the head, like the bad spies did to the good guys in the espionage books he enjoyed so much. He was dreaming. No. This was no dream. This was a nightmare. It shared that sense of building dread every nightmare had. But somehow Pete knew that this was a nightmare from which he would not wake up.

Time passed and nothing happened and the question remained: what should he do?

Unbeknownst to either boy, Wesley was only a few feet away from Pete. For Wesley, nothing had changed. The sky remained a brilliant blue. An autumnal breeze stirred and combed the stalks all around him as he pushed through to the center of the field—to the scaresparrow.

The scaresparrow stood where it should have, its straw body nailed like Christ upon the cross. The sack face and its black Xs for eyes stared off into the distance as if it were reflecting on a past poorly spent. Wesley didn't remember the scaresparrow being so lifelike in presence before today. The clothing looked fuller, inhabited, especially the appendages, so unlike the half-empty limbs Wesley recalled. The boy felt that if he poked at the scaresparrow's leg he'd feel under the jean fabric of the coveralls not the give of crunchy straw but the resistance of human flesh.

He turned to ask Pete if Pete thought there was anything different about the scaresparrow and saw not his friend behind him but the back of a man as the man pushed between the stalks. The stalks closed behind the man like a curtain at the end of a play. The shape of the man couldn't have been mistaken by Wesley, not even on his worst day.

"Father?" Wesley said, meaning Father George. Meaning, he'd seen a dead man in the corn. Meaning, he had lost his mind. He needed to get out of here, and fast, before he became as lost as his sanity.

But which way to go? At some point he'd lost his bearings, and without the sun in the sky overhead he had no guidepost to follow.

The scaresparrow! The scaresparrow always faced south, as did his home. So if he followed the direction of its gaze, and did not deviate from that course, he'd find his way home easily.

He heard a massive cracking sound followed by the thump of something hitting earth behind him. Wesley turned and found the scaresparrow face down on the ground. Its head was on backward, as if someone had snapped the thing's neck. Wesley backed away from the fallen thing as something rose from the stalks.

Pete heard Wesley scream, the sound of his friend's fear echoed from every direction. Wesley sounded both near and far; miles away and directly behind Pete and inside his very head. His skull vibrated with the sound of Wesley's screams. Having no way to pinpoint Wesley's exact location and doubly rooted by his own fear, Pete remained unmoved and mostly immovable. His head snapped from side to side, seeking dangers, but his feet stayed put. He felt that, if he moved, even an inch, in any direction whatsoever, all would be lost: his life, the life of Wesley's father, and Wesley himself, all gone, murdered at the hands of... of what?

The killer in the baby doll mask who had murdered his parents flashed into his mind and Pete almost bolted into the sea of corn ahead of him. By sheer willpower alone, he remained still.

Wesley screamed again, his mind creaking under the strain of the thing rising from the stalks. The great beast was not entirely unlike the scaresparrow; whatever clung to the posts that made up its cross had once been human, or humans, that much was certain. But the body (bodies?) had been burned beyond recognition. In the briefest second before Wesley snatched around and dashed into the cornfield and whatever lay beyond, he thought he saw not one pair of arms but two. He thought he saw four legs as well. But the scorched mass didn't have the right dimensions to have been a man or a woman. Instead, the thing resembled a man and woman fused, as if the man had been poured into the woman. Furthermore, the larger body (the man's?) seemed to be crooked and folded in on itself, as if he'd been in a fetal position when the melding had occurred. Wesley absorbed all of this in under two seconds' time, and then he was off, rushing through stalks of corn that reached for and battered him as he fled.

Where he was going was anybody's guess.

Pete, however, remained where he was. He could hear breathing. Someone breathing. Just over his shoulder, yet he could not move. His legs refused to follow the directions called down from his brain. It were as if he stood waist deep in quicksand: his movement reduced to his torso and arms. He felt certain that his next move would be his last.

Long fingers grasped his shoulder. He looked down on the blackened digits. The skin had split and cracked in several places, and he could see red meat and white bone peeking through charred flesh. Smoke drifted in lazy wisps of black cloud from the nails and knuckles of the smoldering fingers. When it tightened its grip, the hand creaked like a poorly oiled door hinge.

"Please," Pete whispered. Tears streamed down his cheeks. He was on the verge of wetting his pants. "Please don't hurt me."

"Pete? That you?"

Pete sought the voice, his eyes bursting from his head in shock and confusion.

"Dad? Daddy?"

"Right here, son," Patrick Rothsberger said as he stepped from the corn. He looked as healthy and alive as Pete remembered. Pete's father wore a white cardigan and black slacks, what Pete thought of as Dad's Work Clothes. His feet, however, were bare. Strange, but Pete didn't focus too hard on the oddity.

"How are you—you died."

"It's all a lie, son, all of it. Religion. Politics. They give you choices that aren't really choices at all. Do you understand?"

"No, I don't. What are you talking about? I need—Daddy, I need help!"

"Have you had any weird mornings, Petey? Have you woken up and—has your penis been hard?"

"What are you—you—Daddy?" And that's when Pete knew that his father wasn't really here. This was some kind of memory, a loop of dialogue. He'd heard all this before. This most recent bit, the part about erections, had been his father talking to him about the birds and the bees.

Whatever was happening, Pete didn't like it, but now he was more angry than he was frightened.

"Stop it!" he squealed in a shrieking, cracking explosion of breath. "Just stop it!"

Patrick Rothsberger glared at his son. His eyes glazed, became lifeless. He swayed almost imperceptibly with the breeze.

"I was trying to help your passing," said a voice in Pete's ear. It was a voice that Pete associated with vampire movies. Rough yet smooth. A hiss like that of rushing water. The charred fingers squeezed his shoulder. "No one deserves to die alone."

"I don't want to die." Pete sucked snot and hated how weak he sounded.

"No one wants to die. It's the human condition. So very selfish, wanting to live forever. You'll live on, though. In memories. As your parents have lived on in yours."

"Please don't."

"I have no other choice."

And for the first time in his life, Pete thought, *better safe than sorry*, and began to pray, "Our Father, which art in Heaven…"

Wesley had forgotten all about prayer and God and saviors nailed to crosses. He had his very own cross to worry about, and by the sound of the thing (things?) upon the scorched cross, it moved quicker than he wanted to believe it could.

He'd never been so terrified in the daylight. His young mind assumed evil and monsters and creepy-crawlies couldn't come out during the day. Vampires were killed by sunlight, weren't they? Even werewolves couldn't shapeshift without a full moon. Witches never tended their cauldrons while the sun was up. Frankenstein's Monster? The Mummy? Forget about it. Not scary at all in the brightness of daytime.

But this thing on his heels? It was all the more terrifying because he could see it in its every minute detail: from the rolling white eyes in those two scorched faces, to the vibrant meat peeking through the cracks of the charred flesh. The way it moved was the worst: all herky-jerky, twitchy movements as the impossible thing struggled toward him.

Wesley didn't understand how it was moving so fast. Every time he chanced a glance behind him, there it was, mere feet from him, lurching on legs longer than any humans, legs longer than even the body of the cross. The scaresparrow's arms extended twice as far from its body as any human's as well. Those long, lanky arms swiped at the corn, cutting through the field like some kind of demonic harvester.

The last time he looked back, the thing had switched from two legs to all fours. It scurried toward him like a cockroach even as he burst free of the cornfield.

The barn.

He had to reach the barn, where at the very least there would be weapons in the way of farming equipment. Even a pitchfork was a better option than the whole lot of nothing he had to defend himself with.

Wesley was halfway between cornfield and barn when something grabbed his ankle. His leg was snatched backward and could not be pulled forward. He did a painful split and hit the ground, mashing his testicles in the process. Pain exploded in his crotch and radiated out in a corona of agony, souring his stomach.

He was flipped onto his back as easily as a trained line cook flips a flapjack. The scaresparrow crawled over him, sniffing and prodding with its noses, as if it were a pair of inquisitive pups.

"*Nonononono*," Wesley pleaded. "God, no. Please, God, no."

The woman's face slowly moved up to his own face. For a moment he was looking into the blackened features of a slumbering countenance. And then the eyes opened, as did the mouth, and Wesley screamed. Her white eyes rolled in her head. The chipped and cracked teeth in her mouth looked to be nothing short of a death trap. She sniffed at him, and Wesley could hear the man's head, where it hung in the woman's armpit, whimper like a baby denied a bottle.

The scaresparrow grabbed Wesley's arms and ripped them off, like a child removing the appendages of a fly.

Pete was made to watch the murder and dismemberment of his friend. The hand on his shoulder held him in place, and for the life of him he could not close his eyes. The scaresparrow tore Wesley's arms from his shoulders, and then the legs from each hip, as easily as one might tear apart a roasted chicken carcass. There was a fantastic amount of blood. Gallons upon gallons of gore splashed and sputtered and sprayed in every direction. Finally, the scaresparrow snatched up the torso by the shirt and dragged the corpse into the cornfield and out of sight.

Pete looked at the discarded arms and legs and couldn't remember Wesley as he'd looked when he was alive.

"Time to go, Petey," said the voice of Pete's father.

Pete wanted to ask where but did not need to.

"Home, child. Where else?"

"Home," Pete said and followed without another word.

\*\*\*

Hap's first mistake was reaching for Beulah where she lay seizing on the floor of the cellblock's hallway. Once his fingers touched her skin, everything went to hell. Several flashes of light, like lightning in the dark, blinded Hap. He stumbled backward, expecting there to be a wall to stop his momentum, but there wasn't. His speed collected, and he was suddenly reeling, arms pin-wheeling at his side, as he fell and fell and fell...

Hap's second mistake was keeping his eyes open as he was sucked from one place to another. He thought this must be what fluid feels like as it's sucked through a straw. For that's how he felt—sucked—and not in any way that could be misconstrued as pleasant.

On he flew, folded over at the waist, nose to knees, fingers touching his toes, rocketing through one place after another, scenery rushing by, sounds so muddled and mixed up he couldn't put a finger on what were words and what were random snatches of noise.

Time itself seemed to come apart behind him as his backside augered through rock and rubble, dirt and water, and then seemingly backward through a cornfield. A joke popped into his mind. Something about why you shouldn't run backward through a cornfield.

He came to a stop all at once. No slowing down. No deceleration. No whiplash when he snapped to a halt.

He found himself standing in the middle of a street. A street not unlike any other suburb he'd seen. Although the houses on either side were brighter than he was used to seeing: garish reds and yellows, neon pinks and greens. The houses looked like things taken part and parcel from someone's imagination, someone who had never seen a house in real life. The street didn't continue or terminate beyond the last houses. Instead the road curved upward to a building made of steel and glass. The modern structure would've fit right in somewhere else, some cityscape, somewhere like Manhattan or Los Angeles. Here, in what looked to be any old middle-American suburb, wacky-colored houses or no, the building of glass and steel fit in like a donkey in a field of flamingoes.

Hap's final mistake was assuming he was safe in this place, what he assumed was a dream. After all, what else could this be? He assured himself nothing could happen to him because this was obviously not reality. Maybe he'd been attacked and knocked out. Sure. He was unconscious somewhere, dreaming, while whoever had assaulted him attempted to break Kirby Johnson from his cell. Joke was on them, though, because Hap had hidden the key.

"Good luck, motherfuckers," Hap said as he made his way for the spot where the street curved and the hill started. He certainly wasn't going to stand around with his finger up his ass.

"Hello?" he called, thinking maybe that if he interacted with this dream world he might jumpstart the next phase of the dream. Or nightmare. Or whatever this was. Suffice it to say, he couldn't wait to wake up and confront whoever had knocked him out. They had a world of pain headed their way.

Every front door on the block crashed open at the same time. Hap, who'd been expecting something, anything at this point, didn't so much as flinch. Nothing came out of the doors, but Hap felt a multitude of cold eyes studying him.

He moved up the curve, toward the building of glass and steel. Halfway up the hill, lying in the middle of the road, was a crumpled human. A boy, by the look of him. Hap was right up on the kid before he recognized the kid.

"Pete? Pete, that you?"

The boy sat up, arms swinging this way and that, face flushed with the anger of battle, his thin brown hair plastered to his forehead and slick with sweat.

"Whoa, son. Whoa, calm down. It's Sheriff Hap, is all."

"Sheriff?" Pete asked, his eyes troubled with confusion. He squinted into the middle distance between the building of glass and steel and the brightly painted houses below. "Where am I?"

"That's the same question I've been askin myself, son. I was thinkin it might be a dream, but I don't think that's it. Seein you here has set my mind that there's a slight possibility that all this is real. And if it is real, I reckon we're in someone's idea of a game. I bet you the public fund that I know just who might be behind it."

"A game? Huh?" Pete seemed to consider this until his focus abruptly switched. "Wesley! Wesley Haversham is dead!"

"Haversham, you say? The Haversham boy who lives out on 607?"

"Yessir!"

"How'd he die? Did you see it happen?"

Pete started crying. "It tore him apart."

Hap noted that Pete had said *It*; not *He* or *She* or *Them*, but *It*. He didn't like the sound of that. Having seen the state of his deputy, the one splattered all over his office, Hap figured he was dealing with something bigger and meaner than just Kirby Johnson.

"What killed Wesley, Pete? What did it?"

Pete shook his head and sobbed. "I don't know. First—first we thought it was the scaresparrow. Wesley says they don't get a lot of crows out his way so he named it a scaresparrow. But it wasn't the scaresparrow. It was something else. Something big and nasty and all burned up."

"All burned up?" Hap said, his heart racing as film reels of Charlie Marchesini and Mary Robichaux roasting in Marchesini's car played in the cinema of his mind.

"And—and they—It was on a cross. A big one. It was huge!"

"You said *they* there for a minute. What did you mean by *they*? Was there more than one?"

*Please say no, kid. Please. I ain't but one man with only an idiot left for a deputy. I don't have anyone else I can call…*

"I think so. They were kinda fused together. I couldn't tell where one began and the other started. They were two people in one. It had too many arms and legs. They reached too far!"

The kid was losing control, and Hap wasn't sure how much he could trust what Pete said.

"Try to calm down. Calm down so we can find a way out of here. Wherever here is."

"It looks like," Pete sniffled, "looks like Humble Hill. My dad worked—he worked here before he died."

"You been here before?" Hap asked.

Pete shook his head. "Pictures. I've seen pictures. Dad brought one home and sat it on our mantle. Just him and some priest, Dad's arm around the priest's shoulder, both of them smiling. Down there." Pete pointed down to the street and the gate beyond, a gate Hap had yet to notice. "They're standing at the gate and the camera captured them, all those weird houses, and this building in the photo. It's one of the few pictures I kept. That one, one of Mom alone, and one of all of us together."

Hap stood and dusted off his knees. "So maybe all this has got something to do with your old man?"

"What? No. My mom and dad are dead. They got nothing to do with all this… all this weirdness."

"Weirdness. Yeah, I guess you could call it that. Loads and loads of weirdness. Hey, tell me, what were you doing before this scaresparrow thing killed Wesley?"

"Nothing. Nothing important, anyway. We were just—I was about to leave and Wes was walking me out and that's when I turned around and saw the extra cross, like there were two scaresparrows instead of one. That's what made me wanna check. Oh. Oh no. I killed him. I killed my friend. My only friend. I killed him. I kill—"

Hap slapped the boy, and probably a bit too hard. For a second there, what with the way the boy's mouth hung open, lips trembling, Hap feared he might've fractured Pete's jaw.

"Don't crack up on me. I can't have you losing it. I need you with me, ya hear?"

"Yes—Yessir." The boy looked dazed but more put-together than he had before. "What should we do now?"

"I suppose we need to find out how we got here and if we can leave."

"You don't think we'll be able to leave? Why wouldn't we be able to leave? You're the sheriff! They have to—"

"Pete, you're losin it again. Stay with me. I ain't a hundred percent, but I'm confident enough that we're in for some trouble that I don't think you should leave my sight, much less my side. Ya hear?"

"Yessir."

"Good boy. I guess what we should do first is check out this building right here, see if it's got a phone we can use. Once I get my deputy on the line, maybe he can come get us. Where'd you say this place was?"

"I don't know where it is. All I know is what my dad told me."

"And what did he tell you?"

Pete shrugged. "That it was called Humble Hill, is all."

"And what did your father do for Humble Hill?"

"He was in maintenance. He worked with equipment, is all I know."

"Was he a janitor?"

"Nossir."

"Okay. So what kind of equipment did he work on?"

"I don't know!" Pete cried.

"All right, all right. Calm down. Everything's gonna be all right."

"How do you know? Everything wasn't all right for Wesley!"

"You're cracking on me, Pete. Stay—"

"Of course I'm cracking! Look at me! Look at all of this! Look what's happened... A kid gets ripped apart right in front of me by some demonic scarecrow... scaresparrow, whatever, and then I wake up in some strange place with the town sheriff. I'm past losing it. I'm gone!"

"Makes two of us, kid. Listen, I don't have any answers, but I know that losing our shit—pardon my French—is the last thing we wanna do. It's easy to let go and cross the line into Crazy

Town, but don't. Stay with me. Put in the time, and maybe we make it out of this, this... whatever this is."

Pete shook his head until the shaking became nodding. Hap helped the boy to his feet. Pete wobbled at first, but soon stabilized.

Together, they entered Humble Hill.

\*\*\*

The lobby of the main building, what Pete thought of as a hospital, was chilly, as if someone had left on the air conditioning and forgotten about it for several days.

"You could hang meat in here," Hap told Pete. "Bet their electric bill is sky high."

Pete didn't respond. He checked behind the front desk for a phone and found one straight off. There was no dial tone. No operator picked up, either. Pete hung up and gave Hap a shake of his head.

Hap said, "Damn it. Keep looking."

Pete found another phone in an office off the main corridor, where the elevators sat with their doors open, silent and empty. No dial tone on the office phone either. But Pete did find something of interest. He picked up the picture frame from the desk and took it to Hap in the main lobby.

"This is the guy my dad worked for. His name's Lagotti, or something like that."

"Looks like a shady one. Never have trusted foreigners," Hap said, and the boy frowned. "Come on, you can tell he ain't from here. He's Indian, or somethin like it. They got different morals and beliefs than us. Me? I'd trust someone born and bred

363

American quicker than I'd trust some Frenchie or chink, wouldn't you?"

"I've never met a Frenchman or a... Chinese, so I don't know who I'd trust. All I know for sure is, plenty of Americans lie and cheat and steal. I think it's just humans who are horrible. I don't think where you were born has anything to do with what kind of person you'll become."

"How old are you again?"

"Eleven?" Pete asked as if he wasn't quite certain.

"Eleven? Really? Hell, you're dumber than a load of bricks for being almost a teenager."

Pete didn't like being picked on by kids his age much less a grown man who he had up until now respected if for no other reason than because of the badge on Hap's chest. Pete thought maybe that was a mistake, and that perhaps no one deserved blind respect, not even an officer of the law.

"You're a jerk," Pete said, and was proud to have said it.

"Yeah?" Hap said with a grin.

"Yeah." Not *Yessir*, just *Yeah*.

Hap chuckled. "I didn't mean none of that. Just stressed, and when I'm stressed I rag on those around me, is all. You understand?"

Pete nodded because he understood perfectly. Hap was not the man Pete had thought he was. Anyone who picked on a child wasn't much of a man at all.

"What's say we check out this hospital, or whatever it is. How about that?"

Pete, believing there was nothing else to say, said nothing at all. He headed for the doors at the end of the elevator hallway. Hap followed. They'd made it halfway there when the double doors came open and Beulah Blackwood stepped through.

A smile stretched her face and she screamed, "Oh, thank God in Heaven you're alive! I thought you were dead for sure!"

She crushed Pete in a hug.

Into her age-deflated bosom he mumbled, "I'm fine, but they got my friend."

"Friend? What friend?" She pushed him away to look at him but kept hold of his shoulders. "You don't have any friends."

Pete glanced at Hap as if to say, *See what I deal with?*

Hap gave Pete a looked that said, *Sucks to be you, kid.*

"How'd you get here, Beulah?" Hap asked Beulah.

"I don't know. Been here a minute, I reckon. Been all over this damn hospital and ain't another person here. If they is, they ain't answerin my hollerin."

"Nothin? Ain't nothin here? I don't believe that shit. Not far as I could throw you. Why else we here? Huh? What the hell we doin here if'n there ain't shit for us to interact with?"

Pete noted how deep the sheriff's accent became the redder the sheriff's face got.

Beulah said, "There ain't but one door I haven't checked, and it's locked. If you fancy bustin it down, maybe we could get some answers."

"Well, hell, woman, why didn't you say so to begin with? Lead the fuckin way, for Christ's sake."

"Language, Harold."

"I don't need to hear that bullshit right now, Beulah. Just show me where the door is before I shoot you."

\*\*\*

Beulah knew what was behind the door to Exam Room 1 long before she'd found Hap and Petey wandering around in the lobby. There was only one person it could be. Only one person left.

She'd even guessed correctly that the door would open easily now that they were all here. Because whoever had organized this nightmare had a plan, and the only way forward was through their lavish traps.

Doors that didn't open until all party members were in attendance were the least of their worries.

Hap pushed open the door to Exam Room One and said, "I should've fuckin known it would be you."

"Hello, Sheriff," Father George said. "Been an age since we last saw you around here."

"I thought he was dead," Pete said, obviously the only one in the room surprised to see the dead pastor. Although he didn't look dead. Beulah had to give the guy that. For a dead man, Father George was awfully fresh-looking.

"Those who accept Jesus Christ as their Lord and Savior, never truly d—"

"Save the god-bothering for another time, Holy Man. Mind telling us what's going on here and how we opt out of it?" Hap said in a stern voice that sounded mighty silly to Beulah, and seemingly to Father George too, for the man clasped his hands in front of himself and laughed.

Father George said, "On the wall out front, in case you missed it, it says Exam Room One. Did any of you consider what it is we might be examining?"

"Forget the riddles, George. Tell us what you want."

Father George sighed. "So impatient. But patience has never been your strong point, has it, Hap? If you had a little patience, maybe Mary Robichaux would still be alive. Maybe not. *Que sera sera...*"

"I remember that name. Why do I remember that name?" Beulah asked. Damn her memory, never working when she needed it. It was right there, on the tip of her tongue, the edge of her subconscious, if she could only tip it over...

"Don't hurt yourself, Beulah. Here, let me help." Father George snapped his fingers and Beulah saw it all, as if she'd been present the night Hap had murdered Mary Robichaux and Charlie Marchesini.

"You... you killed them? You killed that young couple and got away with it? All this time? You... you..."

Hap said, "Oh for fuck's sake, Beulah, I tried to warn you. I tried. No one can say I didn't fuckin try."

Hap slid his revolver from its holster and permanently fixed Beulah's bad memory for her. Never again would she have to worry about misplacing a name or thought, for now her mind was written on the wall for all to see.

***

"Worthless old bitch," Hap growled. "Now, far as you're concerned—"

Hap turned to face Father George, the dead man who wasn't so dead after all, and was disappointed to see that the pastor had vanished. In his place was the Johnson boy—Kirby—strapped to a chair in the middle of the room. The rig vaguely reminded Hap of a dentist's chair that fully reclined. Beside the chair was a push cart with what looked like a car battery and jumper cables resting atop it, but instead of alligator clamps at the ends of the cables, there were metal paddles the diameter of a coke can with rubber handles.

Scorch marks darkened the flesh at Kirby's temples, and his blank eyes gazed toward the ceiling. Dried tears drew pale lines down his face. He looked like a catatonic clown.

Hap sighed in exasperation. "Now what the fuck is this shit?"

The teenager didn't speak, not in English or any other language Hap was familiar with. He just kinda blubbered and cooed, like a baby. To further add to the image of an infant, the teen's neck was loose on his shoulders, like a newborn's. No doubt about it, the kid was absent from his own wheelhouse.

A feeling of fear and uncertainty overcame Hap. Something was *wrong*, and the worst part about all of it was that Hap had no idea what exactly was *wrong*. He struggled, but the harder he thought, the further away the answer moved. Like he did sometimes when dealing with truly bothersome people, Hap recited the Miranda Rights in his head until his brain reset. Then:

*Where the fuck is Beulah's body?*

The old woman's body, along with the blood and brain matter on the wall, was gone. Hap stood there for a moment, reliving the last minute, wondering if he'd actually killed the bitch. Why had he shot her in the first place? Shit, he couldn't remember.

Fuck.

He was missing something else, meaning Beulah's body was not the only thing missing from the crime scene—examination room; whatever. Someone else had been here.

Father George?

Yes. But not only him. Someone else. Someone smaller. Younger. Chubbier.

"Pete?" Hap asked an empty room. Kirby didn't count as being in attendance because what was left of Kirby, to Hap at least, barely counted as human.

"Pete!" Hap roared like a caged and confused animal. "Pete, you come out now! I don't wanna be chasing you all over this godforsaken fuckin hospital! Pete! *Petey!* Come out, come out, wherever you are!"

\*\*\*

No way in hell was Pete moving. Not only was some psycho sheriff on the hunt for him, but things were all screwed up.

His mind replayed Mama's head exploding and splattering all over the wall of Exam Room One Luckily he'd had the wherewithal to run and not hang around to ask stupid questions like, "Why did you do that?" That's how you got yourself killed. Well, that's how idiots got themselves killed, and Pete was no idiot.

He'd hid under a desk in an office off the main hallway. The desk was big by adult standards and gargantuan by Pete's. He seemed to be in a whole other world under here. He had so much room. If he lived through this, he'd have to get one of these desks for himself.

He wasn't thinking properly. He knew that. Was he going crazy? Had he already gone? Who in their right mind thinks about shopping for desks while playing hide and seek with a madman? Not an eleven-year-old, and certainly not an eleven-year-old such as Pete Blackwood. Yet there it was, that asinine thought, flashing brightly in his cerebral cortex.

He felt like a character in a badly written book, one whose author bends the rules to fit the arc of the plot. Pete had read books like that all too often, mostly of the pulp-paperback variety, the ones his father used to love. A character would go out of their way to do something against character simply so the story could progress.

He could smell something burning. The odor was both irritating and familiar all at once, the scent of burning leaves that, until today, had been nothing more than a reminder of the season. But now he associated the scent with something far less innocent than autumn.

"*Nonononono…*" Pete hissed from under the desk. "Not here. Not now."

\*\*\*

Hap smelled the burning around the same time Pete did. Smoke, thick and black, wafted under the door like sentient fog.

And from that fog rose a horror Hap's mind refused to parse: flesh the color and texture of coal, sickly yellow eyes and teeth, twisted limbs with skin so cracked and warped that the raw red meat below the scorched flesh peeked through.

Hap roared and fired into the cruciform. A bullet struck the head in the thing's armpit. This second mouth creaked open, pouring smoke, to release a squeal that loosened Hap's bowels. A long, thin, blood-red tongue flicked from the orifice to lick at the chasm the bullet had gouged in the charred forehead. Hap could easily see the white of the skull as the tongue licked the wound clean.

In that spread of several seconds, that microcosm of stationary time, Hap saw what the thing was, what it truly was, everything it had been before the fire, and tears came to his eyes, for this thing was more victim than villain, much in the same way Hap was more heathen than heretic.

"Bay?" Hap spoke the words uncertainly but he was certain. He'd never been so certain in all of his life. This burnt and twisted and evil thing had once been a human being. Two human beings, in fact, and that meant only one thing. The stories were true.

Marietta Bay had been burned alive, at the stake, and Francis, her husband, had clung to her in his final moments. What magic had brought them back was of no concern to Hap. All he wanted was to live. So he did the first thing that came to mind; he begged for his life.

"I didn't do this to you. I had nothing to do with what happened to you. Neither did anyone in my family. What happened to you—" The scaresparrow took a lumbering step forward, dragging its wooden tail behind it. "Stop! Just—Just fuckin stop right there!" He pointed his gun to the ceiling in a gesture of placation.

"Just listen a moment. I don't know what you want. But if you tell me—shit, *can* you tell me? Can you even fuckin *talk*?"

Another step closer, smoke rolling off the crossbar and shoulders in sulfuric waves. Hap could see and feel the heat coming off the thing. Tears dried instantly on his cheeks, it was so unbearably hot.

"God, please. Please, no." Hap, backed into a corner, waited for the end.

\*

Jerimiah Fulgore drove the pickup through the security gates of Humble Hill. Metal squealed and tore away, allowing the truck through. The damage didn't matter. No one would stop them because no one manned the guard posts. No one lived in the colorful houses, or worked in the hospital on the hill. This place existed elsewhere, in someone's Someplace, someone dead, and Gertrude Fulgore planned to make it stay dead.

Somewhere in Reality, Waverly Chasm groaned, waiting to be fed.

"Up to the hospital. Up there." She pointed in the direction she wished Jerimiah to drive and only hoped she wasn't too late.

Maybe, just maybe, she could save the day, and this timeline along with it.

\*\*\*

Hap could go no farther. The wall wasn't moving and there was no way he was melting through it. He either had to try to run past the scaresparrow, or give up and let it kill him.

One thing was certain, Sheriff Harold "Hap" Carringer—two RS, please and thank you—was no goddamn quitter. He slid to the right, back against the wall, moving from one corner of the room to the other and effectively putting Kirby, where the teenager lay strapped to the dentist's chair, or whatever it was, between him and the smoking creature.

Oddly, Hap wanted the thing to talk, to threaten him, to do something other than glare and blow smoke. Its silence was more terrifying to him than any drunken slur or shouted ad hominem attack he'd ever faced. This thing was all about its business, and its business was him.

Slavering and puffing acrid black plumes, the scaresparrow skirted Kirby in his chair and inched forward. Hap slid into another corner, a mere foot from the door. He reached for the handle. The scaresparrow squealed and roared and shoved Kirby, chair and all, up against the door, pinning Hap's wrist in the process.

"Fuck!" Hap hollered in pain and frustration. "Fuck you!"

Hap spat in the face jutting from the thing's armpit. His saliva flash-boiled upon the black flesh, sizzling away to nothing. He looked away then, not wanting to see the kill stroke, and saw Kirby's eyes were open and staring. Starting at him.

"Whataya looking at, shithead?" Hap cringed and waited to die.

Kirby spoke. "Not him. Not now. He has a role left to play. The boy. Get the boy." He reached for where Hap's hand was pinched between wall and door and yanked it painfully out.

Hap, confused yet curious, snapped his head to watch the scaresparrow melt into the floor. As it descended, black smoke boiled up and around it. The smoke then drifted under the chair and subsequently under the door and out of the room.

Hap thought he'd rather make a fire extinguisher disappear up his ass before he'd willingly stand face to face with that thing ever again.

When the scaresparrow was good and gone, Hap stumbled away from Kirby and crashed into the far wall. He slid down and brought his knees up and cried like he hadn't cried in a long, long time, not since he was a very little boy. Adrenaline does that to a person. No matter how tough you are, no one is tougher than fear. Fear can be overcome. Fear can be defeated. The strong rise above. The weak crumble. But fear, fear lives on.

"You con—control that th-th-thing?" Hap stammered and hated himself for it.

"It is of me, yes." Kirby looked at each of his straps and they came loose, one at a time.

"What the fuck are you?"

"I am of no import. I am but a messenger. The boy—Kirby—has been gone for some time. Since they—since they did what they did to him."

"Who did what to him?"

"They opened him, allowing me in. It wasn't all that bad. Not really. He feels no pain now, and warrants no reprisals. Leave him be to do what he wants, clean up this mess, and move on. One day, you will be of use. One day, you'll even be a father."

"What the fuck are you talking about?"

Kirby's image flickered and skipped, like a film reel missing several frames, and suddenly he knelt before Hap, his hand holding the sheriff's chin in its palm.

"You will be the catalyst, the spark that starts the fire that burns it all down. Your story will be told and people will believe and not believe, but none of it will matter, as none of *this* matters.

"Your species is so selfish. Each and every individual thinks they are worth more than the bag of flesh that they are. You work and play and fornicate and pray and feed, feed, feed, but none of it matters. *You* do not matter. But I have no control over the will of man. I can suggest and point in the right direction, but I cannot force actions. I can remove pieces from the board, as it were, but I cannot change a rook into a queen. Likewise, I cannot make a king into a pawn.

"I don't know what any of that means," Hap whined. He no longer had control of his emotions. The metallic taste of spent adrenaline tainted his taste buds.

"Be sated by the fact that your understanding or lack thereof means nothing. You are but a stain on the fabric of time. A streak of filth across the loom of the universe. And I for one cannot stand your vileness. But a cleansing fire is in order, and unless you wish to be removed from the board, I suggest you play your part. Ah, ah—no comment is needed from you. There are no instructions, Hap. You simply must do what you will do. When the time comes, you must do what is best for your family, for your boys. I give you only one piece of information. Candy is important."

"Candy? What the—"

But Kirby was already gone from in front of him. The teenager—or whoever was driving Kirby's body—was back in the chair, straps in place, eyes rolling behind closed lids.

Hap didn't want to move, so he didn't. He stayed where he was until the noises outside the room stopped and everything was over.

For him.

For now.

\*\*\*

Gertrude Fulgore walked through the doors of Humble Hill and into another place—a *Someplace*. She'd grown accustomed to the smell of ozone and the pop of her ears when traveling, so much so that she was nearly comforted in her task, knew that she was on the proper path.

People in white uniforms shuffled about the hospital's lobby but no one noticed Gertrude because Gertrude was not here. This was nothing more than the Roaming, the memories of the living. But whose memories? If Father George was truly dead, there had to be someone else. Someone powering this place, this recollection.

Gertrude peered through doors, down hallways and around corners, until she came to a single red door in a row of white ones. She pulled the door open with her mind and moved inside, because for all her intangibility she found she could not pass through solid objects. People in the Roaming didn't notice her, but atoms, the building blocks of everything, knew she was there.

Those inside the room did not acknowledge her presence. One man, who was dressed in an open red lab coat and white dress shirt, sat behind a desk that took up a third of the large office. The man in the red coat leaned forward and said to the other man whose face Gertrude had yet to see, "What did he say?"

"*Everything is horrible now.*" The man whose face Gertrude had yet to see sounded like a man in a trance, like someone had hypnotized him.

The man in the red coat frowned. "Is that all?"

"Yes."

"And they're both dead? The man and woman? The boy is alive?"

"The boy is alive."

"Good, good. I hate that he had to see that, but such is the nature of the world. He'll be stronger for it, later on in life. You've served your purpose. You may leave. When you get home, I'll call you and reset you and—What am I telling you all this for? You're not going to remember a damn word of what I said." The man in the red coat laughed. "You may go home now."

"Yes."

The man in the chair rose and turned to face Gertrude. She stumbled back through the open office door and into the hallway. Connected hard with the opposite wall and damn-near climbed it by sheer willpower alone.

She hated dolls. Had never liked the things. Their dead eyes terrified her.

The man coming at her wore a baby doll mask. Although this was a man and no doll, she could see no spark of life in the eyes peering through the holes in the mask. Those eyes were empty pits—windows looking out over a barren landscape.

The man in the doll mask turned to his left and moved down the hallway and out of sight.

In the office, a phone rang. The man in the red coat lifted the receiver and said, "Lagotti."

After a brief pause, he said, "Yes. Yes, he's gone. No, we still are not entirely sure how they traveled. I imagine it has something to do with the rift the sissy created. I'm sure." Lagotti chuckled as one chuckles at an inside joke. "Unbelievable. Did she really? Well, give her my regards. Goodb—I'm sorry? No, no, I have no idea what comes next. We can make the fixer a piece of marketing but it might take a while to catch on. The longer we wait the more the world will change. Oh, yes, a false sense of security is better than force, always, I agree. Yes," Lagotti laughed again, "It gets better. It does, indeed. Goodbye, now. Yes, yes, bye."

Lagotti placed the receiver back on the phone's base and looked out through his office door and into Gertrude's eyes.

"It gets better. The bandage on the spurting wound. The round peg in the square hole. It's not about the fix. Only the perception that it is fixed. Let them believe it gets better. Let them have their cake and eat it too. What care I, I say. What care I?

"*Que sera sera.*" Lagotti's right eye flashed red before the man vanished.

"The Lord's will be done, Gertrude."

Gertrude turned in the direction of the voice and found Father George in the hallway. His smile seemed genuine, but so much about him had.

"What's the meaning of this? What does any of this have to do with you?"

"Some questions are never answered, Gertrude. Some questions we must give to the Lord."

None of this was new. This was all—what had the boy with the eye patch said?—a recording. A loop of previously spoken words. In what context had Father George said the things he was saying now? And did it really matter?

"His will be done, Gertrude."

"His will be done," she echoed.

"That's right."

"I come here to save you, but you can't be saved, can you?"

"All things in the Lord's time."

"You was a good man, weren't you? Why'd you kill yourself? Why'd you do all that to your baby and your wife? What makes a good man go sour? Will you tell me that, Father?"

"I'd like to think that I can be a father figure in lieu of our true father."

More repetition. She'd heard all this before. What possible good could any of this—

Wait.

This wasn't the Roaming. At least not *her* version of the Roaming.

She glanced back at the office, to where Lagotti had been seated, and instead of the doctor in the red lab coat, she saw a boy lying on a cot in a jail cell.

She knew this boy, didn't she? He was a member of her church. What was his name? Jones? Jackson?

Johnson. Donna Johnson's boy, that's who he was. Donna was a good, god-fearing woman; she attended every service. Gertrude, if nothing else, had respected the woman as a fellow member of her congregation, moreso than that Blackwood woman, anyway.

Gertrude looked away from the boy on the cot and found that she was no longer in the hallways of Humble Hill but inside the boy's cell: bars to her back, cinder block walls on both sides, an unbearable chill coming from everything.

Kirby Johnson, where he lay on the cell's cot, seemed to be crying.

"Boy?"

At the sound of her voice, something changed. Kirby Johnson was no longer lying on the cot but sitting on its edge, eyes to the ceiling, mouth gaping, as if loosing a soundless scream toward Heaven. Above him, the ceiling was gone. Nothing up there but the black void of space. Icy fingers tickled her spine.

"What is this?" was all she could manage.

"Everything is horrible now."

"I'm scared," said she, and knew it was true. There was something up there—*out there*—beyond the stars, beyond any afterlife, beyond eternity. Something ageless beyond sat on its haunches, waiting. She could feel its heartbeat in her chest. Could smell its breath in the vacuum of the Void.

This presence was not God.

This thing had created God.

*In the beginning, there was only me.*

Was it a woman's voice? Why shouldn't it be?

Gertrude, trembling, dropped to her aged knees and genuflected before the presence.

"I live to serve!" she cried into the concrete floor. "I am your faithful servant, Lord God. Bless me, for I am but a humble sinner. Praise be to you!"

Moments passed.

Nothing happened.

Then, a small voice:

"Kill me."

\*\*\*

Pete smelled the smoke long before he saw it. It crept under the desk to wrap around his ankles. With a vicious tug he was torn from his hiding spot. His fingers scraped along the carpet of the office, nails bending back, not catching, palms burning as they dragged over the coarse fabric. The hand of whatever gripped him burned through his pant leg and into his flesh. He could feel his leg cooking.

"Help!" Pete cried, his voice a gurgling mess. He couldn't clear his emotion-clogged throat long enough to get a good, hardy scream out. He was going to die, whimpering and alone.

A profound pressure built up in his head, like a tea kettle with a closed spout gathering steam. No release. His skull pounded. Begged for relief. He screamed and wished for the end.

His ear popped.

Glorious relief.

Exquisite release.

He opened eyes he hadn't realized he'd squeezed shut due to the pain.

*Where am I?*

\*\*\*

"Wait. Where'd he go?" Kirby said in a dreamlike voice.

Hap looked up at the boy through tear-clogged eyes. "What?" he said in a weak voice.

Kirby's voice was barely a whisper, his lips parting just enough to utter two words:

"Find him."

\*\*\*

The smell of smoke lingered, haunted the boy.

Pete was on his stomach, as he had been while trying to scrabble away from the black and reaching cloud, but instead of carpet beneath him there was grass. He rolled over, sat up.

In the middle of an open field a massive pyramid of wood reached skyward, logs jutting toward cloudless night. Although there was no sun, or any sort of light whatsoever, Pete could see just fine. He started to get up but his leg protested.

He reached down and pulled up his scorched pant leg to reveal seared and bubbling flesh. He cringed at the sight. It smelled like burnt grease.

It took everything he had to stand on that leg, but he managed.

Smoke poured from between the logs that made up the massive bonfire. But this smoke wasn't from any bonfire. The noxious black cloud boiled from the base of the unlit bonfire like fog off a lake. The stink of it invaded Pete, clung to him like a scared child. He stumbled away, crashed down on his ass.

From the pooling smoke came the scaresparrow, rising from the ebony miasma like a black angel on the Devil's business. Its skin crackled and sizzled as it lumbered toward Pete; its eyes, one pair in the head up top and the other in the armpit, blazed with uncanny yellow light. Behind it, the tail made of cross skittered and scraped across the grass, gouging a trail in its wake. The unnaturally long legs jerked and stuttered. The forever-long arms reached.

Pressure built up once again in Pete's head and then:

*Pop.*

He stood in a forest gazing down on a horrific scene. A pile of woman lay before him. She looked to be the victim of some kind of explosion. Her features were marred by an obviously broken jaw, but the squint of her eyes easily told her ethnicity: Asian. A claw reached from her chest, as if a great, bony monster had impaled her on its talons.

It took Pete a moment but he finally recognized the claws for what they truly were.

The woman's ribs had burst from her chest.

What had happened to her? Why was he here? Surely he couldn't help her. He couldn't even help himself at present.

Pete looked up, glanced around for help, and that's when he saw the ghost. Had this been any other day, any other normal day, Pete would have thought he was imagining things. But not today. Weird was the soup de jour, and Pete was eating his fill.

A ghost floated amongst the trees. Not a specter. But a Halloween-party ghost. A boy or girl draped in a sheet. Maybe three, three-and-a-half feet tall.

The woman on the ground gurgled. Her right leg twitched, kicked at him. It seemed to be her only working part. The only working appendage, anyway.

Pete didn't want to be here.

Pressure.

Pop.

A new place. Still in the woods. Up ahead, an old man hid behind a tree, watching a scene unfold several yards away. A police car sat on the same side of the road as the trees. Across the street, a line of houses. Pete could hear voices in the distance: a man speaking, followed by a woman pleading. He glanced behind him, for the voices seemed to come from all around, and saw through the trees an unlit bonfire off in the distance. This was a much smaller one—about a hundredth the size, at least—than the great pyramid he'd seen in... in that *other place*, but it was arranged the same way: logs set up like a teepee.

Three kids—two boys and a girl—darted from around the cop car, the boys laughing, the girl looking scared out of her wits. They disappeared into the thicker part of the woods. Then:

*Pop.*

Pete expected to teleport to another location, but he didn't.

Another pop, like small-arms gunfire.

Pete counted six pops in all.

He hadn't moved an inch, and didn't plan to.

Out at the street, a cop came jogging into view. He made like he was about to drop into his car but stopped. He twisted and gazed down into the cruiser and cussed loudly. His head snapped left and right, seeking help.

No. That wasn't right.

The cop looked guilty of something. He seemed not to be looking for help but for witnesses. One of the dead giveaways for Pete was the fact that the cop wasn't crying for help or going for his radio. Something had happened, and the cop was making sure no one had seen.

For the first time Pete saw the long white scar across the cop's cheek.

The old man left his hiding spot behind the tree and went to the cop. Together they walked out of sight. Pete could hear them talking in low voices.

Pete, unsure what else to do, moved toward the car, remaining vigilant of the scene, tentatively checking all around as he went.

He snuck a peek inside the cop car. Four cherry bombs, or the husks of them, anyway. Pete noted that there had been six pops though and looked around for more husks.

An engine started and Pete swung his head up and to the right in time to see a yellow car driving away. The old man was gone, but the cop remained, watching the second car leave.

Pete wasn't stupid by any stretch of the imagination. He knew that, at any moment the cop would turn and head back to his squad car. Then he would see Pete. Pete, a witness. Pete, someone who needed to be silenced.

*Crap.*

Pete turned to run.

The scaresparrow wrapped him up in its fiery embrace.

Pete's hair caught fire first, then his clothes. He tried to scream but flame raced down his throat and cooked his lungs from the inside. His eyes ruptured and dried on his cheeks in the intense heat.

In his final moments, Pete heard his father's voice assure him that Heaven wasn't real. It was a mythical construct created by man. While that might be the case, Pete Blackwood knew Hell existed, for he had stepped into its damning fire.

\*\*\*

"Kill me," Kirby said again, and the old woman in the cell with him glared.

"Who is you?"

"Please, kill me," Kirby pleaded. Tears rolled warmly down his cheeks.

The old woman squinted and studied him.

She said, "I'm Gertrude Fulgore. Name yourself."

"I'm Kirby," he said and dropped his gaze. "You're not going to kill me, are you?"

"I'm the Lord's business. 'Sides, I'm not a killin kind. Are you Donna's boy? The one what went away?"

Kirby nodded. He looked up into the swirling void above, into that darkness bereft of stars, and an overwhelming melancholy sucked the air from his chest in a shuddering breath.

"Everything is horrible now," he said. "They told Sadie it gets better, but I don't believe that. I just wanna die and be done with it."

"Why you wanna die?"

Kirby looked at the old woman with the long silver hair and thought she was pretty, despite her gray flesh and seeping wounds.

"You ever feel like you don't belong?"

"I ain't never belonged anywhere but with my family."

"See, I don't even have that anymore."

"What business do you have in this? You ain't but a boy."

"He said he loved me," Kirby said, bottom lip quivering. "He told me he wanted to be with me."

"He?" she said, a cloak of disgust shadowing her features.

"It doesn't matter what you think of me, what anyone thinks of me. I'm tired of feeling trapped in my own body."

Kirby stood, stepped onto the cot, and reached upward, into the void.

"Take me. Whoever's up there, watching, will you take me?"

"Boy?" the old woman named Gertrude said. Kirby looked down at her. "It were Father George who said he loved you, yes?"

"Yes."

The old woman nodded and the pall of judgment fell away from her face to be replaced by a look of pure understanding.

"Godspeed, Kirby. Godspeed."

Kirby Johnson drifted from the cot and into the airless void above. Passing over the threshold was like slowly sinking into a frozen pond. His muscles stiffened and hardened. Cracks spider-webbed his skin. Teeth shattered. Eyes burst. His mind was the last to be destroyed, but not before a soothing presence bigger than the ominous beast that had chased him from his home this morning came over him and he was filled with joy.

Here, he was welcome.

Here, he would be loved.

Joy would make it all right.

Joy would make it better.

Lo, if he'd only found Joy before the end.

\*\*\*

"I expected more from you."

Hap lifted his head from where he'd buried his chin in his chest. His face was sticky with dried tears and snot. He felt like a mess and looked the part too.

He wasn't a bit surprised to see Father George standing in the corner of the room, to the left of the door Kirby and his chair blocked. Hap was done being shocked. A baboon in a loin cloth selling real estate in Wonderland wouldn't have so much as raised an eyebrow.

"You don't look happy to see me."

"Fuck you," Hap muttered.

"That's not very nice of you to say. I'm here to help you, child."

"I ain't no child."

"Everyone is my child," Father George said, his eyes flashing red, like rubies glinting in the sun, there and gone, just a flicker, but Hap caught it.

"Leave me alone. Haven't you done enough already?"

"What is it I've done, child?"

"Stop calling me that."

"Fair enough. No more patronizing from me. Feel free to call me *Father*, though. The moniker is apt."

"Fuck you."

"Your vocabulary could use some work."

Hap sighed and closed his eyes. All he wanted was to sleep.

He closed his eyes again.

And again…

And again...

No matter how many times he squeezed his lids shut, he could still see. More demon magic, or whatever was going on, he figured. He was so goddamn tired of all these games.

"Kill me, or don't, but just get on with it."

"No one's going to kill you. Didn't the boy tell you you're needed? Far be it from me to stand in his way. He gets testy when he's ignored or left out."

Hap studied the ends of his shoes. They could use a good polish. He wiggled his toes beneath the black leather.

"Hap, I fear you're not here with me."

Hap wondered if Bailey's was open now? He could use a sandwich. A good corned beef with mustard and a dill pickle.

"You're making me angry, child."

"I ain't your fucking child, and I don't give a flying fuck if you behead me and piss down my neck. I ain't talking to you. Last I'm sayin on the goddamn subject, you two-bit magic-unicorn motherfucker."

The thing that looked like Father George laughed.

"Must say, Hap, that's the first time anyone's ever called me that combination of words." Chuckle, chuckle. "Oh, how strange you children become when frightened."

"I ain't scared of you."

"No. But you were. Now you've given up, and I can't have that. The Creator had his fun, but there's more to this game than role playing and skipping stones. We've come to an impasse, a place where time itself is broken and cannot move forward. Mainly because of you."

Hap shook his head. "You're missing the part where I'm saying I don't give a shit."

"You didn't say—"

"I don't give a shit."

Hap caught a glimpse of a second shadow lingering on the wall behind the man before it melded back into the one cast by the pastor.

"And this is why I'm here. All of this comes down to this moment in time, this overlap. We're stuck, Hap, and it's all your fault."

"Go to hell."

"We all, every single one of us, corporeal or ethereal, are in a hell, of a fashion. You, child, are the one who put us there, and yourself along with us."

Hap simply stared at the apparition of Father George, waiting for it to continue.

"You never have been quick on the uptake. Fine, listen." Father George, or whoever was controlling this version of him, cleared his throat. "Time is a pretzel."

The being before Hap traced a figure-eight in the air with an index finger. The finger left behind a smoky crimson haze so that Hap was looking at a bloody cloud in the shape of an eight laying on its side.

"This is time, infinite, ever growing and overlapping on itself. Do you see?"

Hap glanced from the figure-eight to Father George and back again.

"I'll take that as a yes." Another clearing of the throat. "This overlapping timeline is your reality. But my kind—your memories and emotions—live on the fringe. Connected, but apart. See here." Father George drew a drooping line connecting the bottom of the eight's left loop to the bottom of the right loop, effectively connecting the two beneath the twist in the middle and turning the figure-eight into a pretzel.

*I'll be damned*, Hap thought. He'd never look at a pretzel the same way ever again.

"So, you see, time—or if you prefer, reality—is a pretzel. While my kind exists outside of your timeline, we're all connected. Thus, time, my child, is a pretzel. Do you see?"

"What does that have to do with me?"

Father George waved a hand, clearing from the air the crimson pretzel as one might wipe away the writing on a chalkboard. The thing then drew a crimson circle in the air.

"This is us—my kind and yours—right now. My brethren are no longer separate from yours. We're all on the same timeline and repeating. That is why you're here. You're stuck in a moment that happened months ago. Of course, that part isn't your fault. Kirby here is special. Some children are able to…travel, I guess you'd say, between the Roaming and the Withered and Reality and the Void. I see the confusion in your eyes, but follow along as best you can.

"Kirby's potential was unlocked. The problem lies with *how* he was unlocked. When one of my kind unlocks a special child, we can train and direct and stop situations like this from happening. This loop is an anomaly so rare that none of us know how to deal with it. We can see ahead and behind, for all eternity—remember that pretzel?—and we've never come across another oddity such as this. I'm comfortable saying that you, the vile shit that you are, are one of the most important human beings to have ever lived, and you still have forty years before you live up to your true potential. If we can get out of this mess first, that is."

"I still don't see—"

"Because I haven't gotten to the point yet. Do shut up. My patience is beyond stressed."

Hap shut up and listened, if for no other reason than he wanted this asshole to finish and leave him alone.

"I see you're done. Really and truly done. You've given up. And, somehow, you've managed to stall the state of things, the permanent fluidity of the universe has come to a screeching halt because one miniscule dust mote in the vast forever of the Void is not only undecided on what to do next, but he can't even be bothered to decide that he's undecided.

"I know, I know, this is all a riddle to you, but it's hard for me to explain it because you have no way of seeing the entire picture. Only one sees everything at once, and he's an immature little boy with limitless power. Your kind are nothing more than playthings to him. Even I am at his beck and call, for he's the one who created me. I see only what he wishes me to see, and what I see is how you fit into the puzzle. I need you to make a choice, a choice you don't even realize exists, but showing you the outcome would be disastrous."

"Why?"

"Because if you see the outcome your decision will be to the opposite of the actual outcome."

Every bit of what the thing had said might as well have been gibberish for as much as Hap understood the words coming out of its mouth.

"If you see what is to come, you will not make a decision because you, at your basest level, Hap, are a coward."

"I ain't scared of nothin."

"No matter how unafraid you might say you are, there is one thing that you cherish in life, but it is something that does not exist yet. And that is family. You're to have children, Hap, but their fates are locked in time. If you are shown their fates, you will alter the outcome of the end, and that is predetermined. How we get there is not, but the destination is locked. You will end. All of you. The Where of the matter is even decided. It's the When that we're working on. But we cannot move forward without you. So you must make a decision to decide."

"How can I decide when I don't know what I'm deciding about?"

"Child, if I knew that, we wouldn't be here, because, for all my abilities, I cannot affect your will to act."

"I've heard all that before. From him." Hap hitched his chin at Kirby.

"You do realize he's not him, right? The boy that was Kirby Johnson has been buried for months. The Creator's been using him to play a game. Furthermore, I am not—"

"You're not Father George. Yeah, I got that. Thanks."

"They tried to change him," Father George looked to the teenager strapped in the chair and sighed. "They tried to fix something that wasn't broken and ended up unlocking something they had no control over. Because of that, we're here. He opened a door and allowed you into this microcosm of time. You and the woman you shot—Beulah. She dragged the boy-child Pete in with her and now we're all over the place. He's cycling around—" the pastor traced the hazy red circle with his finger—wisps of crimson smoke swirled, "—and around, trying to escape the creature that started the path to the end in motion. Beulah is dead by your hand. And I'm here, trying to motivate the unmotivatable. That this is what it comes down to," Father George clicked his tongue, "is truly mind-boggling."

"What happens if I don't decide?"

"This."

Hap waited for more but Father George said nothing else.

"This what?"

"We repeat. Forever and ever, amen. Don't you find it funny that no time has passed?"

"I hadn't noticed."

"Exactly. Because time isn't moving. As long as you exist in this bubble, none of us can move."

"So if I get up and move, everything rights itself? Easy enough."

Hap shoved off the wall and got up. He raised his hands and let them drop.

"There. Happy?"

Father George shook his head.

"You fail to understand and I can't make you understand. I've existed forever, but you are the first creature ever to test my patience."

"Then I guess we're just gonna stay fucked, because I don't have a clue what you want. Shit, I don't even think you know what you want."

"That's what I've been saying, Hap. You truly are mind-numbingly dumb. Even for a human."

"Fuck you, dipshit."

"You, too, Hap. You, too."

This was getting him nowhere. If he truly was stuck here until he made a decision to decide—whatever that meant—then he needed to be more proactive about the situation. Gears clicked in his head, settling into the first cog they came across.

"Okay. So if Kirby started this, all I got do is—"

Hap yanked his gun from its holster, stepped up to Kirby, placed the gun to the kid's head, and pulled the trigger. The gunshot was deafening in the enclosed space of the examination room. But the sound of the gunshot was the only proof he'd pulled the trigger. No hole opened in the teen's head. Brains didn't splatter all over the door. Kirby didn't so much as flinch.

"Shit," Hap growled.

"He doesn't exist to you, Hap. He was then. You are now. And we are stuck. You cannot affect anything, anywhere, which is why I cannot help you. I can't even point you in the right direction because I don't know how you will decide, or if you will decide, or if this is—" Father George went blank-faced and silent, as if someone had shut him off but forgot to close his eyes.

"If this is what?" Hap asked. "Hello?"

"I needed you to see," Kirby mumbled, his words barely above a whisper, his eyes closed and rolling beneath their lids.

"This is it?" said a voice from behind Father George. The man himself remained expressionless, motionless, vacated. "This is how it ends?"

"Yes," said Kirby.

"I—But I don't want to die." the voice sent sorrow cold as ice all through Hap's bones.

"Nothing lasts forever, Bastard. Nothing stays the same. And, sooner or later, everything ends."

"But—but what comes next?"

Hap waited with bated breath.

"Nothing," said a voice that was now unmistakably female. "All things lead to the end, and at the end we have arrived. Goodbye, my friend."

"No," the puppeteer breathed. "I am a god. I am forev—"

From a distance, barely audible above Hap's own breathing, he heard a bright female voice say, "No. You're not."

Hap, and everything else along with him, ceased to exist.

# 13. Beginnings Can Be Endings Too

Father George, like so many holy men throughout history, was chased from the town in which he'd lived all of his life by a scandal. He'd seduced a local boy of sixteen years, and that same boy had betrayed Father George's trust. The boy had told his parents about the sinful things the pastor had made him do, even if those things had been welcomed. Even if Father George had been, at the time, invited. Father George fled in the night, taking with him his young wife. He'd told her that lies and betrayal had caused their flight, which wasn't entirely a lie; simply a sin of omission.

Molly and he floated around for a while, taking advantage of one family member's kindness or another's, until they landed in Columbus, Ohio. Father George went to work for a milling company, and Molly took work fixing clothes for a local seamstress. Then Father George read about the new church being erected in the small town of Bay's End, seventy miles to the east, and everything, as they say, fell into place.

Father George responded to the ad in the paper, calling the number provided and receiving a clipped, if kind, "Hello." Father George did most of the talking, stumbling about his words and offering more information than was necessarily required. All of this because the man on the other end of the phone was uncannily quiet. Father George was a natural speaker, and natural speakers hate unfilled silence. So he filled the silence, rambling on and on about subjects that did not suit the conversation.

When finally the man on the phone spoke, he told Father George three things: who was behind the building of the church; what his duties would entail; and how much he would be paid. When Father George inquired as to when he would be paid, the man on the phone hung up. The following day, a check arrived in the mail. Father George had not given his address.

A man named Fairchild was responsible for the construction of the new church, and Fairchild's one request was that such information never be revealed. By cashing the check, Father George had agreed to Farichild's terms. He stepped into the role without any further questions. Every month, Father George's bank account grew by a thousand dollars, and soon enough he had more money than he knew what to do with. Not wanting to look a gift horse in the mouth, he never questioned the blind deposits, but some part of him knew it was Fairchild sending the funds, whoever that might be. To Father George, Fairchild was a faceless entity floating in the foggy far-distance of his mind.

Chastity Baptist opened on a Sunday, and it seemed everyone in town came to see who this new pastor was. He shook so many hands that morning that his wrist and elbow were sore for an entire week. Molly iced him and tended to his every need. She made love to him that night, telling him not to move while she rode him until he climaxed. Georgina was conceived from this coupling, and Father George recalled thinking that life was beginning over again—a second-coming seemingly brought on by Father George's coming. God had seen fit to give him a second chance, and Father

George promised the Lord that, this time, things would be different. He would do right by God and lead his flock. He promised to never again stray from his marriage bed, be the object of his affection male or female, young or old. Nor would he look upon men sinfully, covetously, as men were meant to look upon women.

He would, for all intents and purposes, behave himself.

In the seventh month of Molly's pregnancy, Father George received a phone call from what sounded like a girl-child. The girl-child said her name, a name he thought he recognized, but the surname was wrong, so he told her she had the wrong number and said his goodbyes. Hours later, the phone rang again, and Father George answered, expecting—for whatever reason—that it would be the same young girl with her wrong number.

It was Fairchild.

"Your presence is required tomorrow at—" the man's voice droned out an address he was unfamiliar with. Father George wrote it down and then added at the top of the ruled sheet:

*What in the world?*

The following day, Father George drove out to Humble Hill. The guard at the gate allowed the pastor inside without so much as requesting credentials.

"But where do I go?"

"Up to the hospital," the black man, who had the number nine stitched into his red coat, pointed to the building of glass and steel on the hill. "To the hospital. Dr. Lagotti is waiting for ya."

"Lagotti? A man named—" Father George had almost made the mistake of saying Fairchild's name. His benefactor—Fairchild—had requested his name be kept out of all conversation regarding the church but had failed to mention if his name could be dropped in any other conversation. Father George decided to err on the side of caution and omit Farichild's name.

The guard in the red coat cocked an eyebrow.

The pastor said, "Never mind. The hospital you say?"

"Yeah. Just sign in at the front desk."

Father George did as he was told and took a seat in the waiting room. What couldn't have been more than a few minutes—short enough a time that Father George not once glanced at his wristwatch in impatience—another guard—this one a white man in a red coat with a number fourteen followed by a white cruciform on the lapel of his red coat—stepped through and called Father George's name from a doorway. Father George followed the man to Exam Room One, where he was told to have a seat.

The proffered seat looked like any dentist's chair. Aside from the straps, of course. As disconcerting as the straps were, Father George took a seat and waited.

This time, Father George looked at his watch a total of nine times. Forty-seven minutes passed before the door came open and three men came in, two quicker and more purpose-driven than the third. One was the Red Coat with the Number Fourteen stitched into the lapel, while the other was clothed in a red coat with the Number Three. The two red-coated brutes shoved Father George down into the chair as he tried to sit up. Number Three grabbed his throat and threatened him with death, should he move, while Number Fourteen strapped him in. Father George was no fighter. He was, however, a man of God, so he prayed to be elevated and removed from the situation, posthaste. Amen.

Through tear-blurred vision, Father George watched the third man—a wisp of a guy with dark skin and baggy eyes—approach as if floating on a cloud.

"My name is Dr. Lagotti, Father. Pleased to meet you. Sorry about the restraints, but we have a job to do and no time to explain. Greg, if you will grab my cart," the doctor told Number Fourteen. Number Fourteen did as was requested of him, slipping out into the hall and returning directly pushing what looked like a meal cart with a car battery on the top shelf. From the car-battery-looking device came two cables the thickness of a telephone line. At the ends of these cables were rubber handles with metal paddles at the tips. A tube of surgical jelly of which Father George had become well acquainted with during his trysts with the young boy from the previous town sat next to the paddle device.

The rig disturbed Father George on a deep level, although he knew not its purpose. He tried to voice a query, but the brute choking him only squeezed harder, effectively cutting off air and silencing him.

"No, no. No talking, Father. Your input is not needed. All that is required of you is to sit still. For, if you do not sit still, you're liable to not survive the procedure. Do you see?"

Instead of trying to speak, or even nodding his acquiescence, he dropped his eyelids and, internally, said a short prayer, asking for deliverance.

"This'll only take a moment. I swear."

What felt like individual pieces of ice touched themselves to each of Father George's temples and the world went away.

When he came to, he sat in his house, a lamp glowing softly in one corner of the room the only light to see by.

On his lap was a bloody baby doll mask. He cried out and swept the mask off and onto the floor. His hands out in front of him, he was able to get a good hard look at the state of them, as well as the dark clothing he wore: all black, head to foot. The flesh of his hands were stiff with rust-colored blood. His forearms were covered, as well, caked and cracked and in some places clotted and purple where there'd been too much blood to properly dry. The metallic reek of a smelting plant came in offensive waves.

"Honey?" Molly called from the bedroom, her voice thick with sleep. He'd awakened her with his cry, he was sure of it.

Father George bounded from the couch and rushed down the hall, making sure to touch nothing on his way. He used his shoe to close the bathroom door behind him.

Outside, in the hallway, Molly loosed a terse scream.

"Honey? Honey, are you okay?"

He could see her out there, in the dark of the hall, where the lamp in the living room did not reach, holding her immensely pregnant belly, her face contorted in fear and shock, wondering why her beloved had slammed the door in her face.

He hadn't realized she'd been in the hallway.

He hadn't realized how close he'd been to getting caught.

But caught in what? What had he done? How could he possibly explain the situation when he hadn't the foggiest idea as to the whys and wherefores of the situation?

"I'm—I'm fine, Moll. Go back to bed, dear. Please. I've just—I've stubbed my toe. I'm bleeding like a stuck pig. I didn't mean to slam the door on you. Please, just go back to bed. Everything is okay. Everything is going to be fine."

*No,* he thought, *everything isn't fine.*

*Everything is horrible now.*

Molly, silent outside the bathroom door, shifted her weight. Floorboards creaked. Father George held his breath, which was much harder to do at present than it should've been, he thought, and struggled to listen.

Another floorboard creaked, this one farther from the bathroom door than the first. Silence, and then another creak toward the middle of the hall.

She was sneaking toward the living room, the lamp there drawing her as a flame does a moth.

*The mask!*

"I said go back to bed!" Father George roared, covering his fear with uncharacteristic anger.

"I—I just —"

*Oh God no please God please don't let her have—*

"I was just going to make you some tea," Molly lied. He could hear the deception in her voice, the lie as plain and clear as his own.

"Come to bed soon. Please," Molly said in the defeated, worried voice of a wife kept in the dark. He could see her out there, rubbing her belly, heading back to bed, trusting him. Or afraid of him.

Had she seen the mask?

He waited until the bedroom door closed (Molly never had been able to sleep with the bedroom door open; not even the closet door could remain open while she slept—especially not the closet door—a layover fear from childhood, Father George assumed) before moving. Then he stripped, balled up his blood-soaked attire, and jammed it, shoes and all, into the bin beside the toilet. He tied off the trash bag and tossed it in the corner. Then he took a long, scalding shower, trying his damnedest to wash away the blood, and whatever it was that he had done.

Someone was dead. And he had killed them. He knew that much. What haunted him the most was the sense that they had not, in any way, deserved it.

He dried off, retrieved the mask from the living room, returned to the bathroom and stuffed it into the bathroom trash with his bloody clothes. He took the bag of evidence outside, to the aluminum garbage can, which sat alongside the house, and crammed the sack of bloody clothes and mask and other bathroom garbage, down below two other bags. Only then did he go inside and crawl into bed beside Molly. She did not stir, did not move a muscle. She barely even breathed. If Father George didn't know any better, he would have said she was holding her breath.

Somehow, he fell asleep.

\*\*\*

Four days later, he read a newspaper article about a man and woman—the Rothsbergs—who had been slaughtered in their Columbus home. They were survived by their only child, Pete Rothsberg, who was now being cared for by a close relative.

That following Sunday, Father George met Pete, a chubby pale-faced child with bright red cheeks, for the first time. The boy had been taken in by one of Father George's own congregation, the devout Beulah Blackwood. Somehow, Father George managed not to tremble when shaking the boy's hand.

That Sunday was the first and last time the boy attended church, and all the way up until his death, Father George would wonder if the boy hadn't returned because he'd known who Father

George was and what he'd done. For there was no doubt in Father George's mind; he had killed this boy's parents. The blood on his hands had smelled just like the fat boy.

*My God, forgive me.*

\*\*\*

Baby Georgina came and the happiness of creating life buried the sorrow of having taken it. She was a beautiful child. Perfect, really. When they lay his baby girl in the warmer to clean her, Father George reached in to caress his firstborn's cheek. Baby Georgina grabbed his index finger, squeezing tightly, as if she'd never let go. Father George promised her that she'd never want for anything. Never would she know the evil and pain of the world. Not as long as he lived.

The new family of three headed home from the hospital, where life as they knew it drastically changed. Molly's patience was tested daily; the baby's crying unveiling a side of Father George's wife that had, up until now, been unseen. Molly would scream at the infant, tell her to shut up, and even curse at the child; language unfit for a lady screeching from her lips and staining the environment of their once happy home.

Father George spoke with trusted members of his congregation, Gertrude Fulgore especially, about an unnamed woman among them who had seemingly changed overnight. He refrained from telling anyone the woman's name, but Gertrude knew. He could see it in her eyes.

"Does this woman—was she recently with child? Is the child among us now as well?"

Father George, humbled at being caught in his deception, lowered his eyes and nodded.

A gnarled, wound-pocked hand grasped his knee.

"Some women miss the baby inside of them so much that they hate the baby they had. Do you see?"

Father George, thinking he saw perfectly, met Gertrude's rheumy eyes once more and nodded.

"I understand. Thank you, Gertrude."

"That's good, that's good," she said, patting his thigh. "Now, about my boy, Henrik…"

\*\*\*

In time, Molly began disappearing in the evenings, saying she'd needed to walk… that paperwork needed to be done at the church… that this month's bookkeeping wouldn't do itself… that the ladies' group demanded her attention.

They hadn't made love in months, not since she first began showing her pregnancy, and Father George became impatient as a man denied release is wont to do. Sinful or not, he tried masturbating, but Baby Georgina's colicky cries always interrupted him. Their appetites seemed to have synced; her hunger for food trumping his sexual desire.

And then Donna Johnson brought her son Kirby to see him.

He never should have touched the boy, he knew that, but Kirby Johnson was beautiful, and Father George needed the feel of another's skin against his own. He needed to quench the fire of his desire and cool the heat of his unrequited passion.

If Molly would not do her wifely duty, Kirby would.

The evening after he first made love to the Johnson boy, Father George received a phone call from a Dr. Asmai Lagotti. The doctor introduced himself as the head of a new facility called Humble Hill, a place of recovery from life's demons and the devil's influence. Lagotti said he'd found a cure for homosexuality, what he was calling Conversion Therapy, and was wondering if a man of God like Father George might be interested in attending a session. Father George agreed, saying it sounded wonderful, while wondering if he, himself, could be fixed.

The first subject was a girl named Sadie. Father George watched on with macabre interest as the young woman was shocked repeatedly with paddles that extended from a car-battery-like device. He blinked away tears, but said nothing. Lagotti never let on whether or not he could tell how upsetting the session was for Father George.

*So much for being cured*, Father George thought. No way was he going to confess to this Dr. Lagotti only to be willingly electrocuted.

Yet the brutal conversion therapy—if anything of the kind can be accurately called *therapy*—did give him an idea.

Once the procedure was completed, and Sadie was left drooling and strapped in her chair, Father George took Dr. Lagotti aside and told him he knew of another boy, a boy named Kirby, who he'd like to bring in.

"You think he'd respond well to treatment?"

"No, not necessarily," Father George said. Lagotti frowned, obviously disappointed. "What I wanted to do was offer a counterpoint to your process, a control experiment, perhaps." He didn't think that was the correct term, but he pushed ahead anyway. "Say I start a group, speaking with the people who've come to live here. I can try methods of my own, while the most severe cases can be brought to you. If I'm honest, sir, this should be a worst-case-scenario procedure. Don't you agree?"

Dr. Lagotti glanced to the drooling young woman and shook his head. Father George feared the worst, but Lagotti said, "I don't see why not. How long do you think before we try my way?"

"A month? Maybe less. Maybe more. We're working on the Lord's time here."

"Yes, yes. All things at the Lord's pace," Lagotti said but frowned like a man who thought what he'd said smelled like the anal leavings of a bull. "Bring the boy in. He can live in number nineteen. We'll pair him with Sadie. Give the boy a domestic life and see if that helps. Who knows," Lagotti shrugged, "maybe they'll live happily ever after."

So he brought Kirby in. The next morning, less than twenty-four hours after Kirby's intake was completed, Father George was called back to Humble Hill because something had gone terribly wrong. Something, Lagotti had said on the phone, *impossible*.

Nothing had happened like Lagotti said it would happen. Father George had been given no group time, much less alone time with Kirby. His young lover had been brought in, by force, to suffer Lagotti's paddle treatment. Sadie, who now seemed somewhat normal, if a bit off at times, had told Father George this much.

Father George stormed the castle, ignoring the disapproving cries from the receptionist as he barreled through the double doors on his way to Exam Room One. He burst in and came to a stumbling, lurching halt.

Kirby sat in the dentist's chair, leaned back and staring wide-eyed at a ceiling that wasn't a ceiling. A swirling darkness lay above, like a great gaping maw waiting to swallow the world whole. Inside the darkness swirled yellow and red lights, like colorful meteors orbiting an unseen mass.

"Isn't it something," Lagotti said from a corner. "All I did was give him a short shock. Just one. And then this happened. Isn't it beautiful?"

"What is it?"

"You being the man of God, I was hoping you'd tell me. I hypothesize that what we're seeing is Heaven itself. Though it might be a leap. I would ask you to touch the boy before laying down judgment."

"Is it safe? To touch him, I mean?"

"I was touching him when it happened and I'm... fine, I guess you could say."

Father George looked at the man. "You guess?"

Lagotti shrugged. "Try it and see. I wasn't harmed and can only assume you won't be either."

Father George stepped forward and whispered into Kirby's ear a soft "I'm sorry" before laying a trembling hand on the boy's forearm.

A vast sucking sensation, like stretching but without the limitations of your body's flexibility, ripped Father George from his feet. Then he was flying. Streams of consciousness like moving-picture screens unspooled parallel to him, on either side, and on these screens played every minute detail of his life: his birth; his first bath in the sink of his first home; his first meal; his first steps; *first, first, first...* Firsts of everything. Nothing redundant. Nothing repeated. Only firsts. Experience altered perception, and perception altered experiences. The more he saw, the less he found importance in life, and the less importance he claimed the more he saw reality for the overlapping madness that it was.

Insanity wasn't a lack of clarity.

Insanity was knowledge.

Hands on his arms pulled him back into himself. He once more stood beside Kirby in the dentist's chair, staring at Lagotti in the corner. But, if Lagotti was in the corner, who'd pulled him out of the stream? He twisted around and saw no one. Shaking his head in confusion, he faced Lagotti.

Lagotti smiled and said, "I don't know who pulled me out, either, but I will be forever grateful to them."

"I felt like I was losing my mind."

"Oh, I don't think that was it at all. I think that what we're seeing is the acceptance that the universe is bigger and more complex than we could ever imagine. I think someone, or something, was showing us how small and insignificant we truly are. And, in a way, isn't that refreshing? Isn't that so very freeing?"

"But what of God? Where was He in all of that?"

Lagotti blinked several times. "Didn't you see Him?"

Father George loosed a shaky breath. "I don't know what I saw."

"I think you do. I think you do, indeed. That *was* God. That experience. I've never known a holier experience. It was as if I was shown everything."

"But it was chaos."

"Exactly. Beautifully destructive chaos masquerading as insanity."

Dr. Lagotti began to laugh. A maddening cackle that sent gooseflesh up and down Father George's arms.

In mid-laugh, the doctor exploded. Blood splashed. Bone shards pierced Father George's skin, making him look like a prehistoric porcupine. The sack of ravaged flesh that had been Lagotti fluttered to the ground.

Father George fled the room, screaming.

But, at some point, time skipped, and he lost a good chunk of happenings.

In Father George's mind, time was a jumbled up mess of images and circumstances.

Kirby Johnson in his bedroom.

Kirby in the street.

Another man exploding, only this time, just the head.

Flashes of horrors beyond comprehension.

Moving pictures and still life.

Chaos and insanity.

Reality and breath.

Breathing…

*breathing…*

*beating…*

*eating…*

*ring…*

*ring…*

*ring…*

Father George sat on the edge of his bed, rubbing sleep from his eyes. He felt hungover. The last few days were a blur.

*Ring… ring… ring…*

Why wasn't Molly answering the phone? Was she even home, or had she gone for another one of her walks?

Father George, like a man bursting from a pool's surface, shot from the bed, fully awake now, all at once, as if in the grip of a life-altering epiphany. He jogged downstairs, chipper and happy to go about his day.

Nothing was off.

Everything was fine.

What fog?

What hangover?

*Answer the phone and start your day, this day to end all days.*

"Georges' residence, how may I help you?"

A woman crying. Her tearful voice mumbling.

And then: "Everything…"

A pause.

"Everything is horrible now. Everything is horrible now!" she screamed. "Did He do this? Did God do this to me because I didn't believe in you, Father? Am I being punished? Is this what happens when you do not have faith?"

He knew this voice. He knew this woman.

"Gertrude, you cannot—" but her screams cut him off.

"Tell me! Tell me why! Why me? What is so goddamned important about me?"

"Gertrude, what are you talking about? Why is everything— why is everything as bad as you say? What happened?"

"You said you like being called *Father* to remind people that even when God is absent, you'd be there. So why weren't you there for my son? Why weren't one of you there for Henrik?"

"Because you didn't ask." He didn't know what else to say.

"You devil. You charlatan!"

"Gert—"

"I know who you are! I know why you like being called *Father*. You're not fooling me. Not any longer. You're in league with the Bastard! You like being called *Father* because you never had one. You're… fatherless. Or he is. Something. I don't know. But I see you! I see you, Devil! *I see you*!"

The line clicked, and she was gone.

Upstairs, Baby Georgina began to cry.

"Molly?"

Silence.

The more he ignored the infant's wailing the louder she became. Her cries cleaved his eardrums and pierced his brains.

"I'm coming goddamn it!"

He stormed upstairs and into his daughter's room.

There sat Molly, in the rocking chair in the corner of the room, the same one he sometimes used to rock Baby Georgina to sleep. Molly's face was in her hands, her elbows on her knees.

"What—what are you doing? Don't you hear her crying?"

"I always hear her crying," Molly said, her voice muffled by her palms. "*Always*."

"Why aren't you doing something about it?"

With infuriating slowness, Molly dropped her hands and gazed upon her husband with bloodshot eyes.

"I am doing something about it." She rose and, without another word, walked out of the room.

Father George wanted to go after his wife, to snatch her around and slap her face and shove her down the stairs and drown

413

her in her own mutiny, in the betrayal of this family. Their family. The bitch. The ungrateful whore.

These were not his thoughts. Something was wrong with him. He was not this hateful person. Something…*occupied* him, and he couldn't wrestle the entity's grip from his bones. From his soul.

Baby Georgina cried…

*and cried…*

*and cried…*

He looked down into the crib with a father's undying love. He scooped her up and into his arms and she immediately quieted. He held her lovingly to him like the precious treasure that she was and prayed for her to know her own treasure one day. He prayed that she might live a long, healthy life. He asked the Lord that she never, ever know hardship.

Downstairs, the phone began to ring.

Father George lay Baby Georgina in her crib where she went instantly to sleep. He beamed and went to see about the phone, bouncing jovially down the steps.

"I got it!" he called to Molly. "I finally got her down, by the way."

"That's good, dear," Molly said, her voice dripping sarcasm. "She's a daddy's girl, just like I was."

Father George, trying to ignore his wife's tone, a tone almost anyone but him would mistake for true pleasantness and not the vile mockery it truly was, snatched up the handset.

"George residence?"

"Father? Father, it's Kirby."

The smile he'd managed to plant on his face withered and died. "You shouldn't call me here."

"I need help. I'm home and I—I don't know how I got here. Things are happening and nothing makes sense. It's all—it's a mess. In my head. I don't remem—"

"Don't ever call here again. Do you understand me?" Father George whispered into the phone and hung up. He made it three steps from the phone before it rang again.

His face boiled with anger. Usually pale cheeks filled with blood. His fists balled at his sides. He spun and snatched the phone from the base, slammed it down with a grunt.

"Who is it, dear?" Molly sang.

Her tone, that syrupy-sweet faux pleasantness, enraged him to no end.

"Wrong number," he spat. "Must be stubborn, too."

*Like someone else I know.*

"Be gentle, dear."

*Go to hell, woman.*

A roar built in his chest. But before he could loose it, the phone rang again.

"You—" Father George wanted to scream curses, to let out all the pent up vileness in his heart, to allow the vulgar and macabre spew from him in vile torrents. He took a deep breath and mouthed a silent prayer, steeling himself the best he could.

The phone rang twice more before Father George answered it one last time. He'd calmed considerably, had collected his thoughts, but did not speak into the phone when he picked it up.

"Father George?"

"Yes," Father George said, confused. This wasn't Kirby. This was some other man. Some man with a voice he didn't recognize.

"I've been sleepin with your wife. I'm sorry. Please don't be mad at her. It's all my fault. Okay? Bye."

The line died and Father George, staring vacant-eyed into the middle distance between himself and the wall, hung up the phone.

A demon crept up his spine and slipped its cold, wormy fingers over his shoulder.

*She does not deserve this.*

*What doesn't she deserve?* Father George asked the voice inside his head.

*The child, she does not deserve this final betrayal. Her mother has ruined everything. Your Molly is no longer yours, and thus, she is no longer fit to be a mother. Let me fix this. Only I can fix this.*

*What would you have me do?*

*Allow me to take control. Allow me to pull the reins. Allow me, Father, for I wish to sin.*

*Thy will be done, on Earth, as it is in Heaven.*

Father George was little more than a spectator as he shambled upstairs. He took the shotgun from the closet and sat on the edge of his marriage bed to load the damned thing. Then he went downstairs and fixed Molly. Fixed her good.

He would save Baby Georgina as well. He would keep her safe by removing the chance that she would become a whore, like her slut of a mother. Once the deed was done, and his family was fixed, Father George retreated to the porch, where he sat down in his favorite rocking chair, the one he sat in when he wrote his sermons, and lay his shotgun across his lap.

The demon retreated, slowly, slithering down and around his spine like ribbons on a maypole. The creature receded. Its icy grasp on his shoulder vanished, and he was left alone, with himself, with his unbearable self and the tragedy he had wrought.

Gertrude was right.

He was evil.

He was a devil.

She was correct on another count as well.

"Everything is horrible now." He repeated the word like a prayer, as if saying it over and over again would fix something. As if God would glide down from his throne to place a healing touch upon his life and let grace outweigh his sin.

There had been a time in his life when he'd believed God capable of such things. But there was no God. Only horror and sorrow. Joy had fled from him, and he mourned the loss of her as he mourned his own family.

Father George barely noticed the boy in his front yard, the boy calling his name and asking what was wrong. He heard a crying, subtle and haunting, the cries of a hungry baby muted by distance.

He repeated his mantra—

"*Everything is horrible now...everything is horrible now... everything is horrible now...*"

—as he kicked off a shoe and toed the trigger of the shotgun. The end was nigh. The end of it all. Because all things lead to the end.

Father George pushed down on the trigger and became a memory. A memory that started as a wound that would not heal. A memory that festered and poisoned everything it came in contact with. Like Kirby Johnson before him, Father George had simply been something different, and not something broken in need of a fix. But when you try to fix something that isn't broken, you end up causing irreparable damage.

Only the passage of time heals emotional wounds.

But time does not pass.

Time is a pretzel.

It overlaps.

# 14. Joy to the World

Joy stepped from the Void and saw that everything was horrible now. One path of many had been taken and things had ended poorly. Like always.

How many times had the boy and his creation ruined everything? How many times would they, from here on out? You could only push so hard before the subjects shutdown. There was only so much sweeping a dust mote could handle before it obliterated and ceased to be.

Oh well. How did the Bastard put it?

*Que, sera, sera?*

*Whatever will be, will be.*

Joy sighed and breathed life back into the universe. She devoured the darkness with light and populated the Earth. She carved great chasms into the world and filled them with her salty tears. She planted her children and watched them grow.

This was her favorite part.

Even if the endings were messy affairs, new beginnings were beautiful things.

She sang as she worked, painting the peoples of different lands different colors, and molding features to taste. She fed them and starved them. She tested the weak and rewarded the strong, and was good and kind and absent and cruel. She was all of these things. She was Joy, both the presence and absence of happiness, both omnipresent and perpetually sought.

Joy, Mother of the Fatherless, the Lonely, the only god worthy of mankind's worship.

In the end, she left one chasm empty, a doorway to the Void, a Someplace pulsing with possibility and thrumming with chaos.

One timeline ended with this chasm called Waverly, but it had yet to come to pass. She thought maybe she would strum this chord next. Let it ring out and allow it to echo.

*All things lead to the End, indeed.*

She snickered at her own joke.

Bay's End, where Francis Bay had loved an innocent woman and died at her side. This one single act of kindness in the face of hate and horror had ruined everything.

Everything is horrible now, and forever would it be. Of course it would be. But that is the nature of Man. These creatures aren't happy unless they are unhappy. So in that way, she would be the only happiness they required.

The perpetual pursuit of happiness.

*Here, let's get started again and see what comes of it.*

She could have gone back to the death of the Bays, but she quite liked that storyline. The Scaresparrow was something she didn't think she wanted to see the last of, so she tucked it away for future use. The Coat Men were unimportant; the simple imaginings of a broken mind. That she could do without. But that baby doll mask. Now therein lay endless possibilities. Perhaps she could do something with that... Someplace else.

From the Withered came a cry of approval.

*Cruelty, my child, your time has come. This is where your story starts.*

*Right...*

*here...*

She plucked the child from the Withered and placed him where he'd do the most harm, the most good.

For what is happiness without a counter point? If all you ever know is contentment, how can you possibly appreciate the bad? The world needed Cruelty and Regret and Forgiveness. Not one without the others.

Now to see how the dust motes were coming along.

She shined upon them and they danced inside her light.

*Oh, look, a doggy. How cute. Here, girl. Come...*

\*\*\*

Wesley Haversham knelt at the creek and began washing his father's sweat-crusted socks. From the trees traipsed a girl-dog with saggy teats from years of birthing litters. Her clean coat sparkled in the sunlight pouring in through the canopy of trees. Wesley smiled at the dog and went back to his wash.

Gethsemane trotted out of sight, headed for parts unknown, the corners of her mouth raised in what could easily be mistaken for a smile.

\*\*\*

421

Father George awakened to a ringing phone. Yawning, he sat up on the edge of the bed and stretched. Molly's voice floated from downstairs, "Wrong number!"

"Okay!" he called down to his beautiful wife, hoping he wouldn't wake his infant son, who was surely asleep at this time of the morning. Baby Jude never woke before nine, and it was now seven-thirty. God was good, having blessed them with such a peaceful child.

With a smile, Father George stretched and lay back down. He had a sermon due tomorrow, but a little more sleep wouldn't hurt.

\*\*\*

Janice Larson threw up in her toilet bowl. When was the last time she'd had her period? When was the last time her and Eric had made love? Would he believe that he was the father and not—

\*\*\*

Police Chief Harold "Hap" Carringer—*the extra R in Carringer is for Really Good at my Damn Job*—poured himself a cup of coffee and flopped down behind his desk. Another day, another dollar. Hopefully things today were just as boring and uneventful as any other day in the End. The town was really growing, he decided, and that's how it should be. And to think, he'd once wanted to be Sheriff of Pointvilla County. Who needed all that work? Give him locally raised crazy and Friday-night drunks and men who kept their ladies in line. Give him all of them as long as they were his neighbors.

The phone rang.

"Yell-o?"

"Hap," whispered a familiar voice.

"Janice?" he said. "Jan, that you? I can barely hear you."

"Yeah, I think we got a problem."

Hap's heart sank.

He said, "Eric knows." It wasn't a question.

"What? No. Not that. But I've been sick all morning and I ain't had my cycle in—"

"Is that all? Goddamn it, woman, do you think I care? Have it or shove a clothes hanger up your cooz for all the shit I give." He paused, listening to the slut's stunned silence. "Hey, now, don't be mad. Here, lemme help ya out. If ya decide to have the little fucker, whatever you do, don't name him Mackenzie. My mother almost named me that. Thank hell my daddy beat some sense— Hello? You there? Jan? Jaaaaaaaanice?" he sang, chuckling. He hung up the phone. "Did I say something wrong?" Laughing he sipped his coffee and read his paper.

Today was gonna be a good day.

\*\*\*

Gertrude Fulgore admired her perfect skin in the mirror above the sink. And to think, she was seventy-one. God was good. She and her boys were blessed and healthy and all was just fine in the Lord's kingdom under Heaven's watchful eye. She blew a kiss to the lovely old woman in the mirror and went to cook Jerimiah, Malakai, and her youngest boy, Henrik, breakfast.

\*\*\*

Eric Larson sat in his police cruiser a half mile down the road. He saw Molly round the curve. When she saw him, she jogged the last fifty yards. Eric threw open the door and stepped out, catching her in his arms. She smashed her face against his and he kissed her back.

They drove out to Waverly Chasm, hiked to the clearing in the woods, and set up a blanket at the lip of the chasm. They lay down atop the fleece and made love, repeatedly, until they were spent, sticky, and warmly glowing.

When he'd caught his breath, Eric said, "Ya think your man suspects anythin?"

"Not a thing. He's so busy at church—Besides, he's a sissy. Did I ever tell you that?"

"No. You mean he has a thing for—for men?" Eric, in his simplicity, could not wrap his mind around the concept of a man laying with another man.

*I mean, where do they put their whistles?*

"Oh yeah, he does." She rolled over to face him, her cream-colored milk-heavy breasts coming together and pooling before her. "If I tell you something, you promise never to tell no one else?"

"Yeah, I 'spose."

"We was run out of the last town we were in because he was diddling some boy. He don't know I know, but I know. Small towns talk. They might keep secrets from outsiders, but ain't no secrets to be had between members of a congregation. We help our own, and he's my own, I guess. Got the child to prove it."

"So the child's his? Thought he don't like women."

"Nah, Jude ain't his. I'd never sleep with him intentionally. Just sayin us raising that kid together is proof of ownership. I caught pregnant with someone else and needed to fuck him one good time to keep him from thinking anything. Lemme tell you, I washed all my holes something fierce after he squirted off inside me. No telling where all his peen had been."

"Yuck," Eric Larson said. "So who's the daddy?"

Molly reached down and clutched Eric's soft penis. It wasn't soft for long.

"Oh, wouldn't you like to know."

Eric's eyes popped. "It ain't me, is it?"

"Honey, we didn't start sleeping together until a few months ago. Baby Jude is a month old."

"What's that got to do with anything? I ain't ever wore protection, Molly."

"Eric—really?"

He stared at her, anger and ignorance shining in his eyes.

"Oh, honey, you really are as thick as Hap says."

"You know Chief Hap?"

Molly smiled and squeezed his dick. "Wouldn't you like to know."

\*\*\*

Beulah Blackwood never woke up that morning. She died in her sleep. Heart attack. "Off to see the Lord," those who attended her funeral would say.

According to *The End* Times: *Beulah Blackwood is survived by her daughter, Joyce, Joyce's husband Patrick, and their eleven-year-old son, Pete.*

\*\*\*

*This time,* Joy thought, *let's leave Kirby out of it.*

**THE END**

The following short story will be important if you choose to read *No Home For Boys*.

### "Cinder Block"

#### 1.

The morning of the cinder block incident, my mother reminded me before I left for school that I was her angel. The statement was made between swigs of Black Jack. She'd said on more than one occasion, "Daniel's is the drink that makes you think." So why was it she had some strange dude laid out next to her again? Did it even cross her mind that's where Dad used to sleep?

That guy, he was lying on his side, hand stuffed down the front of his tightie-whiteys, scratching himself. He looked at me like I was the stranger. Like I didn't belong. He stuck his chin out at me as if to say hello. I nodded back politely, but in my mind's eye I was stringing him up by those testicles he'd just got through emptying into my mom.

Dad left after the infidelity, but before the alcoholism. I only assumed Mom started drinking because she'd lost the one constant in her life—other than me of course. It started with beer on a nightly basis, then (when the beer didn't work anymore) escalated to whiskey. I could see the disappointment in her eyes as she stuffed an empty case of Coors into the trash bin one night. That look said, "It's not making me forget anymore." The same evening that she figured liquor was a more effective choice with which to drown her sorrows she brought home the first stranger.

But, before all the strangers, there was Charles Nickerson—the guy Mom was blowing when Dad and I came home early from another fishing disappointment. He jockeyed a cash register at the Farad's 24/7 in our hometown, Chestnut. Why my mother had decided blowing some guy who owed more child support than he would ever make in his life had been a good idea still haunts my mind on occasion. Yet, there she was, on her knees in the middle of our living room, acting like she was a Hoover vacuum and old Chuck's wanger was the filthiest thing she'd ever come across.

Dad remained uncannily calm, given the scene he'd just witnessed. He told Charles to "Please leave" while the man was still trying to tuck his pecker into his shorts. Charles, looking very nervous, caught a nut in the workings of his zipper and cawed like a crow. To this day, I've never heard anything like that come out of a human being, and it still makes me smile. My father told me to go to my room, and I did so, even as my mother wiped at her wet lips.

I never saw Dad again. He left that night without saying goodbye. Sure, I ask myself why he didn't take me with him, but the more pressing question was why hadn't he killed her. I think I might have, given the chance. But I guess thoughts like that were the main reason a court said I wasn't fit for society.

My mom was a pretty woman—voluptuous if you won't think me a pervert for saying so—with long, curly red hair. She's where I got the freckles and ginger mop on the top of my head.

Now, she had the bed sheet tucked under her arms, and I could see the slit of her cleavage peeking over the material. The stranger leaned in, licked his finger, and stuck it between her tits. He never took his eyes off me.

I left before I got sick.

Mom called after me, "You're my angel! 'Member that!"

My intention for being in her room that early in the morning was to say goodbye to her before I left for school, but I hadn't said a word.

See reference: One Flew Over The Cuckoo's Nest circa 1975. I was Will Sampson's character, Chief Bromden. I didn't say shit because didn't shit need to be said.

### 2.

I was fourteen the year I came across a pornography catalog while checking the mail. Either the mailman made a mistake in my favor, or Dad had ordered the thing; I didn't know which, but I was fourteen, and I had needs. Even though I was an only child, I slept on the bottom half of a bunk bed my father picked up at a garage sale. I took the more graphic pictures from the catalog, cut out neat little squares with Mom's chicken scissors, and stuffed them in between the boards that supported the top mattress. Plenty of mornings, like most young men, I would wake up with my penis swollen and throbbing—The Sundial, we called it—so, I would slide my pictures out and take care of business.

On one such morning—July 3rd, to be exact—Dad walked in on me during a rather glorious tug-of-war session. Being caught didn't much bother me, but Dad looked like his world was ending.

He said, "I didn't realize," and closed the door. I finished up, wiping off with a crusty sock I kept hidden under my bed, and took a shower. I figured, he was a dude; I was a dude. What was the big deal? I knew my buddies did it—Samson had given me pointers, "Rub your thumb on the tip, and you'll cum like a shotgun." Damn good advice—and I was certain my father must've played with himself at least once.

Mom and Dad were waiting on me in the kitchen when I got done cleaning up. At the table, a steaming cheese omelet made my stomach growl. The three of us ate in silence. Dad didn't mention what he'd seen. Not over breakfast at least.

One town over, every year, for as long as I can remember, Bay's End put on a fireworks show for the 4th; Fairchild Farm being the location for the event. The town had a ground show and an air show not only to celebrate Independence Day, but also in memory of two people that died in the summer of 1992—Emily Harper and Eddy Treemont. Anyone who lived in Pointvilla County knew the story. An author by the name of Trey Parker wrote a book about the happenings and then dropped off the map.

The day after Dad caught me waxing my turtle, he took me to the fireworks show. At first, I'd thought it was a simple father and son outing, but during the festivities, Dad opened up.

We were sitting on the hood of my father's truck—him smoking a cigarette, me eating sunflower seeds — and watching the bombs burst high in the sky. He clapped me on the leg, startling me. When I looked at him, I could see the reflections of fireworks in the glare of his glasses. His eyes seemed to be dancing.

He dragged off his smoke, and said, "Women are like fireworks, Toby. They're dangerous, beautiful to look at, fun to play with, and just as much of a mystery to me on how they work."

I nodded, not knowing how else to respond.

"At some point in time, I missed you growing up. I'm sorry about that. I guess it's time for the talk, huh?"

I shrugged, not realizing where our conversation was heading.

"I was your age when I first started masturbating, so I should've—"

"Dad!" I choked on a seed. The kernel caught in the back of my throat. I'm sure I looked like a cat trying to pass a hairball.

"Calm down. I'll try to make this as painless as possible. Do you prefer jacking off?"

I reached into my mouth and extricated the sunflower casing. "As opposed to what?"

He laughed, "I mean, do you want me to call it 'jacking off' instead of masturbation?"

"Oh, God."

"All guys do it, Toby."

"Nah-duh." I shook my head, face-palming. "Dad, you don't need to do this."

"Yeah, I kinda do. My father never bothered with me." He knocked the cherry off his cigarette trying to ash it. He put the butt back in between his lips and lit it again with his Zippo. "Just don't ever let your alone time replace the woman you end up with. You understand?"

"I 'spose." I didn't.

"Do you have anyone in mind," he jabbed me in the shoulder with his knuckles, "other than Rosey Palmer?"

I rarely ever laughed at my father's bad jokes, but I couldn't help it then. "Naw. Not yet."

"Maybe you keep it that way, huh? Less you have to worry about." Dad looked toward the brilliance happening overhead and smiled. He looked so peaceful.

It was two years later that Dad caught Mom deep-throating Charles Nickerson. I bet Dad wished he'd stuck to Rosey Palmer and her five sisters instead of playing guess-the-affair with Mom.

### 3.

Lauren Walsh should have been waiting for me on the corner the morning Mom reminded me I was her angel, but she wasn't there. I checked my watch. One hour to get to school. That fact didn't bother me—school was only twenty minutes north of where I was—but Lauren's absence didn't feel right.

Lauren worked after school at the Farad's 24/7. She's the reason I knew Charles Nickerson; he would be the one to relieve her in the evenings. I wondered if that slimy bastard thought about my mother when he saw me during those times I would show up to walk Lauren home. That's just me assuming that what my mother and him had going on was more than just a one time thing.

I stood there at the corner for a good five minutes, checking my watch, looking down the street—rinse, repeat—until finally I decided to leave without her. Setting shoe to street, I left the curb and started north. I passed by several homes where people

I didn't care to know resided. I imagined that some were even in their houses wondering about the Corvette sitting in our driveway.

"That isn't Mr. Waldrip's car, is it?" I heard them saying in my head.

"Whose is it then?"

"Mrs. Waldrip's current sperm donor, I would surmise. Mr. Waldrip flew the coop over three months ago."

"Do you think the boy minds his mother fucking everyone this side of Pointvilla County?"

"You know what they say: 'The apple doesn't fall far from the tree.' He's probably messing around behind his girlfriend's back. He doesn't deserve that Walsh girl. Lauren is too sweet for a boy like him."

I wish those self-deprecating voices in my head had been right. That I was the one that didn't deserve her.

### 4.

Lauren and I met in Mr. Hash's third period English class; this was just after Dad left. I managed to dig myself into a pretty dark place—somewhere I believed I deserved to be. I kept focusing in on the thought that Dad and I hadn't been enough for Mom. We were so insignificant that she had to resort to other men for affection; if that's even what you wanted to call it. Samson (I'll get to him shortly) told me that sometimes life just can't find a toilet and ends up dumping on you instead. At that moment in my life, I was just tired of being shit on. Whether it was Mom or life doing the squatting, I wanted to be out of the impact zone.

Lauren knew I was a football player. That was her initial attraction to me. I'd been playing since my freshman year and had become one of the most valuable members of the team. Coach Yuribe constantly reminded me that I was not, indeed, God's gift to the game, but I wouldn't listen. During my time as a center for the Chestnut High Loggers, not one quarterback sack was allowed by me.

Samson, my QB, was actually bigger than me. I weighed in at just under a buck seventy-five and stood at five-foot ten. But Samson, that boy was a good six inches taller, and fifty pounds heavier. I used to use leverage to my advantage though. I'd get in low, push up and away, until I had defensive linemen sucking wind and rolling around on their backs like upended turtles. Now and then I'd play defense, but my bread and butter was offense. It didn't bother me that I enjoyed hurting people. I wouldn't have called myself a sadist, but I did get a certain warm spot in my chest at the sight of some lineman curled into a ball, praying to God he'd never met Toby Waldrip. I would glance back to Samson after driving some kid into the ground, and a massive shit-eating grin would spread across my face. At the sight of me, Samson would shake his head and laugh. More than once he said, "There's something wrong with you, dude."

I guess he was right. The courts would agree with him, anyway.

Lauren made the first contact. I didn't have a cell phone like most kids my age, so she had to go the old folded note route to get my attention. It was a Friday, and Mr. Hash had his back to the class while he drew up our homework assignment for the weekend on the blackboard. Lauren sat three chairs ahead of me in the same row. She passed the note back to Fran Bishop, and then Fran transported it to Ricky Jameson. Ricky had his hand over his shoulder for almost a full minute before I realized what the guy was trying to do. He waved the football shaped paper in my face until it looked like his shoulder might pop out of place. When I finally took it, he sighed loudly and rubbed his collarbone.

He whispered, "Take a hint, Waldrip. Shit."

The note might as well have been an origami swan, Lauren had folded it up so well. It took me a minute to figure out how to open it without ripping the thing. When I finally came across the tucked corner, the college-ruled paper came open like a pop-up book. It was simple enough:

I like watching you smash the hell out of people. You doing anything tonight? Call me. If you want. No biggie.

Yeah, right. No biggie. Even at sixteen, I knew reverse psychology when I saw it. If she made it no big deal, I would be more apt to act on her request. Her number was scrawled at the bottom of the note, in big swooping chick-script. When I got home that afternoon, I dialed her number wrong three times because I couldn't decipher her sevens from her nines. Think about that. How screwed up does your handwriting have to be for someone to mistake those two numbers for each other?

"What's up?" Lauren answered after a full minute of a Death Cab for Cutie tone. I couldn't stand those fucking things— ring tones, that is. I'd much rather listen to the drone of a ringing phone line than someone's favorite song blaring in my eardrum.

Whoever invented that crap needs to be trapped on a railroad trestle overlooking a 200-foot drop with a train fast approaching.

See reference: Rob Reiner's Stand By Me, 1986. But in this version, Will Wheaton's character, Gordie LaChance, has a ball and chain attached to his ankle.

"It's Toby."

"Who?"

I sighed, "Waldrip?"

"Oh yeah. What's up?"

"You wanted me to call you. Here I am." I smiled, even though I knew she couldn't see it. Mom was boozing it up in the kitchen, giving me the curious mother eye, so I tucked the handset of our cordless into the crook of my neck and walked out back to talk to her in private.

"Are you busy tonight?"

"I might be. Plans change though. What're you thinking?" I sat down on the garden swing Dad had hung the previous year. The chain pinched the webbing between thumb and forefinger. I held back my squeak and sucked at the purple wound. It tasted like copper.

"Movies?"

I still had my hand in my mouth, so what I said came out sounding like, "Oven."

"What?"

"Movies. Love'em. Kinda nerd out over them."

"Cool. Everything's starting at eight or after. How 'bout you meet me there around seven and hang out while we go over what to see?" She didn't have to tell me where. Chestnut didn't have but one movie theater. The Glass House was owned by a tall, gaunt man that went by Phyllis. Don't ask.

"Sounds good."

I met Adam Hill that night. A slightly thinner version of Haley Joel Osment in Pay It Forward, Adam posed no threat to me. So when I found out Lauren and he had been friends since fourth grade, I didn't worry about it. Still, I found it odd that she'd brought a friend along to our first date. I just kept wondering if she worried that I might rape her before the ending credits.

We saw the 3D re-release of Titanic. I laughed so hard at the scene where the guy bounces off the propeller and cartwheels away into the ocean that Lauren grabbed my hand and gave it a squeeze. Adam, who was seated in the row ahead of us, turned around and gave me a strange look; it might have said, "You're weird."

He didn't know the half of it.

Back home, my bedroom walls were covered in posters from violent movies and dark comedies. I suppose they didn't help my case later on, but they sure as hell didn't have anything to do with what happened. There was something about horror movies, in general, that really got me off. Films like Friday the 13th and Halloween were my favorite. Stone cold killers stalking hot young people sated my cinematic bloodlust. Never cared too much for Freddie and his Nightmare movies. What was so scary about a dream? In the real world, you woke up. Plain and simple. To each their own, but Elm Street didn't appeal to me.

Of course, Adam had no way of knowing that, so I forgave his inquiring eye. I remember thinking, "Stop judging me and enjoy the movie. The best part is coming."

The popsicle version of DiCaprio clinging to that floating door had me in stitches. Rose knew damn well there was room for her lover on that piece of driftwood, but she still let him freeze. Why? Because it was in the script. People tend to over-think movies. Me, I take them for their end product. Was I entertained, yes or no? It really isn't any more difficult than that. I do miss the days of VHS though. DVD extras almost ruined movies for me, took away the magic. I stopped watching them. Fixed that problem.

One fortuitous thing about a two-and-a-half hour reenactment of a tragic cruise is that the credits are so long because a million people worked on the movie. During that cascade of names, Lauren moved in to kiss me. She tasted like popcorn. Her slippery lips glazed my own, her tongue digging for treasure back by my uvula. I lost track of Adam—didn't care if he watched or not—but when Lauren finally let me breathe, I noticed he was gone.

"Your buddy left." I told her, wiping liquid butter from my mouth.

"I think he's jealous."

The statement caught me off guard. For a moment, I didn't know how to respond. I asked the only logical question I could think of, "Should he be?"

She shrugged. "Guess not."

I cocked my head to the side, finding her eyes in the drab theater lights, trying to size her up.

"Is there something going on between you and him?"

"Fuck no." Oh God, her comeback had been forced. "I've known him, like, forever. He's like a brother."

"Good." I kissed her again. I wanted to take my mind off of a horrible possibility that was growing in the soil of my mind. She was there making out with me, not Adam. He should have been the furthest thing from my mind. But the seed had been planted. And what a tree it would grow into.

## 5.

Lauren should have known I would go the way I did that morning. It was the same route we took to school five days a week.

I couldn't help but think about Mom's recent fling while I walked the streets of Chestnut. I saw husbands and wives kissing in driveways before one or the other left for work. I wondered whether or not one of them was screwing around behind the other's back.

My train of thought changed to questioning if love was real. Love was a strange concept for me. I wasn't in love with Lauren, just like, I suppose, Mom never really loved Dad. You couldn't love someone and hurt them, right? You had to work at love, nurture it, give it the water and sunshine it needed to grow. Once love had grown big and strong in your heart, you could farm it for happiness. Yet, if you thought that way, you wouldn't be happy without another person to share your life with.

Lauren became something to be owned. My idea of her stated that she was a possession of mine. Mom had belonged to Dad after all. That was why Charles Nickerson had been in the wrong. You don't steal from people. It's in the bible. Folks used to shoot your ass in the old west if you stole their horse.

Henry Stoner was leaning against Farad's 24/7 when I rounded the corner onto Booker Street. Everyone called the guy

Stone. If he'd been a pothead, he might have won best name ever in my book. Stone played right tackle for the Loggers. I knew of him, practiced with him, but wouldn't call him anything other than a passing acquaintance. People like to think that just because you're around someone a lot, you must be privy to their complete life's history. Stone and I played on the same high school football team. That was it.

My school sat a quarter mile to the north, on the other side of Chestnut's Sports Hall where all the Loggers' games were played. I should've kept walking. Had I ignored Stone and his off the wall comment, I might've been better off, but who's to know for sure.

"Yo, Waldrip! Don't go back there!" Stone hitched his thumb at the alleyway between Farad's and The Chestnut Report, the home office of the town's newspaper, and then took off running toward the school. Odd as the comment was, something settled in my gut—a certainty, in that exact moment, that his words meant the exact opposite of what he'd said.

I had no reason to go into that alley—none whatsoever—but before Stone had made it ten feet away, I was running too, only I was heading toward the alley he'd told me not to enter.

Someone should have had the foresight to hang a sign above that alleyway, one that read: Abandon all hope, ye who enter here.

My tennis shoes squeaking as I came to a stop five feet from Adam and Lauren caused her to open her eyes. She caught my glare and raised her eyebrows like, "Hey, what's up? Just gimme a minute. Be right with you."

Adam was all over her, his hand up the front of her pale blue blouse, playing with her tits with those long, thin fingers of his. She moaned into his mouth as he kissed her. Lauren's eyes closed again, as if I wasn't even there.

I could feel the heat coming off of them.

I thought about leaving; I really, really did. It would have been the easiest thing in the world to have turned around and left them there. I'd be screwed up for a while, but I would move on, see other people, find another fish in the sea. All that bullshit. Jan Turkleson was pretty damn hot. She shared fifth period social sciences with me. I could ask her to see Titanic, and she would say yes. I'd still be in Chestnut. I wouldn't be a murderer. We might have even grown up and gotten married. Sure. Why not? She would give me a son and daughter and we'd be the perfect happy family, and we'd never cheat on each other and I would never again in my entire life think of that whore Lauren Walsh.

But none of that happened.

Instead, I saw Charles Nickerson with his dick balls deep in my mother's mouth. I saw her cheeks caving in as she sucked him down her throat. I saw my father—so damn peaceful—ask the man politely, if he could "please leave." I saw myself grab Adam's shoulder and rip him away from Lauren.

I heard the caw that came out of Charles as he caught a testicle in his zipper. I heard my mother sucking saliva into her mouth as if she were slurping up a strand of spaghetti. I heard Lauren telling me to stop punching Adam, to "stop fucking hitting him!"

I felt my cheeks flush. I felt the emptiness that had settled in my core, devouring my heart with its dark matter. I felt

Adam's blood, warm on my cheek. I had his shirt balled up in one fist while the other turned his features into hamburger.

Lauren's French-tips stabbed into the side of my arm as she tried to pry me off Adam. I had paid for those nails. That was on date two. Now she used them against me.

I thought about what had come to my mind when Dad found Mom: why hadn't he killed her? In that moment, I knew the answer. It was because Charles Nickerson was to blame. He'd stolen Dad's horse, and he was the one who should've been shot. Adam had run off with my mare. It was time for some old west justice.

Chestnut had a raccoon problem. If you went out of your house at night, you could see them, scurrying about, trying to scavenge for food. To dissuade them from rummaging through our bins, we just had to put something heavy on top of the cans. Some people even secured their lids with bungee cords, but those furry bastards could chew through, if they were desperate enough. My household used a brick. The Farad's 24/7 used cinder blocks.

I reared back and socked Adam a final good one. He folded at my feet. Now, I don't condone violence on women, but Lauren had it coming. I slapped the shit out of her. The impact sent her flying back, onto her ass. With Lauren out of the way, I could finish with Adam.

Adam, on his back—his head less than a foot away from the dumpster—had his hands out in front of him like he could use The Force to keep me away.

See reference: Return of the Jedi, 1983. Adam was Emperor Palpatine hitting me with everything he had. But I was Darth Vader, and wouldn't be stopped.

Murder isn't hard. All it takes is a push; a subtle one at that. A firm palm on cold stone.

If Adam would have covered his face, it might not have been as bad, but he had those arms stretched out, trying to protect himself from me.

I used the flat of my hand to slide that cinder block off the top of the dumpster.

The way that piece of concrete landed didn't help matters. The corner of the cinder block connected with the bridge of Adam's nose and that was that. If it had landed flat, he might have gotten away with a broken nose.

... if

... if

... if

...

Lauren began screaming at that point. She about ruptured my eardrum, she wailed so loudly. I don't remember when she got to her feet, but when I turned around, there she stood.

I'm sorry Lauren. What came next must have sucked.

### 6.

I've heard the bullshit where people say they saw red, blacked-out, or had an out-of-body experience during the perpetration of their crimes. I couldn't have said that, honestly, because it didn't happen. I knew what I had done. I just didn't care.

I was glad Adam was dead. He deserved it.

See reference: A Time To Kill, 1996.  I was Samuel L. Jackson's character, Carl Lee Hailey, and I was on the stand screaming one of the best lines in cinematic history.

Then again, I don't necessarily remember tossing Lauren to the concrete and smashing in her skull with that cinder block. I do, however, recall heading home. I walked like I didn't have a care in the world, my arms swinging at my sides; my give a fuck completely, utterly, irrefutably broken.

I didn't expect mom's fuck-buddy to be there when I got home. I came walking in, and the guy was in the kitchen, grabbing a beer. He wore a dirty white tank top with sweat stains under the arms. He looked at me like I was a ghost. In the middle of twisting the cap off his brew, he dropped the bottle. It exploded against the tile floor, spraying my legs with suds. I didn't know what his problem was. Of course, I had forgotten that I was covered in Adam and Lauren's blood. I'm sure I was a hell of a sight. By the look on Fuck Buddy, I was right.

Mom came out of the hallway, hollering questions, wanting to know if the blood was mine. I shoved her off. She landed a good ten feet away, her back up against the sofa in the living room.

I walked down the hall and into the bathroom. I needed to clean up and get back to school. I was late. I had just killed two kids. I didn't need to add truancy to my list of violations.

It didn't take long for Chestnut's finest to find me. Carl Bartley, editor over at The Chestnut Reporter, had the forethought to call the police when he heard Lauren screaming for me to stop pounding her new boyfriend's face into lasagna. He would testify to the fact that I had walked by his establishment with my arms swinging by my sides like I didn't have a care in the world, covered from the top of my head to the bottom of my shirt in what he thought was pizza sauce. Silly man. He hadn't tried to stop me because, hell, he didn't know if I had a weapon. When asked how he knew I was the perpetrator, he responded, "Because it was a girl screaming. A girl. That bloody kid I saw was, as you already know, definitely not a girl."

James Hendricks, of 1911 Booker Street, told the jury that I passed by his window that morning, whistling a merry tune. He'd seen me walk into the house shortly after Adam Hill was said to have died. His house was directly across the street from mine, after all, and his "windows stayed very, very clean." I still wonder how the hell he heard me whistling through glass. Nice elaboration, if I do say so myself.

My mother said some stuff, too. Mainly how I had about killed her when I "threw her across the room." I was no longer "her angel." She told the court that I had a penchant for violent movies. That she knew they would rot my brain, but I wouldn't listen to her parental guidance. In her mind, Jason Voorhees and Michael Myers drove me to commit my acts of murder. Not the vision of her blowing Charles Nickerson. She left that part out. I'm sure everyone knew the truth of the matter—my mother's promiscuity was no secret around town—but her lack of sexual control had no bearing on the case.

D.A. Abbott said: "Given another incident like the one Toby Waldrip stumbled upon in that alleyway, he could, very well, kill again. Waldrip's temper, and his lack of control over it, are on trial here, just the same as he is. We're dealing with a sociopath here. I would have the jury remember that."

445

Sociopath? Pfft!

The first responding officer had had his gun drawn when he walked in. Mom told the officer, just like she told the court later, "He was going to kill me, I know it! I asked him if he was all right." (She didn't.) "And he told me he was." (I hadn't.) "He just walked off, like one them zombies in the movies. You know what I mean?"

D.A. Abbott answered, "We do."

"Then he went to the bathroom and told the arriving officers where he was. I just can't believe he did it!"

The D.A. smiled. "Thank you, Mrs. Waldrip. You've been very helpful."

Helpful to who? God, I could've choked her to death on the floor of the court room.

The officer who found me in the shower dragged me out and shoved his knee in my back. Then he cuffed me. To this day, my back still hurts in that spot; especially when it storms. He would tell the jury that I was combative. Good on him. Wouldn't want any police brutality charges sneaking up his ass, now, would we?

It's the small stuff I remember after killing Adam. Like how small the back of a squad car seemed; how tacky blood feels at that point when it's not quite dried up; the way the hair on my forearm stuck up in odd patches, like thinned-out trees in a desolate, crimson swamp.

But most of all, how utterly alone I felt.

See reference: Cast Away, 2000. I was Tom Hanks' character, Chuck Noland, but I didn't have a Wilson.

## 7.

My first night in county jail was the hardest. I was put into a solitary cell to keep me away from the adults. Outside my slit of a window, rain dropped from the sky.

The cell wasn't bigger than my bathroom at home. My cot was welded into place on the wall, covered in a green, inch-thick mattress that felt like tarpaulin. Someone before me had ripped half the padding out of it through a tear in the upper right corner. Cotton entrails peeked out of the opening, rising up like tendrils of white smoke. I played with the stuffing, twirling it around my finger, pulling it out, and then shoving it back in. The action gave me something to do, something to focus on other than myself.

I kept wondering when I would go home. I knew my fate, but it didn't seem real. I figured at any moment, I would sit bolt upright in my bed back home. This had all been a terrible dream, and I just had to wait to wake up. Mom would come in, her newest stranger on her arm, and tell me I was her angel again. Lauren would be at the corner when I walked outside. We'd go off to school, holding hands the entire way. Samson was there. So was Stone. And Auntie Em, she was there, too.

By the time I came out of my fantasy, the floor was covered in eviscerated bedding. I laughed. Flat out, fuck-it-all, kind of laughter. It looked as if I stood on a cloud. I frolicked in a sea of cotton, arms out at my sides, some crucified martyr prancing off into forever.

See Reference: Mel Gibson's The Passion of the Christ, 2004. The earth didn't quake. But it should have.

Love, man. That shit's crazy.

## The End

*Speaking of the End…*

## <u>All Things Lead to the End (Reading Order)</u>

Made in the USA
Lexington, KY
01 November 2018